Praise for *One Rogue Too Many*

"Filled with hu⸺ ⸺ ⸺ woos readers in true ⸺ ⸺"

—*Publishers Weekly*

"A merry romp... Grace captures the essence and atmosphere of the era."

—*RT Book Reviews*

"Grace's flair for crafting engaging characters and light touch when it comes to humor and charm result in another sexy, Regency-set historical."

—*Booklist*

"Rivalry, marriage proposals, betrayal, secrets, well-drawn characters, plot twists, romance, and true love all add up to a story that readers will not soon forget."

—*Blue Ribbon Reviews*

"I liked these flawed and unsure characters right away...a charming book."

—*Once Upon a Book*

"A great love story and a wonderful historical romance I believe any book lover will enjoy."

—*Long and Short Reviews*

Praise for *Lady Vivian Defies a Duke*

"Grace supplies another winning marriage of romance and wit in this delightful Regency. The tried-and-true 'will they or won't they' plot gets new life with Grace's trademark humor and charm. This classic love story is absorbing and endearing."

—*Publishers Weekly* Starred Review

"Sprightly, amusing, fun, and quite charming, Grace's latest wins fans over with everything a love-and-laughter romance reader could desire. From first page to last…the characters shine and Grace's talents sparkle."

—*RT Book Reviews*, 4 Stars

"Captivating, thrilling… Filled with steamy, heartfelt love scenes, it is a must-read for anyone who is seeking a wild, romantic adventure! Ms. Grace…creates an inviting landscape that is sure to pull any reader into her divine spell!"

—*Night Owl Romance* Top Pick!

"*Lady Vivian Defies a Duke* has just the right ingredients blended together to give a marvelous vicarious experience that makes the reader give a happy sigh that love wins again. Most enjoyable reading!"

—*Long and Short Reviews*

"Oh my goodness, I LOVED this book!"

—*Smitten Books*

Praise for *Miss Lavigne's Little White Lie*

"The suspense and intrigue are well tuned, and the humor is subtle and charming—much like the novel as a whole."

—*Publishers Weekly* Starred Review

"The characters are colorful, the research on target."

—*RT Book Reviews*

"*Miss Lavigne's Little White Lie* has a special kind of charm and a beautiful love story."

—*Long and Short Reviews*

"It's official. Author Samantha Grace has proven it's impossible for her to disappoint. *Miss Lavigne's Little White Lie* is a dazzling historical romance!"

—*Romance Reviews* Top Pick

"A delightful, witty romance with a dashing sea captain and a stubborn woman bent on protecting her family against all odds that will leave you cheering and sighing with delight."

—*Rogues Under the Covers*

"I loved the story, with its smooth style, dastardly evil counterpoints mashing against all the good, and the hot steamy scenes."

—*Yankee Romance Reviews*

Praise for *Miss Hillary Schools a Scoundrel*

A *Publishers Weekly* Top 10 Romance for Spring 2012

"With heart and humor, Grace delivers a rich and winning Regency debut... Everything Regency fans love—meddling mothers, oppressive high society, subtle wit, steamy interludes, and a bit of intrigue."

—*Publishers Weekly* Starred Review

"Grace's fabulously fun debut will dazzle and delight readers with its endearingly outspoken heroine, devilishly rakish hero, and abundance of high-octane sexual chemistry."

—*Booklist*

"An absolute must-read. [Grace] writes with the elegance and talent of a well-established author... I loved it, I adored it, and I can't wait to read more from this author."

—*Romance Reviews*

"If you are looking for a warm Regency filled with wit and laughter, a bit of mystery, and some wonderful, hot loving, this is a great debut!"

—*Rogues Under the Covers*

"This charming debut from Grace has all the ingredients that make historical romance so fascinating."

—*Library Journal*

Also by Samantha Grace

The Beau Monde Bachelors Series:

Miss Hillary Schools a Scoundrel

Lady Amelia's Mess and a Half

Miss Lavigne's Little White Lie

Lady Vivian Defies a Duke

The Rival Rogues Series:

One Rogue Too Many

In BED WITH A ROGUE

SAMANTHA GRACE

sourcebooks
casablanca

Published by Sourcebooks Casablanca, an imprint of Sourcebooks, Inc.
P.O. Box 4410, Naperville, Illinois 60567-4410
(630) 961-3900
Fax: (630) 961-2168
www.sourcebooks.com

Printed and bound in Canada.
WC 10 9 8 7 6 5 4 3 2 1

For my husband, who shares my quirky sense of humor and appreciation for the slightly absurd

One

SOMETIMES A GENTLEMAN NEEDED A PLACE WHERE NO one knew his name. For Baron Sebastian Thorne, that place was the Black Dagger. And if all went as planned, he wouldn't know his own name by the end of the night.

Draining his ale, he signaled the serving wench to bring another. The East End tavern hummed with chatter, not that he could follow any of it. Perhaps his drunken state explained the problem, or maybe the patrons' butchered English was to blame. He didn't know. Neither did he care, as long as they weren't talking about him or his betrothed jilting him.

The shadowy interior hid the filth, but he could still smell it, and there was something sticky under his boots. Yes, the Black Dagger was perfect. He wouldn't cross paths with anyone he knew among this nest of thieves.

"Damned thieves," he mumbled. Sebastian couldn't escape them no matter where he went. Whitechapel. Mayfair. It made no difference. A thief was a thief, even if he dressed like a gentleman.

Just that morning he'd learned Anthony Keaton, the most callous of thieves, had returned to Town. The Earl of Ellis had recently stolen the one thing Sebastian needed most: a wife with connections. He chuckled, although there was nothing humorous about being deceived by his former best friend, or in Sebastian's failure to protect his betrothed from falling prey to Ellis's scheming.

The tavern wench plunked a tankard down in front of him, sloshing foam onto the scarred table. "Are you havin' a right jolly time over here by yerself, milord? If you be lookin' for company, I know a place."

Sebastian tried to fix his blurry eyes on her, but she spun in circles, along with the taproom. "You are a right tasty morsel. Why don't *you* keep me company?"

She cackled, showing off rotting teeth, and patted her scraggly, graying hair. "I got a man that don't like that sort a carrying-on. A toff like you is temptin', though."

"Damn the luck," he said and graced her with a smile the ladies had always liked. "Well, if *you* are not available, I believe I will make my way home."

He lurched to his feet and stumbled into the table. More ale sloshed onto the table and splattered his waistcoat.

"My apologies, madam."

When he weaved, the wench sidled up beside him and he slipped his arm around her bony shoulders. She smelled of yeast and a hard day's work. "Steady now, milord. Can't have you tearin' up the place. The Dagger was just redecorated."

Sebastian laughed genuinely for the first time in a

week. He held on to the woman as the taproom continued its erratic tilting. She stood about as tall as Lady Gabrielle and tucked under his arm as easily.

He leaned close, underestimated the distance, and bumped his forehead against hers. "I almost married a girl as pretty as you." His words slurred.

"You don't say." The woman gazed up at him with a half smirk. "What happened to her?"

"She eloped with another man."

Her eyes widened for a moment. "Law! Sometimes the pretty ones be real corkbrains. You get yerself an ugly woman next time. She'll make you a good wife."

Sebastian scoffed. "There will be no next time." He released the woman and swayed before he regained his balance.

"Are you sure ye're fit to go, milord? There's a room abovestairs where you can sleep it off."

He groped for the coin purse in his coat pocket. "Your concern for my welfare is kind. Allow me to give you something in return."

Lord knew he rarely experienced kindness from anyone outside his family these days. He wished he could repay his mother and sister as easily as he could the tavern wench. Instead, he had made their lives more difficult by fouling up his search for a wife. Most everyone had forgotten the scandal of his father's madness and his sister's abandonment at the altar until Sebastian's betrothed eloped with his childhood friend. Now the *ton* was convinced there was something terribly wrong with the Thorne family. Bad blood, they said.

Fumbling his purse, he tugged the drawstring and dropped it. Gold pieces scattered at his feet. "Damnation!"

The serving wench fell to her knees quickly for a woman her age and scooped the gold pieces back into his purse. Sebastian helped her off the floor, and she slipped the purse into his hand.

"May the Angel of Whitechapel watch yer back tonight," she murmured.

He'd heard tales this evening about an angel. A heavenly beauty roamed the streets at night giving shillings to the poor. *Angels.* Sebastian wouldn't count on one coming to his aid.

He winked at the serving wench. "Could be the angel stole the blunt."

"Oh, no. Ye're wrong 'bout that. Don't know no footpads be parting with their money out of kindness." She escorted him to the exit and smiled up at him. "The angel has a heart o' gold. She left a basket of bread and milk on my widow neighbor's doorstep early this morning. And her with five mouths to feed."

Sebastian chuckled. "There is our proof then. The Angel of Whitechapel is aboveboard." He extracted four shillings from his purse. "For you, madam. From the Mad Devil of Mayfair."

"Ye're no devil."

"But I am quite mad. Ask anyone." He dropped the coins into her outstretched palm. Tipping his hat, he bid her good evening and stumbled through the tavern exit while trying to shove his purse back into a suddenly missing pocket.

Fog clogged the narrow street outside the door and he stopped to get his bearings. Where would he most likely find a hack at this hour? Perhaps he should have arranged to have his driver return for him, but he hadn't known how long he'd wanted to wallow. A couple hours turned out to be too long.

What is done is done. Self-pity wouldn't help his sister to reenter Society, nor would it complete the work his father began before his death. Sebastian had made an oath to see his father's dream of housing for injured soldiers become a reality, and he was finally making progress this year. To the devil with what others thought of him. He wouldn't allow a bit of nasty gossip to defeat him.

Sebastian stepped onto the street, lost in a muted world of mist that lightly fell against his cheeks. Now, where was that hack he needed? He groped his coat once more.

"There you are." He found his pocket, at least, and replaced his purse.

His boots made a sucking sound in the muddy lane, and he sloshed through a puddle, soaking his pant legs. *Gads.* His valet would be in a mood when he saw the mess Sebastian had made of himself tonight.

His excursion to the Black Dagger had been less than satisfying. He hadn't found the comfort he'd sought in anonymity. And now he was returning home looking like a sow after a mud bath.

A sound, like the scraping of wood against stone, echoed in the street. Sebastian whirled to his right.

"Who goes there?"

No one answered. He strained to hear movement in the dark until a ringing silence filled his head. Then he heard it again. Definitely a scrape and a footfall. The hair at his nape stood on end. A black wall of night hid whoever was out there.

"I am seeking a hack," he called out, on the off chance there really was an angel waiting to help him.

No one answered. His heart slammed against his breastbone. A squish behind him made him spin around, and he wobbled off balance. He shouldn't have overindulged this evening.

Fumbling in his coat, he searched for his pistol. His fingers brushed the polished wood as something hard slammed across his shoulder blades.

He cursed and fell to his knees, his back burning as if on fire.

"Get 'is blunt," a voice growled.

Sebastian reached for his flintlock once more, but a heavy boot crashed into his stomach. He doubled over, groaning. On second thought, he wasn't nearly foxed enough for this kind of treatment. A blow to his head created an explosion of color behind his eyes, and he collapsed in the mud. His assailants ripped the coat from his back while he tried to catch his breath.

"Found it!"

Another kick to his kidney paralyzed him in a cloud of pain. Two men grabbed his legs and tugged at his boots.

"Not the Hessians," he mumbled.

They laughed and ran off, the splash of footsteps growing faint.

"Bloody... hell..." he said between wheezing breaths. He would have given them his purse if they had asked nicely, but no gentleman should have to part with his boots.

He rolled to his back and cried out as his muscles wrenched. If he ever learned his attackers' identities, they were in for a shocking introduction of his foot to their backsides.

✣

Lady Helena Prestwick jumped in response to a sharp whoop from the street. Laughter and the sound of running footsteps approached her hiding spot. She pressed against the stone wall, her fingers trembling as she clutched the dagger Fergus had given her. The men ran past the alley entrance without noticing her. She released her breath and slumped against the wall.

Perhaps she should have listened to her late husband's land steward and stayed behind at the town house while he searched the Wentworth Street brothel tonight, but it had been nine years since she had seen any of her four younger sisters. Waiting one more day to learn of her sisters' fates was unbearable. Fergus—a man who was more like family to her than a servant—had never lied to her, but she couldn't quite trust he would do as he promised if she wasn't present to oversee everything. Her father's and husband's duplicitous natures had taught her the value of caution.

She and Fergus had tracked Lavinia to Whitechapel a week ago. There were an overwhelming number of places to search, but last night they had gotten their first promising lead. A widow with several little ones clinging to her skirts was certain she remembered Lavinia, even though she hadn't seen her in a long time.

The woman had wrung her hands. "Such a pretty girl. It's a shame she landed in a brothel, but it's no surprise O'Riley wanted her." She had no recollection of Lavinia having had any living family.

Helena's stomach turned and she closed her eyes against the horrid images invading her mind. She couldn't allow herself to believe Cora, Pearl, and Gracie might be dead. It was awful enough knowing Lavinia had ended up in the rookery. Their father had wagered it all away, then. Had he also lost Lavinia in a lousy game of cards?

She breathed in deeply to slow the surge of animosity racing through her veins. She had prayed her sisters would escape this fate just as she had with her late husband's help. If only Wickie had allowed her sisters to come with her to Scotland, they could have been saved, too. Resentment swelled within her, but she pushed it down. Lord Prestwick had been under no obligation to take in Helena, much less her sisters. She tried to remember she was fortunate he'd married her and gave her a home, even if she'd often felt like a prisoner at Aldmist Fell.

A low groan carried on the air followed by an almost unintelligible curse. *Almost.* The word *bugger* had been clear enough to make her blush. The man's moans grew louder.

Whoever was out there was in pain, but it was too dangerous to come to his aid. Her fingers gripped her gray skirts. She had promised Fergus she wouldn't leave the alley for any reason.

"Help." The man gasped for air.

She covered her ears to shut out his pathetic moaning, but it did no good. What if he lay bleeding in the road and here she hid like a frightened mouse?

She eased along the wall toward the mouth of the alley and peeked around the building. An indistinct dark lump crawled toward a building with flickering lights in the windows, but collapsed in the street.

"Help me, please." His voice was raspy and weak.

He couldn't know she was there, could he? Yet his plea seemed directed at her.

"Please."

Oh, good Lord above! She couldn't take it anymore. As quietly as possible, she slipped into the street, holding the dagger at the ready, and hurried to where the man lay facedown in the mud.

"Help has come," she whispered as she sheathed the dagger and knelt beside him, "but you must be quiet before someone else discovers you and finishes the task the other men started. Can you roll over?"

Grabbing his shoulder, she pulled firmly. He flipped to his back with a sharp hiss. "Feels like knives when I breathe."

She cradled his head in her lap and wiped the mud from his eyes and mouth as best as she could. "You may have cracked ribs. I know it hurts, but we cannot leave you in the street."

He started to reach a hand toward her face then jerked to a stop with another painful moan.

"Do not try to move yet. We are going to need help."

She looked toward the brothel, hoping Fergus would reappear with the lantern so she could see what damage had been done by the footpads.

"Are you the angel?" the man asked.

"I am no—" He went limp in her arms. "Angel."

Blast! Now what was she to do? She didn't have the strength to drag him back to the alley. He was at least six feet tall and—she placed her hand against his chest to check for breathing—he was solid. Her hand began to wander and she snatched it back.

Her body was practically purring with him close. She eased his head to the ground and scooted away. She couldn't be the only widow to miss intimacy, but that was no excuse for being familiar with a stranger, no matter how well formed he was.

"*Mo chroi*," a harsh whisper carried on the air. "Where are you?"

Fergus. "In the street. Come quickly."

They had decided if Fergus needed to address her on their clandestine outings, he would use the childhood pet name her mother had given her. She would rather no one know she was nobility, although she was a lady by marriage only.

It was strange to hear the gruff Scot refer to her as his heart, but it provided a cover story for them as well. She could play the role of disgruntled wife seeking out her husband at the brothel if need be.

Fergus emerged from the alley with the lantern held aloft. A golden halo surrounded his broad shoulders and highlighted his messy mop of brown hair. He scratched his whiskered cheek and frowned at the man lying in the mud. "Stuck the scoundrel in the gullet like I taught you, aye?"

"Dear Lord, no! Footpads attacked him." She studied the man's sculpted face and recognition sparked. Lady Eldridge, Helena's cousin by marriage, had pointed him out just yesterday when they were shopping on Bond Street. Lord Thorne's name and the circumstances of his jilting had been spoken at every gathering Helena had attended this last week.

"I know him." She pushed to her feet and took the lantern. "Carry him to the carriage. We will take him home."

"He's no' a stray cat," he said as he stooped to heft Lord Thorne over his shoulder. Fergus never ignored her wishes, although he didn't hesitate speaking his mind. "Can't give him a dish o' milk and a scratch under the chin and expect him to curl up on your lap."

She aimed a mischievous grin at her companion. "Are you saying I cannot keep him? Pity that. I bet he would clean up nicely."

Fergus laughed. "Luna would be jealous if you brought this alley cat home."

Luna was the scraggly feline Helena had rescued days earlier during one of their midnight excursions. A bath and a few good meals had worked miracles with the animal's appearance and disposition. But a cat was one thing. Helena didn't need a man in her life to order her about, even if her body tended to disagree.

Fergus jostled the baron to get a better grip and the unconscious Lord Thorne groaned.

"Be careful. His ribs might be cracked."

"He is no sack of flour, lass."

"I know he must be heavy, but please. For me." It was a long jaunt until they reached the Prestwick carriage waiting in a park outside the rookery for fear someone might recognize her berlin. A pang of embarrassment for asking so much of Fergus drove her to reach for his arm. "Thank you."

The Scot offered a gruff "At your service," and trudged along with his burden. "What do you intend to do with him?"

"Return him to Mayfair where he belongs. To Thorne Place on Savile Row." She would see him safely under the care of his family, and her search would have to resume the next night. "Am I to assume you didn't find Lavinia?"

"No, I dinna, but do no' worry yourself. We'll find her."

His voice lacked conviction, and she tried to keep despair from creeping up. She and Fergus hadn't been searching long. Only two weeks. But it seemed they were no closer to finding any of her sisters than she had been hidden away at Aldmist Fell, observing the proper mourning time.

When they reached the carriage, her driver grunted a greeting to Fergus. The clansmen had a strange way of communicating, but she had grown accustomed to their habits after years of living at her husband's estate. She held the carriage door open.

"Take care not to bump his head."

Fergus grimaced. "Are you certain you want him inside? He's covered in mud."

"I am aware, but unless you wish to carry him all the way to Mayfair, there is no other choice."

That settled matters quickly, and Fergus dumped him on the carriage floor. The baron roused long enough to release a string of curses damning the servant's manhood before he slipped back into unconsciousness.

Helena arched her brows at Fergus. "Well, that saves me the trouble of taking you to task for carelessness, I would say."

"Aye, that it does, milady." He took the lantern from her and grinned. With his assistance, she climbed inside and stepped over Lord Thorne to settle on the bench.

Fergus eyed the baron crumpled on the carriage floor taking up the majority of space inside. "I'll be on the box with Robert. Signal if he wakes." He closed the door, shrouding the interior in darkness. When the carriage jerked forward, the motion elicited another miserable moan from her passenger.

When a wheel hit a rut and his head knocked against the floor, she winced. It was bad enough the baron had taken a beating from the footpads. He didn't need additional bruises courtesy of her assistance.

She opened the curtain to allow for light, slid onto the floor, and arranged his head on her lap to cushion any further blows. The scent of ale wrinkled her nose. Perhaps his addled state had more to do with overindulgence than injury, at least she hoped.

She had never made Lord Thorne's acquaintance. He didn't attend the assemblies, but she couldn't blame the poor man. Invariably, details of his jilting were on gossips' lips at balls, garden parties, and every at-home. Helena had begun to feel she knew him personally, and her heart went out to him.

She wiped his lips clean with her handkerchief and sighed wistfully. Such a lovely set of lips. If a duke's daughter had jilted *him*, Helena wanted to see his competition. Lord Thorne was quite possibly the handsomest man she had ever seen, even caked in mud.

He mumbled something in his sleep. On instinct, she smoothed a hand over his hair. "Shh, you will be home soon."

Perhaps if circumstances were different, she would ask for a proper introduction. She shook the thought from her head. No, she wouldn't. Sebastian Thorne was trouble, and she didn't need trouble getting in the way of her finding her sisters and giving them a better life now that she was free of her husband.

The carriage rolled to a gradual stop, and the door swung open. Fergus filled the doorway. With his face in shadow, she couldn't see his expression, but she thought she had heard a small gasp. She supposed she'd shocked him by touching the baron, but there was nothing inappropriate about the situation.

"He didn't wake," she said. "Perhaps he requires a doctor."

"His family will summon one if need be." When the Scot grabbed Lord Thorne's arms and tugged, the baron's head rolled back. Fergus tossed him over his shoulder again. "Thorne Place is around the corner. Robert will take you home, and I'll wait out of sight to make certain his household discovers him."

She scrambled to her feet as Fergus turned. "Wait!"

The servant raised a bushy brow in her direction. She had no idea what she wanted or why she had called out. It was just… Well, something inside of her wasn't ready to let the baron go yet.

"Do not let anyone see you."

Fergus flashed a cockeyed grin. "That is part of the plan, lass."

Two

SEBASTIAN'S THOUGHTS WERE PREOCCUPIED WITH angel's wings and harps as he drifted into consciousness. More precisely, he was thinking the angel from the mist had possessed neither wings nor a harp, which meant his savior had been no angel at all.

From the feel of the thick mattress beneath him and the familiar sounds of the house settling, he wasn't in heaven either. He was in his bedchamber. God only knew how he had gotten there.

He smacked his lips. His mouth was dry, like someone had shoved a wad of muslin in it. With eyes still closed, he fumbled for a glass of water on his side table without success. He cracked open an eye.

"Faith!" He jumped, then sucked in a sharp breath as pain sliced through his ribs.

His younger sister pursed her lips. "What happened *this* time? Did an irate husband chase you out a window?"

"I refuse to respond to such a ridiculous accusation." Gingerly, he probed the bandage around his middle. How had that gotten there?

Eve slid from the edge of the bed and went to retrieve a porcelain pitcher from a tray sitting on a side table. "The doctor said you bruised your ribs and knocked your head. And don't pretend I have insulted you. I smelled the lady's perfume on you before your valet cleaned you up." Despite her scolding tone, her brown eyes were sympathetic when she glanced over her shoulder. "I worry about you, Bastian. God only knows what you are doing that causes you to come home with bruises. And no coat or boots at that."

"Well, it's not bedding married women, not that you should know about such goings-on."

Snatching the glass from his bedside table, Eve filled it from the pitcher. A drop of water slid down the side and dripped to the floor. "You forget I was almost a married woman. I received the talk, fat lot of good it will do me now."

"Thank you," he mumbled as he accepted the glass. He hadn't forgotten she had been abandoned at the altar or that the blackguard had left England without allowing Sebastian a chance to defend his sister's reputation. It mattered not that Eve was blameless. Society had decided Benjamin Hillary must have discovered something untoward about Sebastian's sister and cried off. Eve had been ruined, and Sebastian had been helpless to correct the mistake.

He hadn't forgotten anything. No amount of alcohol—or bumps on the head, apparently—could erase the things he wanted to forget.

The water chased away his thirst, but sitting up to drink it made his head pound. He handed the glass to his sister, eased back against the pillows, and closed his eyes. "Does Mother know of my condition?"

"She was abed when Milo answered the door and found you. After the doctor said you would live, I didn't see a reason to wake her."

From the short shadows on his walls, he guessed the time to be near noon. "And you mentioned nothing when she woke this morning?" It was likely too much to hope this could be kept a secret from their mother.

Eve shrugged. "She wished to break her fast, and a gander at your face would spoil anyone's appetite."

He scowled, but she simply chuckled and pulled the covers up to his armpits. "Not under normal circumstances, mind you. Just this morning you look a fright."

"Thanks," he said flatly. The bruises from his fight with Ellis had only recently disappeared and now he had to heal all over again. "Where is my watch?" It wasn't on the bedside table in its usual place.

Eve set the glass on the table. "You would have to ask your valet. Are you hungry? I could have Mrs. Wilmot prepare a tray."

His stomach roiled at the thought of food, and he shook his head.

"So, what happened last night?"

"Footpads got the best of me. A woman came to my assistance, which explains the perfume." Likely a prostitute, given the location and time of night. Sebastian didn't much care what class of woman she was. If she hadn't come when she had, he might not be safe in his bed now.

He hadn't gotten a good look at her face, but the

pleasing lilt of her voice had been soothing, and her hand on his forehead had been gentle in the carriage. Much kinder than the bloke who had tossed him into it. Sebastian frowned. Of course a common whore wouldn't have transportation at her disposal or a servant to do lifting, which made it seem more likely his rescuer was a lady.

He propped up on his elbows and gritted his teeth. "I believe she brought me home. Perhaps Milo asked her name so I may thank her."

When he sat up and swung his legs over the side of his bed, Eve planted a hand against his chest. "You're not going anyplace right now. The doctor said you must stay in bed until you are healed."

His fingers circled her wrist and he smirked. "Do you really think you can stop me, little sister?"

"I am a grown woman, so stop calling me little sister. Besides, there wasn't anyone at the door, so Milo will not know the woman's identity. It seems your rescuer rang the bell then left you alone on the stoop."

The woman knew him and where he lived. Who was this mystery lady skulking about Whitechapel aiding those in need? He ran through a mental list of ladies he knew and couldn't imagine any of them stealing away to the rookery. Unless his rescuer was in trouble. What sort of trouble, he didn't know, but if she was willing to risk discovery to save him, he owed her a debt.

"Maybe one of the other servants saw something last night. I will have Milo gather them," he said.

"Oh, no, you won't."

He gently swept his sister's hand aside and stood.

His head spun and he plopped back on the bed. "Perhaps tomorrow."

Eve smiled smugly. "I told you. The doctor said to rest."

"How am I supposed to rest with a pesky sister buzzing about?" He tweaked her nose to show he was teasing.

"Very well. I am going, but you'd best stay abed or I will return with Mama. And you know how she likes to fuss over you when you are injured."

"You wouldn't dare."

She grinned. "You know me better than that, Bastian. I *would* dare and I would enjoy every minute of it." With that, his sister spun on her heel and hurried from his room, laughing.

❧

Helena brushed a strand of hair from her forehead and sighed as she tugged one of the double doors leading into St. Saviour's Church. She carefully descended the dimly lit stairs of the side entryway and paused to allow her eyes to adjust.

It had been a week since Fergus had searched the Wentworth Street brothel, and they hadn't received a single lead on Lavinia's whereabouts since. Helena couldn't avoid the church any longer. As Fergus had said, it was the most logical place to check.

She hadn't been to St. Saviour's in many years, but it looked no different, much to her dismay. She leaned against a stone pillar to steady herself and drew in a cleansing breath. Burning wax lingered on the air, mingling with the musty smell of damp wood.

After her mother was buried, her father had stopped bringing her and her sisters to worship. Helena hadn't cared. She'd wanted to forget the place where her mother had been laid out, her body as cold as one of the statues in the Lady chapel. Helena never would have come back except she knew the best chance of finding her sisters might lie in the parish registry. If any of them had married, perhaps she could decipher one of their signatures and learn the identity of her sister's husband. Although their disappearance from London did not bode well, Helena refused to believe her siblings had met the same end as their mother.

A rustling sound came from the front of the sanctuary, and she rounded the pillar to peer down the narrow nave. Candles burned in only the first tier of the iron chandelier, casting the interior in long shadows. A flash of black disappearing into an antechamber propelled her forward.

"Pardon me, sir." She hurried down the aisle, her skirts brushing against the dark woodwork of the enclosed pews.

The man reappeared in the archway. His round face was open and his smile welcoming. "Good afternoon, madam." His rich voice echoed off the vaulted ceiling and was eerily familiar. "Welcome to St. Saviour's Church."

She returned his smile as she neared. "Thank you and good afternoon. I am Lady Prestwick of Aberdeen, and I am hoping you can assist me in a matter."

"It would be my honor to serve, Lady Prestwick. How may I be of assistance?"

"I am searching for a member of this parish, but

there is a chance she has married. I would like to view
the church registry in hopes of learning her husband's
name, so I can pay her a call."

His brows came together and his smile dimmed.
His gaze ran over Helena from head to toe. "A
member of *this* parish, milady? Has she wronged you
in some way?"

"Heavens, no. She is a sister…of one of my
servants. They lost touch several years ago, and I
promised to look for her when I was in Town. To
deliver a message."

Her face heated with the lie. There was probably a
special place in Hell for people who lied to a man of
the cloth, but she couldn't allow anyone to link her
to her past. Admitting she was searching for her sisters
could create all manner of questions she didn't want
to answer, and it could interfere with her mission to
bring her youngest sister into her world when she
found her. Helena would see Gracie become a lady
someday, with all the benefits that position would
entail. Tutoring wouldn't be the same hardship for
her young sister as it had been for her. At age fifteen,
Helena had had much to learn in a shorter span of
time, and her education had been grueling.

Besides, Wickie had gone to a lot of trouble to
create a respectable past for Helena, and she had promised no one would ever learn the truth. Some would
judge him harshly for his actions. He would be seen
as a lewd older man who had seduced a young girl,
which couldn't be further from the truth. Her husband
had behaved honorably, and when she reached the
appropriate age, he had offered marriage as a well-bred

gentleman would. She never wanted anyone to think of her as that poor young girl.

The preacher scratched his head and regarded her. "Forgive me for saying so, milady, but you have most unusual eyes. I feel I have made your acquaintance in the past. Were you also a member of the parish at one time?"

"Oh, no. I've only recently arrived from Aberdeenshire." His features also rang with familiarity, but she hadn't been to London for many years, and she hadn't attended church even longer than that. She couldn't possibly know him. She only remembered one clergyman at St. Saviour's, the one who had officiated her mother's funeral service.

Mr. Cooper had been a middle-aged man with thick blond hair and a round, friendly face.

Helena's heart jumped into her throat. "Mr. Cooper," she whispered.

His smile widened. "We have met, haven't we, milady? Please, refresh my memory."

"I am afraid you are mistaken, sir." She licked her lips, her gaze flickering toward the aisle.

"But you know my name, and yours is a hairbreadth away." He rubbed his forehead. "Is it Mary? Margaret?"

Panic surged inside her. He was getting too close at guessing her mother's name. *Marianna.* Helena had her mother's distinctively large blue-green eyes, but she'd never thought anyone would remember her mother after all this time.

"I—I must go." She began to back away. "I've recalled an appointment I cannot miss. Perhaps I can search the registry another day."

Her elbow bumped the corner of the altar and startled her.

Mr. Cooper's brow wrinkled in concentration. "Marian? No, that is not quite right. It is on the tip of my tongue."

She turned and fled.

❧

Sebastian grimaced at the entrance to the church. His sister, Eve, crossed her arms and returned his scowl. "Well, are you going to be a gentleman and open the door?"

"There are churches closer to home. Why did you have me carry you across town?"

"I am less likely to see anyone we know. Besides, it isn't too far and Mr. Cooper is always in on Thursdays."

"And you fancy Mr. Cooper?"

She burst into laughter and her face lit like a ray of sunshine. These moments had been too rare of late. His foul mood faded as he realized his sister wasn't as broken by Benjamin Hillary's betrayal as Sebastian had thought.

She wrinkled her nose, the light sprinkle of freckles and action reminding him of when she was a little girl. "You cannot be that eager to be rid of me, Bastian. Mr. Cooper is at least twice my age."

"I'm not eager to be rid of you at all, even though you are most vexing at times." He jerked the south entrance door open, smiling back at Eve when a force slammed into his chest. The impact caught him by surprise and he stumbled back a step, hugging the young woman to save her from falling.

"Oh dear," she said. "Forgive me. I wasn't watching where—"

Round, expressive eyes met his and her mouth dropped open. He'd grown accustomed to leaving ladies speechless, but it had been a long time since a real lady had allowed him near her. Pink infused her pale cheeks as she remained in his arms, her perfectly pleasing breasts crushed against his chest.

A full smile spread across his face. "No apology necessary, Miss…?"

She blinked, her thick lashes making her eyes even more extraordinary. "Lady Prestwick."

Sebastian released her, a rush of disappointment leaving him flummoxed. "Begging your pardon, my lady. I meant no offense to you or Lord Prestwick."

"So you know my husband. This never gets easier," she mumbled and smoothed her hands over her skirts. Her delicate brows drew together as if it pained her to speak to him. "There was an accident. A little over a year ago. And he…uh…I am afraid he—"

"Oh! He *died*."

"Sebastian!" Eve hissed and elbowed him.

"I am sorry to hear that, my lady, even though I didn't know Lord Prestwick, per se." Gads, Sebastian was a first-rate clod today. This was what came from avoiding Polite Society. He'd forgotten how to talk with people.

Eve linked arms with him. "Our condolences, Lady Prestwick. I don't believe we have had the honor of an introduction. I am Eve Thorne and this is my older brother, Sebastian."

The lady nodded. A light breeze off the Thames

fluttered strands of golden-brown hair around her face. "I am familiar with you and your brother, Miss Thorne."

Sebastian stiffened, prepared to defend his sister from a vicious attack, but it was unnecessary. Lady Prestwick smiled, two dimples appearing in her cheeks.

"It's an honor to make your acquaintance. Perhaps you and Lady Thorne would call on me when I have my next at-home so I might meet her as well."

The fight drained from him and his easy smile returned. The lady had truly surprised him with her invitation to call on her. Most ladies gave Eve the cut direct. His sister hadn't attended a social gathering in a long time.

Eve squeezed his arm and beamed at Lady Prestwick. "That would be lovely. Mother will be so pleased when I tell her we have met."

Lady Prestwick glanced at him once more and nervously licked her rose-colored lips. "Again, forgive me for not watching where I was going."

"There's nothing to forgive, my lady." A woman like her was welcome in his arms any day, and if his sister weren't present, he would let it be known. He had a fondness for widows and had provided comfort to several over the years. At least before they'd started referring to him as mad and began avoiding him.

The lady smiled once more then bid them a good day. He turned to watch her carriage approach and her climb inside. Her footman glowered at him as he closed the door and took his position before the carriage rolled away.

"Did you see that?" Sebastian asked his sister, his temper rising. "Her servant *glared* at me."

"I am sure he has good reason."

He tore his gaze from Lady Prestwick's carriage disappearing around the corner. "A good reason? What good reason?"

She lifted a slender brow. "Don't you dare be coy with me, Sebastian James Edmund Thorne."

He rolled his eyes at her excessive use of names. "I have no idea what you are talking about."

"Lady Prestwick is your lady. For the life of me I cannot figure out how you sustained such severe injuries, though. Did you fight a round of fisticuffs for the honor of her company, or did she have her footman toss you from her house?"

"I have no lady, so I am not sure what you are babbling on about." He pulled the door open wider and motioned his sister inside. She swept into the dim belly of the church.

"Very well. Be tight-lipped if you must, but I recognized her perfume. She is the lady from that night you claimed to be attacked by footpads."

Eve's revelation hit him square in the gut. He lifted his cravat to his nose and drew in the faint spicy-sweet scent of Lady Prestwick's perfume lingering on him.

Jiminy. Maybe his sister was right, but reputable ladies like Viscountess Prestwick didn't wander the East End, and they didn't fall into the kind of trouble one would find there. He shook his head. *No, Eve must be mistaken.*

His sister reached the bottom of the stairs and looked back over her shoulder. "Are you coming?"

"Why are we here, anyway?"

She shrugged a shoulder. "I am praying for Benjamin, of course."

"He does not deserve your prayers." He scowled and followed her inside despite his protest.

"Now, now. You don't know what I am praying for." Her calculated grin made him forget the mystery of Lady Prestwick for a moment.

He chuckled. "And all this time I thought you were a saint."

"Likewise," she said then snorted.

Three

HELENA OFTEN FELT OUT OF PLACE IN A CROWD, AND the one gathered in the foyer of the Theatre Royal was no exception. She only half listened to the ladies standing around her discussing their latest hardships. Lady Wiltshire's modiste was working too slowly on her newly commissioned gown. Lady Rutland's sojourn to Bath would be delayed by a week. And Lady Teesdale was having a horrible time with her cook, who had taken to bed with a fever two days earlier, which had Lord Teesdale high on the ropes.

Problems of the privileged. How do they cope?

"I told Mrs. Burke no more lazing about unless she wants to be turned out without references. Lord Teesdale was fit to be tied and refuses to eat another bite until the regular cook returns."

Helena smiled to disguise the gritting of her teeth. She didn't even know Mrs. Burke and yet she felt sorry for her. Lord and Lady Teesdale must be the most trying employers in Town.

Lady Eldridge—*Olive*—caught Helena's eye and motioned Helena to join her and her dear friend, the

Dowager Duchess of Foxhaven. The duchess was a cheerful lady who always put Helena at ease, and she was more than happy to escape the present company.

"Please excuse me. My husband's cousin is summoning me."

The ladies offered fleeting smiles, then returned to consoling one another.

Helena nearly wilted with relief when she reached Olive's side on the outskirts of the Grand Saloon. "Is intermission almost over?"

"Soon. We could return to the box if you like."

"That would be lovely." She inclined her head in greeting to the duchess, admiring her vibrant bronze silk gown. "Good evening, Your Grace."

"The duchess thought you looked in need of rescuing," Olive said, fluttering her tortoiseshell fan to create a breeze on her reddened cheeks. Her fine, blond hair lay limp against her head and drew attention to her long face. The evenings had grown warm that week, but Olive refused to abandon her ruffled chemisettes. "Was it the toast story again?"

Helena chuckled in surprise. "You have heard about his lordship's chipped tooth?"

"We all have, dear girl," the duchess said, her blue eyes sparkling. "Other than being bombarded with uninteresting tales of woe, how are you finding London?"

"Very pleasant, Your Grace."

The only reason Helena had traveled to London for the Season was to search for her sisters, but attending social events was necessary to keep up appearances.

Olive's keen gaze swept over the other patrons as if on the lookout for trouble. What kind, Helena didn't know, but she relied on her husband's relation to guide her during her time in Town. Olive had been exceptionally kind and welcoming when Helena arrived, and they got on well despite the twelve-year age difference.

"Lady Eldridge is pleased you decided to summer in London," the duchess said.

Olive nodded. "I wrote to Wickie several times suggesting he bring you to Town. I knew you would enjoy the Season, but my cousin was the most head-strong man I have ever known."

"Wickie preferred the country, and I learned to love Aldmist Fell as much as he." Helena didn't defend her husband out of loyalty as much as a desire to avoid questions about her marriage.

Headstrong was an apt description for Wickie, however. As were obsessed, domineering, and irra-tional at times. One year Helena had begged him to accept Olive's invitation, but he refused. He insisted the journey would be too tiring for a lady trying to conceive. When she had argued that she was in good health, he accused her of trying to interfere with conception and ordered her to bed rest. His accusation had mortified her, because she had wanted a child des-perately. The emptiness of her life had chipped away at her. It still did, but finding her sisters would fill the hole left in her heart.

"I have seen enough here," Olive said, linking arms with her and directing her toward the grand staircase. "Perhaps more exciting things are afoot in the theatre."

Wickie's cousin enjoyed her gossip, but she wasn't

mean-spirited about it. Her shrewd observations made navigating Society easier for Helena. Helena had learned when to hold her tongue and when to turn a blind eye, which had won her several friends among the ladies of Mayfair.

The duchess fell into step on Olive's other side. As they neared the rotunda, Olive froze. "Oh dear."

Helena's head snapped up to locate the cause of Olive's distress and her breath caught. Lord Thorne was standing in the middle of the stairs beneath a massive chandelier, and he was watching her with his captivating dark brown eyes. They had been like mirrors reflecting her image earlier that day, leaving her with the odd sense he saw into her soul and knew her secrets.

Candlelight shimmered off his black hair and cast a shadow over one side of his face, defining his high cheekbones. She was relieved the footpads hadn't caused any lasting damage. Perhaps it was silly to think on such things, but he had a very handsome face.

"It is good to see the baron out again," the duchess said as she continued toward the staircase.

Olive sighed and followed, dragging Helena with her.

"Lord Thorne, how lovely to see you again." The Duchess of Foxhaven offered her hand to the baron as they met at the foot of the stairs.

"Thank you, Your Grace, but the pleasure is all mine." He bowed gallantly over her hand and smiled. Helena melted inside even though it wasn't aimed at her. "I hope your family is well."

"Yes, my lord. We are all fortunate to be in good health."

"Excellent. I understand Lady Gabrielle and her new husband have returned to Town. Please extend my best to them."

A slight tightening at the corners of his eyes made Helena question his sincerity. Yet, she couldn't imagine she would be half as gracious as the baron if her betrothed abandoned her days before their wedding.

"Of course I will, my lord." The duchess patted his hand and smiled sympathetically. "How are you managing these days?"

He ignored the intent of her question and reported on his mother's and sister's health instead. While he and the duchess engaged in pleasantries, Helena studied him without reservation. His black jacket was of the best quality and cut to hug his broad shoulders and trim torso. Everything about his appearance was intentional, from the starch of his collar to his carefree hair made to appear as if he'd crawled from bed looking like perfection, to his high-polished footwear. A lot of effort went into his appearance, suggesting he cared a great deal how others viewed him.

She suppressed a sigh. She'd thought of Lord Thorne often these past seven days.

Too often.

She found herself looking for him while shopping with Olive. When she and Fergus made forays into the rookery, she feared running into him again. And in bed at night she fantasized about seeing him at a ball where they would dance the waltz. Where she hadn't expected to see him was at the church today. And now he was here, looking magnificent and causing her to yearn.

The man was a menace.

His gaze landed on her; amusement twinkled in the dark depths of his eyes.

She looked away quickly, her face growing hot from being caught taking his measure.

The duchess smiled reassuringly at her. "Lord Thorne, may I present Lady Prestwick? The viscountess is a new arrival from Aberdeen."

He took Helena's hand and bowed over it. His full lips grazed her gloved knuckles and sent her heart into a clumsy run, tripping and sputtering. "Lady Prestwick, it is a pleasure to make your acquaintance. Properly, that is." He lingered over her hand with a small smirk as if challenging her.

Helena didn't know what to say. If she explained their encounter earlier at St. Saviour's, Olive would have more questions she didn't want to answer. And if she said nothing, she feared her husband's cousin and the duchess would assume something untoward had occurred between her and the baron.

Olive forcefully cleared her throat, and Lord Thorne released Helena's hand.

"Forgive me, Lady Prestwick. What I meant to say is I had hoped for a proper introduction when I spotted you from afar this evening."

Theatre patrons began filtering through the rotunda returning to their seats.

"We are blocking the way, my lady."

"Oh!" Helena backed up several steps to allow others to pass. Lord Thorne flashed another perfect smile and bid her and her companions a good evening before sauntering away from the stairs, going against the flow of traffic. Helena turned to watch until he disappeared from sight.

Once he was gone, she was faced with Olive's frown. "Do be careful of the baron. He is a scoundrel of the first order."

The duchess chuckled and linked arms with her friend. "Allow the girl to have a bit of fun."

Olive sniffed, clearly not a supporter of fun. "Do not listen to her, Helena." She leaned close to whisper in her ear. "Unless you wish to be added to his list of conquests."

Helena's eyebrows shot up as her stomach pitched. Despite the tantalizing images that came to mind of becoming Lord Thorne's conquest, she needed to keep her distance. Maintaining a sterling reputation was important if she had any hope of bringing her youngest sister into Edinburgh Society. Gossip had a way of traveling even long distances. She banished the annoying voice inside her head telling her she should stay out of the rookery if she was worried for her reputation. Laying eyes on her sisters again outweighed the risks. Besides, she had no intentions of anyone important discovering her in Whitechapel.

※

Damn!

Sebastian wasn't any closer to being certain Lady Prestwick was the Whitechapel Angel than he'd been before his sister's observation about her perfume. He had thought he would be able to tell if she was his rescuer if he had a chance to really study her face and listen to her speak, but he still didn't know. She could have been the woman from that night, but then again, she may be nothing more than she appeared.

She was a pretty little thing. He hated to think she was frequenting the streets of Whitechapel and endangering herself. If she was the woman who had helped him, she was too sweet to be in any trouble. He'd seen her kindness with his sister. He might have even been the recipient of that kindness the night he was set upon.

He felt more unsettled than he'd been that afternoon. Seeing her again had only stirred up more questions. This was the reason he was lurking outside the theatre waiting for the performance to end instead of headed to the Den of Iniquity as planned.

Lord Prestwick hadn't kept a house in Mayfair, which meant his widow was either staying with relatives or she had let a town house for the Season. If she were engaged in clandestine activities, staying with Lord and Lady Eldridge would pose problems. She would need a place of her own unless she wanted to explain her late-night excursions.

The rub of it was Sebastian couldn't imagine any lady being so harebrained as to risk her reputation— Hell, her *life*—by stepping one foot in Whitechapel. Was she acting out of a misguided sense of charity? Reports of the angel's generosity made it seem a more likely scenario than anything else he'd envisioned. Regardless of her intentions, she would get herself killed if she kept this up, and he couldn't let that happen. Not if she had saved his life.

Perhaps following her this evening would put the matter to rest. Eve did have a tendency to allow her imagination to run wild, and he was probably a fool to entertain her silly notions. Still, a niggling at the back of his mind wouldn't go away. There was something not quite right about the Widow Prestwick.

As ladies and gentlemen began spilling from the theatre, carriages lined up to collect their owners. He kept a lookout for Lady Prestwick's green gown; his pulse jumped as he recalled how the silk creation teased with a peek of her modest décolletage. She wasn't as well-endowed as many ladies of his acquaintance, but she was soft and round enough to make for a pleasing bed partner.

He ran his fingers through his hair and exhaled slowly. Damn, he needed a good tup. He seemed incapable of thinking on anything else since his encounter with the lady earlier.

When a carriage bearing the Eldridge coat of arms rolled up to the curb, Sebastian pushed away from the wall. Peering through the crush, he spotted Lady Eldridge's peacock feathers first and then Lady Prestwick's pearl-draped coiffure. As the ladies strolled to the carriage arm in arm, any urgency to follow her faded. Obviously, she had arrived with her relative and would leave with the countess, too. Turning to find his own carriage and abandon this fool's mission, he stopped mid-spin.

"Do be careful, Helena. London is no place for a lady to travel alone."

"I have Fergus and we haven't far to go." Lady Prestwick embraced Lady Eldridge before the older lady climbed into the carriage with her footman's assistance. As the door closed, the countess swept the curtain aside to speak through the open window.

Sebastian eased closer to catch all of their hushed conversation. It wasn't well done of him, but he couldn't help himself.

"I do worry so about you," Lady Eldridge said. "Won't you reconsider staying at Eldridge House?"

Sebastian's ears pricked up. She wasn't staying with relatives.

Lady Prestwick smiled, dimples piercing her cheeks. "I would be underfoot too much. Besides, I became accustomed to being alone much of the time at Aldmist Fell. I don't mind the solitude."

"Wickie was adamant about keeping you all to himself in that rambling castle, the selfish man."

A slight grimace wrinkled Lady Prestwick's forehead, but she smoothed away the lines with an absentminded sweep of her hand. "Good night, Olive."

"Indulge me a little, Helena. At least allow me to accompany you next time. *I* grow weary of solitude."

Lord Eldridge rarely escorted his wife anywhere. Sebastian experienced a pang of sympathy for the countess, even though she was responsible for his sudden betrothal weeks earlier when Lady Eldridge had entered the drawing room to find him kissing Lady Gabrielle.

He tried to shrug off his guilt for taking liberties with Gabrielle, but it clung to him like the stench of a drunken night.

Lady Prestwick raised a hand to bid the countess farewell. "I will call tomorrow and we will go shopping."

As the carriage rolled away, Lady Prestwick blew out a breath that lifted a curl lying on her forehead. She turned and startled when she saw him.

"Lord Thorne, I thought you left an hour ago."

The tips of his ears began to burn. It wasn't like him to spy on others. Perhaps the knock to his head had turned him batty. He grinned to hide his embarrassment. "I didn't realize you kept such close watch on me."

She lowered her gaze and he was certain she blushed, though he couldn't see pink in the dim light from the street lamp. "Yes, well, you are not exactly unnoticeable."

He offered his hand as her carriage arrived at the curb. Her footman narrowed his eyes when Sebastian led her to the stairs instead of turning her over to the servant's care. Sebastian leaned into the carriage, waiting for her to settle on the bench. She adjusted her skirts and offered a terse thank-you.

"You catch a man's eye as well, Lady Prestwick," he said with a wink.

As he turned away, she mumbled something that sounded like "blasted handsome scoundrel." He smirked in response to her footman's scowl. "See the lady home safely, my good man."

He headed toward his carriage.

"Home?" The footman's voice carried on the air. "Aren't we searching tonight?"

The servant's words slammed Sebastian like a fist to the jaw and his step faltered.

Lady Prestwick hushed the man. "Of course I am going home," she said with false brightness. "*Ladies* don't traipse about London at night."

Oh, but at least one lady did. And Sebastian had discovered her identity.

He stalked toward his carriage but halted before climbing inside. "Follow the berlin," he said to his driver, "but keep your distance."

"Yes, milord."

Four

As Helena approached the front door of her rented town house, she looked back over her shoulder to Fergus and her driver. "After we change into more suitable clothing, we will reconvene in the foyer."

Fergus's eyebrows pulled together. "But you said——"

"I know what I said, and I'd thank you to be more careful of what *you* say in public."

His shoulders slumped. "Aye, lass. I wasna thinking."

Remorse flooded through her and her step faltered. She hovered on the edge of pretending she hadn't been harsh with him and asking his forgiveness. Fergus was in London pretending to be a servant well below his high rank of land steward because he was the kindest man she knew. When she had told him that she wanted to find her sisters, his response had filled her with hope and gratitude.

Blood ties shouldna be severed.

Her husband had told her the opposite. He'd said to think about the future and what their children would need—those strapping sons he had wanted so badly.

The past and future cannot exist side by side, Helena.

Remember where you would be if I hadn't taken you away and provided you with a home. Leave it behind you.

Tears pricked her eyes, and she turned toward the only man who had ever treated her as if what she wanted mattered. "Forgive me, Fergus. I don't know why you tolerate me so."

A corner of his mouth turned up as he held a handkerchief out to her. "You are a mite surly at times, but I tolerate you well enough."

She dabbed at the tears before they spilled over. "Thank you. I mean that sincerely."

His toothy grin appeared. "Run along, lass. We could have a long night ahead of us."

She nodded and returned his handkerchief. "I will be back in a wink." This was a frequent promise she'd made as a girl when Fergus agreed to take her and his sister fishing. Helena had been grateful for the moments she could forget about her lessons and earn a bit of freedom for a while.

She rang for her maid as soon as she reached her room. Ismay arrived with her characteristic smile, despite her eyes still being cloudy from sleep. Ismay was Fergus's younger sister, and Robert, the coachman, was his cousin. In fact, every servant at Aldmist Fell was some relation to him. Only Helena's governess had been an outsider.

When Wickie first brought Helena to the castle, he'd left her in the care of his servants. He rarely visited Aldmist Fell the first three years she had lived there, and when he did, their audiences were brief. He would demand an accounting of her progress from her governess, ask Helena if she needed anything, then dismiss them both.

Wickie wasn't unkind in their encounters, but his intensity had made her squirm. It was like he was inspecting her for flaws. She had been relieved to see his carriage driving away from the castle at the end of each visit.

She had met Fergus about two weeks after her arrival. He worked as Wickie's land steward and Fergus's mother was the cook, which meant he took all his meals at Aldmist Fell.

In the beginning, Helena dined alone in the drafty hall, but the day she screwed up her courage and made her way to the servants' dining room, Fergus had welcomed her. Being the highest-ranking servant, he'd overruled his mother and her governess, filled a plate for Helena, and made a spot beside him at the table. She ate every meal with the staff from that moment until Wickie returned and made her the lady of Aldmist Fell.

"Godspeed, milady," Ismay said as she secured the last fastening on Helena's boot.

"Thank you, my friend."

They shared a quick hug, then Helena rejoined the men. Tonight she and Fergus would be searching another brothel. More aptly, he would be searching while she waited close by biting her nails.

Blast. She hated having to rely on a man, even if he was a good one. But what choice did she have? She couldn't waltz into the brothel and demand information on her sister, or at least Fergus said she couldn't.

He assisted her into the carriage then climbed inside for the ride to Whitechapel as he always did when he wasn't pretending to be her footman. His brows lowered over his dark green eyes. "You should wait with Robert tonight. It's not safe. I promise to return with any information I learn about Lavinia at once."

She offered a bland smile. They had the same conversation every night. "If you find my sister and she's reluctant to come with you, how do you propose to get her to the carriage without her sounding the alarm?"

The man rubbed his whiskered jaw as he pondered her question. Eventually, his eyes lit. "I will bind her hands and stuff a handkerchief in her mouth. That oughta keep her quiet."

Helena wrinkled her nose at him. Fergus was teasing, of course. He might be a near giant, but he wouldn't hurt a soul. Well, not a woman anyway. He *was* a Scot, and like most of his clansmen, he enjoyed a good brawl on occasion when he was deep in his cups.

"I told you time and again, lass, I will invite her to come speak with her sister."

Helena rolled her eyes. She hadn't known about the letter her husband had written to her family until he was gone, but her family thought she was dead.

"I am sure that will be well-received." She did her best imitation of a Scottish brogue and made her voice deep. "Your ghost of a sister willna go away until you speak with her, lass."

He chuckled. "I do no' sound anything like that."

"Aye, you do."

When he crossed his arms over his barrel chest and jutted his chin, she laughed too.

"I admit I never picked up the accent, but it's not from a lack of trying." She patted her thigh where she had strapped the dagger he had given her. "I am coming with you, and I will be fine."

His scowl deepened. "You may not have the brogue mastered, but you possess the Paterson women's stubbornness."

Since she admired his kinswomen very much, she considered this a high compliment. She just wished it hadn't taken so long for her stubborn streak to develop. Perhaps then she wouldn't have allowed Prestwick to run roughshod over her during their marriage.

Of course, she hadn't been privy to his lies during their marriage. And even if she had learned the truth, she'd had no power to change things. But she could have been less accommodating.

Robert stopped the carriage on the edge of Whitechapel. She and Fergus would walk the rest of the way.

"Please stay with Robert, lass."

"No, thank you."

Fergus huffed in exasperation and mumbled something about stubborn women being God's curse on men.

As they moved deep into the belly of the rookery, foul odors took on a life of their own. The smell of urine and soured scent of rotted food seared her nostrils and throat. She covered her mouth and nose with her handkerchief and pressed on.

At the entrance to a winding alley, a small fire burned. A man was slumped over before the fire, his mouth hanging slack. Orange flickers revealed deep valleys in his gaunt face. A child was curled into a ball at his side. Heaviness settled in her heart as their misery carried across the street in waves. Were her sisters hungry too? Did they sleep cuddled together on the street? The thought nearly overwhelmed her, and she stopped to catch her breath.

"You canna wait in the alley this time," Fergus said as he turned toward her. "No playing the angel tonight, lass. You've a good heart, but it is just as likely to be cut from your chest in this place. Leave the man and child be."

Even though she knew it was unwise to reveal herself to the poor and forgotten people of London, she couldn't help wanting to take care of them. Every time she gave to someone else, she prayed someone was doing the same for her sisters. She nodded reluctantly.

The light from the fire licked over the uneven cobblestones, and Helena's and Fergus's shadows stretched grotesquely on the brick walls of the tenements. No candles burned in the windows, but she knew the buildings were occupied. Angry voices rose in argument and a baby's wail pierced the darkness.

The sounds filled her with deep sorrow and shameful relief. She was but a visitor passing through the squalor. Tonight she would lay her head on a clean pillow and fall asleep secure in the knowledge she was safe. She might risk her life every time she ventured into the East End, but she wasn't always in danger. Her sisters had no way of escaping this life without her assistance, so it was a risk she must take.

"Just a bit farther," Fergus said softly. "Then we'll find a hiding place."

They fell into step together and headed in the direction of a dimly lit establishment. Delicate notes from a pianoforte drifted from the brothel. She was struck by the irony of the beautiful sound originating in such an ugly place.

A scuff sounded behind them. She snapped her head around, but the dark hid everything. Hairs on the back of her neck stood on end and goose bumps chased down her arms and legs. Fergus didn't stop walking. She strained to hear signs that someone was there as she crept along in his wake, but there was nothing more.

Trying to shake the uneasy sense they were being followed, she focused on the brothel. *Please, let us find Lavinia tonight.*

About a hundred yards from the establishment, Fergus stopped and deposited her in an arched door-way as deep as a wall niche. Her heart hammered as the uneasiness refused to go away.

"Remember what I taught you, lass. If anyone gives you trouble, do no' hesitate to bury the blade in him."

She wet her lips. "Please, be quick about it. I must know if we've found her." She couldn't admit she was frightened, or he might not leave her. Sometimes Helena felt as if they were chasing a specter. They never came any closer to the end of their hunt.

She watched until he entered the brothel, then leaned back against the door to wait and listened some more. Her fear dissipated as she detected no more evidence anyone was stalking her. Time dragged, and when she tired of watching the brothel, she glanced toward the alley where the man and child were. The street was deserted and the only sounds were the ones she had grown accustomed to hearing in the rookery.

The man and child seemed so alone, forgotten.

Their sadness called to her. She glanced back at the brothel. No one was coming from that direction. If she hurried, she could slip the man a few coins and return without anyone being the wiser. She hesitated a moment, but then made up her mind and pushed away from the building to head for the alley.

∽∾

Sebastian ducked into a dark doorway when he heard light footsteps quickly approaching. A figure passed him without detecting his presence, and when it crossed the street and entered the ring of light created by the fire, he could see it was Lady Prestwick. A halo lit her hair and surrounded her lithe figure. Her manservant was mysteriously missing.

As she neared the man and child, the outline of her body showed through the thin muslin dress. Sebastian smiled, appreciating her form. He wished his sister had been right about his association with the lady. He would have liked to share Lady Prestwick's bed, but alas, she had only saved his life.

She spoke briefly with the man before bending over and providing Sebastian with a better view of her behind. The man thanked her profusely for whatever it was she handed him, then she turned to make her way back down the lane. She barely made it two steps before another man shot out of the alley in pursuit.

Sebastian sprang from his hiding place, which was too far away to reach her first. "Look sharply, Lady Prestwick."

Her cry of surprise pierced the air. The lanky form lunged for her, but before Sebastian knew what was happening, she grabbed the man's ears and her knee slammed into his groin. He crumpled to the cobblestones, groaning in agony. She lifted the hem of her skirts and dashed away.

"*Mo chroi*, where are you?" a man called.

"Fergus! I am here." It was her servant looking for her. Their voices faded as they hurried away in the opposite direction.

Sebastian crossed the road and nodded to the wide-eyed man and child. "Good evening."

When the footpad began to stir, Sebastian pulled his firearm from his jacket and cocked the hammer. "Stay where you are."

He held the man at gunpoint until he was certain Lady Prestwick and her servant had escaped.

The Scot had called her *mo chroi*. *My heart*. What exactly was the nature of her relationship with the man? An irrational surge of jealousy raced through him, and he turned it on the thief.

"Do you have a pair of Hessians that don't belong to you?"

The man responded with a confused grunt.

"Consider yourself fortunate." Sebastian nudged him with the toe of his boot. "Stand up and take your leave before I finish what the lady started."

He struggled to his feet and limped away, disappearing into the alley again. Sebastian turned his attention to the man before the fire and the young boy.

The boy held out his palm to reveal a coin. "The angel gave it to me, sir. I didn't take it."

Sebastian grinned. So she was out performing good deeds. "Well, you should tuck it away where it will be safe. Don't mind me. I am just here to protect the angel." On second thought, he could do his own good deed. He pulled out a pound note and gave it to the man. "You both could benefit from a good meal and a place to sleep."

The man took it reluctantly at first, then shoved it into his pocket. "God's blessings, sir."

Five

SOMEONE HAD RECOGNIZED HELENA LAST NIGHT. IT seemed impossible anyone would know her identity, much less see her in the dark, and yet it had happened. Someone had called her name in time to save her from being accosted. Her attacker had been a menacing shadow pouncing when she'd spun around and reacted. Fergus's training had saved her skin, but now she faced a new danger.

Someone had followed her to Whitechapel.

Despite the grittiness of her eyes, her body refused to stay abed. She rushed through her toilette without bothering Ismay and made her way down the corridor. Her movements were graceful and controlled as she descended the staircase. The morning newssheet was folded neatly on the heavy walnut table just inside the entry where it always awaited her, along with copies of *The Informer*, *The London Observer*, *A Lady's Companion*, and *The Talebearer*. Her heart slammed against her breastbone as she forced herself not to run.

Picking up the stack of gossip sheets Fergus had purchased that morning and tucking them under her arm, she glided toward the breakfast room as if it were any other day. If there was mention of her encounter last night, she didn't know what she would do.

Once she was seated at the small, round table, she muttered a desperate prayer. *Please don't let me see my name. Please don't let me see my name.* When she couldn't ignore the distasteful task any longer, she slowly opened *The Informer* and scanned the columns for mention of Lady P. and late-night excursions to the rookeries. Her pulse raced as she dragged her finger over the words, but each inch she covered without seeing anything remotely connected to her eased the tightness in her chest. She quickly opened the next paper. And the next. After reading all four, she melted against the seatback.

There was nothing. Not a hint of her late-night activities. She released a pent-up breath and chuckled, relieved. She couldn't believe her luck.

In a better frame of mind, she paid closer attention to the victims who hadn't been so lucky to escape having their reputations sullied. The second to the last tidbit caught her eye.

> *Lord Thorne was seen leaving the theatre in a rush after an encounter with a certain paragon of Society last night. Could it be the lady gave the baron the proper set-down he richly deserved for making her daughter so unhappy that she had no choice but to run away?*

Helena closed the paper with a disgusted huff. Really, couldn't Lord Thorne make an appearance anywhere without exciting the gossips? And how terrible to imply the Dowager Duchess of Foxhaven had been anything less than kind to the baron or to remind everyone his betrothed had eloped with another man.

Hardly a day passed without hearing some salacious tidbit about Lord Thorne. She considered the sources and frowned. Perhaps he was partly responsible, although he was clearly the wronged party.

No matter what was said about his mental status or reputation, everyone agreed he was a handsome devil. Several women had gone so far as to imply they would welcome his company any time or place, but Lord Thorne was not accommodating. He ignored the assemblies and thwarted any chances these ladies might have to lure him to their beds. Helena suspected this was the source of their ire and the reason there was often venom behind their words. Feeling slighted, they took pleasure in uncovering his flaws and pointing them out to everyone. Helena supposed it was human nature to disparage what one couldn't have, but it was still very nasty business, indeed.

Fergus entered the breakfast room, holding out his hand as he approached. The gold watch glinted in the sunlight when he passed the window. "Robert found this in the carriage."

Helena took the piece with a frown. The hinge had been knocked askew and she was barely able to pry it open. The face of the watch had a crack across it. She turned it over, looking for a marking, but didn't see one. "It must have fallen from Lord Thorne's pocket the other night." She closed it as best as she could.

"Would you mind too much taking it to the watch-maker? Once it has been repaired, it can be returned to him anonymously."

Fergus scowled. "He can replace his watch."

"But if it has sentimental value... Please. The poor man has suffered enough. Surely a little kindness will do him good."

"You are too kind, lass. It addles your brain." He tucked the watch in his pocket. "I will take it to the watchmaker today."

"Thank you, Fergus."

He left, grumbling under his breath, but she knew it was for appearances only. He rarely denied her anything, which made him addled by kindness as well.

Feeling much relieved by the absence of her name in the paper, Helena retired to her chambers to sort through her correspondence, but Luna had other ideas. The gray cat leaped onto the small writing desk, turned a circle atop the letter Helena was trying to read, and plopped in the middle.

"You naughty girl," Helena playfully scolded as she scratched Luna's head and smiled when the stray began purring. Helena's correspondence would have to wait, it seemed. A knock sounded at the door.

"Enter."

It was Ismay and Fergus.

"You have a visitor, milady." Ismay crossed the chamber and held out a calling card. Helena took it, expecting Olive had come to check on her well-being, as she often did. Helena fumbled the card.

Sebastian Thorne? The black ink screamed in warn-ing. What was the baron doing here? In the middle of the day, no less. An unrelenting heat engulfed her as the alternative hit her. A nighttime visit would be a thousand times more damning. Her mouth was dry and she licked her lips.

"Did he state his business?"

Fergus frowned. "He didna. I should toss him out on his arse." He looked too happy with the prospect of manhandling the baron, but she didn't care to draw more notice to his presence at her doorstep than necessary.

She couldn't receive a bachelor, of course, especially one with his reputation for being a rogue. Even if curiosity would drive her mad all afternoon.

"Don't do anything hasty, Fergus. Tell him I am not in, but see if you can determine his purpose in calling."

The large Scotsman snorted. "A man like Thorne has one purpose for calling on a lady."

Helena shot a censorious look in his direction. Fergus glanced at his younger sister and sobered. "As you wish, milady." He bowed then spun on his heel and stalked from the room.

She scratched Luna behind the ears once more before making her way to the window to see if Fergus would follow her orders about not making a scene. Ismay scooped the cat in her arms and came to peer out the window too.

The boulevard was free of carriages, thank goodness. Lord Thorne had arrived a little before calling hours, which meant he'd either given thought to how his appearance at her door may be viewed, or he had no manners.

"Does he wish to bed you then, milady?"

Helena gasped.

Ismay smiled and cuddled Luna. "I know about the carrying-on between lads and lasses. Fergus may treat me like a child, but just because I am no' married does no' make me naive."

Helena didn't question her claim. Ismay had a beau back in Aberdeen. "When are you going to marry your Terrence? I know he has asked you."

Ismay shrugged. "Not till I see you settled, I suppose."

"If you are waiting for me to remarry, please don't. I am widowed and I have money at my disposal. I am as settled as I will ever be."

"You havna been loved yet, but you will. Then I will marry Terrence. He is waiting for me."

Helena bit her tongue. They could discuss it once they returned to Aldmist Fell with Gracie and any of Helena's other sisters who wanted a new start.

Muffled voices carried to the second floor, and the front door slammed, rattling the window.

"That didna sound good."

Helena held her breath as she awaited the baron's reaction. He stepped onto the walkway and paused, his back to the town house. A smart hat hid his raven hair except for a few wisps brushing the collar of his burgundy coat.

"My, he cuts a dashing figure in his buckskins."

"Aye." Ismay chuckled as she set Luna on the ground. "His tailor should be commended."

Heat climbed Helena's neck as she realized she'd spoken aloud. *Blast.* Why must she too want what she couldn't have?

"Are you certain you want to turn him away?"

"No," Helena murmured. "But I must. Lord Thorne is a distraction I cannot afford."

The baron glanced over his shoulder toward the window. Her heart stopped. Her feet became rooted to the mahogany floor. He turned slowly, his gaze locked with hers. His dark eyes narrowed and his lips moved.

What are you about, Lady Prestwick? he seemed to say.

Her heart leaped, pounding against her ribs and in her ears.

"Dear heavens, it was him. He followed me to Whitechapel last night."

Ismay issued an outraged cry and yanked the curtains closed. "We'll just see what Fergus has to say about the bloody Sassenach stalking you."

"No!" Helena grabbed her maid's arm. She hadn't told Fergus about someone calling her name before the footpad tried to attack her, and she didn't want him to know Lord Thorne had followed them.

"Why not?" Ismay's green eyes widened. "Ooh, you like him."

Helena shook her head. "Fergus would get in a lot of trouble if he attacked a nobleman. Please, say nothing to him. I can handle Lord Thorne."

It was a bold statement. She had no experience in handling rogues, and rumors had it the baron was a notch above average when it came to being roguish.

Avoidance. That was the only action she could take. She could never see Lord Thorne again, which meant she must hand over control of the search to Fergus. It didn't sit well with her, but with the blasted baron dogging her heels, she was left in a position she hated.

With no choice.

❦

Four days had passed since Sebastian was turned away from Lady Prestwick's door, and she had refused to see him each day since. Every evening the lady attended balls he wasn't invited to attend, returned to her town house, and didn't venture out again. A lack of adequate sleep made his mind fuzzy, and he'd begun to wonder if he had imagined following the viscountess to Whitechapel. Perhaps he should hire a man to follow her.

He shook his head. People might think he was as insane as his father if they found out. In truth, the only thing separating his brand of madness from his father's was that Sebastian didn't forget where he was or battle demons no one else could see.

Oh, no. *Sebastian* was engaged in a different type of fight. A battle of wills with an angel. The Angel of Whitechapel, no less. And she was winning.

Devil take it! He squeezed the bridge of his nose as he stood before a glossy black door with a sparkling brass lion knocker. He couldn't believe he was doing this, but God help him, Lady Prestwick was all he could think about morning and night. He needed help, even if it meant swallowing his pride.

Before he could change his mind, he grasped the knocker and banged on the door. It took but a minute for the servant to answer. Perhaps that meant she was receiving today.

Sebastian handed his calling card over without ceremony. "Lord Thorne to see Lady Ellis."

As the manservant showed him to a tidy parlor, Sebastian's stomach turned to stone. If his former fiancée refused to see him, his humiliation would know no bounds.

He was left alone while the man went to see if Gabrielle was in. A decanter filled with amber liquid winked in the sunlight, and he made his way to the sideboard to pour a glass. The warmth of the brandy had begun to loosen the knots in his body when Gabrielle swept into the room.

"Sebastian, how lovely to see you." Her voice held wonder and perhaps a touch of relief.

They hadn't spoken since the night at the inn when she'd chosen his rival over him. The familiar slow burn of anger flickered in his chest, but it didn't combust as usual.

He allowed himself a good look at her. Her gray eyes held a sparkle again, and her cheeks boasted a healthy, rosy glow.

"You look radiant." It sounded more like a concession than a compliment, but it was the truth.

"Thank you, my lord." Her smile faded a bit, and she gazed at him from beneath her dark lashes as if she were ashamed to be happy in his presence. "I see you have a drink already or I would offer one."

He lifted the glass in salute. "Convey my compliments to your husband. He always had fine taste in brandy and women."

She crossed her arms, closing off to him before he'd even had a chance to solicit her assistance. Not that he blamed her. He was behaving like an arse.

"Forgive me, Lady Ellis. I am not here to dredge up old grudges." He gestured toward a chair. "May I sit, please?"

She pursed her lips. "I suppose, so long as you aren't here to cause trouble."

"I promise trouble is the furthest from my mind," he said, then smiled because part of him was pleased to see her again. At least his doubts could be laid to rest. "You look happy. It pains me to say, but it seems I was wrong about Ellis."

The softness returned to her face, and she claimed a chair so he could finally sit as well. "I should be the one asking forgiveness. I never meant to—"

He lifted a hand to signal her to stop. "I am quite well." If she said she hadn't meant to hurt him, he would feel compelled to tell her she hadn't. He'd been fond of Gabrielle—she had seemed a pleasant means to an end—and he would have treated her very well, but he hadn't loved her. And compared to how blissful she appeared now, she hadn't loved him either.

She folded her hands in her lap.

"There, now isn't that better?" He relaxed against the seatback. "Just two old friends having a nice chat?"

"Perhaps *you're* old," she said with a saucy toss of her head and the hint of a teasing smile.

He laughed, feeling more at ease.

"Do you want to tell me the real reason you have called, Sebastian?"

He took another sip of his drink to stall. She would want explanations, and he wasn't certain how to explain his curiosity about Lady Prestwick.

Obsession is more like it.

Gabrielle sighed. "I do not have all day."

"I need you to speak with your mother. I would like an invitation to Lady Eldridge's annual ball this week."

Her mouth formed a silent O.

"Since your mother is Lady Eldridge's closest friend," he said, "I had hoped she might speak with the countess on my behalf."

"And you think Lady Eldridge's ball is the best time to reintroduce your sister to Society?" Her wrinkled brow revealed her reluctance to help. "If I may be so bold as to make a suggestion, perhaps a smaller venue would be more tolerable to Miss Thorne. Large crowds make her nervous."

"*I* want to go," he snapped.

He closed his eyes and took a slow, deep breath to contain his temper. He didn't need advice from someone who'd met his sister only a handful of times, but he did need Gabrielle's help. Opening his eyes, he forced a half smile. "As I was saying, the invitation is not for my sister."

Gabrielle's frown deepened. "Why, in God's name, would you want to attend Lady Eldridge's ball? You called her a busybody."

He gritted his teeth. Leave it to Gabrielle not only to remember things he said weeks ago, but also to remind him. He could see he would get nowhere unless he told the truth. "Lady Eldridge has a cousin visiting from Scotland. I made Lady Prestwick's acquaintance at the theatre recently, and I would like to further the association."

She leaned back in her chair and steepled her fingers in a manner her father used to practice. "The Widow Prestwick." She emphasized the word *widow* as if that alone explained his interest. Did his former fiancée truly believe he would come to her for help in seducing a woman?

"Her marital status is one small part of who she is."
Not that he really knew much more about her—other
than she was adept at protecting herself and had a
penchant for midnight strolls in the rookeries—but
he *wanted* to know more. And it had very little to
do with wanting to tup her, although that would be
acceptable too.

"I'm sorry, Sebastian. Whoever you wish to know
better is none of my concern. I think it is wonderful
you have an interest in Lady Prestwick. Mama has said
such nice things about her."

He scowled and Gabrielle chuckled.

"I will speak to Mama this evening. I'm certain she
will be able to persuade Lady Eldridge to invite you."
She bit her bottom lip, her merriment fading.

He nodded in encouragement for her to say what
was on her mind.

"Anthony and I were also planning to attend. We
don't receive many invitations, and I…" Her gray eyes
shimmered and she blinked away tears.

He had known when she eloped with the earl her
reputation would suffer, but he didn't wish her ill.
His smile was tight, even though he would like to put
everything behind them. "It seems like the perfect
opportunity to show the gossips there are no hard
feelings between us, wouldn't you agree?"

"Not even with Anthony?" She looked so hopeful
he couldn't bear to disappoint her.

"The evening will not end in fisticuffs. I can promise you that much."

"Thank you, Sebastian. Considering everything
that transpired, that is gentlemanly of you." A sweet

smile eased across her pretty face, reminding him of the reason he'd thought she might be the one for him. "Anthony misses your friendship. Maybe someday…"

He shrugged. "Maybe."

He and Ellis had a long way to go before Sebastian would call the earl a friend again, if they ever reached that point. Still, he had other matters claiming his attention, and fighting over something he couldn't change would do him no good. It wasn't until he left Keaton Place that he realized he wouldn't change the past even if it were possible.

Six

HELENA WAS READY TO CRAWL OUT OF HER SKIN BY the time she arrived at Olive's annual ball. She had turned over every possibility in her head, and she had gained nothing but a throbbing at her temples. How could Lavinia be so close and yet completely out of Helena's reach?

Earlier that morning Fergus had returned after a night of prowling the East End with both good and bad news about her sister. One of the girls at a George Street brothel had been more than willing to talk once Fergus handed over a fat purse. She said Lavinia had worked there a short time, but she'd been traded to a fashionable brothel that catered to gentlemen of means. The girl hadn't known which one, not that Helena would have allowed *that* to deter her. She was willing to search every one until she found her sister.

It was the *gentlemen only* rule that presented an obstacle.

"Gentlemen," she grumbled under her breath as she approached the ballroom entrance. She hardly considered any man who frequented a brothel a gentleman, but that was neither here nor there. She needed a man of good breeding and prestige, one who knew how to keep a secret. And she wasn't convinced such a creature existed.

Blast! Perhaps she should forgo the ball and return to the town house until she solved this problem. There had to be a way to gain access to Lavinia. Surely the brothels received deliveries, but could Fergus slip away unnoticed to question the women about her sister? It was far-fetched, but pursuing outlandish ideas had almost become commonplace for her.

As one of the footmen turned to ask her name, a thought occurred to her. Perhaps Olive's husband knew a thing or two about visiting brothels. Her face heated. Approaching Lord Eldridge about the subject would require more gall than Helena had. Nevertheless, the idea was better than anything else she'd come up with today.

She spotted Olive several steps inside the ballroom engaged in conversation with the Dowager Duchess of Foxhaven and a young woman with ebony curls and exotic eyes. When the footman announced Helena's arrival, Olive looked up with a welcoming smile. She gestured to her to join them.

Perhaps Helena could cut the night short if she first spent a little time chatting with Olive and her friends. She didn't want to insult her husband's cousin, but she was in no state of mind to enjoy a ball.

"Helena, how lovely to see you." Olive grasped her hands and pecked her cheek. "Allow me to make introductions. You have met the duchess, and this is her daughter, Lady Ellis."

The lady who had jilted Lord Thorne was stunningly

beautiful. A pang of envy seized Helena, but she quickly banished the unwelcome sentiment. She couldn't care less about Sebastian Thorne or whom he found to his liking. At least that was what she'd been telling herself all afternoon. Seven days in a row, he had come to her door requesting an audience, and he had been turned away each time. Today, however, they had seen neither hide nor hair of him. She hated to admit she had been disappointed.

Interest lit Lady Ellis's gray eyes, and Helena had the impression the countess was taking her measure. "It is a pleasure to meet you, Lady Prestwick. I've heard much about you."

Before Helena could wonder what tales Olive had been spreading, a handsome gentleman with dark blond hair approached. Lady Ellis linked arms with him. "Anthony, *this* is Lady Prestwick."

Helena could only assume the gentleman was Lord Ellis, given the lady's familiarity. His blue eyes were kind and warm just like his wife's. Olive introduced Lady Ellis's husband and everyone exchanged pleasantries.

Even after the duchess excused herself, and Olive left to attend to her hostess duties, Lord and Lady Ellis remained at Helena's side.

"Have you met anyone interesting in London?" the lady asked.

Helena blinked. "Interesting?"

She nodded, her dark curls bouncing slightly. "Yes, I found quite a few interesting gentlemen are in Town for the Season. Has one in particular caught your eye?"

"Uh…" Words abandoned Helena.

Lord Ellis smiled fondly at his wife. "Subtlety has

never been your strength, love. Do you not recall our conversation in the carriage about minding our own affairs?"

"I recall it, but we never reached an agreement."

"I am fairly certain we did, Gabrielle."

She patted his arm and batted her lashes at him. "Now, dear husband, you mustn't argue with me, or Lady Prestwick will think you are a terrible bore."

He laughed and the affection in his gaze warmed Helena's heart. She had no idea there were married couples who behaved this way. Lord and Lady Ellis seemed to genuinely enjoy one another's companionship.

The orchestra began to play a waltz.

Lord Ellis smiled at Helena. "I believe that's my cue to whisk away my meddling wife. I will keep her occupied while you find a place to hide."

"Anthony!" Despite Lady Ellis's protest, she beamed at him. If ever a love match existed, Lord and Lady Ellis were living proof. The countess took Helena's hand between hers. "It was lovely to meet you, Lady Prestwick. I hope we can speak again soon."

"I would welcome your company anytime, Lady Ellis." Awkward questions and all. The countess seemed the most genuine person Helena had met in London. It was refreshing.

She bid the couple a good evening then sought out a quiet place to think. No sooner had she turned her thoughts back to solving the problem of gaining access to her sister than a rich baritone interrupted.

"I thought they would never leave."

Helena's heart slammed against her ribs. She didn't need to turn to know the baron had come up behind her. The air was heavier, more electrified when he was near.

"Lord Thorne, I didn't expect to cross paths with you this evening."

He moved closer, his body heat saturating her back and yet causing a chill to race down her spine. If she shifted an inch, their bodies would come in contact.

"The ballroom isn't our usual rendezvous location, is it, angel?" he whispered, his breath whisking across her nape.

She could barely swallow. Pretending a calm she didn't feel, she tossed an amused look over her shoulder only to come up short. His mouth was entirely too close. And tempting beyond reason.

An image of Sebastian Thorne's elegant fingers grazing her cheek, sliding down her neck and along her collarbone before cupping her breast, and his lips nibbling the slope between her neck and shoulder made her legs tremble.

Blast! If she swooned, she would never forgive herself.

"What is it you want, my lord?" Her voice had grown husky.

A small smirk played upon his lips. "I want my curiosity satisfied."

She returned her attention to the dancers and shuffled a step forward to create a little distance between them. "I don't take your meaning."

"We both know what you have been up to, Lady Prestwick. You don't want me to spell it out in front of witnesses. The *ton* does enjoy a good scandal, but not as much as I relish denying them pleasure."

She wheeled around to face him. If she'd had

doubts that he had been the one to warn her of the footpad's attack, they were eradicated looking into his intense brown eyes. He knew her secret, or at least he knew one piece to it. How long he would keep it, she didn't know. Perhaps she could buy his silence.

"Come to the town house tonight, but please be discreet."

She tried to sweep past, but he captured her elbow and guided her toward the dance floor.

"What are you doing?" she whispered harshly.

"Dancing with you."

❧

The lady bristled as Sebastian led her into the waltz. It was the middle of the dance and he wouldn't have long to hold her, but he would savor every moment.

Her eyes narrowed at him. "*Why* are we dancing? I already invited you back to my home."

"And if we leave now, tongues will begin wagging. You have a reputation to protect, do you not, Lady Prestwick?"

A crimson blush spread across her face, and her lashes fluttered as she looked everywhere but at him. Tonight she wore a sheer robe trimmed in embroidered black ribbon over an ivory silk gown. Her attire was uncharacteristically demure for a widow, as if she shied away from drawing attention to herself.

Sebastian couldn't take his eyes off her.

"I believe you can see the logic in remaining at the ball, madam. Enjoy the festivities. Dance with other gentlemen." His voice thinned. He cleared his throat and pretended it meant nothing. "Later, you will depart for home and soon after I will leave as well, but only when I'm certain no one will link our names."

Her gaze snapped up. "It sounds as if you have had your fair share of secret liaisons, my lord."

He couldn't hold back a grin. "What exactly did your invitation entail? I thought we were just going to talk."

She turned a deeper shade of red and pressed her lips tightly together.

He didn't push her to answer but drew her closer on the spin. Her sweet scent filled his head with memories of her soft breasts crushed against him when they had collided outside St. Saviour's Church. She had smiled at him that day, dimples winking up at him. Her plump mouth ripe for tasting.

If she offered more than conversation tonight, he might forget about wanting answers, but only temporarily. The mystery of what she had been doing in Whitechapel was eating at him. If it were nothing more than a charity mission, there would be no reason for her servant to leave her alone.

The music faded; the waltz finished too soon. They still held each other, neither of them moving even as the other couples began filing from the dance floor. She glanced up with wide eyes. Her pink tongue darted across her lips. God, he wanted this woman. But a vulnerability about her held him in check.

He released her and led her into the promenade. At the end of the line, he lifted her hand to his lips. Eyes that reminded him of the blue-green waters off the Spanish coast regarded him warily. The same optimism that had overtaken him as he'd stood on the sands as a younger man and viewed the vast sea filled him again in that moment. It was irrational. Unexpected. Marvelous.

"Thank you for the pleasure of your company, my lady, but I must bid you farewell. For now."

A slight frown turned down the corners of her mouth.

As he sauntered away, he could feel her eyes on him and he smiled.

Seven

SEBASTIAN HEADED TOWARD THE CARD ROOM TO PUT distance between him and Lady Prestwick. If he stayed in the ballroom, he feared he would be unable to ignore her, and he didn't want anyone speculating about his association with her. From the snippets of conversation he had overheard while waiting for Ellis and Gabrielle to take their leave, Lady Prestwick was well thought of by the *ton* at large, and he didn't wish her any harm.

Her connection with Lady Eldridge afforded her some advantage, but her participation in the Mayfair Ladies Charitable Society had secured her place among the ranks. Apparently, the ladies found her quite demure and amenable. The footpad she'd unmanned would probably disagree. He chuckled, finding he liked that she was more than she seemed to be.

Sebastian's jovial mood carried over to the card room and improved even more when an old school-mate waved him over to join a game of loo. With his mind preoccupied by his coming meeting with the intriguing Lady Prestwick, he lost several rounds, but even parting with his money didn't put a damper on his mood.

The Earl of Ellis's arrival, however, did the trick.

The last time Sebastian had laid eyes on Ellis, they both had been bloody messes from fighting over Gabrielle. His temper flared as the entire affair came back in vivid detail. Sebastian's fiancée staying with his longtime rival and onetime friend. Gabrielle as bare as the day she was born underneath her cloak. Her hand linked with Ellis's as she declared her intentions to stay with him. It was too much to forgive and forget.

As Ellis neared the table, Sebastian snatched his stack of money and pushed to his feet.

"Where are you going?" one of his competitors asked in a harassed tone.

"Away." He ignored the protests, brushed past Ellis, and stalked from the card room. He made it halfway down the corridor when a door closed behind him.

"Thorne, I would like a word." It was Ellis.

Sebastian came to a halt, his fingers curling into a fist. The sounds of muffled music and laughter beyond the double doors at the end of the corridor reached him. He should keep moving. If they came to blows at a ball, Sebastian would only make things worse for Eve and Mother. Instead, he turned to face his adversary.

"Lying. Traitorous. Jackass." Sebastian bit out each insult. "There are three words for you. I think they all fit."

The muscles in Ellis's jaw bulged and fire flared in his eyes, but the earl doused the flames. His smile was grim and forced. "I could say those words fit you as well, but I promised Gabby I would mind my manners."

"What do you want?"

Ellis took a step toward him, his footfall silent on the thick Turkish carpet. "My wife suggested we try to make amends."

"Has your bollocks in hand, does she?"

The earl's brows dipped low and he crossed his arms. "I refuse to exchange insults. I only meant to tell you I didn't intend for matters to end badly for you."

"Are you trying to say you are sorry?"

"For doing what I did? *Never.* I need Gabby as much as the air I breathe."

Sebastian scoffed. "The chit has turned you into a sap." He continued toward the ballroom, dismissing Ellis.

"I'm sorry for what my actions did to you, my friend."

Sebastian paused with his hand on the door handle. The word *friend* was bittersweet. In all his years of competing with Ellis, Sebastian had never realized the earl was the only real friend he'd ever had. Now there was nothing but anger in Sebastian's heart.

"I want to help," the earl said.

"I never needed your help, and I don't need it now."

Ellis's assistance had made his life hell years ago at Eton. When the earl had intervened in a fight between Sebastian and three older boys who had been tormenting Sebastian since his arrival at the school, he thought he'd made a lifelong friend. Then Ellis hadn't arrived at the stables the next morning to ride with him as planned. The bullies had ambushed him. Their leader had taunted him. *Where is your wet nurse, Thorne?*

No one else had been in the building. Not even a groom could be found. The biggest one had smacked a riding crop against his meaty palm. *Ellis won't be here to save you today. He has better ways to spend his time.*

Sebastian took a beating like he'd never known that day, and the attacks increased in intensity and duration over the next few weeks. He had lain in bed at night with the taste of his own blood feeding his desperation. He couldn't stop fighting back. If he had, he would have always been seen as a victim in need of rescue from the heroic Anthony Keaton. Sebastian's only hope had been to become better than Ellis.

At fisticuffs. At riding. At anything and everything.

Eventually, Sebastian established a reputation for fighting like the devil's spawn, and the other boys began to give him wide berth and grudging respect. By the time he no longer needed to prove his superiority over Ellis, challenging the earl had become a game. One Sebastian enjoyed playing and winning until Gabrielle.

He met his former friend's shuttered gaze. The sting of betrayal was as sharp as the moment Sebastian learned Ellis had run away with Gabrielle. As hurtful as the day the earl hadn't come to the stables as promised.

Sebastian would be a fool to trust the man ever again. "Bugger off."

Eight

HELENA WAS ASHAMED TO ADMIT SHE WAS HIDING from Lord Thorne. In the ladies' retiring room, of all places. It was the one place she felt certain she wouldn't bump into him again.

Unfortunately, one could only do so much primping before earning curious stares from the retiring room attendant. Helena glanced up to catch the young woman goggling her in the looking glass for the third time. The attendant averted her gaze.

Helena swallowed a resigned sigh. Hiding was pointless given he would be standing in her drawing room before the night was over. Carefully, she replaced the lid on her lip rouge, slid it into her beaded reticule, then slowly gained her feet.

The retiring room door swung open and Celeste, Baroness Lovelace, entered. Her step faltered when she spotted Helena, but she covered her hesitation with a pretty smile. "Lady Prestwick, I thought you had gone."

"I will be leaving soon." Helena avoided looking in the mirror. If she didn't see the blood rushing to her cheeks, she could deny she was blushing. She had definitely spent too long loitering in the retiring room if a mere acquaintance had noticed her absence.

Lady Lovelace strode to the dressing table, and Helena shuffled out of her way. The widow's regal bearing caused a sick tumble inside Helena. Even though she knew Society saw her as one of them, she couldn't help from time to time still seeing herself as the common girl her father had cast away.

She rolled her shoulders and held her head high. Her dealings with Wickie had taught her never to show weakness. *It's like blood in a shark-filled ocean*, he'd said when she asked to come to London. *The* ton *will pick your flesh from their teeth.*

Her experiences so far suggested her husband had held a skewed view of Society. The ladies of Mayfair extended many kindnesses to her, but she was always cautious, never speaking of anything controversial and keeping her opinions to herself. Her aim was survival.

"I saw you dancing with Lord Thorne." Lady Lovelace plopped onto the tufted stool and smoothed a hand over her hair. "If you've a rendezvous with Sebastian, you will not regret it."

Helena's breath hitched.

The widow's eyes gleamed in the looking glass. "Just as I suspected. He is worth the risk, so long as no one else finds out. Most every lady desires him in her bed, but she would be mortified if others knew she'd been bedded by a Bedlamite."

She twittered at her joke, but Helena didn't find her amusing in the least.

"Forgive me, my lady, but you are mistaken about

Lord Thorne and me." Helena headed for the retiring room door, brushing past the attendant who wasn't even bothering to pretend she wasn't eavesdropping. Her owl-like eyes blinked several times at Helena.

"Oh?" The widow swiveled on the seat. "You haven't succumbed to his charms yet? You would be the only woman whose skirts he has chased but failed to lift."

"I don't know what you are babbling on about." Helena stalked from the retiring room. But she did know what the widow meant.

Obviously, Lady Lovelace had been Lord Thorne's lover at some point—perhaps even now he paid her visits—and she thought Helena would be his next conquest.

God help her, she wished her association with the man was as simple as that, but Lord Thorne wanted something more than a tumble between the sheets. What that was, exactly, she didn't know. Money? A special favor? She could pay for his silence, but the true cost would be surrendering her pride. She'd vowed never to be at a man's mercy again, and Sebastian Thorne had her at a decided disadvantage.

❧

Sebastian searched for Lady Prestwick inside the crowded ballroom. The Countess of Eldridge's theme for the evening was "excess." Rivers of lavender silk flooded the great room, and there were enough white gardenias to choke a man. The concentrated aroma clawed at his throat. He covered a cough with his fist as he circled the dance floor.

Lady Prestwick wasn't with her kin or among the ladies gossiping together. She wasn't visiting with Gabrielle either, who stood surrounded by her brothers' wives, the current Duchess of Foxhaven, Lady Phoebe, and Lady Lana. He had little doubt his former betrothed would recover from scandal no worse for the experience, thanks to the support of her kinswomen.

He felt a pinch in his chest. That was what his sister lacked, a powerful circle of women to protect her. A man could only do so much. Eve could have had that if he hadn't failed in his bid for Gabrielle's hand.

When he was certain Lady Prestwick had taken her leave, he sent a footman to call for his carriage. Lady Lovelace, an attractive widow he'd spent a few entertaining nights with early in the Season, was standing in the foyer with her prim and very respectable mother-in-law. He understood the widow's reluctance to let on they knew one another and didn't expect her to acknowledge him, but she surprised him.

"It's rather stifling in the ballroom, is it not, Lord Thorne?"

He returned her polite smile with a bemused one. "Er. Yes, it is."

The elder Lady Lovelace peered at him through her quizzing glass. "You danced with Lady Prestwick this evening."

"The lady was kind enough to grant me the privilege," he said, expecting the conversation had run its course.

She nodded. "She is a lovely young woman with a generous heart."

Is she implying dancing with me is an act of charity?

"I didn't realize you were friendly with Lady Prestwick," Celeste said. The sardonic twist of her mouth left no doubts what *she* was implying.

"The lady is friendly with my sister," he lied, although it wasn't a complete fabrication. She had been friendly with Eve outside St. Saviour's.

The older woman's drawn-on brows rose on her wrinkled forehead. "Mercy. I had no idea Lady Prestwick and Miss Thorne are close friends. I must speak with Lady Eldridge and insist she invite your sister to the next charitable society gathering. Lady Eldridge is hosting next week."

Sebastian blinked, certain he had misheard her. Eve never received invitations to anything.

The footman entered the foyer from outside. "Ladies, your carriage has arrived."

The younger Lady Lovelace ushered her mother-in-law toward the door but stopped at the threshold to peer back at him. Her gaze traveled the length of his body and she tossed a smile in his direction. "It has been a long time, Lord Thorne. I hope our paths cross again very soon." She mouthed the word *Tonight*.

He was tempted. This type of unwritten invitation hadn't been extended to him in quite a while, but he'd already agreed to meet Lady Prestwick this evening. And her invitation proved most intriguing.

Nine

HELENA HAD CHANGED INTO A COMFORTABLE DAY gown and requested the lamps lit in the drawing room in preparation for Lord Thorne's arrival. She glanced around the small space with a nagging sense something was missing. Her gaze landed on the empty fireplace. Perhaps a little ambiance would be nice, but it was too warm for a fire.

"Oh bother!" She made a dismissive flick of her wrist, disgusted with herself. Ambiance would be nice if the baron were set on seduction, not blackmail, which, now that she'd had more time to think about it, seemed like the most logical scenario.

Many gentlemen with titles and entailed estates needed money. The baron probably saw her as an easy target. The question she had been asking herself since the ball was would anyone believe him?

She'd heard the gossip about Lord Thorne tonight. The words "insane" and "family trait" had circled the room more times than the dancers. Only she didn't believe for one second he was unbalanced. His eyes were too clear and sharp. He was intelligent. *Cunning*.

And he would make a formidable foe if she crossed swords with him.

Paying him seemed the wisest course, but it made her tremble with repressed rage. No doubt the baron expected her to play the frightened victim, and blast it all, she *was* afraid. Afraid of losing her standing in Society, of never being able to give her youngest sister the life she deserved.

But Helena would be damned if she admitted her fear to anyone.

Fergus entered the drawing room without knocking and crossed his arms over his broad chest. She didn't want to hear his warnings against receiving the baron.

"What do you think?" she asked, feigning cheerfulness. "Should I set out the cordial?"

His shaggy brows dropped dangerously low over his forest-green eyes. "You shouldna be receiving him at all."

"It is either now or later. I would prefer to hear his terms as soon as possible and send him on his way."

Fergus yanked the dagger from the holster at his hip. "Highlanders do no' extend hospitality to black-mailers. The vermin are greeted by the sharp bite of metal between their ribs."

The last thing they needed was a dead lord on the Aubusson. "You will not raise a hand toward the baron unless you want both of us sent to the gallows. This is not Scotland. You cannot kill a lord willy-nilly."

His frown deepened, but he replaced the dagger. "Aye. A wee bit of planning first is sensible, lass."

She sent him a quelling glare. "*No* killing, Fergus. I mean it."

Luna, who'd been curled into a ball on the tufted footstool, woke from her nap with a sweet mewl. She blinked her amber eyes twice, then stared at Helena as if to ask what all the fuss was about.

"It is nothing, sweetheart," she cooed. "Go back to sleep."

Fergus smirked, his surliness giving way to amusement for a moment. "You realize the fur ball canna understand you."

"You don't know that."

Luna was having none of their nonsense. She jumped from her perch and pranced from the drawing room like the Queen herself.

A light knock sounded at the front door. Helena narrowed her eyes at Fergus. "Not even one hair on his head is to be harmed. Do you understand?"

He sniffed in response and stalked from the room to answer the door. She quickly chose a chair facing the drawing room door, arranged her skirts, and prepared to meet the enemy.

The front door creaked when Fergus tugged it open.

"Lord Thorne to see Lady—"

"I know why you're here," Fergus snarled.

She winced. Her loyal Scot was itching for a fight, but she couldn't allow him to do anything foolish.

"This way, Lord Thorne," she called.

The rich carpet in the entry muffled the baron's footsteps, and he was in the threshold before she had properly prepared herself. Her breath caught at the sight of him, his dark eyes gleaming and a hint of whiskers creating a shadow on his defined jaw. He was much too handsome for a blackmailer.

A humorless laugh slipped from her. *Who ever said scoundrels had to be ugly?*

He leaned against the doorjamb, unperturbed by Fergus lurking behind him. "Do I amuse you, Lady Prestwick?"

"Not particularly, my lord. Thank you, Fergus. You may go."

The Scot gritted his teeth and looked for one moment as if he might pounce on Lord Thorne.

"*Please*. I will call out if I need you."

Fergus withdrew, but not before locking a death stare on the baron.

Lord Thorne lifted an eyebrow in her direction once they were alone. "You will call out? I believe my honor has just been besmirched."

"Is it a first, my lord?" She smiled sweetly.

He chuckled and pushed away from the doorjamb. Her insult had shot wildly over his head.

"There aren't many firsts left for me, Lady Prestwick. May I have a seat?"

She held up a hand to stop him. "This will not take long. How much do you want?"

His step faltered and his brow wrinkled. It was almost worth enduring the interview to see him flustered. "I beg your pardon? How much of *what* do I want?"

"Must you pretend ignorance, sir? You are here to demand money, so speak your price. I would like to resolve this matter at once."

One side of his mouth twitched. "It's not your money I want."

What was he saying? Her heart bounced off her breastbone, drumming furiously and making her light-headed. There had been more rumors whispered about Lord Thorne tonight, ones that made her shiver with shameful excitement. Whispers of his conquests, mostly widows. Very happily conquered widows.

She fidgeted with the locket around her neck, her body consumed with prickly heat. "I was prepared to pay with money. N-not…" She concentrated on breathing, which had become a monumental task.

"I see." A wicked grin slowly slid across his face. "Then you should be relieved to learn I have no need to resort to blackmail to find a bed partner."

Her face burned hotter as if she'd been doused in oil and set afire. She grabbed the ivory fan resting on a side table and snapped it open.

Not asking for permission this time, he claimed the armchair across from her. "I am not here to threaten you, Lady Prestwick. Believe me when I say I've no love for the gossips and would rather cut off my left arm than toss them a juicy bone to gnaw."

He lounged casually on the chair, his elbow propped on the padded armrest, eyeing her. Odd that she should trust him on this much at least. His name had been dragged through the muck often enough these past weeks to convince her that he wouldn't conspire with gossipmongers.

"You came here for some reason," she said, "and I'm sure you want something." Even if it wasn't her money or her body. And why didn't he want her body? Not that she was offering it.

"It's true I am here for a reason." He nodded. "But it is nothing to warrant animosity. I would like to extend my gratitude for coming to my aid. Had you ignored my calls for help, I might have had my throat slit for my efforts. So, thank you."

She simply gawked, shocked that he knew it was she who had helped him in the street.

He uncrossed his legs and leaned forward, his expression animated. "I cannot fathom what you were doing in Whitechapel, but I've asked myself many times if maybe you are actually an angel come to earth."

"That's ridiculous."

"I thought the same the first time I heard talk of the Whitechapel Angel, and then when we collided outside the church, I knew you were real enough. And yet, you were there when I needed help. A *lady* in the rookery. What are the odds?"

Helena recovered from her surprise and narrowed her eyes at him. What game was he playing? She didn't believe for one moment he had come to thank her.

"I don't concern myself with odds, my lord. I'm not a gambler." And she never would be. Having watched her father lose everything, she couldn't even bring herself to play a game of whist with no stakes attached.

"You've been gambling your reputation—your very life—by entering the rookery. What are you about, Lady Prestwick?"

She pushed from her seat and stood behind it, creating a barrier between them. She rested her hands on the cresting rail. Her fingers betrayed her frazzled nerves by repeatedly skimming the ornamental details carved into the wood. "I will ask you once more what it is you want from me. An honest answer, or I will have Fergus toss you from the premises."

❧

Sebastian frowned. Was there no one to believe in his honor? What sort of gentleman would he be if he demanded payment for his silence? "You seem set on being blackmailed. Why don't you tell me what it is I should demand?"

Her mouth dropped open, but no sound came out. When she issued a resigned sigh, he eased back against his seat.

"Very well," she said tersely. "If I have misjudged you, I beg your forgiveness."

"*If?*"

She ignored his protest and barreled on. "But a gentleman doesn't waylay a lady at a ball, insinuating he knows something untoward about her, then arrive at her home in the middle of the night for no reason."

He wanted to argue that she had invited him, but she had a good argument. The rub of it was he didn't know why he had come. She had been plaguing his thoughts morning to night ever since their first encounter. For some unexplainable reason, he couldn't walk away without knowing what she was doing in Whitechapel.

"Tell me what you were doing, and I will go. There will be no need to summon your ill-tempered servant."

She clamped her lips together, and he thought for one moment he was no match for her stubbornness. "I am searching for someone. My—my servant's sister." She waved her hand as if shooing a fly. "Not Fergus's sister. Another servant. One who isn't here, so do not ask to speak with him—*her.*"

She had told the truth when she said she wasn't a gambler. She was the worst liar he had ever met, but at least she was talking.

"Fergus and I tracked her to Whitechapel, to a brothel."

His eyebrows shot up. "Couldn't he have searched alone? Perhaps during the day?"

She shook her head and crossed her arms. "He has never seen her. What if he brought back some woman pretending to be Lavinia? She could have come to search for valuables at the town house and report her findings to her associates. I'll not place the servants' lives in danger."

"Only your own. Not to mention your footman's."

"Fergus can take care of himself." She hugged her arms around her waist as if trying to hold herself together. "Really, Lord Thorne. This conversation is pointless. I won't be returning to Whitechapel, so you may set your worries aside. If indeed you are worried."

He blinked in surprise as the realization hit him that he *had* been concerned for her. She was a woman alone in the world, and breakable despite her iron will. Her skin was pale and smooth like porcelain, the bones in her face delicate. And she was small. Not a robust woman accustomed to fighting back. Only she had, hadn't she? Someone had taught her to defend herself, but her luck wouldn't hold forever.

"So you have found this Lavinia," he said. "Your goal is accomplished."

"Not exactly, but since all paths lead to..." She frowned. "Well, I don't know *where* the fashionable brothels are. I am certain, however, they are not in Whitechapel, so I assure you I am perfectly safe. Although I may never gain access to her now."

"Ah." Sebastian nodded in understanding. If the girl had truly been sold to a high-end brothel, she would be working in the West End. Perhaps in St. James or Covent Garden.

"Even if I did know the location, it would be pointless to go there. As you can see"—Lady Prestwick gestured toward her lithe curves—"I am not a gentleman."

Far from it, he would say, but considering she thought he had come to take advantage of her, he refrained from commenting on her very feminine and inviting figure. "Your man, Fergus, cannot help either." Without a title or lands, he would never gain access to the madams' girls.

"No, he can't." She lowered her gaze, her expression so downtrodden, Sebastian nearly left his chair to wrap his arms around her for comfort. Instead, he gripped the padded arms and forced himself to stay seated. This girl was important to her, and for some inexplicable reason, she suddenly became important to him too. But if the girl was simply a servant's sibling, why did she care enough to risk her life?

Lady Prestwick fidgeted with the locket around her neck, refusing to look at him. She had an emotional attachment to this girl. Perhaps they had been raised together. It wasn't unheard of for children to form friendships before an adult informed them they were not equals.

The idea boosted his opinion of Lady Prestwick. She was no mindless rule follower, and yet she effortlessly navigated the *ton*, charming the matrons of Society. The same gossipmongers who'd turned their backs on Eve, believing she'd been sullied and fearing their own reputations would suffer from associating with her. The women were nothing more than sheep trotting wherever they were led, and Lady Prestwick had their ears.

A rush of exhilaration coursed through his body. What if the solution to Eve's problem was standing before him? He hadn't hoped for a second chance to do right by his sister, but what if Lady Prestwick had appeared from the mist not to save his life but to give Eve's back to her?

Her blue-green gaze flicked up and discovered him staring. Pink rushed into her cheeks, but she didn't look away. He gave her a tentative smile.

Slowly he rose from his chair and mimicked her earlier motion, sweeping his hands down his body with flourish then holding his arms out to his sides. "Hopefully this doesn't come as a shock, but *I* am a gentleman."

Her blush deepened to a dark red.

So she *had* noticed. He bit back a pleased grin. They were on more familiar ground now.

"I believe we can help one another, Lady Prestwick. What say you? Shall we form a partnership? You sponsor my younger sister Eve, and I will search the brothels on your behalf."

Her eyes flared wide briefly, then narrowed to suspicious slits. "Why would you do that for me?"

Good Lord. Maybe he should demand money so as not to disappoint her. She gave a new definition to mistrustful. "I'm not offering for you, Lady Prestwick. I'm not even doing it for me. My sister needs help and she is the most deserving person I know. So can we reach an agreement or not?"

The hard lines of her face softened, and her extraordinary eyes glimmered in the candlelight. "Miss Thorne seems like a nice young woman. I have no reason to deny her my assistance."

"Splendid!" Sebastian came forward and extended his hand. "Should we shake on our agreement like gentlemen, or would you prefer to seal it with a kiss?"

Her frown returned, and she hesitantly grasped his hand. "This does not mean I trust you, Lord Thorne."

"How could I ever think otherwise, Lady Prestwick?"

Ten

Two days later, Helena arrived at Eldridge House with guarded optimism. She still didn't quite trust Lord Thorne or his intentions, but she considered entering into an alliance with him a necessary risk. Besides, her part in the partnership was pleasant enough. Eve Thorne was a delightful young woman.

With Miss Thorne's mother and Olive admiring Olive's prized orchids in the conservatory, Helena was allowed a moment alone with Miss Thorne. Helena sank against the seatback, realizing she was no longer dreading the afternoon ahead.

Her companion beamed, her rich brown eyes alight. "I don't know how I can ever repay your kindness, Lady Prestwick. I still think I am dreaming and any moment I will wake in my bedchamber."

Helena returned her smile. "Please, call me Helena. You've no need to repay me. I am honored to sponsor you."

Yesterday when Helena had called on her husband's cousin and requested her assistance in reintroducing Miss Thorne to the *ton*, Olive had brightened considerably. With Lord Eldridge remaining at the gentlemen's club most of the time, Olive often seemed at a loss with how to fill her time. She had clapped her hands and declared with much enthusiasm that she loved taking on a project.

Miss Thorne is not a project, Helena had said with a disapproving purse of her lips, but Olive hadn't paid her any notice. Instead, she had launched into a long list of actions that must be taken at once. First Helena was ordered to send a message to Lady Thorne expressing her wish to act as Miss Thorne's sponsor, which received a gracious reply in a matter of hours. Then Olive invited Lady Thorne and her daughter to tea and informed them she had secured an appointment with the most sought after modiste in Town through Lady Norwick.

It is my mission to see that young woman's name on every guest list from now until the Season's end, Olive had promised. *Perhaps she will even receive an invitation to the country. Everyone who is anyone of importance retires North for hunting.*

Helena had been surprised by this revelation. Wickie hadn't discussed life in England often, but he had led her to believe ladies' activities were less adventurous.

Do ladies hunt?

It depends on whether she has landed a buck during the Season, Olive had responded with a smirk.

Helena smiled with fondness at the baron's sister.

"If I am to use your Christian name," Miss Thorne said, "you must call me Eve." Her hand fluttered to her chest. "And a personal recommendation from Lady Norwick? I never once thought Madame Girard would allow *me* an appointment."

Helena's heart warmed as a dreamy expression crossed the woman's lovely face. Perhaps someday Helena would be able to put that same dreamy look on her own sister's face.

"Lady Eldridge is responsible for the recommendation to Madame Girard. She knows Lady Norwick from their involvement with the Mayfair Ladies Charitable Society."

The Countess of Norwick was a generous benefactor of the charity and apparently one of the modiste's favorite patrons, since she had been able to secure an appointment for Eve. Rumor had it ladies waited months to see Madame Girard.

"I must send a letter around to the countess to thank her," Eve said. "I am overwhelmed by everyone's kindness. Thank you again for sponsoring me. I can't imagine the reason you would choose me, but I am so very grateful."

Helena smiled and sipped her tea as Eve launched into tales of her foray into Society two years earlier. She suspected the young woman wished to warn her of the huge undertaking it would be to act as her sponsor, but Helena was unconcerned. Even if Lord Thorne withdrew his promise to help her, she couldn't stomach the thought of disappointing his sister.

She eased the saucer and cup onto her lap as Eve began to describe her first waltz.

"Sebastian made the poor man sign my dance card. Of course, that is what friends do each other. They dance with younger sisters so the brothers don't have to do it themselves." She laughed, obviously reliving that evening, and Helena couldn't resist joining in.

"Lord Ellis watched his feet the entire time and was counting under his breath. It is a wonder he didn't dance us into the wall."

Helena sobered. "I had no idea your brother and Lord Ellis had been friends."

"I'm not certain friends is the correct term. They were always challenging each other to the most ridiculous contests, but Bastian seemed to like the earl well enough before…" Miss Thorne's gaze strayed to the mantel and she sipped her tea.

Before the earl stole away with Lord Thorne's fiancée. Everyone knew what had happened and talked about it freely, all except his loyal sister. How unfair that Lord Thorne should bear the brunt of a scandal he didn't cause while Lord and Lady Ellis appeared mostly unscathed. But Lady Ellis had a large, influential family to stand beside her, and Lord Thorne only had his mother and an ostracized sister.

Helena sat up taller. Well, Eve had *her* now too, and with Olive's support, Helena would see her new friend restored to her place in Society. Perhaps Lord Thorne would be judged less severely if his sister made a good match and proved what Helena already knew: there was nothing distasteful about the Thornes.

A small shiver traveled the length of her back when she recalled just how appealing she had found Lord Thorne as they had danced together.

It was difficult to believe he wanted to be her ally, but as far as she knew, he had begun his investigation last night with a visit to one of the most popular brothels. She wrinkled her nose in disgust, preferring not to think about his activities. Although she couldn't help wondering what he had learned. About Lavinia, that is. He already seemed to know a lot about...*activities* and such. Unfortunately, she didn't know when she would cross paths with him next.

She and Lord Thorne had agreed there could be no more meetings at her town house—after all, her reputation must remain intact to help anyone—but waiting for word and not knowing when it would come chipped at her patience.

She sat her cup aside. "How is your brother? Did you see him this morning?"

Eve's brows arched over clever eyes so similar to her brother's. "Sebastian is well. I think he was pleased when I told him of Lady Eldridge's invitation to tea and the visit to Madame Girard's dress shop, but he was racing out the door with the newssheet and did not say much." She sighed. "I don't think there is anything he wouldn't do for Mama and me, but I want to wring his neck for stealing the newssheet every morning."

"He steals the newssheet?"

Eve rolled her eyes. "He thinks he is shielding us from gossip, but if we venture from the house, we still hear whispers and notice the stares."

Did he truly do that? Helena's heart softened toward him a little more. He loved his family and wanted to protect them just like Helena wanted to protect hers. Perhaps she had misjudged him.

"I assume they are speaking about me again," Eve said, sounding unexpectedly serene. "Heaven only knows why my story would be of interest after two years. It must be a slow Season."

Helena studied the lady across from her. Eve smiled

and sipped her tea. She truly didn't know what the gossips were saying, did she? Well, Helena wasn't going to be the one to tell her, especially when her brother made efforts to protect her.

Everyone said the former Lord Thorne suffered from madness, but it was obvious insanity didn't run in the family as people claimed. Eve and her brother seemed well balanced, but there was usually some basis for rumors. Perhaps someday Eve would trust Helena enough to volunteer the information. Until then, she would mind her own affairs.

"People can be ignorant and cruel," Helena said. "It is best to ignore them."

"And some restore my faith, like you and Lady Eldridge."

"Thank you," she demurred.

Lady Thorne and Olive rejoined them moments later, and they passed the time pleasantly discussing upcoming entertainments until the mantel clock struck the half hour.

"We should leave if we want to make Miss Thorne's appointment with Madame Girard," Helena said.

Olive waved off the invitation. "I have correspondence demanding my attention. Shopping is a young ladies' pastime. Go, enjoy yourselves."

Lady Thorne nodded, smiling. "I couldn't agree more, and quiet afternoons lying about are for *old* ladies. I have a fainting couch awaiting my return."

Outside, Eve bid her mother farewell with a kiss to her cheek then eagerly climbed into the Prestwick coach with Helena for the short ride to Bond Street.

They climbed from the carriage and stood on

the walk outside Madame Girard's dress shop. It was snugly wedged between a haberdashery and a sweetshop. Harnesses rattled and struts squeaked as carriages carrying fashionable ladies traveled the busy thoroughfare. Helena closed her eyes for one moment to savor the scent of coffee hanging on the air from the coffeehouse across the street. Such a heavenly scent for such a foul-tasting brew.

"Sebastian!" Eve's surprised call startled Helena and her eyes flew open.

Lord Thorne was in the middle of the street. When an opening presented between carriages, he dashed forward to join them on the walkway.

"What brings you to Bond Street, dear brother?"

"You will need an account set up with Madame Girard, so I decided to meet you." He grinned at Helena and tipped his hat. "Good afternoon, Lady Prestwick."

Helena offered a small curtsy. "Lord Thorne."

Eve looked from her brother to Helena, her smile widening. "What a perfect opportunity for you to become better acquainted with Lady Prestwick. I think you will get on well." If Lord Thorne recognized the scheming glint to his sister's eyes, he pretended not to notice and offered Eve his arm.

Helena turned toward the dress shop before either sibling could spot the heated flush rising in her cheeks. The bell suspended above the door tinkled merrily as she preceded them inside. A shopgirl greeted them then bustled away to retrieve Madame Girard.

The modiste emerged from a back room, head held high. She was bone-thin with chiseled features and a wide forehead, but her appearance proved to be the only thing sharp about her. With a voice like warm molasses and the gentleness of a mother with her babe, she took Eve under her care and ushered her to the platform beyond the curtains to take her measurements. Madame Girard's assistant yanked the curtains closed, blocking Helena and Lord Thorne's view.

"This could take some time." He gently took Helena's elbow to guide her toward a corner of the shop where lace was on display. He absently lifted a loose end dangling from the bolt then let it flutter from his fingers. "Very nice."

Helena smiled wryly. "Are you having a petticoat made, my lord?"

"I was considering drawers," he said with a waggle of his eyebrows.

She chuckled as she imagined him in ladies' drawers and pulled down a bolt of frilly red lace. "I believe this is more suited for your coloring."

He winked. "Who said I was purchasing the drawers for myself?"

Helena's breath caught as his meaning hit her. He must keep a mistress. Her reflection in Madame Girard's oval looking glass rivaled the red lace. She shoved the bolt back on the shelf and moved on to something less scandalous.

Leather gloves seemed innocuous enough.

He joined her and leaned casually against the counter. "I hope you realize I was teasing. I have no need for ladies' drawers, either for myself or anyone else."

She sank against the glass countertop, almost laughing in relief. She had no say in what he did in his spare time. In truth, she had no reason to be bothered by what he did at the brothels on her behalf either, but she was.

He leaned close to her ear, his nearness making her heart skip. "I didn't just come to set up an account for Eve. I thought waiting for a report from last night might be difficult."

She swiveled in his direction, her breath shallow and quick. "Did you find her?"

"I'm sorry." He shook his head slowly. "I hate disappointing you, but there has never been a woman by the name of Lavinia employed at either place."

"Oh." Tears burned her throat, but she swallowed them. It had been naive to think Lord Thorne would find her sister immediately, but she had gotten her hopes up anyway.

He gently patted her shoulder. "We will find her. We have only begun looking."

We. Not I.

His gaze was earnest and gave her a sense he understood how important this was to her. Her heart melted even more. He had a way of lowering her defenses, and although it seemed unwise to allow him a step closer, she couldn't help herself.

"Could she be using a false name?" he asked.

"I don't think so. Fergus tracked her using her Christian name."

"True." His smile was comforting. "I will search again tonight after the House of Lords adjourns for the day. I will let you know what I have learned as soon as possible."

Without stopping to think, she reached for his hand and squeezed his fingers. "Thank you. I mean that sincerely."

The damask curtains flicked open again. Helena dropped his hand and came forward with a bright smile as Eve emerged from the back room.

"Lady Eldridge has ordered me to make certain you commission at least five new gowns," Madame Girard said.

Eve's gaze flicked toward her brother. "I have several gowns in my wardrobe already. Five seems extravagant."

Lord Thorne nodded at Helena. "I am trusting you to make certain she commissions twice that many. A beautiful young lady deserves beautiful dresses."

"Sebastian, that's too much. Really, I have what I need."

"You heard your brother, Miss Thorne." Madame Girard clapped her hands, the matter apparently resolved in her mind. "Come along."

The modiste commandeered Eve, practically dragging her to a long table with fashion plates scattered over the surface.

"Oh my!" Eve held up a sketch. "Helena, you must see this gown. It is spectacular."

Lord Thorne detained Helena before she could comply. His dark eyes sparkled and made Helena's knees shake. "Thank *you*, my lady. She hasn't been this happy in a long time."

Helena could barely think to form a response with the heat of his touch searing through her sleeve. "It— it's my pleasure."

He flashed a smile, then took his leave as Helena joined Eve and Madame Girard at the table. The shop seemed less lively with him gone, as if he took the warmth and light with him. Butterflies stirred in her belly as she anticipated their next encounter. And she was ashamed to admit the prospect of receiving news about her sister only partly accounted for her excitement.

Eleven

Sebastian took a moment to savor the mouthwatering aroma of ham and eggs the footman at Brooks's set before him. Even though he was ravenous from his morning ride, he delayed satisfying his appetite. He had learned taking his time often wrought the most pleasure when he finally rewarded himself.

Lady Prestwick's plump bottom lip came to mind and he smiled. Their daily encounters over the last week to report on his search for the servant girl increased his hunger for the lovely viscountess, and when he finally had her beneath him, it would be the sweetest of rewards.

He lifted his fork in preparation of devouring his meal just as the Earl of Ellis entered the room. Sebastian's appetite vanished.

The earl scanned the room, locked his gaze on Sebastian, and headed in his direction with a determined set to his jaw. Several members of the club abandoned their activities to gawk.

God's blood! He didn't want to deal with Ellis or the curious stares. Before he knew it, he could be at the center of a ridiculous wager not of his doing, which was typically the case where he and Ellis were concerned.

Sebastian snatched up his knife with a snarl and vigorously sawed the ham on his plate.

Ellis stopped at the table and lifted a brow. "I don't know what the ham did to earn your displeasure, but I'm sure it meant no offense."

Sebastian popped a piece in his mouth, ignoring the earl and his oh-so-clever quip.

Ellis sat across the table as if they hadn't had a falling-out. A ripple of whispers traveled the room and several gents perked up. Eyes locked on them, perhaps hoping for some excitement. Sebastian ignored them.

"Have you seen this yet?" Ellis pulled a bundle from under his arm and plopped it on the table. It was a copy of the ladies' magazine *Le Monde Couture*.

"Following ladies' fashions now, are you?"

Despite his irritation with the earl, Sebastian couldn't help smiling as he recalled his conversation with Lady Prestwick about ladies' drawers. The attractive pink that had infused her cheeks had been worth the risk of shocking her. It reminded him of that just-shagged flush ladies got.

Ellis opened the magazine and pushed it toward him. "She looks lovely."

Staring back at him in glorious splendor was Eve in one of Madame Girard's elegant gowns. The engraving caught her likeness in fine detail and the caption made him choke up. *Miss Thorne turned heads at the Marblewick Ball in a stunning creation by talented modiste, Madame Girard.*

When he looked up, Ellis grinned. "According to my mother-in-law, Miss Thorne drew many compliments at Lady Langston's soiree last week too. I know it's not your habit to read the Society column, but your sister's beauty, charm, and amiable disposition have been mentioned several times recently."

Sebastian glanced at *The Morning Times* lying on the table. After his failed attempt to stop Ellis and Lady Gabrielle from eloping, he had changed his habits and began scouring the gossip column for any mention of his name. He had even begun purchasing the gossip rags, much to his embarrassment. The tidbits written about him were mean-spirited and often fabrications, such as the last report he'd read in *The Informer* that claimed he arrived at "Lady L's" door in the middle of the night naked and babbling nonsense.

Celeste denied any involvement in feeding the story to the paper, and her utter bewilderment had convinced him she knew nothing about it. If he could discover who owned the reviled paper, he would put a stop to the bloody lies. These last few days, however, Sebastian had been too preoccupied to care what was written about him.

"There is mention of Miss Thorne in the newssheet again today," the earl said. "Very complimentary. Your sister has made quite the splash. Congratulations."

Sebastian wanted to reject Ellis's conciliatory gesture, but he couldn't bring himself to be rude. "Thanks." He slid the magazine back across the table. "I will purchase a copy on my way home. Eve will be beside herself."

"Keep it. It's a gift. Gabby and I wish her the best."

Politeness was one thing. Sebastian refused to accept the earl's charity. "Return it to your wife. I can afford a copy for Eve."

"You know that wasn't my meaning." Ellis's mouth turned down. "What will it take to make things right between us, Thorne?"

More than a bloody magazine. And yet, Sebastian felt more at ease in the other man's presence today. Perhaps delivering this good news hadn't been Ellis's worst idea.

Sebastian shoveled more food in his mouth before he said something ridiculous like perhaps he no longer held a grudge against the earl. The past was less relevant now that Eve was back in Society and turning heads. She would receive an offer of marriage before the Season's end, and Sebastian could rest easier knowing her future would be secure. Besides, he had more important matters on his mind, such as meeting Lady Prestwick at Finsbury Square in an hour. Still, he wasn't ready to ease Ellis's conscience by offering forgiveness.

The earl sighed after a time. "You haven't been attending the assemblies with your sister. I am surprised."

"A fool is easily caught off guard." Sebastian didn't want to ruin his sister's prospects by reminding everyone they were related. It was best to keep his distance for now. "Mother and Lady Prestwick are adequate chaperones."

"I didn't think you trusted anyone besides yourself when it came to your sister's well-being."

Sebastian hunched over his plate and avoided eye contact. He didn't need anyone reminding him that he should be watching over Eve, but she was better off if he kept his distance. "Could I break my fast in peace now? I've never known anyone who nags as you do."

"I was not nagging." Ellis pushed back from the table, grumbling under his breath. "This was a waste of time."

"I couldn't agree more." Sebastian nodded toward the magazine in the earl's hand and gentled his tone. "Extend my gratitude to Lady Ellis. It was a thoughtful gesture, sending her messenger boy."

Ellis's tense posture eased and he cracked a smile. "Sod off, Thorne."

Sebastian chuckled under his breath as his longtime rival sauntered from the room. For a moment, it seemed like old times. And it felt good.

His fellow gents were still staring, so he glared in return. With nothing more to see, they resumed their activities. He supposed they missed his and Ellis's antics, and strangely, he was beginning to miss challenging the earl, and besting him.

When Sebastian left the club, he set off for The Temple of the Muses, where he and Lady Prestwick had been meeting almost daily for the past week under the pretense of browsing for books. Even though he looked forward to seeing her, he dreaded delivering disappointing news again. Her mystery woman, Lavinia, was proving to be as elusive as a ghost.

The hopeful glimmer in Lady Prestwick's eyes dulled each time he had nothing positive to report. So far he had been able to tease her out of the blues, but he still hated causing her distress. He often fought the urge to hold her close and offer comfort. Aside from the public spectacle he would make of them, she didn't seem amenable to accepting sympathy.

He entered the bookstore and headed for the novels written by Maria Edgeworth. The authoress seemed to be a favorite with Lady Prestwick. Perhaps Eve would enjoy the books as well. He would choose one to take to her along with the magazine.

As expected, Lady Prestwick was tucked into a corner with a book already in hand. He sidled up beside her and pretended to peruse the same shelves. A quick glance at the book cover revealed her selection.

She offered a shy smile. "Good morning, Lord Thorne."

"Lady Prestwick," he responded with a tip of his hat, then returned his attention to the bookshelf. "I hope you don't think me forward, but I couldn't help noticing your book selection. Is *Belinda* one of those mawkish gothic novels favored by silly young ladies?"

She slanted an impassive glance in his direction. "Do not pretend scorn for gothic fiction, my lord. I have it on good authority you devoured *Glenarvon* in one sitting."

A shocked laugh burst from him and echoed in the high-ceilinged room. Two ladies frowned at them, and Lady Prestwick turned her back on him, pretending to search for another book.

"My apologies," he whispered as he eased closer to her. "What other secrets has Eve revealed about me?"

"I am sure you would love to know, but I would never consider betraying my friend. But they are shameful indeed, my lord." She tsked. "Falling from a lady's window?"

His jaw dropped. "Balderdash!"

She shushed him as the two ladies glared in their direction.

"She lies," he hissed as he followed her to a different section of the store. "When I get my hands on my sister…"

Lady Prestwick chuckled. "I am teasing. Eve confessed she thought we'd had a liaison the night you came home bruised and beaten. She was quite embarrassed by her assumption. I, on the other hand, was amused by the absurdity of such a situation."

Absurd? "Why would such a scenario be absurd? There is an attraction between us."

She stopped abruptly and he bumped against her. An intense current where their bodies met sent his blood gushing through his veins. A furious blush consumed her and she shuffled to create space between them. "This is not proper conversation, my lord."

She wasn't denying the attraction, not that he would believe her if she did. The quickening of her breath and high color in her complexion told him everything he needed to know.

Licking her lips, she stole a glance at him from beneath her lashes. "Perhaps you should just tell me what you have learned before we draw any more attention."

"Not until you answer my question. Why do you find us"—he wagged a finger from her to him—"absurd?"

"Please, lower your voice."

He smirked. "I will start shouting if you make me ask again."

"Why are you doing this to me?"

"All I've said is I find you attractive." He lowered his voice to match hers. "Why do you find it impossible that we would ever—?"

She gasped. Her face glowed red.

"Well, I needn't continue. I'm certain you know my meaning."

"You are teasing me, sir," she whispered harshly. "I couldn't be any more different from Gabrielle, Lady Ellis."

Thank God for that. "True, but how does that mean I am teasing you?"

Wariness flared in her eyes. "I don't know what pleasure you get from this, my lord, but I will say it so we may put this to rest. Your former betrothed is breathtaking. She is exotic and yet fashionable in the way gentlemen prefer."

Ah, so she thought he preferred Gabrielle's curves. While there was no denying his former fiancée was a beauty, Lady Prestwick was twice as stunning. She had a delicateness to her beauty that made her seem not of this earth.

As he leaned to speak in her ear, tendrils of her hair tickled his cheek and her breath became uneven. "I prefer you, madam. Perhaps someday you will allow me to prove it."

He was close enough to hear her swallow. "I—I will take you at your word," she murmured.

This conversation wasn't over. Sebastian glanced around the store in search of her escort. "Where is your man?"

"Fergus is waiting outside. He never learned to read and he grows impatient with the bookstore."

"Meet me on the walkway in a moment." He took the book from her hands.

"Wait. I wanted to purchase that."

"Go." When she blankly stared at him, he made a shooing motion with his hands. "Off with you, madam, before I cause a scene."

Her lips thinned and he expected he was in for a row, but she turned on her heel and stalked away. Quickly, he selected a book for Eve and retrieved a copy of *Le Monde Couture*. As the clerk wrapped his and Lady Prestwick's selections, he had an idea. "Do you have a quill and ink I may use?"

"Yes, milord." While the clerk retrieved the writing tools, Sebastian unwrapped Lady Prestwick's book. He used the quill to scribble an inscription on the inside cover and wrapped the book again.

The lady was waiting with her servant just as Sebastian had requested. The Scot merely glanced at him in irritation rather than his usual murderous intent. They were making progress.

Sebastian held up the book. "For you, but please allow me to carry it."

She pursed her lips, but took his arm when he offered it. He didn't often walk her home, but it would allow them more time to speak in private. He glanced over his shoulder at her menacing shadow. *Well, relative privacy.*

Perhaps sensing his reluctance to having an eavesdropper along, Lady Prestwick addressed her servant. "Lord Thorne and I need to speak alone, Fergus. Perhaps you would walk ahead?"

The man nodded. "Aye, milady." His long strides

built distance between them quickly and the crowd swallowed him.

Sebastian's brows lifted. "Your man is almost agreeable today."

"Fergus is perfectly agreeable, sir. You, on the other hand, try my patience. Why did you purchase my book? I have the funds."

He drew her closer as two men jostled past. "I know you do, but I wanted to buy it for you. I rarely buy gifts for ladies, which is in direct conflict with what you believe about my preferences."

She rolled her eyes.

"Are you calling me a liar?" He held the books over his heart as if he'd been wounded. "Me? A pillar of Society?"

She chuckled, relaxing on his arm. "I didn't say a word, so how could I have insulted you?"

"Oh, you have your ways." He winked and she glanced away. "The attraction is mutual. *I* have no trouble admitting the truth."

She sighed. "I answered your question. Could we please change the subject?"

For now. But he was far from finished trying to get her in his bed.

∾

In silence, Helena and Lord Thorne passed hawkers shouting out their wares and a woman with a basket of flowers. Carriages and wagons clattered along the boulevard in a rush to get to their destinations, while she and the baron strolled arm in arm. The contact sent tingles racing through her.

Fergus kept a respectable distance ahead of them, close enough to provide protection if needed, but far enough away to allow them to speak freely. Only she didn't know what she wanted to say.

Discussing her attraction to him was out of the question. If she admitted she was drawn to him, it would be a mistake. That would be the first step in becoming another of his conquests, and even though they had no future together, she didn't relish the thought of him moving on to another lady once he had bedded her. It was best to keep their association friendly, but not *too* friendly. Then she could return to Scotland no worse for the experience.

The overcast sky provided little respite from the muggy day, and Helena's undergarments soon grew damp and clung to her body.

"It smells like rain," she said.

She should ask about Lavinia, but she already knew the answer. After days of receiving nothing but disappointing news, she had learned to read Lord Thorne's body language. There had been reluctance in the lines around his eyes and the muscles in his arm twitched when she had mentioned changing the subject. Their last two meetings she had begun to sense he shared in her sadness. Although it was most likely a trick of her imagination, she felt he understood her, and her guard was slipping. It was a dangerous development, but she was enjoying his company too much to fortify the wall she had built around her heart.

As they entered a residential area, the crowd thinned. "Do you have any family besides your mother and sister, Lord Thorne?"

"Mother has distant cousins in Dorset, but we rarely see them."

She nodded, nibbling on her bottom lip. She wanted to tell him the truth about her past and Lavinia, but she feared him withdrawing his offer to help. If he knew about her father's gambling and learned her sister was a whore, he might use her scandalous relations as an excuse to break his promise. Or worse, he could expose her as a fraud. All the friendships she had built and valued—Eve, Olive, the duchess, Lady Norwick—would be destroyed.

His brow furrowed. "Is something troubling you, madam?"

"Not at all." She breathed a sigh of relief when he nodded, seemingly content with her answer. "We are nearing my home. I suppose we should dispatch with the unpleasant task of you telling me your search continues to be fruitless."

"I am sorry to bring you no news yet again, but there are still several places to check. If she isn't working at one of the West End brothels, I will expand my search. Stay hopeful." He flashed a dazzling smile. "I promise to visit every one, if I must."

The thought that he might actually enjoy his part of their bargain made her stiffen. She tried not to imagine him mixing pleasure with business he conducted on her behalf, but flashes of him touching some faceless woman invaded her mind. *A different woman each night.*

A wave of nausea swept through her as a fine sheen covered her body. Her knees wobbled and she stumbled.

"Lady Prestwick!" He caught her under the arms

to keep her from falling. Fergus swung around, saw her slumping in Lord Thorne's embrace, and came running.

"What happened, lass?"

"She collapsed," Lord Thorne said. "It's too warm. I should have ordered a hack."

"Don't be ridiculous." She tried to stand, but her head spun and she swayed.

Fergus's concerned face loomed close. "We are almost home. Can you make it a little farther?"

"Yes," she choked out, mortified by her weakness. She tried to pull away from the baron. "I can walk."

Lord Thorne frowned. "If stubbornness came bottled, I would accuse you of overindulging."

"Aye, she is as headstrong as the day is long." Fergus smirked as he accepted the books the baron held out.

Helena frowned at them for joining forces against her. "I am not—"

Lord Thorne scooped her into his arms and she squealed. The town house was only a three-minute jaunt at best. She could walk. *Maybe.*

She gawked as Fergus fell into step with the baron. He shrugged and smiled sheepishly. "His lairdship means you no harm, lass."

She bristled at his betrayal and Lord Thorne's high-handed ways. She was a grown woman, per-fectly capable of deciding if she had the strength to walk. When they reached her address, Fergus hurried ahead and held the door open. Lord Thorne carried her inside.

"You can put me down, sir."

He headed for the drawing room without pause,

deposited her on the couch, and knelt beside her. "Do you want to remove your bonnet?" He reached for the tie at her chin.

"I can do it," she snapped.

His hand dropped to his knee and when she looked up into his anxious eyes, it was like spotting a ray of light breaking through a stormy sky. Lord Thorne wasn't her husband and he wasn't ordering her about. He appeared genuinely concerned.

"I didn't mean to upset you," he said softly.

Her head bowed with remorse. "Forgive me. I didn't—" She swallowed her apology. How could she explain she had misunderstood his intentions when even Fergus had realized they were good?

He bobbed his head until he was in her line of sight. His grin melted her heart. "There is nothing to forgive, Lady Prestwick. I overstepped my bounds."

"No, you were being a gentleman."

She reached for a ribbon's end and slowly pulled. The bow released and she slipped off her bonnet. Removing it did make her feel better. She tugged off her gloves too and handed everything to Lord Thorne. It was a symbolic surrender, at least partly. He likely didn't interpret her actions that way, but it required great effort for her to trust a man to take care of her after her husband's suffocating type of caring.

He placed her bonnet and gloves on the table then removed his own hat and gloves. "Would you like something to drink?"

"Please."

Pushing to his feet, he smiled at her once more, then left her alone. She barely had time to miss him before he was back. "Fergus will bring a glass of lemonade."

"And one for you, too?"

He fingered the fichu clinging to her. "May I?"

She nodded and he unwound the damp lace from her neck. His fingers brushed her skin, making her light-headed again. "Thank you."

His ring caught the light, a white star appearing in the dark jewel. She reached out to skim her fingers over the stone. "It is beautiful."

"It was my father's." A muscle in his jaw twitched.

She wanted to ask him about his father—the report of the former Lord Thorne knocking his wife to the ground during a ball or the claim he'd shouted obscenities during a meeting of the House of Lords and threatened a fellow peer—but she didn't dare.

Sebastian frowned. "Are you well enough to attend the musicale with Eve? I could step in if you are under the weather. Did you eat anything this morning?"

"Not as much as I should have. That is likely the trouble." Heat singed her cheeks. She would die if he learned the real reason for her near-swoon, although the heat likely played some role. "I'm well, really. I will see your sister this evening as planned."

"Send a messenger if you change your mind."

She wouldn't. Eve was counting on her to play chaperone, especially with Lady Thorne's rheumatoid acting up the last few days.

Lord Thorne raised her hand to his lips. They were warm and soft against her bare skin. She wanted to feel them on her lips. Her breath caught in her throat as she leaned slightly toward him.

A sharp knock broke the spell and Lord Thorne released her hand with an exasperated sigh. He stood and turned toward the door where Fergus was just inside the threshold. His eyes narrowed at the baron. He had only one glass of lemonade.

"You aren't staying, my lord?" she asked.

He smiled. "I have much demanding my attention this afternoon, madam. Perhaps another day."

She managed to eke out a farewell and experienced a pierce of disappointment when he was gone.

Twelve

SEBASTIAN ADJUSTED HIS CRAVAT IN THE FOYER LOOK-
ing glass and tipped his head to inspect his jaw for
wayward whiskers. As usual, his valet had done an
impeccable job with Sebastian's shave, but one could
never be too fastidious. People were judged on appearances, and he took pains to set himself apart from the
disheveled mess his father had become in his last years.

Nodding with approval, he fleetingly wondered
what Helena would think of his new waistcoat.

Lady Prestwick.

He really must remember to address her appropriately, even though her name created the loveliest
sound. "Helena," he said softly. The name rolled off
his tongue.

A rustle on the stairs snapped him out of his reverie
and he spun around. Heat inched up his neck as
he spotted his sister. If she'd heard him murmuring
Helena's name, she gave no indication.

Eve reached the landing, flung her arms to her sides,
and twirled. Her daffodil skirts flared, revealing her
new slippers. "How do I look?"

She looked amazing, as usual. "Ladies don't ask for compliments, poppet."

"If gentlemen offered them freely, a lady wouldn't have to resort to asking," she said with a lift to her chin. "Besides, I want to know if I am dressed appropriately for Lady Norwick's salon."

"How am I to know? I've never attended the ladies' circles."

Even if he had, he wouldn't know what to expect from Lady Norwick. The countess was known for her outlandish gatherings.

Eve huffed and wrapped her shawl around her shoulders before marching toward the door. "You are no help at all, Sebastian."

"You look lovely," he called after her. "Is that better?"

"Only marginally. Next time employ a touch of sincerity."

He chuckled as he followed her to the carriage. His sister's surly mood didn't last beyond the next corner. "Helena and I have been having a wonderful time getting to know one another. I do wish you would stay and become better acquainted with her."

"It's a *ladies'* circle."

She arranged her skirts and smiled. "You like ladies. Very much, from what I gather."

"The company you keep, Evie." He rolled his eyes in jest. "I will stay long enough to give my regards, then I will hie off to the gentlemen's club until it is time to collect you."

Perhaps he could pull Helena aside to arrange a meeting for later to update her on his search. There was still no sign the girl had ever come to the West

End. He was beginning to suspect her man Fergus had been duped, but Sebastian didn't want to alert her to his suspicions. There were other places to search yet, and he wouldn't abandon the task until he found the girl, or at least had a good accounting of her fate.

The drive to Norwick Place was quicker than he'd anticipated. He alighted from the carriage and offered a hand to his sister. After the evening shower, the air had cooled and a refreshing breeze stirred a curl at Eve's cheek. He could walk to Brooks's, then return for her later.

"What do you say to a stroll after the gathering?" he asked his sister.

"That sounds lovely."

He sent his driver home, then joined her at Lord and Lady Norwick's door. As he reached for the knocker, the door flung open and Lady Norwick's sunny smile greeted them.

"Miss Thorne, you are here at last. And you've brought your brother. Splendid." She looked Sebastian up and down with an assessing sweep of her chocolate brown eyes. "Yes, you will do perfectly."

He arched an eyebrow. "Will do for what exactly?"

"This way, Lord Thorne." The countess latched on to his arm and urged him inside with Eve hanging tight to his other arm. He felt like a man being led to gaol. His head swung around in search of the butler to appeal for help, but the foyer was empty.

"Do you answer your own door?"

Lady Norwick ignored his questions and issued a steady stream of chatter as they wound through the town house. "How fortuitous that you brought Lord

Thorne along. Jasper had promised to stay, but I think the whole trance scenario frightened him in the end."

"Trance? What is going on?"

Sebastian needn't have bothered speaking since Lady Norwick was obviously deaf to his words.

"Sir Jonathan Hackberry is set up in the drawing room. He recently returned from an expedition abroad and his work is fascinating."

"Yes, fascinating is the word." Eve made the appropriate responses and smiled graciously as if she understood Lady Norwick's babbling.

"What do you know of his work?" he grumbled to his sister. Eve scowled in return.

They passed through the double doors into a grand drawing room, and his gaze landed on a drum that stood nearly as tall as Lady Norwick. He was vaguely aware there were others in the room, but an assortment of circles covered in tanned animal skin and scattered on a table demanded his attention.

"What is all this?"

Lady Norwick flicked a hand toward the circles. "Those are frame drums, my lord. They are quite ancient and came all the way from Mesopotamia."

"They are well-traveled, aren't they?"

Helena's soft chuckle behind him warmed his insides. He turned toward her, the light she had sparked in him coming out in a smile.

Her eyes twinkled with amusement. "Have you agreed to help Sir Jonathan Hackberry? He needs a gentleman to give us a demonstration, since ladies are too suggestible and mentally fragile." There was an edge of sarcasm in her tone, but she maintained her pleasant expression. "I would think those qualities would make us good subjects for an altered mental state, but alas, the method only works on males."

"I should think so, Lady Prestwick. It is common knowledge gentlemen are even *more* suggestible and mentally fragile." He crossed his eyes, earning her laughter. "Very well. You've convinced me to stay. The ladies must have a demonstration."

Lady Norwick clapped. "Marvelous, Lord Thorne. How brave you are."

More like daft.

The countess excused herself and crossed the room to greet a new arrival, Lady Lovelace. Celeste met his gaze and grinned like a cat that had stumbled across the cream unattended. For once, her mother-in-law wasn't at her side, which left her free to play. And from the sultry look Celeste gave him, she was ready to play with him.

Weeks earlier he would have obliged her, but he could barely spare her a thought today. When Helena was near, he was drawn to her like an ocean wave to land. The light-green dress she wore flattered her golden-brown locks and brought out her eyes. Her bottom lip was moist as if she had just licked it.

Helena cocked her head at an angle, her fingers toying with the silver pendant around her neck. "You are staring," she murmured.

"I am."

Her eyelashes fluttered as she shyly averted her gaze. "Well, you should stop before someone misinterprets your bad manners for interest." Even though she delivered a reprimand, there was amusement in her tone. Her gaze traveled slowly over him, her lips curling contentedly. His blood heated and there was a tightening in his lower belly.

"Now who is staring?"

His body screamed interest and it was mutual. The faint impression of taut nipples poked through her thin muslin dress. His mouth watered at the thought of sampling them.

A succession of sharp raps on a drum broke his Helena-induced trance. He inclined his head in her direction. "I believe that is my cue, Lady Prestwick."

Sir Jonathan Hackberry came forward to introduce himself and shake Sebastian's hand. The baronet wore no gloves, and his browned skin bore deep grooves, even though he couldn't be any older than Sebastian. "I cannot thank you enough for volunteering to be my assistant today, Lord Thorne. The ladies are an eager audience."

"Mesopotamia, eh?"

The gentleman puffed out his chest, preening like a peacock. "Uncovered them near the Tigris. Of course, the region is better known as the Ottoman Empire now. Please, come have a seat."

He led Sebastian to a Chippendale chair and urged him to sit. "I need you to have an open mind, my lord. Concentrate on the beat of the drum and allow your spirit to wander wherever it wishes. You shouldn't be caught off guard if you feel yourself floating above your body."

Sebastian nearly rolled his eyes but stopped himself in time. Clearly Sir Jonathan Hackberry was one of those—uh, what were they called again? *Oh, that's right. A crackbrain.* Sebastian had met several on his grand tour.

Eve slipped into a seat beside Helena and clasped hands with her. "I cannot believe he agreed. How marvelous." His sister's excited whispers carried on the air. Both women looked at him with expectation shining in their eyes. In fact, every woman seated in the semicircle seemed to be holding her breath, waiting for something spectacular to happen.

Never let it be said Sebastian was a disappointment to women.

∾

Helena found the content of Sir Jonathan's lecture interesting. His monotone voice, however, was becoming tedious. She shifted position on her chair and leaned closer to pretend attentiveness out of regard for their hostess.

"The frame drum emerged at the center of mystical religious traditions in the great civilizations of Mesopotamia, Anatolia, Greece, Egypt, Rome. Many of the relics uncovered in the excavation of these once thriving cities depict women as a priestess or goddess leading the religious ceremony through their drumming. Days of nonstop drumming and dance were intended to alter consciousness, to let go of earthly restraints so they could be one with their gods."

Sir Jonathan moved behind the tall drum and stroked it like one would a lover. "This is a kettledrum and it was used for the same purpose."

Suddenly, he smacked his palm hard against the

surface. Eve jumped and cried out, then covered her giggle with her hand.

Helena exchanged an amused glance with Lord Thorne.

Sir Jonathan's discourse continued between lively beats on the drum, his manner becoming less stiff.

"And this, dear ladies, is the frame drum I mentioned." He hurried to the table, snatched a large round disk, and swung his head toward Lord Thorne. "Are you ready to demonstrate, my lord?"

With a half smirk, the baron nodded.

Sir Jonathan lifted the drum and knocked his hand against it. "This is called a thumb roll. Listen for the difference."

There was a definite difference when he struck it a second time, although Helena didn't know how to describe the sound. Wickie hadn't thought it necessary for her to study music.

In rapid succession, Sir Jonathan tapped out a rhythm. It reverberated in her chest as if challenging her heart to match it. His drumming became more aggressive, but the rhythm stayed the same. Eve drew in a shaky breath beside her and eased to the edge of her seat. Helena didn't know if the beat of the drum was affecting Eve, or if the attractive glow that had come over Sir Jonathan's face accounted for her sudden interest.

Helena's gaze strayed to Lord Thorne and lingered, enjoying a moment to study him while he was preoccupied. His eyes were closed and dark lashes fanned against his olive complexion. For a moment, she allowed herself the luxury of wondering what it would be like with him sleeping in her bed.

Not the act of making love, but actually watching him in slumber. Never was one more vulnerable than when one slept, and succumbing to sleep in the presence of another required great trust.

Longing was a faint beat in her heart, gaining strength as she drank in his magnificence. His slender fingers rested casually on the arms of the chair. His broad shoulders appeared capable of holding up the world. His arms and chest a safe haven. Her longing grew more unbearable by the moment. She wanted to trust him in the worst way and believe he wouldn't look at her differently once he knew she was seeking her sister and not a servant girl. But she was afraid, and her fear grew in proportion to how much she liked him.

Helena frowned at the low hum accompanying the drum. Eve clutched her arm. "It's happening," she whispered. The noise was coming from Lord Thorne.

Helena blinked, uncertain what to make of everything.

The drumming grew more vigorous; a fire ignited in Sir Jonathan's eyes. Lord Thorne began to moan and sway on the chair.

Sir Jonathan stepped toward him, smacking his palm on the drum at a feverish pace. "Surrender your spirit, my lord."

The baron moaned louder. He rocked and swayed.

"He is fighting it," Lady Banner hissed.

With a cry, he pitched forward and fell on his knees. Everyone gasped.

But then Helena saw it, a tiny twitch at the corners of his lips. Lord Thorne, the scoundrel, was putting on an act. She sat back and crossed her arms to enjoy the show.

His eyes flew open and stared blankly at his audience. Murmurs traveled the small group. Sir Jonathan urged Lord Thorne to give himself over to the trance.

"No." He flung his head to one side and then the other. "I can't. I must fight it."

"I told you he was fighting it," Lady Banner declared, sounding proud.

Helena snorted softly.

"Don't fight." The drummer rushed forward, beating the drum with all he had. "Surrender, my lord. Let go of your inhibitions."

Lord Thorne went still. Everyone shifted to the edges of their seats. Slowly, he rose, silent and unblinking. Sir Jonathan missed a beat, his mouth hanging open.

"It worked." Eve gripped Helena's arm. "He is in a trance."

The excited murmurs grew louder.

"I've really done it!" Sir Jonathan sounded as surprised as Lady Norwick's guests.

"What now, sir?" Eve asked in a rush.

A baffled expression crossed his face. "Um…"

"Dance," Lord Thorne intoned. "Must dance."

Sir Jonathan nodded. "Yes, that's it. Dance is an integral part of the trance."

"Play faster," Lord Thorne commanded.

The drumming accelerated, and then as if given a directive straight from heaven, Lord Thorne threw his head back and flung his arms wide. He moved them in the air like undulating waves and twirled in a circle. Shaking his hips in a most improper fashion, he raised his hands above his head.

Jaws dropped. Sir Jonathan even stopped his drumming. A giggle sounded from across the room.

"Oh!" Eve released Helena's arm and bolted from her seat. "Sebastian James Edmund Thorne, you are incorrigible. How could you?"

He cracked one eye and grinned. "You remembered the gypsy dance."

"How could I forget when you never let me?" There was a touch of merriment to his sister's hassled voice.

"The gypsy dance?" Lines creased Sir Jonathan's forehead. "But I don't understand."

Eve smiled ruefully. "I am so sorry, sir. I know you were hoping for my brother to channel the spirits, but I'm afraid he only managed to resurrect a naughty little boy."

Lord Thorne's grin widened. "It was *your* dance, Eve." Then he turned his charming smile on the other ladies. "Forgive me, Lady Norwick. I couldn't resist teasing my little sister. When we were young, we saw gypsies at a carnival and Eve decided she wanted to join a band when she grew up. She forced me to watch her dance for weeks until our mother informed her ladies do not become gypsies."

"And what a pity." Lady Norwick joined Eve at Sir Jonathan's side and patted her hand fondly. "I should think gypsy dancing more stimulating than watercolors any day. Bravo, Lord Thorne! This is the most entertaining salon we've had yet."

Amelia Hillary, Lady Norwick's close friend, gave him a standing ovation and the other ladies joined in. When the baron bowed theatrically, Sir Jonathan's scowl deepened.

Lady Norwick was quick to notice and hurried

to smooth his ruffled feathers. "And Sir Jonathan, upon my word, there cannot exist another drummer as exquisite as you. I was completely mesmerized. Another round of applause, ladies?"

Her guests complied, clapping with no less enthusiasm for the poor man.

He flushed a deep red and his scowl disappeared. "You flatter me, Lady Norwick."

"Not at all, sir." While Lady Norwick flattered him more, Lord Thorne approached Helena and Eve.

When Eve looked up at her brother with devotion, she reminded Helena of a puppy wagging its tail. "You are too silly sometimes, Bastian."

He shrugged. "It's worth acting like a fool to see you smile. Are you having a good time?"

"The very best. Thank you." She pressed his hand between hers. "But I think Sir Jonathan's feelings were hurt. I should go speak with him." She wandered over to speak with the man and their hostess, leaving Helena alone with Lord Thorne.

"You love her very much," she said.

"I would do anything for her." The muscles in his jaw shifted, a sign of strong emotions he held in check. "She was all I had some days."

Helena didn't have a chance to ask his meaning before Lady Lovelace sidled up to him.

"Sebastian, I didn't expect to see you again so soon. Are you following me?" She threaded her arm with his in a too-familiar gesture that made Helena's stomach dive. Turning, Lady Lovelace gasped softly and covered her heart with her hand. "Oh dear! Lady Prestwick, I didn't see you there."

The widow boldly met Helena's gaze with a defiant lift to her chin that said she had been perfectly aware of Helena's presence and didn't like her near her lover.

Lady Lovelace batted her lashes as if embarrassed, but no blush colored her cheeks. "I'm afraid you caught Lord Thorne and me at an awkward moment. I hope you don't think me forward. It is just Lord Thorne and I are old friends."

A bitter taste coated Helena's tongue. "You should catch up then." She spun on her heel and stalked toward the terrace door before she said something she would regret, such as telling the woman to take her hands off her man.

Thirteen

"Now, now. That wasn't nice misleading Lady Prestwick," Sebastian said to the young widow attached to his side like a leech. The other ladies had adjourned to the far end of the drawing room where refreshments were being served, giving him leave to speak plainly.

"How did I mislead her?" Celeste asked. "I simply informed her that we are old friends."

"*Old* as in the past. I believe you were implying otherwise."

Celeste was a pretty one with auburn hair and peaches-and-cream skin, but she was lacking in too many ways to maintain his interest. She wasn't especially kind and her dotty act was getting under his skin.

She tipped her head at a flirtatious angle. "It mustn't remain in the past," she murmured. "Meet me at my town house in an hour? The dowager Lady Lovelace is taking tea with her sister and will be out all afternoon."

Celeste had refused to see him after Lady Gabrielle tossed him over. Even though she seemed to have forgotten about turning her back on him, his memory was intact. "I am afraid I must decline your generous offer, madam."

Lightning snapped in her eyes, but she offered a smile, strained as it was. "I don't understand. We have such a fun time together."

"Perhaps my idea of fun has changed."

Celeste's face hardened, and she appeared on the verge of a tantrum, but she wouldn't dare make a scene for fear of someone learning he had refused her.

"When you come to your senses," she hissed, "you know where to find me."

"I doubt I will ever return to my senses, or haven't you heard? I'm as mad as a March hare." His brows shot up as it dawned on him she was quite adept at employing the innocent act. "You *were* responsible for the piece about me arriving on your doorstep buck-naked, weren't you?"

"No!" Her eyes flared. "I already said it was not me."

He leaned closer and her breath hitched. "I don't believe you, madam. Set your sights on some other poor sod. Our *friendship* has ended."

She nailed him with an icy glare before going to join the other ladies for tea.

Good riddance. Sebastian lingered by the terrace door waiting for Helena to return. He wasn't sure what to make of her sudden departure. Under normal circumstances, he might think she was jealous of Celeste, but Helena wasn't like other women. Most ladies of his acquaintance were easy to read. They wanted him between their legs, and if they weren't already spoken for, he was happy to be there.

Helena, on the other hand, was as difficult to

decipher as hieroglyphics in a dark tomb. He had no doubt she found him attractive. He just didn't know if she *liked* him. She certainly kept him at a distance.

He checked for Eve and discovered she was engaged in an animated discussion with Sir Jonathan and Lady Norwick several feet away. The man even allowed her to pound on one of the frame drums. With his sister occupied and content, he slipped outside to find Helena. If she asked why he had followed her, he could say he wanted to report on his search for Lavinia.

He didn't find her on the terrace, so he descended the stone stairs to wander the gardens. Norwick Place had a small garden, but there were many cozy places to hide. He came upon her sitting on a marble bench beneath a pergola. Ivy weaved through the trellis and created a natural roof to block the sun.

She froze when she spotted him, her round eyes larger than normal. He held his arms out at his sides and moved slowly as if approaching a frightened animal.

"Don't hurt me," he said in a soothing voice.

Her nose wrinkled. "Don't *hurt* you?"

"I saw how you handled that footpad, and I'd rather not wind up in a heap at your feet."

She laughed, her wariness dissolving. "Unless you intend to rob me, I promise you are safe."

He sat on the bench beside her. "And if I steal a kiss?"

"From me or Lady Lovelace?" The way she spat the other woman's name gave him the answer he wanted and placed him on familiar ground. He knew how to relate to women who desired him.

"Why, Helena, I think you are jealous."

Color drained from her already-pale complexion. "That's—I am not jel—*Who* gave you leave to use my Christian name?"

He flashed a grin. "You gave permission to my sister."

"And you are not your sister, Lord Thorne."

"I am not." He made it a practice never to argue with women, especially since he hated losing. "You may call me Sebastian if you like."

"I *don't* like, my lord."

Damn, she tried his patience. Why couldn't the lady admit she wanted him? There was nothing standing in the way of them having a very pleasant friendship of their own. Nothing except her stubbornness.

"Then you must forgive me for being too familiar, Lady Prestwick." He took her hand and smiled when she allowed him to turn it palm up. His fingers moved to the tiny pearl button on her glove and pushed it through the small loop of fabric. Her breath escaped in a soft wheeze as he inched the satin free of her fingers.

She closed her eyes on a sigh. "Your apology seems less than sincere."

With no barrier present, he turned her hand over and raised it to his lips. Each perfect knuckle received a kiss.

Then her palm.

Her inner wrist. Goose bumps rose along her silky skin.

Her eyes flickered open, but her lids had grown heavy. "Olive warned me about you."

"And her warnings fell on deaf ears, did they not? We know you have a taste for danger," he teased, his lips returning to her wrist and nibbling toward the crook of her elbow.

"That's untrue." She frowned, her brows lowering over her blue-green eyes. "If anything, I have lived too cautiously, and any risks I take are calculated."

He released her arm and sat up straight.

A breeze flowed through the arbor; whisper-like flutters surrounded them. Neither of them spoke, their gazes locked. Was she trying to tell him skulking about in the dead of night where cutthroats roamed was less risky than becoming involved with him? He'd never heard anything more ridiculous.

She swept a strand of hair behind her ear. "It is none of my concern, but are you and Lady Lovelace…?"

He blinked. Was this the barrier between them? Helena believed he was still involved with Celeste? "Lady Lovelace is no one to me."

Her eyes darkened. "She is 'no one.' You share her bed, but she means nothing to you. Is that how affairs are with you? No attachments?"

"I said no such thing." Her disapproving tone heated his blood. He had never taken advantage of anyone's feelings. "And you *are* jealous."

She opened her mouth to argue, but he cut her off.

"Don't try to deny it. And for your information, I am not having an affair with Celeste."

"*I* am not jealous."

"Egads! You are infuriating, woman."

She squared her jaw. "Well, so are you. You keep insisting I am jealous when I am not. You and I have a business arrangement. Nothing more."

Her hand shook as she pushed the silky strand of

hair behind her ear again. Her body betrayed her lies at every turn. There was more between them than business. *Much* more. Or there could be if she would only admit the truth.

As he leaned toward her, her eyes widened, but she didn't retreat. The tip of her tongue flicked across her plump bottom lip and he stifled a groan.

"Those sweet lips were made for kissing. Not lies."

Her hand came to rest on his chest and she eased closer, her eyes drifting to half-mast. His heart thudded hard beneath her palm. "I'm not lying," she whispered.

If he shifted, her lips would be against his, and he would finally have what he'd been hungering for since that moment outside St. Saviour's Church. But more than he desired her taste, he needed her to admit she wanted him too.

"Prove there is nothing between us, Helena. Kiss me."

"I've nothing to prove." She swayed into him, her lips brushing softly against his.

Good enough. His hand slid to her nape and gently encouraged her to kiss him like she meant it. She sank into him with a pleasurable sigh. The feel of her lips was heaven, her mouth moving with his in a sensual dance. He swept his tongue along the crease of her lips, savoring this reward for his patience. She opened her mouth and her tongue met his, intensifying his hunger. He wanted more. *Much* more.

His mouth traveled to her neck and nibbled a path to the supple flesh of her ear. She gasped when he took the lobe gently between his teeth, then melted as he laved it with his tongue. He wanted to taste her everywhere. The hollow of her collarbone. The valley between her lovely breasts. Her puckered nipples. The sweet spot between her thighs. But he couldn't do any of those things here in the garden.

Running his tongue lightly along her ear's rim, he whispered, "Someone might come upon us, sweetheart. I promise to make it up to you tonight."

Her eyes drifted open as he eased her away. "Tonight?"

He kissed away the bewildered lines between her brows. "I'll come to you tonight where there's no danger of anyone interrupting."

She stiffened in his arms. For one horrible moment, he thought he had hurt her. Her cheeks were flushed and her eyes still cloudy with passion but clearing quickly. She licked her lips and his cock twitched, excited by the possibilities of what her mouth could do to him.

She held her hair back from her face with both hands. "W-we agreed you wouldn't come to my town house again. If someone sees you…"

He smiled. Was it wrong to feel pleased she wasn't casual about allowing him in her bed? "No one will see me. I know when to practice caution."

She shook her head. "No." She scooted farther away, her eyes darting as if searching for an escape. "We agreed you wouldn't come to my town house again. It's a bad idea. Lady Bellwyn's garden party is tomorrow. We will see each other then."

"Along with a hundred other guests. How am I to get you alone at a garden party?"

"You aren't." She hopped from the bench. "I am sorry, Sebastian. I—I don't think I can do this."

She lifted the hem of her skirts and ran.

❦

Helena tried to stay ahead of the panic, but it threatened to overtake her as she neared the Norwicks' home. How had she gone from supremely put out with Sebastian to nearly allowing him to bed her? In a stranger's garden, no less. And it was *daylight*, for pity's sake.

Slumping against the terrace railing, she tried to catch her breath. She curled inward, her shame too heavy for her shoulders. If one kiss made her forget herself, what would happen if she allowed him in her bed? She would become hopelessly dotty and perhaps follow him around like a pup. Not only would that be undignified, falling in love with him would ruin her plans.

She must stay strong and focused on her goal. Providing a home for her sisters and a future for Gracie was the highest priority, and becoming involved with another man who might interfere with that goal was unacceptable. She didn't judge Sebastian to be anything like her late husband, but all men expected to be in control, and the risk was too great. Barring Sebastian from her house and bed was the wisest course, even if she wanted him there desperately.

Taking a fortifying breath, she straightened and patted her hair. She caught a glimpse of her reflection in one of the windows. The run-in with the baron hadn't left her nearly as disorderly on the outside as it had inside. She approached the French door and entered the great room with what she hoped was a calm smile.

Eve looked up from the kettledrum where she was

standing with Sir Jonathan. "Come watch, Helena. Sir Jonathan is teaching me to play."

She pounded out a rhythm as the gentleman nodded. "Perfect, Miss Thorne. You've a natural talent for drumming."

Eve beamed in response to his praise.

"I am impressed." Helena joined them and tried to focus as Eve chattered about all she had learned from the baronet on Mesopotamia, priestesses, and gods Helena had never heard of.

Helena swore the man issued a dreamy sigh when he gazed at Eve. It seemed the poor man was love struck. He likely had it as bad for Eve as Helena did for Sebastian, which made her feel a sort of kinship with him.

The gentleman moved closer to Eve's side. "Shall I show you the thumb roll?"

"That would be splendid."

Helena took a seat to oversee the lesson, feeling rather neglectful for having left Eve unsupervised earlier. A movement from the corner of her eye caused goose bumps to rise on her arms. It had to be Sebastian returning, but she forced herself not to look.

Eve brightened. "Where have you been? Sir Jonathan has been teaching me to drum and you've been missing all the fun."

Sebastian's deep laugh washed over Helena and filled her with that same blasted longing she'd run from. Without asking permission, he slipped into the chair beside her. "I suppose that depends on one's definition of fun," he murmured. "Isn't that correct, Lady Prestwick?"

Helena shot him a quelling look, but he only raised a brow as if challenging her to contradict him. She snapped her gaze forward, her hands gripping the arms of the chair.

What was he doing? She had essentially told him she wouldn't become involved with him and he acted as if they hadn't spoken.

"I don't understand you," she whispered. "I told you there can be nothing between us."

"I fully support a lady's prerogative to change her mind." He leaned back in the chair, extending his legs and crossing them at the ankles. "And I'm told I can be persuasive."

"Have you also heard you are arrogant?"

"A time or two, yes."

Helena folded her arms and fought back a smile. She didn't want to encourage him, but she couldn't help feeling flattered that he would want to change her mind. Her gaze traveled the length of his strong legs and her heart missed a beat.

Stop it! There was no room for a man in her life, no matter how amazingly handsome he was. She was doing the right thing for her family and herself.

Eve quit drumming. "I have a great idea. We should invite Helena and Sir Jonathan to join us for a stroll this afternoon."

"I'm afraid I must—"

"I would be honored." Sir Jonathan cut off Helena's response.

"That is a splendid idea, poppet." Sebastian grinned at Helena, and she had a sinking feeling she would be subjected to his persuasive powers very soon if she agreed.

Eve's doe-eyed gaze pleaded with her to accept. "Surely you can join us, Helena. We have barely spoken all afternoon."

Helena did feel rather guilty for ignoring her friend, but if she didn't know better, she might think Eve was conspiring with her brother.

She suppressed a sigh. She hoped she wouldn't come to regret this. "A stroll sounds lovely, Eve. Thank you."

❧

Sebastian would have to thank his sister once they reached home, although he didn't delude himself into thinking Eve had asked Helena and Sir Jonathan to join them on a walk for his sake. His sister had linked arms with Sir Jonathan and dragged him several paces ahead the moment they left Lady Norwick's. Eve's laugh was a little heartier, her gestures more animated, and when she slanted her head to smile at her escort, the poor man stumbled over his own feet.

"She likes him," Helena said softly.

"Yes, she is rather obvious, but it's sweet."

A slight smile curved Helena's lips. "Sir Jonathan allowed her to play his drums, even though he wouldn't put her in a trance. I am sure that says something about his regard for her, too."

"I've no doubt he is smitten, but I'm unfamiliar with the gentleman and his family. Until I know more about him, I will not encourage a match."

"He seems kind."

Sebastian's teeth ground together. She had known Sir Jonathan Hackberry for all of three hours and she had already deemed him kind. And yet Sebastian, who had willingly given his time to help her search for a servant's sibling, was arrogant. A completely unfounded accusation. He was *confident*. There was a difference.

When ladies began propositioning him at age sixteen, he had known he was different from his friends. Granted, nine years of women fawning over him hadn't made him humble, but the experience with Gabrielle had knocked him down a few pegs. Now there was Helena, a woman he desired more than any other, and she refused to have anything to do with him, which made no sense.

He glanced sideways at her. Her gaze remained straight ahead and her posture was as stiff as a soldier marching in a parade. Sebastian had never been one to dance around a topic. In fact, he'd been told on occasion he had no tact, but he'd always found asking straight questions usually reaped straight answers.

He cleared his throat. "What impediment keeps you from becoming involved with me? I know you are as attracted to me as I am to you."

"Sebastian." Surprise and censorship was clear in that one word.

"Be honest. I deserve the truth." He held his breath, dreading her answer. If she mentioned anything about his family history of mental frailty, he wasn't certain he could stand to hear it. Not from her.

Her steps slowed until the gap between them and his sister grew even greater. Eventually, Helena stopped. He turned to face her, preparing for the harsh truth and unsure how he would respond.

"Sebastian." She forcefully exhaled and a pink flush climbed her face. "It's *me*. I am the impediment."

He blinked, not following her.

"I'm afraid."

"Of me?"

She shook her head. "It's not like that, at least I'm not afraid of you in the sense you mean. I am afraid of what I might lose if I become involved with you. I never had a moment of freedom until recently and I can't risk my independence. I just can't."

A surge of affection flowed through him. She had nothing to fear from him, and now that he understood her reluctance, his patience returned. "I don't want to control you, love."

She gave a rueful laugh. "You would be the only man who hasn't. First it was my father and then my husband. This is the only time in my life I haven't had a man making decisions for me, and I've found I like that very much."

"I understand the appeal."

He wasn't being sarcastic. Having grown up mostly with his mother and sister for companionship, Sebastian didn't hold some of the same ideas about ladies and their places in Society as his fellow gents. He believed in protecting and providing for Mother and Eve, but he would never force them into doing something they didn't agree to. He wanted to ask Helena about her father and husband, so he could reassure her that he was nothing like them, but the middle of the walkway was not a place for such a discussion.

For now, he would just have to prove himself, and he would start by accepting her refusal.

"I promise not to place you in a difficult position again, Lady Prestwick, but know I will be waiting." *As long as it takes.*

Despite his father's long periods of isolation, he had managed to impart some of his values to Sebastian. *Hard work and determination reaps rewards.* Determination was in Sebastian's lifeblood. He had never been one to surrender without a fight or back down from a challenge, but that didn't mean his only weapon was brawn. He had the advantage of charm and wit, and that was what he needed to win over the ever-more-desirable Helena.

"Shall we?" He offered his arm and a disarming smile.

Her eyes narrowed on him as she accepted his escort. "Thank you, I think."

"Now, now, Lady Prestwick. No more flattery or I will become too arrogant by half."

Her smile returned. "Too late, my lord."

Fourteen

HELENA SMILED FONDLY AT EVE AS SIR JONATHAN Hackberry led the young woman to the dance floor. Somehow Sir Jonathan had managed an invitation to Lady Bellwyn's garden party yesterday, where Eve had spent most of the day paired with him in games, and now he'd made a surprise appearance at Lady Chattington's ball. He obviously had connections one would not expect a mere baronet to have.

Helena suspected it wouldn't be long until Sir Jonathan requested an audience with Sebastian. Whether Sebastian would entertain an offer from the gentleman remained to be seen. The stubborn set to his jaw when he had spoken of investigating Sir Jonathan indicated he would leave no stone unturned. Not that Helena could blame him after Eve's disastrous engagement to Mr. Benjamin Hillary.

But if Sir Jonathan proved to be a worthy suitor for Eve, what might that mean for Helena? If Eve made a match, Helena would have fulfilled her part of the agreement with Sebastian. She had no way of holding him to his side, and she didn't have another gentleman to take his place. Her stomach churned and she took several deep breaths to rein in her worry. Sebastian had given his word, and he'd done nothing to make her question his honor. She owed him the benefit of the doubt.

She sensed Sebastian's approach before he spoke. Prickles raced along her skin as if every inch of her was aware of him.

"May I have this dance, Lady Prestwick?"

She glanced sideways at him, her heart sputtering a moment before recovering its steady rhythm. Giving him the benefit of the doubt did not require her to dance with him. His touch would only complicate things and muddle her thoughts.

He held out his gloved hand, and she placed hers in his. Her fingers tingled and she swayed into him.

He caught her by the elbow, smiling down at her. "Careful."

Good Lord, she was trying to be cautious, but he had an invisible pull on her that made resisting him impossible.

He led her to the dance floor as the quartet began a waltz. She sighed softly when his hand pressed against her back. Her mind might believe it was unwise to be so close to him, but her body clearly disagreed. When his fingers wrapped around hers to guide her along the parquet floor, it was as if a lost piece of her had returned.

"You look beautiful tonight, madam." His eyes flared like the black star sapphire ring he always wore.

She mumbled her thanks, uncertain if her dry mouth had formed the correct words.

He urged her closer as they twirled, her head spinning just as fast. She caught a glimpse of Eve laughing with Sir Jonathan.

"Eve may have an offer soon," she said. "Did you learn anything about the gentleman?"

"He seems aboveboard. Although he has been out of the country much of the time, his estate is in good condition and yields a decent yearly income. He is not squandering his fortune with his travels."

"It sounds as if you've made a decision already."

He shrugged. "It's not my decision to make. If Eve chooses to accept him, I would have no qualms about negotiating a contract with the gentleman."

Her eyebrows shot up. It was hard to imagine a man who would allow his sister a choice, and yet he met her gaze directly. There was no guile behind his dark eyes. Her heart skipped.

Helena had been given no choice when Wickie had come to their door to claim her. She had been fifteen and acting as a mother to her four younger sisters. Her father woke early that morning, stumbling into the kitchen looking like Lazarus raised from the dead. In a rare show of kindness, he had smiled at her. She should have known then something was amiss. Instead, she had returned to stirring the morning porridge with Little Gracie on her hip. Her baby sister had been teething and fussy, and refused to allow anyone but Helena to hold her.

Lavinia, Cora, and Pearl's happy chatter at the battered kitchen table had stopped when their father entered the room. Cora and Pearl had watched him with distrust in their almost identical blue eyes.

When the knock came at their front door, bile had risen in her throat. It was the same every time her father played at the tables. She had beaten her father to the door, eager to bargain with the debt collector to save their meager belongings, but it wasn't their usual type of visitor.

The pain slicing into her heart had nearly doubled her over when she learned what her father had done. With tears blurring her vision, she had turned to Lord Prestwick before climbing into his travel coach. *Please, if I cannot stay, could my sisters come too?*

He'd lightly grasped her chin and smiled sadly. *I only need one of you, Miss Kendrick. You will have a better life with me. You'll have no regrets.*

Wickie had lied, of course. Or perhaps he didn't know the meaning of regret. Or family. Or heartbreaking grief that stripped one of hope. It felt like the ultimate betrayal that she had grown to care for him in the end.

Sebastian's lips gently touched her ear. "The music has ended, love."

"Oh!" She blinked, embarrassed to have been lost in her thoughts and feeling awkward just standing there, gripping his hand as if he were her lifeline.

❧

Sebastian didn't want to release Helena. She had the most haunted look on her face, and it took every bit of his self-discipline to refrain from pulling her into his arms. He recognized that look. His father had gotten a similar look when anyone mentioned the Irish Rebellion. Only once had Father spoken to Sebastian of his days in the cavalry. Sebastian's grandfather had been boasting of his son being a war hero and Father pulled Sebastian aside.

I'm no hero, Son.

Sebastian still recalled the haunted vacancy in his father's stare.

What terrible things could have happened to Helena to account for that same vacant look? His thumb brushed against the bare curve of her shoulder blade, slowly bringing her back from wherever her mind had taken her. "Let's take refreshment."

She nodded and dropped hands, but he retrieved hers and slipped it through the crook of his elbow. He worried she might need the support to stay on her feet. He led her toward a smaller sitting room off the great room where Lady Chattington served punch in silver cups and sweets on delicate china plates. Sebastian retrieved two drinks, handed one to Helena, then guided her to a vacant settee in the corner.

People entered and left the refreshment room in a steady stream, too caught up in their own goings-on to pay attention to them.

His knuckles grazed her leg. "Do you wish to talk about what is troubling you?"

She crossed her arms tightly across her waist as if creating a shield around herself. Something was definitely out of sorts this evening. He held his tongue while he waited for her to determine if she wanted to confide in him. Her eyes cleared and she offered a slight smile. "Forgive me for being such poor company, my lord."

Very well. She didn't want to discuss it, and he

understood it wasn't the most appropriate place for an intimate conversation. "Someday, if you wish to tell me what has caused you such sorrow, I pledge to keep your confidence. You may tell me anything, Helena."

She sighed and slowly unfolded her arms. "I believe you, truly I do, but it is nothing I want to remember. Would it be acceptable to change the subject?"

"Of course."

Her gaze darted to his and she licked her lips. "Please, don't take this the wrong way, but I cannot help wondering what will happen once your sister has an offer of marriage, what that will mean for us."

He grinned. "Well, we will no longer be forced to attend the assemblies, which should leave more time to look for your Lavinia."

The worry lines on her forehead disappeared. "I wasn't certain our partnership would continue."

"Before I've fulfilled my end? You hold a poor opinion of me, Lady Prestwick."

"Not of you, Lord Thorne. Of men as a whole, with the exception of Fergus. He has proven to be a very loyal sort."

Sebastian cocked an eyebrow. "And? Haven't I earned my place as your loyal champion yet?"

She chuckled softly, her face losing the last signs of tension. "I suppose you have. Forgive me for doubting you."

"I meant what I said earlier. If you ever want to tell me what those men did to turn you against all of us…"

She shrugged one shoulder. "I would rather forget about it."

Only she hadn't forgotten. Even if she didn't dwell

on the specific ways she had been mistreated, these men who had come before him colored her decisions. Their acts made her wary and kept her isolated and alone.

His hand found hers between them on the settee. "I will never hurt you, Helena. You have my word."

She turned her hand palm up and twined her fingers with his. "I know."

Did she really? He supposed he would have to have faith in her too if there was any hope for them. "We shouldn't have left Eve alone this long. There is no telling what kind of mischief she has gotten into," he said.

He grinned, knowing his younger sister wasn't inclined to get into trouble. She was uncommonly astute for a girl of one and twenty. And he had taught her to stay in the ballroom under the watchful eyes of the matrons while not allowing any particular gentleman to monopolize her time unless she would welcome a match with him.

When he and Helena entered the ballroom arm in arm, he didn't immediately see his sister, but she wouldn't have gotten far. As he and Helena completed a turn around the room, his confidence began to falter.

"There is Sir Jonathan. Perhaps he knows where she is," Helena said.

The man was in conversation with the Duke and Duchess of Foxhaven and the Earl and Countess of Ellis.

Splendid. Just what he needed, another encounter with his former fiancée and her husband. Well, there was no help for it. If Eve was missing from the ballroom—as it appeared she might be—Sir Jonathan could know where she had gone.

Gabrielle's brother, the duke, greeted Sebastian with a friendly smile, which was the decent thing to do since Sebastian hadn't sued for a breach of contract. To be fair, the duke hadn't killed him for compromising his sister either, so Sebastian considered them to be on good terms.

Ellis took Helena's hand and placed a respectful kiss on her knuckles. "Good evening, Lady Prestwick. Lord Thorne."

He ignored Ellis's greeting on principle and turned to Sir Jonathan. "Have you seen my sister, sir?"

"Uh…" Sir Jonathan glanced around the ballroom, his weathered forehead wrinkled in confusion. "She was dancing a moment ago. Some gent recently returned from Delhi asked for her dance card. A former acquaintance, I believe."

"An acquaintance?" Eve's social circle was small, so whoever had danced with her was likely one of Sebastian's associates. But he couldn't think of anyone who had been abroad recently.

Sir Jonathan nodded. "The gentleman intimated it had been a long time. I believe his name is Hillary?"

Sebastian's gut seized. There were several Hillary men—all brothers—but only one could claim to know Eve.

Ellis met his eye; a knowing glance passed between them. The earl clapped Sir Jonathan on the shoulder. "Sir, have you spoken with Lord Hollister about your expedition to Egypt? He is quite fond of hounds. I'm certain he will be enthralled with the history of Anubis."

The gentleman brightened. "I haven't had the honor."

Ellis pointed to Lord Hollister and nudged Sir Jonathan in the man's direction.

Sebastian nodded his thanks. His old friend had deftly handled Sir Jonathan. The fewer people who knew Eve might be with Benjamin Hillary, the better.

Ellis fell in step with him as he stalked for the terrace. "They couldn't have gone far," he muttered. "We will find them."

A low growl rumbled in Sebastian's chest. "When did that coward return?"

"Two days ago. He was listed on the ship's manifest in the newssheet."

Damn! Sebastian would have to begin reading the paper again. "I'm going to kill him."

Benjamin Hillary, the man who had abandoned Eve at the altar, was worse than dead. Sebastian was going to rip him limb from limb.

"Anthony, wait." Gabrielle hurried after them with Helena close behind.

Sebastian halted midstride and turned to the women. "You will only draw attention if you follow us," he whispered fiercely.

Gabrielle raised a haughty brow. "As if two grown men dashing off like hounds after a fox is inconspicuous."

Sebastian's sarcastic retort died away when Helena threaded her arm with his. "She has a point, my lord, but escorting ladies to the terrace shouldn't raise any alarms."

Her touch calmed the storm brewing inside him. He didn't wait to see if Ellis took his wife in hand. Instead, he forced himself to smile pleasantly at the lady on his arm and pretended he wasn't going mad with worry.

Once they cleared the ballroom and found the terrace abandoned, Helena dropped his arm and gave him a gentle shove. "Check the garden."

Surely Eve wasn't that dim-witted. Hillary had already proven he had no honor. She couldn't expect him to do the right thing if they were discovered together.

Sebastian raced down the steps into the dark garden. A sliver moon peeked between heavy clouds, shedding little light on the garden path.

Ellis caught up to him at a fork in the path. "I'll search the west side and you take the east."

Sebastian nodded sharply. He veered to the east, going deeper into the garden. Fireflies were random beacons in the darkness. He could see nothing but the outlines of bushes. The spiced scent of myrtle was thick on the humid air. A rustle sounded to his left. He froze.

"Go away, Ben. I mean it." Eve's exasperated command from the bushes set Sebastian's blood on fire. With red shrouding his vision and muscles tensed for a fight, he stormed toward the large shrub.

"I'm not leaving until you come back inside, Evie."

"Just leave me be."

A stick snapped under Sebastian's boot.

"What was that?" Eve whispered harshly.

Hillary shushed her. What the hell was the bastard thinking, taking her into the gardens?

Sebastian barreled around the bush, sighted a taller shadow, and slammed the man to the ground. The impact shuddered through him, but he felt no pain. He scrambled to get his feet under him before Hillary could recover from surprise, grabbed the man's cravat, and drove his fist into his face. Eve's scream was like a mosquito buzzing in Sebastian's ears.

He had two years of pent-up fury for the man who had broken his sister's heart and ruined her. Hillary fought back and got a solid connection with Sebastian's cheekbone, but the hit only fueled his rage.

"Sebastian, stop!"

He landed another facer and slammed his opponent in the ribs before someone grabbed him and jerked him off Hillary. He struggled to break free of the arms trapping his.

"Not here, Thorne," Ellis growled in his ear. "Ladies are present. Your *sister*."

Eve. Sebastian stopped fighting. His chest jerked with each breath. Hillary attempted to push up from the ground.

"Stay down," Ellis said. "Or so help me, I will let him tear into you again."

Hillary plopped back down.

"Release me." Sebastian broke Ellis's hold and stalked a few paces away, trying to gain control of his temper. He shoved a shaky hand through his hair.

A lithe body rounded the shrub and collided with him. It was Helena. Her scent eased his anger, and he pulled her close.

She reached a hand toward his cheek. "Are you hurt?"

He angled away from her, but she touched him anyway. Her fingers were gentle and she took care to avoid his cut. His remaining anger drained from him.

"You are going to soil your gloves," he murmured.

"I have plenty more."

Once she had determined he would survive, she

joined Eve on the grass where his sister sat hugging her knees. Helena wrapped an arm around her shoulders. Eve was uncommonly composed, considering what she had witnessed. He heard no evidence of tears and she hadn't swooned.

"Did he hurt you?" he asked.

She waved away his concern. "No, I can only imagine what you must have thought, but this isn't how it seems. Benjamin—"

"Not now," Helena said with a quick hug. "You can explain later."

"He was only trying to coax me to come back inside. I should not have left the ballroom alone. I wasn't thinking."

She had been trying to escape from Hillary, no doubt.

Gabrielle tentatively peeked around the bush, then hurried to Ellis's side when he held out his arm.

Sebastian dusted off his breeches and straightened his jacket. Hillary was still seated on the grass, seemingly following Sebastian's movements.

"Choose your second wisely," Sebastian said.

Hillary nodded sharply.

"No!" Eve struggled to her feet. "There has been a mistake. Nothing improper occurred. Please, Bastian." She clung to his arm, her face turned upward.

"This man left you at the altar and ruined your reputation. He will answer for his deeds."

"But you are talking about *killing*." Her voice broke and the sobs came at last.

Faith. Her tears always had a way of ripping into him.

Helena came to offer his sister comfort. Eve turned into her shoulder, her cries muffled. "Dueling is illegal, my lord," Helena said. "Isn't there another way to settle this?"

"Thorne is within his rights to defend his sister, Lady Prestwick," Ellis said. "Mr. Hillary wronged Miss Thorne when he jilted her. The only way to restore her reputation is to beat him on the field."

Sebastian felt a smile of gratitude on his lips for Ellis even if he was loath to acknowledge it. Before their dispute over Gabrielle, he and Ellis had been decent friends. Many times the earl had taken Sebastian's side in disagreements and helped even the odds when more than one man tried to get in licks in a fight with Sebastian. He had forgotten that fact for a time.

"You will need a second, too," Ellis said. "If you will allow me…"

Gabrielle huffed. "What in God's name is wrong with you men? Why must you always resort to violence and bleeding? It's a most unattractive trait."

Ellis held his hands up as if surrendering. "Now, now. Don't get in a dither. I have a suggestion that might appease everyone."

Sebastian frowned. He didn't much care for Ellis's suggestions. They usually made one or both of them look foolish, like the time he wagered he could knock an apple from Sebastian's head with a rock in less throws than it took Sebastian to hit Ellis's apple. Sebastian had better aim than his friend, and Sebastian had sported a bloodied nose to prove it.

Ellis inclined his head toward him. "Allow Miss Thorne to choose the weapons."

Sebastian and Gabrielle cried out in protest. That was the most asinine suggestion he'd ever heard. How was Eve to feel any better about choosing the weapon that would lead to her former betrothed's death?

Eve's tears began to dry and she sniffled. "Anything I want?"

"If Mr. Hillary agrees," Ellis said. "He has been challenged, so he has final say in the matter."

Sebastian's frown deepened. He had mistakenly thought Ellis was taking his side.

Benjamin Hillary slowly stood. "I place my life in your hands, Miss Thorne."

She sniffled again and swung her head toward Helena as if seeking guidance.

"Anything you like, Eve. I know you will choose wisely."

Eve turned back to Sebastian. "Do you agree to the terms? You can have your duel, but I will choose the weapons and terms?"

"No one said anything about the terms."

She crossed her arms. "Well, who decides the terms?"

Ellis raised his hand. "It is my responsibility to negotiate it with Mr. Hillary's second, but I promise to take your wishes into consideration."

"Judas," Sebastian grumbled, but no one paid him any attention.

"Very well." Eve sniffled once more then lifted her chin as if daring Sebastian and Hillary to argue with her. "I choose gloves."

"Gloves?" Sebastian and his opponent said at the same time.

Helena and Gabrielle laughed. They probably thought his sister was clever, but he could easily wrap his gloved fingers around Hillary's neck.

"What type of gloves, Miss Thorne?" Ellis asked.

"Well, I don't suppose ladies' evening gloves would have the desired effect. I assume the goal is to hurt one another." She drummed her fingers over her lips as she considered the question. "Perhaps leather riding gloves? Gentlemen's, of course."

Ellis had the gall to chuckle too. "Gentlemen's leather riding gloves. Excellent choice."

"But they cannot wear them. Knowing Bastian, he is already searching his mind for a loophole."

Sebastian scowled, irritated that his sister knew him so well. "And how are we supposed to duel with gloves?"

Eve tugged off her glove, held it aloft, and whacked it against his cheek. "Like *that.*"

"A slapping duel?" Even Hillary sounded appropriately appalled.

"Yes, but remember, no hands inside the gloves."

"I've never heard of anything more ridiculous," Sebastian said.

Her hands landed on her hips. "Trying to kill each other over nothing is twice as ridiculous."

"It's not over nothing," he ground out. "He ruined—"

"I am *not* finished speaking." She shook her finger at him as if he were the younger sibling. "What would happen to Mama if you weren't alive to take care of her? Surely you don't expect Sir Jonathan to take on responsibility for both of us."

"But—" Sebastian's argument died away as her meaning became clear.

Her laugh was breathy. "Sir Jonathan indicated he

wishes to speak with you soon. He knows about my broken betrothal, and he doesn't care."

Hillary's groan reminded Sebastian of a wounded animal. The blackguard didn't know the meaning of pain, but he would once Sebastian was finished with him.

He glared at the man. "You heard my sister. Have your second meet with Ellis to settle the terms. And, uh…" Heat flooded his face and he was thankful for the dark. "Gloves it is."

When Ellis laughed, Sebastian wanted to slap him too.

Fifteen

THE SUN WAS JUST PEERING OVER THE EASTERN HORIZON when Sebastian arrived at the edge of the field to face Benjamin Hillary. In the light of day, Eve's demands weren't any less absurd, but he had given his word.

Sisters. The chit had him wrapped around her finger. He almost felt sorry for Sir Jonathan Hackberry, except he knew the man would be receiving a prize when he married Eve.

A crowd had gathered to witness the spectacle, their jovial manner grating on him.

"What are they doing here?" he grumbled to Ellis.

"You want others to know you have successfully defended your sister's reputation, don't you?"

The earl had a valid point, but Sebastian still wasn't keen for an audience. He could just imagine what the gossip rags would write about him after this spectacle.

"He came," Ellis mused, nodding toward Hillary. "With his history of cowardice, I wouldn't have been surprised if he had fled the country again."

Sebastian grinned, appreciating Ellis's show of loyalty.

Hillary's stare was sullen as Sebastian and Ellis

crossed the tall grass, their boots glossy from morning dew. Hillary's brother Jake was holding a wooden box one would use for pistols and exchanged a smirk with Ellis.

Sebastian's gaze narrowed on his own second. "I should start on you once I've finished with Hillary. Fighting like ladies. How am I to show my face at Brooks's after today?"

The earl laughed. "Come now, ladies don't fight. Besides, you've made a bigger fool of both of us in the past. Don't you remember the time you bet me that you could knock the apple from my head?"

"That was *your* idea."

"Well, you got us in trouble for stealing the vicar's wife's bonnet and dressing their cow in it."

"It looked better on the cow." Sebastian laughed too. "We were lads. You cannot hold the mistakes of my youth against me."

"And the time you challenged me to a drinking contest? That was only a year ago."

Sebastian waved his hand. "Oh, do stop prattling on. I have a duel to win."

The gentlemen who had come to gawk cheered as Sebastian squared off with Hillary. No doubt they had already placed their bets. His actions often inspired others to gamble, even if they sometimes bet against him.

Sebastian's steely glare bore into the man who had abandoned and humiliated his sister. His lip curled as he swept his gaze from Hillary's head to his toes. This piece of rubbish made Eve cry, and he was going to pay.

Ellis stood between them, one hand on Sebastian's shoulder and the other on Hillary's. "Jake and I negotiated the terms late last night. Each man will exchange blows in turn until one of you surrenders. If Ben yields, Thorne will have successfully defended his sister's reputation and the matter will be put to rest."

A muscle in Hillary's jaw twitched, but he held Sebastian's gaze.

"It has been decided Thorne, as the challenger, will be allowed the first strike."

One side of Sebastian's mouth kicked up. And he would make the first blow count.

"No fists, elbows, head-butting, kicking, or otherwise," Ellis added. "Leather only."

Sebastian's smirk became a scowl. *Blasted sisters.*

Jake Hillary stepped forward with the wooden box and flicked the lid open. A single pair of black leather gloves lay on the blue silk where dueling pistols should have been.

Sebastian grabbed one of the gloves. With a resigned sigh, Hillary took the other and frowned at his brother. Jake lifted one brow and Hillary sighed again.

Turning his back on his opponent, Sebastian marched to a section of the field where he'd seen pebbles and scooped a handful.

"What are you doing, Thorne?" Ellis asked.

He dropped the pebbles into the glove and smirked. "My sister said no hands."

Several of the men who had come to watch laughed, and new wagers began to travel around the group.

Hillary joined Sebastian and knelt to snatch some pebbles too. "I won't be unevenly matched."

"You already are," Lord Corby called. "Thorne has outwitted you."

Hillary glared at Sebastian as he tested the weight of his glove. When they were both satisfied, they squared off. Their seconds moved to a safe distance and declared the match active.

Sebastian jiggled the glove to get a good feel, adjusted his stance to distribute his weight accordingly, then raised his arm above his head and swung down hard and fast. There was a brief swish followed by a thud so loud it disturbed a covey of quail several yards away. They flew into the air amid frantic beating of wings and alarmed calls.

A welt appeared on Hillary's cheek. He gingerly probed the area and hissed through his teeth. His eyes hardened as he anticipated his turn.

Sebastian braced himself, but nothing prepared him for the surprising bite of the leather. The crowd winced on his behalf. Half his face felt on fire. Even his eye stung and began to water. But the pain only made him more determined to make his next hit more devastating.

This time when the glove whacked Hillary's cheek in the same spot, his opponent growled. A few gentlemen cheered.

The other half shouted for Hillary as he delivered another blow.

"Stop hitting like a lady," Ellis goaded Sebastian.

He swung his head toward his second, tempted to tell him he'd seen a lady take down a man not long ago and not to underestimate them. Instead, he told him to bugger off.

After the fifth smack, Hillary looked up with hell-fire raging in his eyes. "I hope you enjoyed that, you bloody jackass, because it's the last hit you're going to get in."

His brother cleared his throat and his eyebrows shot to his hairline. Hillary's lips pressed tightly together, tremors making him shake. His slap nearly left Sebastian cross-eyed. He shook his head to clear the ringing from his ears. There had definitely been a bit of knuckles involved that time.

Sebastian gritted his teeth. His fingers clenched around the glove and he drove it through the air with all he had. The slap echoed and several men issued laughing groans. A trickle of blood slid down Hillary's cheek from a thin slit.

He swiped at the cut then examined the blood on his fingers. With a guttural growl, he threw the glove to the ground. "First blood. That is what you wanted, wasn't it? I hope I have satisfied your need for revenge."

Sebastian tossed his glove to Jake then jabbed a finger in Ben Hillary's direction. "If you come around my sister again, she won't be choosing the weapons."

He turned on his heel and stalked away. Ellis fell into step with him. When they reached the edge of the field, he stopped Sebastian with a hand on his arm. "Would something like this right the wrong I dealt you?"

Sebastian studied him, trying to imagine Ellis with Gabrielle to stir his anger, but he could barely conjure an irritation. Eve was back in Society, which had been his aim all along. With thoughts of Helena filling his mind at all hours, Ellis and Gabrielle's betrayal had lost its importance. Sebastian desired Helena beyond reason, and if he were being honest, she was the only one he had ever desired. It would be unjust to despise Ellis for loving a woman Sebastian hadn't.

"Tell me you have brandy in your carriage, and we will be on the right path."

Ellis pulled a flask from his jacket pocket and handed it to him.

Sebastian took a long swill before passing it back. "Much appreciated. My face is in excruciating pain."

Ellis smirked. "You're not the only one pained by that ugly mug."

"You are just happy I look more like you."

The earl laughed and took a swig from the flask too. Their bantering continued as they climbed into Ellis's coach. It felt familiar and good, so Sebastian left his anger for the earl on the field along with his need to defend his sister's reputation.

❧

"Is something troubling you, my dear?" the Dowager Duchess of Foxhaven asked.

Helena jerked out of her reverie and realized her crossed leg was swinging wildly under her skirts. She froze, mortified, and was tempted to hide in the retiring room until the opera started.

Gabrielle, Lady Ellis, turned curious gray eyes on her. Never had Helena felt more unrefined and out of place than sitting in the Duke of Foxhaven's box with ladies who wore their ranks as comfortably as the King wore his crown. If not for Eve, she probably would have feigned illness to get out of the invitation, but she couldn't deny her friend this fortuitous opportunity. Even if it meant her own discomfort.

Helena uncrossed her leg and smoothed her skirts. "I expected Lord Thorne and his sister to have arrived by now."

As the dowager duchess's guest, Eve would enjoy a coveted position and a powerful statement would be made. There was no bad blood between the families.

Lady Ellis smiled sympathetically at her. "If it is any consolation, Anthony said Lord Thorne was well when he left him this morning."

"And was his morning successful?"

If Sebastian had lost, Eve's reputation would remain sullied. Perhaps the damage would be even worse since the scandal had faded from most everyone's memory, but Sebastian had been unwilling to listen to reason.

"I will not lose," he'd stated with unwavering strength.

But Helena knew even the strong could fail. Her husband had seemed as solid and lasting as the crags surrounding Aldmist Fell when he left to hunt stag. It wasn't until Fergus arrived with the cart bearing Wickie's broken body that she understood her husband had been a man and not a god she must please.

"Everything is well, Lady Prestwick. I am sure Lord Thorne and his sister will be here soon."

"Thank you, madam. My mind is at ease now." She hadn't really been worried for Sebastian's safety, thanks to Eve's clever thinking, but Helena desired his success. When he had looked her in the eye and declared his love for his sister days earlier, she'd seen his heart. He cherished his family as much as Helena valued hers. She had to believe he saw her heart, too, and was leaving no rock unturned in his search for her sister.

The duchess frowned at her daughter. "Have I missed an important piece of gossip? Olive will be most unhappy if I do not deliver on my promise to tell her everything that happens this evening."

Lady Ellis hugged her mother and kissed her cheek. "I promise to tell you everything later, Mama."

Helena smiled sadly, missing her mother more than usual.

Lord Ellis swept the red curtains aside, holding one side open to allow Eve to enter the box. "I located Lord and Miss Thorne."

Eve's brilliant smile lifted Helena's heart. She stood to greet her friend, taking her hands. "You look lovely, dearest."

It was an understatement. Eve's dark curls were artfully arranged to fall softly around her face, and her pale blue gown with its intricate cream inlay displayed her figure to perfection. Madame Girard was more than a seamstress. She was a master artist.

"So do you, Helena." Eve placed a featherlight kiss on each of Helena's cheeks before accepting the dowager duchess's warm greeting and exchanging pleasantries with Lady Ellis.

Helena's gaze remained fixed on the opening in the curtains, waiting for Sebastian to appear. A soft gasp slipped past her lips when he did. The duchess and Lady Ellis turned to look.

A faint blue bruise marred his cheekbone, but that hadn't surprised her nearly as much as his dazzling grin. And it was directed at her. Her heart leaped into her throat.

Lady Ellis's mouth twisted wryly. "Why, Lord Thorne, whatever happened to your cheek?"

"Gabrielle," her mother scolded softly then waved him into the box. "Pay her no mind, my lord. Growing up with brothers, one would think she would learn not to ask questions that likely cannot be answered in mixed company."

Sebastian chuckled, then offered in a stage whisper, "I had a run-in with a glove, Lady Ellis, but if you think I look bad, you should see the glove."

The lady laughed with him, her eyes bright. It was clear she liked Sebastian even if she hadn't married him in the end. A rushing noise filled Helena's ears, and her vision narrowed until all she could see was Sebastian touching the countess's elbow as he helped her to her seat. He moved aside for Lord Ellis to sit beside his wife and turned to Helena. His smile fell. She pushed down her feelings of jealousy and forced herself to smile calmly as she chose a chair.

Dear God, what is wrong with me? Increasingly, she slipped into that in-between place where she was neither mad nor fully sane. Nights were the worst, though. While he was frequenting the brothels in search of her sister—her flesh and blood—Helena was pacing her bedchamber, her gut twisted in knots, sick with the knowledge he was lying with another woman.

Their kiss had only made the feeling stronger and she hated it. Hated being at the mercy of her emotions. Sebastian had been correct that day in the Norwicks' garden. She *was* a liar. A jealous and apparently poor liar at that.

He sat in the chair beside her and glanced her way with his brow wrinkled. She turned her gaze toward the stage and pretended she didn't notice his confusion. She could hardly admit to what she was thinking.

Eve sat in the front row where everyone could see her and know she was an honored guest. Helena studied the other patrons as they sent pointed looks in their direction. Some smiled kindly while others hid their own jealousy behind haughty lifts of their noses. Lady Lovelace's soured frown jumped out at Helena, but when the widow noticed Helena watching, her expression transformed with a self-satisfied smile. Without trying to hide her interest, she eyed Sebastian as one would a plum pudding. He glanced up, caught the widow staring, and inclined his head in acknowledgment. When he looked away, Lady Lovelace smirked at Helena and mouthed the word *mine*.

The air whooshed from Helena as if she'd been punched in the stomach. She blinked against the sting of approaching tears. Crying was a ludicrous response. Sebastian was no one to her. She had refused to become his lover, and if he so chose to pursue his entertainment elsewhere—even with that harpy—Helena should be happy he was no longer pursuing her. She wasn't.

She kept her attention focused on the empty stage and prayed the opera players would begin performing soon, so she wouldn't be forced into conversation. Her prayers were answered when a short while later Madame Beaudry took the stage in a gown reminiscent of a Roman toga and a crown of gardenias on her loose curls. Helena had never seen anyone appear in public in such disarray, at least not in Polite Society. Madame Beaudry's imperious voice invaded the theatre, holding everyone spellbound. Everyone except Helena, who couldn't stop thinking about Sebastian and whose bed he would visit once they parted this evening.

Her visions were vivid and unsettling. And the harder she tried to banish them from her mind, the more invasive they became.

"How was your day, Lady Prestwick?" Sebastian asked close to her ear.

She jumped. "Fair, my lord. And yours?"

"More painful than I anticipated, but well worth the effort. Benjamin Hillary will no longer be bothering Eve."

Her gaze strayed away from the stage and found the light bruise on his cheek. How she adored those cheekbones. It was silly, she supposed, but their prominence made her want to place her lips against them. She clamped them tightly together. Someone else would be soothing his hurts tonight, and she hated that she wanted it to be her.

He discreetly touched her hand, his smile charming. "I've plans to set off on my nightly mission as soon as the opera ends. Perhaps you and Eve could ride home with Ellis so I may get an early start."

Disappointment settled in her belly. She had been looking forward to the short drive back to her town house with just his and Eve's company. His eagerness to visit the brothel was too much to handle.

"I should find the retiring room." She jerked her hand from his hold, hopped from the chair, and hurried into the corridor. It was deserted. She was halfway down the staircase, uncertain where the retiring room was, when Sebastian appeared at the head of the stairs.

"Is something wrong?"

She shook her head and kept moving. She didn't trust herself to speak without her voice cracking.

He trotted down the stairs faster than she could escape and caught her at the landing. His hand on the small of her back sent tingles racing through her. "Helena, stop a moment."

She hated his effect on her. She didn't want to be one of *them*, one of the multitudes of ladies who lost their wits when he was near. She didn't want to fall in bed with him, and yet her body insisted she did.

She swung her head around in search of someplace to run. Why couldn't she recall where the retiring room was?

His hand slid around her waist and held her in place. "Come with me."

He steered her away from the vestibule and down a dimly lit corridor leading backstage.

"Someone might see us."

He pulled her closer to his side, perhaps thinking she might try to run, but she was hopelessly caught like a fly in a spider's web. The pleasurable tingles radiated from his touch and enveloped her in a dreamy haze. She couldn't run even if he wasn't holding her. Or perhaps because he was, she didn't want to flee. Heavens, she didn't know anymore.

Quite a racket came from behind the door leading

to the actors' domain. Voices were raised in alarm, warnings to hurry because someone was due onstage. A crash, then a curse.

"We can't go in there," she said at the same moment they reached a side door and Sebastian flung it open. He pulled her outside into the dark courtyard. The sounds grew muffled when the door closed.

Away from censorious eyes, she struggled to suppress the urges that had been an undercurrent every time they had been together. Slumping against the wall, her legs quivered as if her bones were turning to aspic. She clung to the bricks, desperate to deny the need to touch him. His firm chest, his sculpted jaw, his lovely mouth. She cleared her throat. "What are we doing here? What do you want?"

She stiffened when he stroked her cheek with the backs of his fingers. His touch was light and undemanding. The tenderness hammered at her resistance. His dark gaze searched her face and she forgot how to breathe.

"I want to know what I have done to upset you."

"Y-you've done nothing. I told you I was looking for the retiring room."

"Helena." He leaned toward her to place his lips against her temple. She closed her eyes, her chest aching at the intimacy of his kiss. "When a lady is upset, she often hides in the retiring room. Please, tell me what I have done."

His voice was soothing, and his mouth so warm and soft when it touched her forehead. She struggled not to melt into his kiss, but her surrender was dangerously near.

"It is not you. It...it is *everything*."

The women at the brothels. Lady Lovelace. Every widow who had ever captured his attention.

He sighed and shifted to create space between them. "You are discouraged about Lavinia, but I will find her. I have given my word, and I will not stop searching until I have news for you. If she isn't at one of the high-end brothels, I will expand the search."

No. She pressed her palms against her head as if she could stop the rush of images flooding her thoughts. There must be another way to find Lavinia, because Helena couldn't tolerate another night of torment. Her imagination proved too relentless and cruel. Her throat tightened as if trying to hold her words inside, but they burst through anyway. "I realize I have no say in which lovers you choose, but please, don't let it be her."

He drew back. "*Her?*"

"Lady Lovelace. Or—or those women at the brothels. Or anyone." *Good Lord, this is mortifying.* But she couldn't stop talking or keep herself from throwing up her hands and gesturing like a madwoman. "It kills me knowing you frequent such places, even if you are going there on my behalf. I cannot sleep, and I pace the floors until my legs are too weak to move another step. I hate it. I am sorry, but I do. And I realize how ridiculous this sounds, but you should know the truth about—"

"Enough." The word echoed in the courtyard.

Her breathing ceased as she awaited the harsh reprimand she was due, but his soft chuckle carried on the night air. "Thank you, Helena."

She blinked, trying to make sense of his response. "Thank you?"

"I have wanted to hear those words for days." His smile was a flash of white in the dark. "Perhaps not those *exact* words, but anything that confirms you desire me as much as I do you."

Was that all they had? Lust? Even though she knew there was nothing more between them—that there could never be more—his admission stung. He thought of her no differently than any of the others who had come before her. She lowered her head, trying to sort through the mess of emotions inside her.

"Look at me, Helena."

As much as she wanted to defy him, she couldn't. She was just another feebleminded lady powerless to deny Sebastian Thorne anything.

He pressed his lips to the corner of her mouth. Helena closed her eyes and leaned her head against the hard wall. He teased the other corner of her mouth then kissed the tip of her nose. She was in trouble. *Deep* trouble. As she anticipated the next touch of his lips, her pulse became a rapid pounding in her ears.

He pulled back, still cradling her face. Her eyes flickered open.

"Since you have been honest with me, I will be with you as well. I have no interest in those women in the brothel. I haven't bedded a single one. I meet with the madam and pay *her* to answer my questions."

She frowned even though his answer relieved some of the tension that had built inside her. He paid for information? Why had he never mentioned this to her? When their time together ended, she didn't want to owe him anything. "How much?"

"Christ." He turned his gaze toward the sky as if

appealing for help. "I am pouring out my heart, and *she* wants an accounting of my funds."

"I do not!" Heat crept into her face as she realized how ludicrous her response must have sounded. She gave a dismissive wave of her hand. "We will sort it out later. Please continue."

Amusement glittered in the depths of his eyes as his thumb traced the curve of her cheek. He placed a light peck on her mouth, and she drifted forward, not ready to lose the warmth of his kiss. Their lips lingered together, tearing down the last of her defenses. When he finally withdrew, she barely held back a disappointed groan.

"As to Lady Lovelace," he said, "I've already told you there is nothing between us."

"But she wants there to be."

"She will be disappointed then, won't she? The truth is, even if every lady in Mayfair offered herself to me now, I couldn't accept."

"Is that so?" An odd stirring began in her chest and expanded until she was too full to hold it inside. She smiled widely, dottily. "Why not?"

"You know the reason." He hauled her against him in one quick move, causing her to cry out in surprise. His mouth grazed her ear. "I only want you," he whispered, his breath hot enough to singe her skin, and yet shivers raced through her body.

"Sebastian." His name sounded like a reluctant surrender. Like it or not, she was good and conquered.

Capturing his face, she kissed him hard. Her back arched to bring them closer.

Sebastian hungrily returned her kisses; a low growl

rumbled in his chest. He backed her against the wall and pushed her arms above her head as he plundered her mouth. His fingers circled her wrists. She could have pulled free, but it was incredibly arousing. She had never been kissed like she was being claimed.

He shifted his weight to hold her firmly against the wall with one hand. His other skated down her arm and side, then skimmed the underside of her breast. Prickles invaded the tips—pleasurable pain—and she strained toward him. He plucked her nipple through her dress, sending a strong current to her core. She gasped.

He tore his mouth from hers and placed his at her ear. His warm breath on her neck heated her blood. "I want to make you come, angel."

Her heartbeat almost drowned out his whisper, but she had heard him and his words made no sense.

"C-come where?"

His lips stopped nibbling her neck and he pushed back to bring his face into view. His eyes gleamed in the moonlight. "Have you never had an orgasm, love?"

She had never heard of any such thing. "I don't know."

He grinned before his mouth came down on hers for a sound kiss. "You have made me a happy man, Helena, for I get the honor of introducing you to the first of many."

"I don't underst—" His fingers massaged her nipple and cut off her thought. Her head rested against the wall as he created the loveliest sensations with his touch. His mouth found hers again and kissed her until she was breathless.

Capturing her bottom lip between his teeth, he gently tugged, then smiled again. "I've wanted this luscious mouth for so long, I used to dream about it at night."

Her body was awash in heat. "You did not." Her voice sounded husky and sensual. She didn't know where it came from at first.

"I did too." He kissed her again, then tugged off his gloves and tossed them on the ground. "Now I will dream of all the lovely ways I will teach you to use it."

Despite the embarrassing nature of their dialogue, she couldn't help returning his teasing smile. "I already know how to talk, so show me something I don't know."

"Lady Prestwick." He chuckled and gathered a fistful of her skirts. "Must you always have the last word?"

She didn't answer as her dress inched up her calves and over her thighs. The cooler air on her bare bottom made her feel exposed and vulnerable, but in her heart, she knew he wouldn't hurt her. Moonlight emphasized his cheekbones, and she placed a light kiss over his bruise.

He paused and stared at her with lips parted.

She averted her gaze, embarrassed to meet his eyes. "Does it hurt badly?"

Cradling her cheek, he tipped her face up. "My kindhearted Helena, always concerned for someone else." When he kissed her, his lips were tender and filled her with achingly sweet affection. It satisfied and made her desperate at the same time. She grasped his coat and pulled him into her.

His finger forged a slow trail along her inner thigh until she was squirming in anticipation.

"Be still or I'll have to start over." His smile

widened to show he was teasing, but serious or not, she pressed against the wall and tried not to move as the exquisite torture continued. When his fingers brushed her curls then cupped her, she sucked in a sharp breath, but she held her position.

"Good girl." He kissed her again, then knelt at her feet. "Hold your skirts."

She did as ordered, eager for whatever reward he would give her in return. His finger traveled to the apex between her legs and lightly circled the bud there before slipping inside her.

She softly moaned when his wet finger returned to that sweet spot and swept over it again. He nudged her legs farther apart, then placed a kiss on her inner thigh, just above her knee, as his finger slid back inside her. He repeated the pattern as his lips kissed a path up her leg and his other hand kneaded her bottom. The sensations flowed through her, disorienting and heavenly.

His hand slid down the back of her thigh to her knee and lifted it over his shoulder. With the wall behind her and his body bracing her, she felt secure. He lifted his face and grinned. "Now, don't forget to hold still, sweetheart."

A retort rose in her throat but came out in a strangled cry when his mouth touched her. His fingers opened her to his tongue, which stroked over her moist flesh. With each slow sweep, her body responded. Soft moans escaped on every breath and her hips began to undulate. She no longer cared about being compliant or good. She wanted the pleasure his touch promised. His strong hand clasped her bottom and encouraged her movement. His mouth worked in unison as his fingers stoked a fire inside her. A fire that was burning her from the inside out.

When his tongue flicked over her bud, the intensity made her arch her back. Sebastian held her tighter and did it again and again until flames licked her belly, spreading to her breasts and up her chest. The fire climbed her neck and roared in her ears until she had no more room for it. It escaped on loud cries that echoed off the walls of the courtyard.

Slowly withdrawing his finger from her, he licked it, his wicked grin making her heart skip. He rose and kissed her, his smile never fading. "I told you to be still, Lady Prestwick. Now you've mussed your hair."

"Oh?" She released her skirts and absently patted her hair.

He wrapped her in his arms and for one moment, she allowed herself to lean against him. Allowed him to support her when she was determined to be strong enough to stand on her own. "Don't let any scoundrels waylay you on the way to the retiring room this time, or you will miss the entire first act."

Good Lord, the opera. She'd forgotten all about it. "How long have we been gone?" she asked.

He released her with a sigh and backed away. "Long enough that you cannot afford to spend more time with me."

The wall at her back felt cold without his heat surrounding her. She reached for his perfect white cravat, pretending it needed straightening to create an excuse to touch him again.

"Helena." His voice was strained, pleading. She slid her hands over his arms as his mouth skimmed across hers. Desire coursed through him, his muscles straining beneath her touch. It seemed unfair to leave him in such a state.

She didn't want to go. Now or later.

The truth was like being doused with a bucket of cold water. Her hands dropped to her sides. She couldn't allow her good sense to be overcome by a handsome face. What had occurred tonight could not alter her plans. Scotland was the only place her sisters had a chance for a new start.

Sebastian embraced her once more before she could step away and lightly kissed her forehead. "You are frowning. Have I made you unhappy?"

"No." She sank against him, closing her eyes and savoring the feel of his body pressed against hers once more. "You've made me feel…"

Alive. Marvelous. Weak-minded. Unsettled.

She eased from his arms with a shy smile. "This was all very agreeable, my lord."

"Very agreeable." His chuckle was forced. "Next time I will aim for splendid indeed."

Heat washed over her as she realized how blasé she sounded. "I did not mean to imply tonight was not lovely." She pressed her palm to her brow and silently cursed her inability to say the appropriate thing. "I should go before someone wonders what I have been doing all this time. What if Olive hears I disappeared during the first act?"

A smile spread across his face, and he playfully chucked her on the chin. "Chin up, wench. Perhaps no one noticed we disappeared at the same time."

She rolled her eyes. "I am certain someone noticed."

Lady Lovelace, perhaps? The idea gave her a burst of sat-
isfaction, although she would never gloat as the widow
had with her. Well, perhaps a little.

"Deny until your last breath. If no one finds us
together, there is no proof." He kissed her once
more before sending her back inside the theatre with
a promise to arrange an escort home for her and Eve.
The door closed behind her and she was alone in
the corridor. She took a deep breath in an attempt
to restore her calm, then hurried toward the retiring
room, suddenly recalling the location. Once she was
composed, she made her way back to the theatre
box. Lord Ellis spared a quick glance, but didn't
make any comment.

Helena tried to settle and enjoy the singers, but
her senses were overwhelmed with memories of
Sebastian's lips on hers. His hand caressing her breast.
His mouth playing over her skin. He hadn't asked to
come to her town house tonight and she regretted not
inviting him.

Several moments later an usher appeared at the
entrance to the box and summoned Lord Ellis. They
spoke softly in the corridor, then the earl resumed his
seat and whispered something to his wife. Since they
both appeared unalarmed and returned to watching
the performance, Helena soon forgot about it.

Sixteen

At intermission, Eve swiveled in her seat and frowned. "Where is Sebastian?"

"He was called away on a matter," Lord Ellis said. "Lady Ellis and I will be happy to see you and Lady Prestwick home."

Sebastian's sister met Helena's gaze and slowly shook her head. "I don't understand what matter would call him away in the middle of the opera."

Helena shrugged as heat crept into her cheeks. Admitting he had left to do her bidding at a brothel had a bad ring to it.

As the group made their way to the grand saloon to mingle during the break, the dowager duchess stopped to speak with an acquaintance, leaving Eve and Helena alone with Lord and Lady Ellis. Lady Ellis nudged her husband. "Tell us what happened today. And leave out no details."

His brow furrowed. "I thought you despised fighting. You said it is for heathens."

"It is, but I still want to hear about it." Lady Ellis directed the next to Eve and Helena. "Anthony refused to say anything about the duel all day, except that Lord Thorne was the victor."

"And that is all you need to know, darling." His blue eyes twinkled in the candlelight and radiated affection for his wife. "If you will excuse me, I will retrieve drinks for everyone."

"You will need help carrying the glasses," Eve said. "Allow me."

Lady Ellis sighed as the earl and Eve walked away. "And to think I love that impossible man." She turned her exotic, expressive eyes on Helena, and Helena tried not to fidget under her intense stare. "He likes you very much."

Helena started. "Lord Ellis?"

The countess laughed and hot tingles invaded Helena's body. Lady Ellis meant Sebastian. Helena's mistake made her feel foolish.

Lady Ellis's merriment faded and her eyes shone with compassion. "Forgive me, Lady Prestwick. I didn't mean to make you think I was laughing at you. It has been awhile since I've been a regular member of Society. I am hopelessly out of practice on how to converse with others. Either I laugh about my blunders or I might cry."

Helena's heart went out to the young woman. "I find you charming, madam. No need to shed tears on my account."

"You are very kind. I see Sebastian has chosen well." She leaned close, her sculpted brows lifted in question. "You will make him happy, won't you? I wouldn't like to see him suffer again. I feel so very bad for how things progressed between us. I should have refused his offer from the start."

The hot tingles turned into flames licking Helena's face. She didn't know what the lady meant by making him happy, but it implied they had a future together, which was improbable. Once Helena found her sisters, they would return to Scotland and need never come back to London again. It held too many bad memories for all of them.

Besides, Sebastian's interest was fleeting. His reputation for enjoying a lady's company for a time and then turning his attentions elsewhere was often a topic of conversation with Olive.

She smiled politely at Lady Ellis. It truly was none of the young woman's concern, but Helena appreciated her directness. She decided to return the favor. "I'm certain I will make him happy for a time. Until he is ready to find his happiness elsewhere."

Lady Ellis frowned and shook her head. "I hate to contradict you, my lady, but I have it on good authority the baron is smitten with you."

"And what authority would that be?"

"My husband spent most of the day with him. Lord Thorne spoke of nothing but you all afternoon. Anthony said he has never known the baron to wax poetic over any lady. *Ever.*" An impish grin appeared. "Which should make me very cross to hear, but I am pleased beyond measure that he has found someone to love."

"Love?" Helena practically squawked the word. What a fanciful imagination the countess had. *Love indeed.*

Eve and Lord Ellis approached with glasses of lemonade, cutting off any further conversation with the countess. As Helena sipped her drink, she watched the earl and his wife together. The way he touched her elbow. How he smiled into her eyes. How he leaned into her when she spoke, as if he feared missing a single word. Everything he did was evidence of his love for her.

Realization hit her like a lightning bolt, and the hairs stood up on the back of her neck. Sebastian behaved the same with her. But he couldn't *love* her, could he?

No. Now who was being fanciful? It was impossible he would form an attachment to her. They had known each other such a short time.

Oh, why must everything become complicated?

Her hands shook so badly she almost spilled her lemonade. Quickly, she drained her glass. "Please excuse me, I would like to visit the retiring room before the opera begins again."

Eve took the glass from her and placed hers and Helena's on a footman's tray. "Splendid suggestion. I believe I will join you."

She linked arms with Helena and led her away. Leaning her head toward Helena's, Eve whispered, "You won't believe what happened when Lord Ellis and I were retrieving refreshment. Lady Wiltshire deigned to speak with me. She has always looked at me as if I were a bug squished on the ballroom floor."

"That is wonderful." Despite her words, Helena couldn't feel Eve's excitement. She was still reeling from the possibility Lady Ellis might be right. What if Sebastian did hold a *tendre* for her? This presented all types of trouble.

Once she told him the truth about her background,

he would put distance between them quickly. Why would he take a chance on damaging his reputation again now that it was beginning to recover?

She hadn't planned to ever tell him about her family. She would just disappear and that would be the end of it, but she couldn't leave without a word if he had feelings for her. It would be too unkind.

Oh, blast it all! Who was she fooling? She had feelings for him too, strong ones that made her half mad most days. She didn't want to leave him, but what choice did she have? Once she found her sisters, they would need her and the security of Aldmist Fell. She couldn't be selfish.

Eve was chattering about an invitation to Almack's, and how Sebastian had defended her honor earlier that day, as they entered the retiring room. Helena's gut seized when she spotted Lady Lovelace at the dressing table applying lip rouge. Several other ladies formed a queue waiting for their turns for a peek in the looking glass.

Lady Lovelace's red lips twisted with a sneer. "What is this I hear of Lord Thorne's ridiculous slapping duel with Mr. Hillary? I heard it was quite the spectacle, but I'm not surprised. I fear it's true what everyone says. The baron is prone to madness just like his sire. The poor man."

Eve stiffened on Helena's arm, and Helena drew her closer to her side. Sebastian would protect his sister if he were here, and since he wasn't, it fell to Helena to be Eve's champion.

"You speak out of turn, madam," Helena said. "The baron is perfectly sane."

The woman's sneer became more pronounced. "Is that so, Lady Prestwick? How is it you come by this knowledge? Have you known many Bedlamites?"

Helena lifted her chin, her stubbornness rearing its head. Lady Lovelace would not come out the victor in this altercation. "I know Lord Thorne is sane because he wants nothing to do with you. What better measure of sanity is there?"

A few twitters traveled through the line of onlookers.

"Lady Prestwick has a valid argument," a voice from behind the folding screen piped up. Lady Norwick circled the screen and smiled sympathetically at Widow Lovelace. "You do have a tendency to chase off any gentlemen with their wits about them, Celeste."

Lady Lovelace's blush matched her lip rouge. "Bianca, how could you?"

The countess lifted her shoulders in a sheepish gesture. "I couldn't very well allow you to disparage Miss Thorne's brother, especially when you know you are in the wrong. Lord Thorne has been nothing but kind to you. Don't be bitter because his interests lie elsewhere now."

The widow huffed and bolted from the chair. "I—we—I've never had anything to do with that man." She stormed for the door and slammed through it, leaving several eyebrows raised in her direction.

Lady Norwick smiled sweetly at the lady who had been waiting to use the looking glass. "It is your turn, Mary."

"Thank you, my lady. I thought I might be here all night." As soon as Mary sat, gossip began to fly around the room, but this time it wasn't about

Sebastian or Eve. Lady Lovelace had made herself the center of attention.

"I almost feel sorry for her," Helena murmured.

Lady Norwick scrunched her nose in distaste. "Don't you dare. It is time Celeste had a taste of her own medicine. Perhaps she will think twice about spreading rumors about others now."

"I thought Lady Lovelace was your friend," Eve said.

Lady Norwick placed her arm around Eve's shoulders as if the countess were a mother bird taking a hatchling under her wing. "True friends never talk behind your back, my dear. It pays to keep those people close, however, then you know what they are about."

Helena had mixed emotions as she watched Eve and Lady Norwick together. On the one hand, once Helena left Town she need not worry how Eve would fare with Lady Norwick at her side. But Helena also experienced a hollowness in her gut. She would miss Eve a great deal.

And God help her, she would miss Sebastian even more.

❦

Sebastian was in the breakfast room perusing *The Morning Times* when Eve and Mother joined him the next morning. He hadn't rushed off to the club with the newssheet before they came belowstairs like he usually did, because he expected the matter of his sister's virtue had been settled now.

There was an advertisement issuing an apology from Benjamin Hillary to Sebastian and his family. The scoundrel accepted responsibility for his "unconscionable actions" and proclaimed Eve blameless. The apology was late in coming, so Sebastian would have no mercy on him if Hillary should cross him again, but at least he could rest easier knowing his sister's reputation had been cleared.

Thankfully, there was nothing in the gossip column about their ridiculous duel. Sebastian supposed everyone knew about it already, since half the gentlemen of Mayfair had attended, and those who hadn't witnessed it heard about it by the time he had arrived at his club. His name did appear in the gossip pages, but he wasn't painted in a bad light for once. Apparently a jealous widow with a vicious tongue made quite a scene over him at the theatre the previous night. At first, he feared the rag was referencing Helena, but all descriptions of the widow pointed to it being Celeste.

Eve paused at the head of the table, her mouth turned down in a puzzled frown. "What are you doing here?"

"I live here," he said with a raise of his eyebrow. "My name is on the deed, in case you've forgotten."

She stuck out her tongue, then bounded around the table to plop in the chair beside him.

He leaned back as if affronted by her nearness. "There are five other chairs. Must you sit on my lap?"

"I am not on your lap, but you are in my usual spot. Your name isn't on this chair too, is it?"

Mother clucked her tongue. "Now, children, no quarreling." A bright smile accompanied her scolding. She moved slowly to the closest chair and lowered into it with a grimace.

"Her rheumatoid is bothering her more in the

mornings," Eve confided in him. "She didn't want me to tell you so you wouldn't send for the doctor."

Mother narrowed her gaze at his sister. "Eve Lorraine Elizabeth Thorne, I told you not to trouble your brother."

Sebastian turned to the page with Hillary's apology and slid the newssheet to his sister. "It is not troubling me to know about your ailments. I'll send for Dr. Campbell this afternoon."

Mother harrumphed and settled her napkin in her lap. "He will only tell me to take a nip of brandy at bedtime. I don't need his expertise, thank you."

"And have you followed his recommendation?" Sebastian asked.

"Ladies do not partake of brandy."

Eve looked up from the newssheet with a sigh, but he couldn't tell if it was a happy or sad sigh. "It is really over now, isn't it?"

"What is over?" Mother asked.

He addressed her question rather than leaving it to Eve to explain and let it slip he'd been involved in a duel, however non-life-threatening it was. "Benjamin Hillary has issued an apology in today's paper and proclaimed Eve blameless in their broken betrothal." He held up a staying hand when he saw the panic on his mother's face. "He didn't use her name."

Mother wilted on the seat, her age suddenly showing in the lines of her face.

He patted his sister's shoulder. "It is over, and I expect you will have a wider selection of gentlemen from which to choose your husband. You could do much better than Sir Jonathan, so there is no need to make a hasty decision."

"I like Sir Jonathan. He's interesting." Eve flipped through the pages until she found the gossip section.

He ruffled her hair. "Well, you may marry whomever you choose."

"Oh, look!" She sat up straighter. "There is something about the run-in with Lady Lovelace in here. She was abominably rude, but Helena defended you quite well. Then Lady Norwick took up our cause. But Helena was magnificent." Her gaze darted to him before returning to the column. "You would do well not to cross the lady, Bastian."

"I haven't crossed anyone." He bent over his sister's shoulder to read the piece again. "Helena was involved?"

His mother cleared her throat, sending him a quelling look across the table.

"Pardon me. Lady Prestwick, I mean."

Eve paid no attention to their mother's censorious ear and continued to prattle. "You couldn't very well expect her to hold her tongue when Lady Lovelace insulted you. The harridan said you were mad, just like Papa."

Mother gasped at the same time Sebastian winced. He hadn't wanted either of them to know what others had been saying about him or to remind them of Father's last years.

Eve blinked her big brown eyes innocently. "Papa was not mad, and neither are you, Bastian. Helena quashed that rumor at once, so you needn't worry about hearing it again."

He smiled affectionately at his younger sister. He didn't believe the rumors would never surface again or that their father had been sane, but he was happy to support her fantasy. "I must thank Lady Prestwick when I see her next." His heart sped at the reminder he would see her again soon.

Eve tipped her head to the side. "What is that?"

"What is what?"

"That *look*. Your face got all soft and dreamy when you spoke of Helena."

"It did no such thing." He scowled and picked up his toast.

"She is correct," Mother said quietly. "And you did use her Christian name a moment ago. Have you developed an attachment to her?"

He shoveled a bite of eggs into his mouth, followed by a hunk of toast. He refused to be teased this morning. Yes, there was attraction, but an attachment? Hardly.

Maybe he had gone a little soft at the thought of seeing her again, but another place was hard with anticipation. And *that* was lust. He'd experienced it enough times to recognize it for what it was, but it wouldn't do to argue his position with the females in his family.

But this is different. Sebastian shook his head slightly, trying to dislodge the annoying thought from his mind. How was his association with Helena different? Because he wondered what churned behind her troubled eyes at times? Because he wanted to hold her and soothe her hurts when she mentioned her husband?

The bloody bastard. Sebastian would like to drive his fist into Prestwick's fat face, even though he didn't know what the man had done to Helena, and it was ludicrous to want to fight a dead man.

Fine. That part was different, but nothing else.

"It's odd," Eve said, "but Helena had that same soft look on her face last night when she spoke of you."

His gaze snapped to his sister's face to see if she was laughing at him, but she looked pensive, as if trying to puzzle out what she had seen on Helena's face last night.

It was called sexual contentment, but he didn't want to discuss such things with his mother or sister.

"I'm sure it was nothing, poppet. Eat your egg before it gets cold."

"No, it was something. Of that I am sure." She drummed her fingers against her lip. "I hadn't thought much of it at the time, but now I am thinking it's possible she has formed an attachment to you too, Bastian."

A soft chuckle slipped from his lips followed by a heartier laugh.

Eve drew back with a scowl. "I wasn't making a jest, and I don't see what is funny about love."

Laughter spilled from him again, earning a darker look from his sister. He stifled his humor. "You are right, of course. There is nothing funny about love. Forgive me."

But Helena? In love with him? That was laughable. Eve knew nothing about the goings-on between men and women, so he could understand how she would get attraction and affection confused. Not wishing to disillusion his sister, he returned to his breakfast. "If you don't want your egg, I will eat it." When he reached for her plate, she smacked his hand.

"Your name is not on my plate either."

Seventeen

SEBASTIAN ENTERED MAGGIE MONTGOMERY'S FASHION-able brothel that evening in a less than pleasant mood. His duties at the House of Lords had consumed most of his day and evening, so that he hadn't had time to call on Helena before setting off on his nightly rounds.

God, he missed the smell of her skin and her taste on his tongue. If she weren't so skittish about him calling at her town house, he would go there after his search was completed. Perhaps she felt differently about allowing him into her home after their encounter at the theatre, but he would be wise to wait for her invitation. She felt strongly about being in control of such things. Not that he blamed her. She was an independent woman with no need for a man.

He smirked. Or so she thought.

A beast of a man dressed in livery blocked the doorway to Madam Montgomery's receiving room. "Greetings, Lord Thorne. It is a pleasure to welcome you this evening. This way, if you please."

"Thank you… Charles, isn't it?"

"Yes, my lord."

It had been a lucky guess. As far as Sebastian could tell, every man under Maggie Montgomery's employ was named Charles. Sebastian followed her man through the large room where two young bucks waited to be entertained. One was red-faced and perched on the edge of a gold brocade chair as if he was waiting to be called before the headmaster to answer for an infraction.

Sebastian raised an eyebrow at him. "Does your nurse know you've escaped the nursery?"

His blush deepened and as soon as Sebastian passed he hissed, "This is foolish. I'm leaving."

Charles held the door open for Sebastian, and he entered a cozy sitting room outfitted with plush crimson fabrics. "Madam will not be pleased you are scaring away her clientele."

"I will pay her doubly for any lost business I caused."

"Very good, sir."

Maggie strove to create an air of sophistication by dressing her men in finery and tutoring them in proper speech, but just as in every brothel, the men were employed to keep order. If a gentleman were to forget his manners, Maggie's men would give him a refresher lesson in the back alley.

Sebastian had always been a gentleman through and through when he'd visited the brothel in the past, which afforded him special treatment. He would be wise not to jeopardize his position as one of the madam's favorites. Not that he had been there in years or intended to return after tonight. Brothels were a young man's playground.

Charles moved to a sideboard and poured two

fingers of brandy into a tumbler before carrying it to him. "Is there anything more I may do for you, my lord?"

Sebastian raised his glass to him. "You've been a great help already."

The man hadn't been gone long before a side door opened and Maggie swept in with four girls trailing in her wake. "Lord Thorne, how lovely to see you again."

He rose in deference to her and kissed her hand as he would with any lady. Her spicy lavender perfume burned a trail up his nose and he rubbed it absently. She smiled, her face more handsome when she was happy, and motioned him to take a seat.

"Come along, girls."

The hired girls hustled to do her bidding and lined up in front of him.

"I have selected only the best for you, my lord. You may choose whichever pleases you."

Sebastian fought to keep a frown from showing on his face. He wouldn't want Maggie to mistake his displeasure as any of the girls' fault. "They are all beautiful, madam, but I was hoping for an audience with you."

Her mouth puckered and her green eyes appeared as dull and hard as malachite. She obviously felt slighted by his request.

Maggie had always been touted as a tasty morsel, and with her flaming tresses and voluptuous figure, she had collected many admirers. But she had given up whoring when she became a madam. It must have been around the time he'd stopped wearing short pants, he imagined.

"I only wish to talk, madam, and I will pay well for your time for I know how valuable it is."

Her expression didn't alter. For a moment, he wondered if she intended to call Charles in to teach him a lesson in manners. She snapped her fingers, and the girls scrambled to leave the room, two bumping into each other. Once they had cleared the room, she sat in a chair across from him and folded her arms. "I don't do dirty talk no more either, Lord Thorne. What is this about?"

Ah, there was the streetwise woman she kept hidden from most.

"I'm looking for a girl."

She glowered. "I just showed you four. Did you find fault with all of them?"

"I am looking for a *particular* girl. Rumor has it she was traded from a brothel in Whitechapel."

A tiny tic showed at her eyebrow.

"Her name is Lavinia. Perhaps you've heard of her."

She shook her head.

"Come now, Mags. You are not a good liar. Is she under your employ?"

She hopped from the chair and strode to the sideboard to pour herself a brandy. Her back was rigid. "There are no girls by the name of Lavinia working for me. What do you want with her?"

"What concern is it of yours if you don't know the girl?"

She turned with the tumbler in her hand. As she sipped the drink, she watched him carefully.

"She is important to someone who is important to me," he said. "All I need is to know how to reach her. My, uh…friend would like to reconnect with her. They were childhood playmates."

The hard lines around her mouth eased. "You have a mistress. Now I understand why you've been away so long. I suppose they became close friends working together. That happens, but it's best for your ladybird to say farewell and forget her friend."

He would let Maggie think he was doing his mistress's bidding. It seemed easier than explaining about Helena and her connection with one of the madam's girls, not that he fully understood it himself. "It's not for you to decide what is best for my friend," he said.

"Fair enough, but I'm afraid I cannot give you information about Lavinia. I was paid well to keep my mouth shut."

Once Maggie mentioned money, negotiations were at hand. Sebastian hid his pleasure behind a mask of indifference. "And how much to open your mouth again?"

"I gave my word, Lord Thorne. My word is my bond." She slanted a smile in his direction. "I did not, however, promise I wouldn't write down her address in exchange for a hundred pounds."

"My, that is a well-defined promise you didn't make." Sebastian returned her smile. "How fortuitous that I happen to have a hundred pounds I can spare. Shall we complete our business now?"

Her hard eyes bore into him. "We have no business, Lord Thorne. You were not here and never spoke to me. Do we understand each other?"

"Perfectly. Who are you again?"

She rolled her eyes and a reluctant smile spread

across her ruby lips. "I hate that I've missed having you around, my lord."

"I hear that often."

An hour later, Sebastian stood outside a modest town house on the edge of Chelsea, trying to make sense of the darkened windows and silence. He'd been certain the address would lead him to a lively gathering of the demimonde where one engaged in all sorts of debauchery and merrymaking. Instead, he found what appeared to be a respectable household.

Bollocks. If Maggie had lied, she would have to answer to him, hulking beasts in livery be damned. He returned to his carriage. His footman opened the door for Sebastian to climb inside and awaited instructions. Fleetingly, Sebastian considered stopping at Helena's on his way home despite his earlier concerns. She would be thrilled to learn he had gotten a lead on Lavinia. She might even be grateful.

A slow grin spread across his lips. Perhaps *exceedingly* grateful.

His eagerness faded as he considered the possible impact the evening could have on her, however. He didn't know yet if the information Maggie had given him was real. How could he raise Helena's hopes when there was a chance of disappointing her?

He couldn't. He swiped a hand down his face, weariness seeping into his bones, and sank against the carriage cushion, then peered at the house once more. Before involving Helena, he should discover who resided at the town house on Walpole Street.

"Take me home," he said with a sigh. A hollowness

expanded in his chest as he realized it had been over twenty-four hours since he'd held Helena.

Very well. He could admit that was different too.

꿏

Helena listlessly twirled her parasol as she, Eve, and Lady Norwick meandered through Hyde Park with Fergus trailing behind them. He claimed he had no interest in ladies' chitchat, but she had twice caught the Scot chuckling over one of her companions' quips.

Eve and the Countess of Norwick were equally matched in wits, and Helena enjoyed their company a great deal. *Usually.* Today, however, all she could think on was Sebastian. She'd been trying all afternoon to inconspicuously introduce the topic of what business kept him away from her.

He had not attended charades at Lady Orham's town house last night, and today Eve had arrived at Helena's home with only Lady Norwick in tow. Since their encounter at the theatre, she'd seen neither hide nor hair of him. Was he done with her so quickly? She knew his attachments were short-lived, but surely not this soon.

She glanced sideways at Eve and swallowed hard. She couldn't bring herself to ask after him for fear her companions would know how hopelessly smitten she was. It was a sickness, pining for him as she did. How had it come to this? She had been determined not to succumb to his charm like every other lady in Town, but there was no help for it. Sebastian Thorne was irresistible, and worse, he knew it.

A light honeysuckle-scented breeze grazed her hot

cheeks, and she tried once again to attend to Eve and Lady Norwick's conversation.

"Has Sir Jonathan professed his feelings for you yet?" the countess asked.

Eve's dark lashes blinked in agitation. "Heavens, no! We've barely known each other a sennight."

"There is no specific time allotment for love, dearest. One can fall in love quite quickly, isn't that correct, Lady Prestwick?"

Helena startled at her question. "I...uh... Well, I cannot speak to such things."

Lady Norwick's smile was too sweet and innocent while her chocolate brown eyes sparked with mischief. "Can't you, my dear? What a pity. I thought for certain you were woolgathering about a particular gentleman a moment ago."

Eve covered a giggle with her hand.

"I wasn't woolgathering." Helena fanned herself with her free hand, her body aflame now. "I was thinking."

The countess and Eve burst into laughter.

"Not about Lord Thorne," she blurted and winced. "I mean, I was considering what gown to wear to Almack's next week."

Eve linked arms and hugged Helena to her side. "Don't be embarrassed. I would be pleased to call you my sister."

Even as she shook her head to dispel any notions of a future with Sebastian, warm tingles radiated within her chest. How she would love to have a lasting relationship with him and claim Eve as family, but it couldn't be. Not unless she abandoned her dream of finding her sisters and providing a better life for them. And she would rather die than give it up.

Eve gasped, startling her from her reverie. "It's Sir Jonathan. What is he doing here?"

"Enjoying this lovely weather, I imagine." Lady Norwick gave her a nudge. "You may go greet him, Miss Thorne, as long as he remains a respectable distance."

Eve didn't require further encouragement and hurried ahead while Lady Norwick and Helena slowed their steps.

"I've known Sir Jonathan since I was a girl," Lady Norwick said, "and I've never seen him as taken with a young lady as he is with Miss Thorne."

"He seems like a decent man." Sir Jonathan was untroubled by Eve's broken betrothal and even less so by her unladylike curiosity. Helena appreciated that about him.

"He is one of the better ones, I must admit. I felt certain he and Miss Thorne would get on if only they made each others' acquaintance."

Helena stopped in the middle of the path, as did Lady Norwick. "You played matchmaker for Eve?"

The countess shrugged one shoulder and a pleasant pink color tinged her cheeks.

Lady Norwick had a reputation for being a force to respect, but rarely did anyone speak of her gracious spirit.

Helena brushed a strand of hair behind her ear. "Please don't be offended, my lady, but what led you to help a young woman you had never met until recently?"

"I could ask you the same, Helena."

A heated blush swept over her face. She resumed walking to avoid answering. She couldn't admit to her agreement with Sebastian.

Lady Norwick matched her pace and entwined their arms. "Forgive me if I was too forward. Naturally, I assumed we had similar motives. I know what it's like to be judged by others, but whereas I earned my reputation for being bad *ton*, Miss Thorne did not. If *I* was given a second chance, how much more deserving is she? Everyone deserves a second chance at happiness, don't you agree?"

Tears pricked Helena's eyes. The countess likely had no idea how much her words meant to Helena. Suddenly, she felt as if she had someone to confide in about her sisters. Someone who would understand and not judge. Yet, Eve needed Lady Norwick more than Helena did.

"Yes," she said on a breath. "Eve deserves a second chance."

And Helena could be a liability. If Society learned of her past, Helena's association with Eve could make her an outcast again.

She shook her head slightly. She couldn't do that to her friend.

Sebastian should know the truth about the woman he was seeking, and if he chose to withdraw his help, Helena must understand. She was willing to put her sisters above her happiness. If Sebastian put his sister ahead of Helena, she had no cause to complain.

But the prospect still hurt.

Eighteen

AFTER A BIT OF ASSISTANCE FROM HIS SERVANTS, Sebastian learned the town house on Walpole Street belonged to the Marquess of St. Ambrose, a bachelor every marriage-minded mother dreamed of snagging for her daughter. It wasn't the home where he resided—St. Ambrose lived in a grander house on Park Street bordering Hyde Park—but it was rumored the marquess paid calls to the young woman letting the town house.

From all accounts, she was a great beauty who mostly kept to herself. Some speculated she was St. Ambrose's mistress, but since she was never a nuisance to her neighbors, everyone tended to their own affairs. Despite Sebastian's attempts to learn her name, her identity remained a mystery. This was the reason he was standing on her stoop, ready to go to the source for an answer.

Late afternoon sun reflected off a brass knocker engraved with the initial *S*. It was warm to the touch when he grasped it to rap twice. He stood with his hands linked behind his back, waiting. There were sounds of movement from within, but several moments passed before the heavy oak door creaked open. A bespectacled woman with graying hair pulled back into a tight knot blinked at him through the crack.

"Yes, sir?" Her voice quivered.

He offered a disarming smile to ease her worries and pulled a calling card from his case. "Good afternoon. I am Lord Thorne and I am here at the behest of Lady Helena Prestwick. May I speak with the lady of the house?"

The woman stared at him with parted lips. "The lady of the house, milord?"

"Your mistress, Miss Lavinia..." Helena had never supplied him with a last name. "Uh, just Lavinia, I believe. It is important I speak with her."

Grooves in the woman's forehead deepened, and the sound of heels clicking on the marble floor caught his attention before a soft voice reached them. "Who is it, Edith? Delivery men are to come to the back."

A woman with a face very similar to Helena's came up behind Edith. She shared Helena's eye color too, but there was a jaded light to hers Helena didn't have. "I will see to the gentleman while you return to preparing our tea."

"Yes, ma'am."

The taller woman patted Edith on the back, then filled the doorway to block his view. "What is it you want, sir?"

"Are you Lavinia, the young woman formerly under Madam Montgomery's employ?"

Her glare would have struck him dead if she had

that power. "I am no longer in the business of entertaining," she hissed. "You should leave at once."

Sebastian balked. "Egads! You have misjudged the situation, miss." How many other men had arrived at her door demanding special treatment? And she thought he was one of them. He felt slightly queasy. "I am here on Lady Prestwick's behalf. Not to be *entertained*."

"I don't know Lady Prestwick, so I'll send you on your way."

As the door was being closed in his face, he called out. "Helena! Your sister, Helena, is looking for you."

He was guessing at their relationship, but the strong resemblance made it clear they were family. It wasn't unusual to have illegitimate half siblings, nor was he concerned about what Helena's father had gotten up to.

The door froze an inch before it closed. Slowly, it eased open and frigid eyes narrowed on him. "How do you know about Helena?" she asked in a fierce whisper. "My sister died nine years ago."

He lowered his voice to match hers even though the street was deserted. "The devil she did. She is here in London, and she has been looking for you, risking her life in Whitechapel until her search led to Madam Montgomery's."

The woman's breath hitched and the moment it dawned on her that he was telling the truth showed in the softening of her face. She was a beauty, just as rumors suggested, but she lacked Helena's warmth and hopeful air. He supposed he couldn't blame her, though. Helena's sister couldn't have lived an easy life.

"Please, I just need a moment of your time."

"Helena *is* alive," she said more to herself than him and stepped back to allow the door to open. "Please, come in, Mr...?"

He held out the calling card Edith hadn't taken. "Thorne."

"I am Lavinia Kendrick." She read the black script then glanced at him again. "We may speak in the parlor, my lord. Did you say my sister hired you to find me?"

"I volunteered my assistance. We are close friends."

She arched an eyebrow and closed the door behind him. "I see."

No doubt Miss Kendrick had seen a lot in her life, which accounted for her sardonic tone. She led him to the parlor and began cross-examining him with the skill of a barrister. Her distrust reminded him of Helena and the haunted look he had seen in her eyes. His patience for Miss Kendrick increased. She was another wounded bird, perhaps hurt by the same father who had hurt Helena.

"Prestwick lied," Miss Kendrick said with a frown. "Our father received a letter a week after he let that coldhearted bastard take her. It said Helena contracted a fever and died at an inn along the way. Since we never heard from her, I assume he wouldn't allow it. I am guessing he is dead now."

"Prestwick is dead."

A small smile played about the corners of her mouth. "Good."

Questions crowded his head and he didn't know what to ask first. Yet, even if he did know where to start, he wanted answers from Helena. He wanted her to trust him enough to share her past ordeals, and reuniting her with her sister could be the first step toward earning that trust.

"How is my sister?

"Well, but she misses you."

Miss Kendrick nodded. "She misses who I was, and I am no longer that girl."

Sebastian knew that wasn't true. Helena's only desire was to reunite with Lavinia. "She knows about you, Miss Kendrick, and she is driven to find you despite your circumstances."

"She wants to find Cora, Pearl, and Gracie. I am a link to our sisters."

Sebastian hid his surprise at learning Helena had more than one sister. "And do you know of their whereabouts?"

She sat up straighter, her wariness returning. "They are safe. Now I will interview you, my lord."

He wasn't able to answer many of the young woman's questions, since he didn't know what Helena's life had been like with Prestwick. But he told Miss Kendrick about her stubborn streak, how she loved to read, her generosity with the old man and child in the rookery that evening, and how she had been dubbed the Whitechapel Angel and came to his aid. He spoke of her bravery when she fought off the footpad, and her loyalty to him and Eve when she defended them against Lady Lovelace. The more he spoke of Helena and all the ways she was unique, the more his heart swelled with admiration.

He didn't tell her sister about the tenderness with

which Helena had placed her lips against his bruised cheek, or the soft glow in her eyes when she looked at him. The way his pulse sped when she was near, or how he wanted to hold her and absorb her hurts. His throat felt tight and scratchy all of a sudden.

Maybe Eve was right. Was he falling in love with Helena?

"It wasn't until a year after we received word Helena was dead that I learned the reason she had been taken." If he thought Miss Kendrick's eyes were cold earlier, they were shards of ice now. "Our pathetic sire had wagered her in a game of loo like she was livestock and lost, just as he always did. The gentleman came to collect his winnings the next morning."

Sebastian cursed under his breath. More than ever, he wanted to wrap his fingers around both men's necks. "No gentleman I know would accept that wager, much less collect the debt."

"Which is the reason I consider him a fiend, but our father was even worse."

What kind of depravity made a man gamble with his daughter's freedom? He could see Helena's reluctance to trust in a new light. The one man she should have been able to count on—her own father—had betrayed her. He couldn't think on it without a harsh pain in his chest. He cleared his throat. "She will want to see you as soon as she learns I've found you."

"Of course, and I want to see her," Miss Kendrick said, "but that is impossible. She can't be seen with me. Not if she is a lady. Perhaps you could deliver a message to her instead."

Sebastian agreed it was important to protect Helena's

reputation, but he couldn't agree with keeping her away from her only family. "Perhaps an inconspicuous meeting place would suffice. It is easy to find privacy in the pleasure gardens. I could bring her there tonight."

"No, it's too risky. I could be recognized by any number of gentlemen."

"She would never agree to stay away, Miss Kendrick. She has been searching for you for weeks."

"I know you are right. There are many things I remember about my sister, and her stubbornness is among them." Her smile was affectionate as she stood and moved to a small desk in the corner. "If you brought her here after dark, it would be safer than the gardens. St. Ambrose comes tonight, but I will tell him he must postpone his visit."

Sebastian raised an eyebrow. "And he will heed your wishes?"

Miss Kendrick stopped writing and glanced over her shoulder. "The marquess cares for me, Lord Thorne. Don't you heed the wishes of the woman you love?"

He smiled sheepishly. "I wouldn't be here if I didn't."

Nineteen

HELENA HEARD SEBASTIAN'S CARRIAGE DRIVE UP TO HER town house and her heart beat a little faster. She had been pleased to receive word that he would be joining her and Eve this evening. The empty ache inside her eased for the moment, but it would return soon enough, and she feared it might swallow her whole.

She didn't want to contemplate never seeing him or Eve again, and yet that was exactly what she was going to recommend to him tonight. He needed to protect his sister by putting distance between her and Helena.

Perhaps he could recommend a reliable investigator to assist her in finding her family. She couldn't be selfish any longer by accepting his help.

A knock on the door was followed by Fergus's gruff reception. Sebastian's murmured reply didn't quite reach the drawing room.

"Crivvens!" Fergus's exclamation startled Helena.

"Shh…"

When a hushed conversation ensued, Helena's curiosity drew her toward the foyer. "What is all the whispering about?"

Fergus's grin stretched ear to ear. "Just last week you accused me of not knowing the meaning of a whisper, lass. You said my voice could wake the dead."

She pursed her lips in mock disapproval. "I was referring to Lord Thorne."

"I will tell you in the carriage," Sebastian said as he came forward to collect her. After assisting her with her wrap, he placed a protective hand on the small of her back. "It's a surprise, and you are trying to ruin my moment."

She couldn't help basking in his attention, turning her face toward him. He smiled and pulled her closer. "I will bring her home safely, Fergus."

"If you value your life, you will." Even though Fergus grumbled, his smile didn't leave his face.

Sebastian chuckled as he escorted her to the carriage. His footman assisted her inside and she froze in the doorway. "Where is Eve?"

"Have a seat, Helena." Sebastian came up the steps and she scrambled to move out of his path.

She plopped on the bench with a soft grunt. He closed the door, then instead of taking the opposite seat, he sat beside her and pulled her into his arms.

"Seba—"

His lips found hers before she could finish her protest.

She moaned into his mouth. He was going to make this difficult. How was she to end their association when he created such a lovely buzz in her head and delicious tingles all the way to her toes? His fingers glided along the back of her neck and goose bumps traveled in a wave down her back, arms, and legs. She clutched his jacket and pulled him to her, deepening the kiss. His tongue flirted with hers until her breath left her in rapid gasps. He paused, his lips still so close if she shifted, she could have him.

He smiled. "I think you missed me."

She blew out a breath and flopped against the seatback. "Yes." Denying it would be pointless. Her body had spoken the truth already.

The carriage wheel hit a rut and tossed her against his side. She hadn't realized they had left her town house, but Sebastian had a way of distracting her. He put his arm around her shoulders.

"I missed you too, sweetheart." Before she could gather her wits, he was kissing her again. His hand cupped her breast, his touch so light, she hungered for more and pressed against him. He pulled back with a smile, then placed a kiss on the swell of her breast peeking above her neckline, his breath tickling her flesh. "Tonight these little beauties will receive the attention they deserve."

Her body heated at his playful teasing. If only she could forget about everything and become lost with him… But she couldn't allow him to distract her further or she would never do the right thing.

Easing from his embrace, she folded her trembling hands in her lap. "I had hoped for a moment alone with you tonight." His grin widened and she added, "To talk."

He opened the curtain more on his side to allow light from the carriage lamp to spill into the interior. "Our wishes are in perfect alignment. I want to talk to you, too, but ladies first." He winked. "Later, we can continue what we started."

She frowned. There wouldn't be a later for them. "I've something to tell you, but I don't know where to begin."

He turned toward her and folded his hands in his lap, imitating her. His playfulness disappeared. "You can tell me anything, angel."

She blinked against the burn of impending tears. "I am no angel." This felt like the only truth she had ever told him. "I am a nobody. A blacksmith's daughter."

His brows twitched, but otherwise his expression remained neutral. She rushed on before she lost courage.

"My father was a gambler, and a very poor one at that. He lost everything. Every shilling he made. His tools, so he couldn't earn anything. Our home. If not for Mama, we would have been tossed on the streets, but she arranged with the new deed-holder to allow us to stay. She took in sewing, cleaned for our neighbors. Anything to keep a roof over our heads. I'm certain we would have starved, but she was a good provider."

A dark frown marred his face, but he didn't speak.

She moistened her dry lips. "W-we were managing well enough while Mama was alive. I helped by caring for my younger siblings and keeping up our house. We had a maid for a time when I was much younger, but Mama let her go when we didn't have the funds to pay her. I don't think Father ever noticed Betsy was gone."

"How many siblings?"

She started. "There are five of us. Mama didn't live long after Gracie was born. She died of childbed fever. I did my best to take her place. She had taught me to sew and I knew how to budget. I was making a decent go of it, too, until—"

Her voice broke as memories of that day she left her family flooded her. Sebastian wrapped his arms around her and tears slipped from her tightly closed eyes. "Dear God, Helena. This is much worse than I imagined."

"I know. I'm so sorry I let you believe I was a lady. I understand why you can't have anything more to do with me. If someone finds out…"

He tipped her chin up so she had to look at him. "Your past doesn't concern me, sweetheart, and you *are* a lady. You married a lord and nothing can change the fact you are Viscountess Prestwick."

"But my father—"

"Is a blackguard and I will meet him with more than a leather glove if we ever cross paths."

"You won't cross paths. Fergus and I returned to my home when we first arrived to Town. A neighbor's elderly mother remembered my family and said my father died. She didn't know what had become of my sisters, but her son pulled me aside and said he'd heard talk that Lavinia moved to Whitechapel." His image blurred as tears filled her eyes. "Lavinia is my sister. My sister is a whore."

The word filled her with shame. She should have fought to stay instead of begging for Prestwick's mercy. Her pleas had meant nothing to him.

Say your good-byes, Miss Kendrick. We've a long day of travel ahead.

Her sister Cora had charged him. *You can't have my sister.* Her child's fists pounded against him, likely hurting herself more than him.

He'd held Cora at arm's length. *I promise to take good care of your sister, little one, but she is not safe here.*

Lord Prestwick's glare had skewered their father. Father had ducked his head and grabbed for Cora, his fingers digging into her shoulders as she struggled to break free. A storm had brewed in their father's eyes, causing Helena to hold her breath, silently pleading with him not to hurt Cora again.

Go with him, Father had barked. *He owns you, girl.*

Helena had held her hands out in surrender. *I'll go, but please, release Cora. She did nothing wrong.*

Lord Prestwick had nodded sharply, and their father complied. Cora ran to toss her arms around Helena's waist. *Don't go. Please, Helena. Don't leave me.*

"I failed them." Helena met Sebastian's serious eyes and burst into tears.

He held her tighter, his embrace a haven from the memories she wanted to forget. He whispered soothing words as her tears came, washing away some of the pain she held inside. He smoothed his hands over her back. Even when her tears subsided, he held her as if she were precious.

His lips caressed her temple. "You didn't fail them, my love. You were just a child. Your father is to blame. He was a piece of rubbish for wagering you in a card game."

She gasped and sat up, breaking his hold. "How do you know about that?"

He reached into his jacket and withdrew a handkerchief. She took it and dabbed at her eyes. "Do you recall I said I had a surprise? I've found your sister Lavinia. We are on our way to see her now."

Her heart dropped into her gut. "You found her? Is she well? Where has she been? How did she end up in a brothel?"

"Slow down." He held up a hand as the carriage rolled to a stop in front of a charming little town house. "You may ask her anything you like. I promise we won't leave until you are satisfied, but we have arrived."

"Lavinia is here?" Fear sliced through her and left her trembling. She'd thought once Sebastian found Lavinia she would have time to prepare. They hadn't seen each other for nine years, and she was struck with the thought that maybe they would have nothing to say to each other. "I—I am uncertain this is a wise plan."

"Your sister wants to see you, Helena. But if you want to leave, we will."

She glanced at the town house as the carriage door opened. Lavinia was inside, only several steps away. She shook her head. "I don't want to leave."

Sebastian gently took her arm to help her from the bench. "We should move quickly. It's dark, but we still don't want to draw attention."

He guided her to the carriage steps and the footman offered her a hand down.

It was a short walk to the town house's front door. "But Sebastian." Helena clutched his arm before he grabbed the knocker.

His brow wrinkled as he turned his dark eyes on her. "What is wrong? I thought you wished to find her."

She nodded, a scratchiness beginning in her throat. "What if my sister hates me for not trying to find her sooner? Look what happened to her."

He smoothed a hand over her hair, his eyes glittering from the light of the carriage lamp. "Miss Kendrick doesn't hate you. She only learned today that you are still alive."

Helena's hand fell from his arm and her lips parted. She should have sent word the moment she could, but her sister wouldn't have gotten it, would she?

The door creaked open and a young woman who looked remarkably like their mother stared back at her. "Lavinia?"

A large smile broke across the other woman's face, and she reached for Helena's hands to draw her across the threshold. "Come inside, Helena. It is me, your sister."

They hugged, both of them laughing. When Lavinia pulled away, she frowned. "You've been crying."

"She had to endure my company from the other side of town, Miss Kendrick. Can you blame her for crying?" Sebastian winked at Helena.

Lavinia accepted his answer with a brief smile, then invited them to join her for refreshment. The foyer was long and narrow so they had to trail behind Lavinia in a single-file line to a cozy parlor. Hand-painted gold leaves on green graced the walls, and a grand walnut grandfather clock stood sentry at the door. Helena allowed her gaze to travel the room, taking in the plush velvet sofa and thick carpet cushioning her steps. How was it her sister could live in such luxury? Unless... Her stomach turned over. Her sister was a courtesan.

Lavinia gestured toward the sofa. "Edith will bring refreshments in a moment. Won't you have a seat?"

They moved through the motions of civility as if it gave them an anchor in this unknown sea. Helena and Sebastian sat on the sofa.

"Are you certain you want me here?" he asked.

She grabbed his hand and pleaded with her eyes for him to stay. He nodded, offering an encouraging smile.

Lavinia sat adjacent to Helena and arranged her skirts. Helena eyed her sister's modest gown, confused by the picture she presented. She hadn't known what to expect when she finally found Lavinia, but it wasn't this self-possessed young woman who could be mistaken for a lady. In fact, she was more convincing than Helena had ever felt herself to be.

Pink raced up Lavinia's face and disappeared into her hairline. Helena broke out of her trance. She had been staring.

"Lord Thorne told me you know about Madam Montgomery and Whitechapel. You shouldn't even be in the same house with me, much less—"

"How did it happen?" Helena dreaded her sister's next words, but she had to know if their father had wagered away Lavinia's freedom too.

Her sister's gaze dropped to the carpet. "I tried to take care of everyone just like you asked, but I am not you. I didn't know how to sew, so I had to find work elsewhere."

Her heart squeezed. "Oh, Lavinia. I never meant to place that burden on you. Was there no place else you could find work?"

Lavinia's head snapped up and there was a defiant spark in her eyes. "Do you think I wanted to become a whore? I fought it like the devil himself, but eventually—" Her sister's throat worked as she fought against the emotions bubbling to the surface. "I worked as a cleaning woman for a time and that kept us from starvation, but it would never provide a better existence for the younger ones. I took a position in a tavern because I could earn a better wage. That is where I met John O'Riley and my future was cast in stone. Every day he would come to the tavern and try to lure me into the brothel. He made promises that I knew were false, so I refused his offers for weeks.

"Then one morning, the son of a longtime family friend came to call. Father had been an invalid for almost a year at that point. He was very ill when Mr. White appeared."

"How did Father become an invalid?"

Lavinia's gaze cut to Sebastian as if to question his presence when they were discussing family matters. Helena nodded that it was all right to proceed. He would need to know the ugly truth about her father, so there was no doubt he should cut ties with her.

"He…uh, fell…from the Westminster Bridge."

"You mean he jumped." It wouldn't have been the first time he was deep in his cups and feeling sorry for himself. Helena had never been so happy her father was such a poor hazard player as the day he tore the house apart searching for his firearm only to remember he had wagered it away a month earlier.

Lavinia sighed. "Yes, he jumped, although it seemed wise to repeat his version of having fallen. As luck would have it, he dove from the bridge in the middle of the day when travel on the Thames was at its peak. He was fished out of the water and brought home with a broken back. He couldn't move his arms or legs and had to be cared for like a baby. I wanted nothing to do with him, so Pearl took it upon herself to be his nurse. She has Mama's patience."

Helena perked up at mention of her other sister. "Where is Pearl now?"

"Cora said Pearl is living in Haslemere. She answered an advertisement to play nursemaid to an injured farmer. Apparently she likes caring for others and is good at it." Lavinia shrugged. "It isn't the life I wanted for her, but it is better than most alternatives."

Helena didn't know how to respond. If she again expressed sorrow for how Lavinia's life had turned out, she feared angering her. Instead, she focused on what they had in common, a love for their sisters. "Where are the others? Cora and Gracie?"

"Cora is married and Gracie is here. She is asleep abovestairs, but I can take you to see her if you like."

Her sisters were alive. Gracie was here, in this very house. Tears burned in her throat and she swallowed to ease the ache. "I—I do want to see her, but I have many questions yet."

Lavinia nodded. "As do I, but you are eldest. I will answer whatever you wish to know."

Helena's sisters had deferred to her in all things when they were young. Time and distance hadn't changed much, it seemed. "You mentioned an old family friend paying his respects."

"Thomas White, he is a butcher in Clerkenwell. Our fathers apparently entered into an agreement some years ago that Mr. White would marry one of us. Before Father began gambling. He'd promised a ridiculous dowry, too. I considered chasing Mr. White away with the broom when I learned the real reason he had come, but Mr. White was posing a solution I couldn't afford to throw away. I agreed to consider his offer, but he'd set his heart on Cora."

"But you were the next oldest. Why didn't he offer for you?"

Lavinia glanced at Sebastian then cast her eyes down. "Cora was beautiful beyond compare at sixteen and had that air of innocence men like. I understood why he wanted to offer for her."

Yet the honorable thing to do would have been to offer for Lavinia. Then her sister would have been saved from this life.

"Mr. White agreed to marry Cora for the fifty-pound dowry promised him, and for an additional twenty pounds, he allowed Pearl and Gracie to live with them too. It wasn't part of our agreement, but he paid a solicitor to write up Father's will. Mr. White has guardianship of our youngest sisters."

"Seventy pounds would be hard to come by working in the tavern," Sebastian said softly.

The hard lines in Lavinia's face melted and her eyes shimmered with tears. Helena held tightly to his hand to fight the urge to go to her. Her sister had somehow maintained her pride, and Helena sensed she would retreat behind her impenetrable wall if she moved.

Lavinia sniffled. "I never would have earned that type of money at the tavern. I saw but one choice to save our sisters. I sought out John O'Riley. For seventy pounds, I would come to work at the brothel."

Sebastian frowned. "Men like O'Riley do not part with money easily. Working at the brothel couldn't have been the extent of your promise."

"No, I became his property until my debt was settled."

Helena's disgust must have shown, because Lavinia's eyes narrowed. "I don't regret anything," she said through clenched teeth. "Our sisters were protected from the life I've lived. I would make the sacrifice a thousand times over to see them happy."

Helena's bottom lip trembled. "I blame myself for not protecting you too, Lavinia. I hate that you have suffered, but I understand why you did what you did. I have nothing but respect for your unselfishness."

Sebastian's arm slipped around Helena's shoulders. "You both made great sacrifices for your sisters. Just this afternoon Miss Kendrick told me that you went with Prestwick to save Cora from a beating."

Lavinia blew out a breath and the rigidness in her shoulders eased. "Forgive me. I only wanted to do as you asked and take care of our younger sisters. I've always worried you would be disappointed in me if you knew."

"Never." Helena scooted to the edge of her seat and reached for Lavinia's hands. Her sister readily curled her fingers around Helena's. "A day hasn't passed without me missing you. I wanted to write, but Prestwick reminded me you wouldn't be able to afford the post. I asked him to send money, but he said he had taken on the burden of supporting me and had done his duty already."

A low growl rumbled in Sebastian's chest.

Lavinia lifted a brow in his direction. "Lord Thorne and I are in agreement. Your husband was an arse."

Helena's face flamed and she released her sister. She hadn't allowed herself to think unkind thoughts about her husband, because he had saved her from her sister's fate. He had hired a tutor to turn her into a lady and given her a home and a respectable position in Society.

It seemed too ungrateful to speak poorly of him, but she couldn't defend him to Lavinia. He could have saved them all and had refused.

A petite gray-haired woman appeared in the parlor doorway with a cart. "Are you ready for refreshments, Lavinia?"

"Please, come in and join us, Edith." Lavinia caught Helena's curious look. "We are dear friends and Edith stays on as my companion."

"St. Ambrose provides well for you," Sebastian said.

"I owe him everything. He found me at Madam Montgomery's and brought me here after paying my debts. He made a home for Edith too."

The older woman smiled fondly at Helena's sister and began pouring tea.

Lavinia accepted the first cup and passed it to Helena. "When Cora heard of my improved circumstances, she insisted I take Gracie. Her husband has several mouths to feed already. St. Ambrose arranged for our youngest sister to come live here as well, although this is no place for a child. That was eight months ago."

It seemed her sister had found a generous benefactor, but Helena didn't know how long Lavinia would receive his protection. According to Olive, gentlemen tired of mistresses quickly and discarded them. Helena sat up straighter. Her sister would never need to worry about her future again. Wickie had left Helena a fortune and there was no heir to inherit.

"Do Pearl and Cora remember me?" she asked.

Lavinia chuckled. "Do you truly think any of us could forget you? You were like a mother to us."

A deep longing tugged at her, the feel of their baby sister's weight on her hip. Her chubby fingers tangled with Helena's hair. She hadn't felt it this strongly since those first months away from her family. "Could I see Gracie now?"

Lavinia set her cup aside and stood. "Of course. Lord Thorne, is there anything Edith could get for you while you wait? St. Ambrose keeps brandy in the study. I'm certain he wouldn't mind if I offered you a drink."

"A brandy would be lovely, Miss Kendrick."

At the doorway, Helena glanced back at Sebastian and he shooed her away with a grin. "Go see your sister."

Twenty

SEBASTIAN PACED THE PARLOR AS HE WAITED FOR Edith to return with his drink. His fingers curled tightly into fists at his side. If Prestwick were still alive, he'd call him out. How the bastard could look into Helena's soulful eyes and refuse to help her family proved how dark his heart had been. And her own father gave her away. Sebastian cursed him under his breath.

A door slammed and he jumped.

"Where is he?" a man demanded.

"My lord, it's not how it appears."

"Lavinia!" Angry footsteps stomped down the foyer and started up the stairs.

Bollocks! It was St. Ambrose, and he was going to discover Helena. Sebastian dashed for the parlor door. "Are you looking for me?"

The marquess halted near the top of the stairs, turned, and slammed back down the stairwell. "What the hell are you doing in my house?"

Edith cowered at the edge of the foyer. Her gaze was trained on the stairs as if contemplating the odds of reaching the upper floor before the marquess overtook her.

Sebastian lifted a haughty brow as the man approached. "Clearly not what you think." He spread his arms wide and indicated his clothed state. "But you have a wicked imagination, St. Ambrose."

The man bore his teeth and drew back his fist. Sebastian bobbed to the left just in time to dodge. The marquess's punch merely grazed his ear. His miss fueled his rage and he charged Sebastian. Sidestepping, Sebastian kicked out his foot to catch St. Ambrose's ankle. The marquess lurched forward into the parlor and landed hard on a side table. The fragile piece splintered.

The man was older than Sebastian's five-and-twenty years, which gave Sebastian a slight advantage, but the marquess was still fit in his early thirties.

"If you will listen instead of trying to kill me, St. Ambrose, I can explain my presence." Only Sebastian hadn't thought that far ahead. He couldn't think of anything other than getting Helena out of this situation unscathed, which might mean admitting to something he wasn't guilty of doing.

The marquess wasn't interested in an explanation anyway. He lumbered to his feet, his face redder than Sebastian thought humanly possible. "I know who you are," he said with a jab of his finger in Sebastian's direction, as if that explained the man's mad behavior.

This time when St. Ambrose barreled toward him, Sebastian hooked an arm around his neck and swung behind him to lock the man in a hold. The marquess struggled and Sebastian tightened his grip. He didn't want to cut off the man's air, but applied pressure to his windpipe to show he could if he wanted. This didn't slow St. Ambrose. He cursed and bucked as Sebastian threw his weight against him in an attempt to knock him to the ground. St. Ambrose's leg kicked back and struck Sebastian's shin.

"Damnation!" He jerked the marquess to the side in one last effort to take him down and they both stumbled into the tea cart.

The porcelain pieces fell one after the other and shattered on impact with the wood floor. A feminine screech made them both jerk upright and spin toward the door. Miss Kendrick stood in the threshold, her fists punched to her hips.

"Gus, what the devil are you doing?"

Helena came up behind her sister. Sebastian mouthed the word *go*, but she stared at him in bemusement. Did the stubborn chit ever listen?

"I was going to ask you the same, Lavinia." St. Ambrose wrenched free and dusted off his trousers. His gaze landed on Helena. "Lady Prestwick, are you here with Thorne?"

Sebastian winced. They were in a pickle now.

Miss Kendrick lifted her chin. "She most certainly is. Now why are you attacking my guest? I've never seen you behave in such a manner."

A young girl with eyes as big as Helena's padded into the parlor. Bare feet stuck out beneath her white night rail. She cocked her head to the side to study Sebastian. "Do we have an intruder?" She was strangely calm about the situation.

Miss Kendrick hugged her. "No, my darling. Lord Thorne is not an intruder."

"What is he doing here?

Sebastian offered a slight bow. "I'm sorry we frightened you. You are Gracie, are you not? My name is Sebastian."

"I wasn't frightened." The girl's smile was identical to Helena's. "It is nice to meet you, sir."

Miss Kendrick smoothed a hand over Gracie's honey-colored curls as Helena watched with a pained look. "Lord Thorne brought a visitor to see you," Miss Kendrick said. "Do you remember hearing about your oldest sister, Helena?"

St. Ambrose sucked in a sharp breath, his gaze shooting to Miss Kendrick, then Helena. Gracie turned assessing eyes on Helena too.

"Yes, she was the best sister any girl could want and she loved me very much. She died when I was a baby."

Tears pooled in Helena's eyes. Sebastian went to her, unable to stand by while she suffered. She sank against him. Her trust was welcome and he silently vowed to never betray it.

Miss Kendrick pulled the girl in front of her and rested her hands on her shoulders. "There was a mistake. Our sister didn't die. She is here now. Gracie, I would like to introduce you to Helena, Lady Prestwick."

She tilted her head back to look up at Miss Kendrick. "Should I curtsy like I do with Lord St. Ambrose?"

Helena swiped a tear as it fell on her cheek. "Heavens, no. I am your sister. No one curtsies to one's sister."

The girl smiled. "I'm not very good at it anyway."

St. Ambrose came forward and ruffled her hair.

"You do a very fine job of it, but your sister has a point. I don't want you to curtsy to me either."

Her smile widened showing matching dimples. "But you aren't my sister."

The marquess chuckled, the remaining tension melting from his posture. "Well, I'm family, so that should matter."

Miss Kendrick's lips thinned. Apparently, she didn't agree he was part of their family, but she didn't contradict him.

Edith tentatively peeked into the parlor. "I have that brandy for Lord Thorne, and I poured one for Lord St. Ambrose too." She lifted two tumblers into the air as if presenting a peace offering.

"Thank you, Edith," St. Ambrose said. "I apologize for startling you earlier."

She ventured into the room, handed a glass to Sebastian then the marquess, and made a quick exit.

"You are supposed to be in bed," Miss Kendrick said to Gracie. Her chide was gentle and she made no move to send her away despite her words.

"I was in bed until the noise woke me. I want to visit with Helena."

Miss Kendrick kissed the top of her head. "I'm sure she would like that."

The girl grabbed Helena's hand and urged her to the sofa. Sebastian hung back to allow them time without him getting in the way.

Miss Kendrick gestured to St. Ambrose. "May I speak with you in the foyer, my lord?"

He followed her and mumbled an apology to Sebastian as he passed.

"I sent you a message," Miss Kendrick hissed as soon as they cleared the doorway. "Why are you here?"

"You never ask me to stay away. I was concerned something might be wrong with Gracie or Edith. I thought you might need a doctor."

She sighed. "Gus, when are you going to accept I'm capable of taking care of my family?"

"But you don't have to anymore. I want to take care of you. I have asked you—"

"Stop. I refuse to have this conversation now."

Sebastian felt a measure of pity for the man. He couldn't imagine how difficult it must be to want to care for someone who wouldn't allow it. He eased away from the door in an attempt to provide the marquess and Miss Kendrick privacy, but he couldn't escape overhearing them.

"You cannot tell anyone about Helena. If anyone knows she was here…"

"Lavinia, you know me better than that. I would never do anything to hurt you or your family. I love you."

There was a long pause. Sebastian pretended interest in a nearby painting, expecting the couple to return and not wanting them to realize he was privy to their conversation.

"I know you would never hurt us, my love. You are the kindest man I have ever known." Miss Kendrick's voice assumed a teasing tone. "Although your kindness doesn't extend to side tables and tea services."

They laughed softly together.

"I will send replacements tomorrow. Forgive me

for behaving like an animal this evening, but the thought of you with another man…"

"I would never. I swear it upon my mother's grave. You must know I love you too, August."

Sebastian's cravat had become too tight and he tugged to loosen it. Over the last day, he had come to acknowledge his love for Helena, but until he overheard St. Ambrose and Miss Kendrick speaking of their problems, Sebastian had not realized loving another person did not guarantee a happy outcome. Helena had made it clear she was content living as an independent woman, which did not bode well for a future together. Dizziness drove him to join her and her youngest sister around the low table.

Too many sensations swirled inside him—in his head, gut, and chest. He sipped his brandy, preferring to observe rather than participate in their conversation as he tried to sort the unfamiliar feelings.

Gracie blinked her deep blue eyes at him. "Lord Thorne, are you Helena's lover?"

Helena gasped. "Heavens, no. How do you even know about such things?"

Sebastian arched his eyebrows as if to say, "Isn't it obvious?" A courtesan was raising the girl. She would be exposed to situations other young girls wouldn't, at least none in their circle.

"I don't know. I am sorry." Gracie picked at her night rail, avoiding eye contact.

"Oh, Gracie." Helena patted her knee. "It is all right. You caught me by surprise, but no harm done. Lord Thorne is an acquaintance. He agreed to help find you and Lavinia, and he has fulfilled his promise admirably."

There was a sinking feeling in the pit of his stomach. He thought of them as more than mere acquaintances. He could understand how their association might be difficult to explain to a young girl, but identifying him as a friend would have been preferable. Helena hadn't even spared him a warm glance.

The marquess and Miss Kendrick returned with Edith. "It is past your bedtime, young lady," Miss Kendrick said with a smile. "Say good night."

Gracie smiled shyly at Helena. "May I hug you?"

"That would make me very happy." After Gracie collected hugs from Helena and Miss Kendrick, Edith ushered the girl from the parlor.

Silence descended over the room. No one spoke for some time until it began to feel awkward. Finally, Helena cleared her throat. "I will visit Cora and Pearl to make certain they are well-situated, and then I will return to collect Gracie as we agreed upstairs."

Sebastian held his tongue. Helena was emotional from her reunion and not thinking clearly. She couldn't bring an unknown girl into her home without stirring up rumors, especially one who shared similar physical traits.

Pain flashed in Miss Kendrick's eyes. "I know it is for the best, but—"

Helena stepped forward to embrace her sister. "I am sorry, Lavinia. I wish there was another way. You have a place with me too, if you would accept it."

Miss Kendrick kissed her cheek before withdrawing to dash away her tears. "I can't. I belong here."

After Helena said her good-byes to Miss Kendrick, Sebastian escorted her to his carriage. They hadn't made it to the corner before she touched his arm. "Are you angry with me?" Her voice was soft, but the emotion echoed in the small space.

He stroked her cheek and smiled. "For not leaving when I said? No."

"I meant for lying to you about my past. I should have told you the truth before we reached this point."

Half her face was in shadow from the carriage lamp, reminding him of the side of her that she kept secret from most. He had known her past held some darkness. He'd seen the haunted reflection of it in her eyes. Now he understood the origin of her mistrust, and he wouldn't condemn her for trying to protect herself.

"At what point would that be, love?" His hand moved to cradle her nape and his lips grazed hers.

Her eyes drifted shut, her breath growing uneven. "Before we became physically involved."

Her answer was like a punch in the gut. He hadn't considered it possible he was the only one falling in love. "Are you implying our connection is only physical? That you care nothing for me?"

"Of course not," she said on a rush of breath. "I value our friendship very much, which makes it difficult to give you up."

Sebastian drew back, his hand falling to his lap. "What do you mean by give me up?"

"I—" She swallowed hard. "I won't be staying in London now that I have found my sisters. I can give Gracie a new beginning in Scotland just like my husband did for me."

Sebastian's jaw clenched. "Like Prestwick did *for* you." The bloody Scot had been an opportunist who took advantage of a weak man and stole his daughter. "You make it sound as if you were a charity case, Helena. He took you from your family. Do not assign him heroic qualities he doesn't deserve."

"I know he wasn't perfect, but he still saved me. Isn't that the mark of a hero?"

Her admiration for Prestwick collided with Sebastian's hatred for the blackguard, and a destructive storm brewed inside him. The carriage interior crackled with tense energy as she held his gaze, presumably awaiting an answer.

"How many times did he remind you that he saved you?" A low growl underscored his words. "Did he lord it over you every time you bucked his authority?"

"No, it wasn't like that." She rubbed her forehead, her eyes squeezed tightly together. "I never questioned his authority, and I regret every moment I submitted to his will."

Sebastian let go of his anger for the man who had hurt her, because feeding the rage would only cause her more pain. Her guilt already weighed on her shoulders, leaving her slumped forward as if closing out everyone. She appeared so downtrodden and alone.

He put his arm around her. Her vulnerability was never so apparent than when she curled her small frame against his, seeking comfort. He exhaled in relief and drew her against his chest. His lips brushed her temple. Her feelings for him were stronger than she was willing or able to admit, so for now, he could love enough for both of them.

But he couldn't let her go. Not just for his sake,

but hers. If she returned to Scotland, Lavinia would not be part of her life. This couldn't be what Helena truly wanted.

She lifted her face to him and he burrowed his fingers into her silky hair, knocking a pin loose, as his tongue teased her luscious mouth. She opened on a breath and dissolved against him. Her surrender was a sweet victory. She returned his kiss with the same passion she had shown outside the theatre.

He sensed the carriage slowing, then drawing to a stop. His lips traveled to her cheek, her temple, and finally to her gently curved ear. "Invite me inside, Helena."

She eased from his embrace. The tip of her tongue flicked across her lips. Did she still taste him?

The carriage door flung open and Fergus glared at him. "What took you, lass? I havna been able to think on anything but if you found yer kin."

Helena scrambled from the bench to hurry down the steps without extending Sebastian an invitation to join her. He gritted his teeth, ready to come to fisticuffs with the Scottish oaf for interrupting.

When she reached the ground, she smiled up at the giant. "Lord Thorne found them. Lavinia, Gracie, Cora, Pearl. They are all alive and well."

The man released a lively whoop and lifted her in a hug. Sebastian didn't have a chance to react before Fergus set her back on her feet and lobbed a grin at Sebastian. "Well done, my laird. You have made the lass verra happy."

"He exceeded all expectations. I'm grateful for all he has done."

Sebastian's heart lurched. Why did that sound like a good-bye? "Helena…"

Her gaze shot in his direction but she didn't respond to him. "I will call on Cora tomorrow then visit Pearl. By the week's end we will begin our journey back to Aldmist Fell with Gracie."

Her words were as powerful as a strike from Thor's hammer.

Fergus frowned at him. "Are you certain, lass? There's no urgency to return home. My cousin will take care of the land as long as necessary."

"I'm sure you and Ismay are anxious to see your kin. There is no reason to delay."

Devil take it! Sebastian would be damned if he was sent away like this. "We had a bargain, madam, or have you forgotten your end?" He climbed from the carriage.

In a surprising move, Fergus yielded to him, allowing Sebastian to stand toe to toe with the infuriating, stubborn, maddening woman. Her eyes widened.

"What about your promise to help my sister?" Sebastian said.

"B-but I fulfilled my promise. She is out in Society. You said she is likely to receive an offer of marriage soon."

Sebastian lifted a haughty eyebrow, knowing his arrogance would engage her in a battle of wills. But a battle meant she was still engaged with *him*, and that was his only hope in keeping her. "The prospect of a marriage proposal is not the same as securing a match. Given the history of broken betrothals in my family, surely you understand my reluctance to release you from our bargain before my sister has married."

She issued an outraged cry. "I never said I would help her make a marriage match."

"It was implied, Lady Prestwick. What other reason is there for a young lady to join the assemblies?"

"I never said—"

"Ahem!" Fergus cleared his throat loudly. Helena blinked up at him. "Now, lass. It seems to me Laird Thorne has done you a good service finding your sisters. It isna right to break your word to him."

"But I'm not breaking my word."

The Scot kindly patted her shoulder. "If Miss Thorne receives an offer of marriage as expected and marries the lad after the banns are cried, Laird Thorne has no reason to feel slighted."

Her puckered face nearly made Sebastian laugh aloud. It was as if she smelled something rotten. He detected it too. It was called conspiracy, and to him, it smelled sweet.

She threw her hands in the air. "This is ridiculous. I don't know what you expect from me."

"I expect you to remain in Town until my sister marries. If she requires more assistance, I can't very well expect you to travel back from Scotland at a moment's notice. Eve needs you *here*."

Hell, Sebastian needed her in London if there was any hope for a future together. He couldn't leave England and continue the work his father started before he became unfit for Society. Sebastian's responsibilities were here, but he wouldn't ask Helena to sacrifice her dreams for him. He would find a way to make them come true while keeping her where she belonged, by his side.

"Well," she said with a slight huff, "if you expect me to sit around waiting for Sir Jonathan to come up to scratch, you are mistaken. The day after tomorrow, I am traveling to see Pearl and you cannot stop me."

He allowed a lazy grin to spread across his face. "I wouldn't dream of keeping you from your sister, madam. In fact, I look forward to making her acquaintance."

She hitched her chin. "*You* are not invited."

He took a step toward her, tempted to claim her bottom lip when it mutinously pushed out. Unfortunately, the Scot wasn't likely to look the other way while Sebastian overstepped his bounds. He forced his hands to his sides, even though he ached to touch her. "If you think I am letting you out of my sight until our bargain is fulfilled, madam, you are mistaken. Would you like to invite me inside so we might discuss this further?"

When she glared, he smiled. "Insufferable beast," she said and stormed inside, closing the door behind her.

Fergus chuckled. "You've riled her now, my laird. Very wise."

"How so?"

"When the lass finally gives in, she will feel satisfied for having given a good fight. Carries too much guilt, that one. For kowtowing to Laird Prestwick, but she was just a girl. She couldna have won the battle."

Sebastian's nostrils flared at the mention of Prestwick. "Did he ever raise a hand to her?"

"No, his lairdship never abused her. She was afforded the same kindness he extended to his breeding mares." Fergus's derisive sneer revealed his poor opinion of his former employer. The Scot obviously cared for Helena, which made his overbearing manner less offensive all of a sudden. Her man inclined his head toward Sebastian. "But I've seen you with the lass. You listen to her wishes and treat her with kindness. Allow her to choose you and her heart will be yours forever."

Sebastian sighed, considering the older man's words. Fergus had known Helena for years. He was like family to her. If Sebastian were truly wise, he would heed the servant's advice. "Perhaps I shouldn't go to Haslemere with her."

"I didna say let the lass run roughshod over you, my laird. Give her the fight she needs, so she can redeem herself in her eyes. Then it's only a matter of time before she lets herself love you in return."

Sebastian smiled ruefully. "Am I that obvious?"

Fergus cackled and slapped him on the back. "Aye, like a jackass at a garden party."

Twenty-one

THE NEXT MORNING HELENA AND FERGUS CLIMBED into a hack to head for Clerkenwell to call on her younger sister Cora. Today she needed a friend, not a pretend footman. As much as Helena tried to stir up enthusiasm for her visit to Cora, she couldn't shake the dark mood hanging over her like a rain cloud.

Fighting with Sebastian had her insides twisted in a snarl. She had known leaving him would be difficult, but parting on bad terms didn't make separating any easier. It made her feel like a spoiled, ungrateful brat.

She had been honest with him about her plans, believing she owed him at least that much. But she wished they could have kissed each other good-bye and ended their association on friendly terms.

Liar. She adjusted her position on the carriage bench, trying to wrestle the truth into submission. Eventually, she tossed her hands in the air. "Very well. I am one." She didn't want to end things with Sebastian, but what other choice did she have? At some point, he would tire of her, and she couldn't see delaying her plans when they had no future together.

Fergus's chuckle reminded her she wasn't alone. Heat rushed into her cheeks. But instead of drawing attention to her embarrassing habit of talking to herself, he asked a question. "How old was Cora when you were brought to Aldmist Fell?"

"She had just turned eleven. Cora was always small for her age. Not surprising since it was nearly impossible to get the girl to sit still. Mama used to say she was going to nail Cora's skirts to the chair if she didn't sit down and eat. She never followed through, of course."

Helena relaxed against the seatback with a fond smile. Even when Mama was struggling to keep them fed, clothed, and sheltered, she had kept her sense of humor. Helena's younger years had been happy ones because of her.

"What about Pearl? How old is she?"

Helena tapped her finger to her lip, quickly calculating Pearl's age. "She is nineteen. Only a year younger than Cora."

"Close in age like you and Lavinia. Were they the best of friends like you two?"

She shook her head and smiled at the kindhearted man across from her. He was trying to distract her, perhaps sensing her nerves. Or maybe he thought she was angry with him for taking Sebastian's side last night. She didn't understand what had made him champion Sebastian's cause, but she knew he meant well.

Fergus looked at the shop windows as they passed. "I think we have arrived, lass."

The hack began to slow and stopped in front of a

brick building with a large display window filled with sausages and hams. A sign above the door read White's Butcher Shoppe.

Fergus clambered from the carriage before assisting Helena. Men and women bustled along the walkway with determined strides. Passersby swerved around her and Fergus with naught but a curious glance here and there. A bell jangled as Fergus pushed the door open and held it for Helena. Smoked meats dangled from the ceiling by various lengths of rope by the unattended counter. Dull thwacks of a cleaver against wood came from a back room, and a rusty scent assaulted her nose. She breathed through her mouth to minimize the nauseating smell.

Helena met Fergus's gaze and he shrugged. Approaching the counter, he peered over it to check if someone had ducked behind it and shook his head to indicate no one was there.

Helena cleared her throat. "Excuse me," she called to the person in back.

A louder whack made her jump. "Mrs. White!" The bellow echoed in the small room and rang in Helena's ears. "Mrs. White, we have customers."

When no one responded, the man muttered, "Where have you gotten off to now?" He tried once more to summon the woman. "Mrs. White! *Cora!*"

Helena's heart stalled as she realized the man was calling for her little sister. Grumbles floated from the back room. Wiping his bloody hands on a towel, a man who appeared to be in his early thirties entered the shop just as the front door banged against the wall. Helena spun around with a gasp. A plump young

woman hustled inside with two loaves of bread cradled
in her arms.

"I have returned, Mr. White," she sang out cheer-
fully, swept past Helena and Fergus without really
looking at either of them, and headed for a set of stairs.

The man's face softened as his gaze followed her.
"We have customers."

Mrs. White stopped on the first step and nailed
him with a scathing look. Helena had no doubts this
was her sister. Although her outer appearance had
changed drastically in nine years, she had retained
her contemptuous countenance. It had earned her a
beating from their father on more than one occasion.
"My arms are full, Mr. White. Why can't you see to
the customers?"

Helena held her breath as she waited for Cora's
husband to storm across the shop and deliver a strong
clout to her ear as their father had often done. Instead,
Mr. White held up his red-stained hands and smiled as
if indulging a child. "I need your assistance, dearest."

Cora sighed heavily.

"We can wait," Helena offered.

Her sister's gaze snapped toward her and narrowed.
She came back down the stairs. "I will take care of
them, Mr. White. You may return to cutting meat."

He thanked her and disappeared into the back room
again. Helena's eyes widened at how easily he was
ordered about by his much younger wife.

Cora's mouth puckered as she slowly looked her
over from head to toe. "You look like Lavinia, only
fancier. I thought you died. What are you doing here?"

Fergus stepped forward as if to take her in hand,

but Helena held out an arm to stop him. "Show some respect for your betters," he snapped.

"I am not her better. I am her sister." She smiled kindly at Cora. Her sister had always been temperamental and difficult, but Helena loved her dearly. Lavinia had told her Cora was affected by Helena's leaving, and although Cora blamed their father, she'd still been angry with Helena for not fighting to stay.

Her sister moved behind the counter and set the bread aside. "How may I help you, milady? We've a nice blood sausage and our smoked hams are always in demand."

"Is there someplace we may speak in private?"

Her gaze lifted to the ceiling, then landed on Fergus. She frowned. "There are rooms abovestairs, but *he* is not welcome."

"I'm certain Fergus won't mind waiting."

Her loyal Scot crossed his arms and glowered in return, but he didn't argue. "I will be outside the door, lass. Holler if you be needing me."

She opened her reticule to retrieve a few coins. "I saw a tavern on the corner as we passed. Perhaps you would like an ale while you wait."

"I will be outside the door," he growled before stalking from the shop without taking her money.

Helena sighed. Although she appreciated his protective instincts, there was no danger when she was with family.

She turned back to find Cora's soured frown gone. "Forgive me for being surly, Helena. You caught me by surprise, but I'm glad you came. Come abovestairs and I will serve you tea."

Helena followed her sister up the solid staircase, taking note of her surroundings when they entered Cora's living quarters. The main room above the shop was twice as large as the one they'd shared in their childhood home. It was tidy and filled with light from the tall windows. A ruckus in the other room erupted as soon as the door closed.

"Quiet down," Cora hollered. "I have a guest."

"Mama! Mama!" A little girl with curls like Cora's raced into the room and threw her tiny arms around Cora's legs. A small boy tottered behind his sister with his thumb in his mouth. His hair was so light and soft-looking, it reminded Helena of down. Her throat grew tight as she looked at her niece and nephew.

"You have children," she murmured.

Cora wrinkled her nose, a reluctant smile on her face. "Three in almost as many years. Emma, what have I told you about running in the house?" Cora freed herself from the little girl's arms and patted her head. "Mother White, you are supposed to be watching the children."

An older woman with graying hair had entered while the children distracted Helena. She held a sleeping baby wrapped in a knitted blanket.

"They move too fast for me, Cora."

Helena's sister swung the boy up in her arms when he reached for her with his sweet, chubby hands. "You know what Mr. White says. You must make them mind."

"I will try harder, my dear." Cora's mother-in-law smiled at Helena. "Who is your guest?"

Cora crossed her arms. "None of your concern.

Now take Emma and Mathew to the other room so we can talk."

Helena's eyes widened at her sister's disrespect. The woman's smile fell away and her eyes hardened, but she rounded up the two children and ushered them from the room. It was clear who ruled at the White residence.

"Have a seat." Helena sat down at the solid dining table while her sister removed her fashionable bonnet, tossed two small logs in the firebox, and placed the kettle on the stovetop.

Helena traced the slight gouges in the wood, nostalgia almost bringing her to tears. They'd had a similar table when they were children. "The children could have stayed. I wouldn't have minded."

"We wouldn't have a chance to talk if they did." Cora joined her at the table. "What brings you to Clerkenwell? You are the last person I ever expected to see."

Helena smiled sheepishly. "I am sorry to arrive unannounced, but I am unaware of the proper etiquette for coming back from the dead. I hope I didn't shock you."

Cora laughed. "I always suspected the blackguard lied. I knew I would have felt it if you were gone. We were always close, you and I." She leaned against the carved seatback and tipped her head to the side. "Where is the mighty lord now, and what possessed him to release you from his castle dungeon?"

"How did you know he had a castle?"

"I thought all lords had castles." Her keen gaze swept over Helena. "He dresses you well. I suppose he is wealthy."

Helena shifted uncomfortably. She didn't wish her sister to know how accurate she was about Prestwick's influence. He had never been unkind to Helena, but she had been his to command. Every decision—what she ate, what she wore, how she arranged her hair, what she read—was dictated by him.

"My husband died a little over a year ago," she said.

"Oh!" Cora's eyes widened. "Have you lost your home then? My Thomas is a good man, but as you can see, he has many mouths to feed already."

"Thank you for the kind offer, but I have a home in Aberdeenshire, and I've let a town house in Mayfair." Helena wasn't certain her sister had actually extended an offer, but she chose to pretend she had. "I came to see you, Cora. Nothing more."

"Ah, I see. You gave his lordship an heir."

Helena shook her head, swallowing her shame over her inability to give her husband a son. Olive had reassured her the problem must have been with Wickie, who had suffered from a severe case of mumps as a boy. "Prestwick left no heirs. He was the last of his line."

Cora's eyebrows shot up as she pushed away from the table to pour hot water into a pretty teapot and add tea. "I suppose you have the castle all to yourself now. It must get lonely."

"Gracie will come live with me, so that will make it less lonely. And Pearl, if she likes. I leave for Haslemere tomorrow."

"So Gracie and Pearl will have run of a Scottish castle, wear expensive dresses, and learn to put on ladylike airs." She snorted. "I'd wager that would be a sight."

"Perhaps you could come visit. Scotland is nice in the summer."

She wished the old fantasy of having her sisters at Aldmist Fell warmed her heart as it used to do. But she would only have half her family with her, and she would miss the friends she had made in England. And Sebastian. Not quite a lover and yet more than a friend.

Cora rejoined her at the table. "Gracie lived with Thomas and me until several months ago. I hated to send her to Lavinia, given the circumstances, but I didn't know what else to do. My husband was working hard to take care of us all. I feared for his health."

Helena reassured her Gracie was well cared for, then asked her about her life.

"Thomas is a good provider and he treats me with kindness, which is more than I ever had at home with our father."

"I am happy for you, Cora."

Toward the end of Helena's visit, Cora brought her children to meet her and introduced her mother-in-law. Helena supposed her sister wanted to be certain about what she wanted before exposing her family to her. She could understand wanting to protect them.

"This is my oldest sister, Lady Prestwick. She's a real lady," Cora said with a proud tilt to her chin. "Your son married into an important family."

Mrs. White's smile was tight. "I daresay Thomas doesn't care a whit about your lineage. He is devoted to you. No offense intended, milady."

"None taken." Helena was pleased with how well her sister had done in her marriage. She had a nice home, beautiful children, a gracious mother-in-law, and a husband who doted on her. Helena couldn't imagine a better life. If she didn't love her sister dearly, she might be envious.

After collecting hugs from the children, Helena bid them farewell. Opening her reticule, she pulled out all the bills she had and held them out to her sister. "For the children. I didn't bring gifts, but I would like to give them something."

Cora smiled. "That is kind, but unnecessary."

Her mother-in-law stepped forward, taking the money, and thanking her on the children's behalf. Helena didn't miss the slight glare Cora tossed at Mrs. White. It seemed there was perhaps some question about who ran the household after all.

Cora walked her downstairs.

"Will you come visit again before you leave for Scotland?" she asked.

"Nothing would make me happier." They embraced and Helena kissed her cheek. "Cora, I am so pleased we have reconnected. I've missed you."

They hugged once more.

Fergus was waiting outside, just as he'd promised. "How was yer visit with yer sister, lass?"

Helena couldn't contain her smile. "Perfect. It has made me even more anxious to see Pearl."

And perhaps she could make peace with Sebastian on the short journey. It would certainly lessen her guilt if she could properly express her thanks. If not for Sebastian, she wouldn't have her sisters back, and she didn't want to part with him believing she was ungrateful.

Twenty-two

SEBASTIAN UNAPOLOGETICALLY STARED AT HELENA across the carriage. They had been traveling for almost two hours on their way to reunite Helena with her sister Pearl, and she hadn't said a word since the carriage pulled away from her house.

Her greeting that morning had been polite and her manners impeccable, but he would rather have her railing than ignoring him.

When her maid Ismay turned from the sights outside the carriage window, she caught him staring at her mistress and lobbed a grin in his direction. Her eyes twinkled with mischief. "Interesting scenery today, aye, milaird?"

"Stunning," he agreed.

Helena's eyes snapped up from the book she held on her lap. Either she was pretending interest in the book to avoid him, or she was an exceptionally slow reader since she hadn't turned the page in the last half hour. Sebastian's lips inched up as he held her gaze. She swiped a lock of hair behind her ear and returned to her book, her cheeks infused with a lovely rose color.

Very well. If she wouldn't engage with him, he would have to rely on her maid for entertainment. "Is the scenery very different in Scotland?"

Ismay cocked her head and studied Helena. "Less flustered, I'd say."

A laugh burst from him. He liked the chit's audacity.

Helena wrinkled her nose at her maid. "Ismay, behave."

"Forgive me, milady, but I thought his lairdship was referring to you. You're the only scenery he has been admiring since we left London."

A darker flush made Helena's face glow. She closed her book. The gilded lettering on the cover caught the morning sun. She'd brought *Belinda*, the book he had purchased for her in Finsbury Square.

"I thought you would have read *Belinda* by now."

She turned it to view the book spine as if she'd forgotten what she was reading. "I only found it in the foyer yesterday. Fergus must have set it aside in the excitement that day."

She said nothing about the inscription inside. Perhaps she hadn't noticed his message. "Is it any good?" he asked.

"I just started it. I thought it would help pass the time today."

Instead of talking to me. He crossed his arms with a slight frown. "Some people pass the time in conversation."

She raised her brows toward Ismay. "Shall we discuss the weather, my lord?" She was using the girl as a shield to avoid discussing anything important.

"There's nary a cloud to be seen," Ismay said, ducking her head to peer at the sky.

Sebastian chuckled. "Now that we've exhausted that topic…"

He wanted to present an idea to Helena. It had formed after a conversation with his sister yesterday. Eve knew nothing of Helena's background—at least not the truth—but she had heard quite a tale from Lady Eldridge at tea last week about how Prestwick met Helena. The viscount had been an imaginative liar, and his tall tales might work to Helena and Sebastian's advantage. But he would have to wait until they changed horses to speak with her about his idea.

Helena returned to her book, and Sebastian resumed enjoying the scenery. The sun set ablaze silky tendrils of Helena's hair that had fallen around her soft cheek. His gaze lingered on the velvety lobe of her ear, recalling her soft gasp as he'd taken it between his teeth. Her sweet moans echoed in his memory. Her fingers tentatively touching his hair as he put his mouth to her quim. Her nails sliding against his scalp as she began to lose herself, moving in time with his tongue.

She glanced up, her large eyes widening when she caught him watching her. He grinned wickedly, amused when she fidgeted with the edge of her book before slapping it closed and turning toward the window.

"W-we are almost to our next stop," she said.

Sebastian swiveled on the bench. An idyllic village lay snug in the valley along the road they traveled. The carriage pitched when a wheel hit a rut, and Helena's maid squealed as they were both almost tossed to the floor. By the time they reached the village, having bumped over every hole along the way, Ismay was holding her stomach and her complexion had a decidedly green tint.

Fergus swung the door open, took one look at his sister, and ushered her into the fresh air. "Take deep breaths, lass."

Helena clambered out ahead of Sebastian without waiting for assistance. Fergus helped his sister sit on a barrel and hovered over her like a mother bear while Helena stood by as Ismay's shaky inhales and exhales began to even out. When the maid's color returned to normal, she smiled weakly.

"Would you like to come inside for refreshment?" Helena asked.

Ismay shook her head. "If it's all the same to you, milady, I would prefer to sit outside."

Sebastian held his arm out to Helena. "Come with me."

Her fingers curled around his forearm, and she allowed him to draw her toward the coaching inn. "C-come where?"

"Inside, of course." He slanted a glance at her and lowered his voice. "Unless you would like to come someplace else."

Just as he had intended, his comment elicited a brilliant blush and her hand sought out a strand of hair to thrust behind her ear. He loved that she retained a bit of bashfulness, and yet she could be uninhibited and sensual when the time called for it.

Light spilled into the dark interior of the coaching inn when Sebastian held the door open for her. She preceded him, but stopped only a few steps inside. As his eyes adjusted to the dimness, he could see the room was filled with fellow travelers.

"I will see to a private room." He approached the innkeeper and was pleased to learn a private dining room was available.

Helena followed the man but tossed a look over her shoulder. Sebastian winked. She hesitantly turned back and nearly collided with the doorjamb. She cried out in surprise, then lowered her head and hurried inside the dining room.

Sebastian paid the man. "See that we are not disturbed."

"Yes, sir."

When the door clicked, he raised a brow. "Alone at last."

Her tongue dashed across her bottom lip, leaving it shiny and irresistible. He slowly stalked her as she backed away. "Are you running from me, angel?"

"No." She shook her head as she continued to retreat. Her backside banged into the table and she startled. Sebastian took advantage of her momentary distraction and pounced. His hands spanned her narrow waist and lifted her to the table.

Her eyes flared as a breathy laugh escaped her. "Is *this* where you wanted me?" She sounded both appalled and intrigued.

He flashed a grin. "This table looks sturdy enough." He stood between her knees, his arms slipping around her back. Her hands landed on his chest as if to push him away, but perhaps she thought better of it because they just rested lightly against his jacket. His pulse sped as her index finger drew a small circle over his heart.

She angled her head and peeked at him from beneath her thick lashes. "Sebastian, I don't think this is wise."

"Because someone might discover us? That is part of the excitement, love. Remember the theatre?"

She laughed, her blush returning. "I liked the theatre."

His grin widened. "Did you now? I had no idea."

"Stop teasing." She lightly whacked his shoulder. "I'm certain your prowess has been complimented once or twice in the past."

He didn't care what other women before her thought. She was the only one who mattered. He placed a kiss on the tip of her pert nose. "I am more than tempted to prove myself worthy of any compliment, madam, but Fergus will come searching for us soon. And I value my life."

"Besides, I am sitting on a table."

He leaned toward her, hovering close enough to capture her mouth but delaying their kiss. "And who says the bed gets to have all the fun?"

"I—I don't know." She wiggled to create space between them, but she couldn't go far with his arms still encircling her. Her gaze became fixed on something beyond his shoulder.

He checked to be certain Fergus hadn't come in behind him. They were alone. Only they weren't really. She had that faraway look she sometimes had when she became lost in her memories. Fergus's words echoed in Sebastian's head. *She was afforded the same kindness he extended to his breeding mares.*

Hatred rampaged through his veins. Helena deserved better than she had ever received in her life. She deserved someone to love her, to take pleasure in her companionship and appreciate her body.

He gently caught her chin between his thumb and

finger. "Sweetheart, you do know sexual relations are meant to be enjoyable. There is nothing unnatural about a man and woman delighting in one another."

She smiled. "Delight sounds so carefree, playful even."

"Playful is good, too."

"Very well, the table is not an issue. But there is another reason I don't think we should do this."

"Do what exactly?" He wanted to hear her say the words. *Making love.* Swaying into her, he grazed his lips over hers. She tasted like heaven, smelled like vanilla. And he wanted her.

Here.

Now.

Bare on this table.

And to hell with the Scot. Sebastian had survived more than his share of beatings at Eton, not to mention a few this Season. He could handle himself well enough in a fight.

Helena's eyes drifted closed. "This," she said on a breath. "Tupping."

Tupping? Sebastian drew back. He couldn't believe a lady would use such crude language. No matter that he used it on a regular basis, but never with Helena. "Is that how you think of us? Like rutting animals?"

She pursed her lips, her displeasure radiating from her blue-green eyes. "Why in God's name would I associate us with rutting animals? That's so—so...*base.*"

Sometimes she frustrated him beyond reason and yet he still wanted her so much it hurt. He paced several steps away, shoving his fingers through his hair, then spun on her. "I didn't use the word *tupping. You* did."

"I don't know what else to call it. We are not married, so it would be incorrect to refer to it as amorous rights."

But they could be. If she stayed in London, they could marry and he could be the husband she deserved. Nothing like that bugger who had kept her locked away at Aldmist Fell. Why did she even want to return to that place? "I expected you to say making love, Helena. That is the appropriate term."

She averted her gaze. "Isn't lovemaking reserved for people who love each other? I don't think brief affairs qualify."

Her refusal to see the truth incited his temper. He marched back to the table and captured her face between his hands before she could scramble from the table. He pressed his face close so they were eye to eye. "*I* love you, Helena."

Her lips parted and he couldn't be sure she was breathing. She certainly wasn't repeating the sentiment, which elicited a tight squeeze in the center of his chest. Well, she didn't need to say it for him to know she loved him too. She had expressed it many times without saying a word. Love was in the gentleness of her touch when he was bleeding after his fight with Benjamin Hillary in the garden. It showed in the softness of her eyes, her kind words to his sister, and her fiery defense of him at the theatre.

"And you love me, but you're too stubborn to admit it, aren't you?" He brushed his thumb over her bottom lip, unable to resist touching her even though anger still burned inside him. "I am very put out with you for making me tell you this when I am mad."

She blinked, her brow scrunching as she eased from his touch.

"It made sense in my head," he said. Perhaps he had loved her from the moment they collided outside the church, or maybe he had fallen for her the day she took Eve shopping. When she had looked into his eyes with such hope and trust, he wanted to be her champion. He still did.

"You love me?" Tears shimmered in her eyes and his fingers intercepted them as they slipped onto her soft cheeks.

"I'm sorry, Helena. I planned to use sweet words and tenderness. I wanted to kiss you first, and then declare my heart. But I've messed it up."

She shook her head, her exquisite eyes still bright with tears. "No, you did splendidly. It was the best declaration of love I've ever had. That it is my first doesn't lessen its value."

Sebastian had never blushed a day in his life, but heat crept into his face. "It is my first time, too."

Her arms slid around his neck and a shy smile spread across her lips. "An innocent."

"Hardly." His mouth touched hers as a bang sounded at the door. Helena jumped.

"Lass, are you in there?"

Bloody Scot.

Helena scooted from the table. "I-I'm coming."

"Liar," he said low enough for her ears only.

She laughed softly, patting her hair then sweeping her hands over her skirts as she moved toward the door. Her hand paused on the handle and she turned back to him. Her smile faded. "Sebastian, I promised myself I wouldn't lie to you again. I want to tell you I love you too, but I cannot."

Cold seeped into his churning gut. If she didn't love him in return, he'd made a fool of himself again. Just like with Gabrielle. And even though no one would know outside of Helena and him, he knew. Steeling for her answer, he asked, "Why can't you say you love me?"

Her gaze dropped to the floor. "If I say it, I can't retract the words. They will be forever between us, binding me to you even when I leave. I fear my heart would shatter if I let myself love you."

Hope swelled within him and drove him to go to her. He took her free hand. "I may know a way we can be together."

"Sebastian, come with me to Scotland. We can make a life there, after Eve is settled in marriage. Your mother could come with us."

He sighed. If only the solution were that easy, but he couldn't leave. His father's sacrifice couldn't be for naught. Sebastian was a baron and his duty was to his King and country. "Helena, I have—"

A louder bang shook the door. "Lass, is there a problem?"

"Only if you call a soon-to-be-dead Scot a problem," Sebastian grumbled.

Helena's smile didn't reach her eyes. "No killing. I made him promise, and I'm holding you to the same standard."

Twenty-three

HELENA AND SEBASTIAN WERE ALONE IN THE CARRIAGE since her maid had begged to ride in the open air after her bout of nausea. Ismay had never tolerated bumpy carriage rides very well, and this leg of the journey qualified as bumpy in more ways than one.

As the carriage shimmied and lurched over the lane, Helena braced herself against the wall and tried to think of something to say to Sebastian. His profession of love had knocked her off balance. It changed everything, and nothing.

The thought of leaving him carved a hole in her heart, an ache similar to the one she'd experienced those first months at Aldmist Fell knowing her family was out of her reach. Only this ache was worse somehow.

She loved him. Whether she held her tongue or shouted it to the world, the truth wouldn't change. She loved him and she was going to lose him.

He arched a brow. "Do you want to talk about why you're abusing your bottom lip?"

What? Releasing her lip, she ran her tongue over it to soothe it. She hadn't realized she was biting it. "No."

The carriage wheel hit a deep hole and jolted her from the bench. She released a sharp cry when her bum smacked the edge of the bench and she slid to the floor.

"For the love of God." Sebastian grabbed above her elbows and tugged her toward the seat beside him. His arm went around her, holding her in place as the carriage dipped again. His thigh and hip pressed against hers, interfering with her heart rate. As hard as she tried, she couldn't slow her shallow breaths.

His hand slid to her nape. "Hold tight and you won't be hurt."

She closed her eyes as his fingers played with the loose hairs falling on her neck, intensely aware of the tingles raining down her body. Longing surged through her blood. She wanted to hold tight to him. To never let him go.

His free hand caressed her jaw. "Everything is going to be all right, Helena. I promise."

How could he promise something out of his control? Blind optimism wouldn't help anyone. "It's not going to be—"

He tipped her chin and kissed her, holding her securely until her nerves began to calm. His mouth coaxed her to surrender and she wanted to fight—knew she *should* fight giving in to her desires—but she sagged against him. His warmth surrounded her and she sighed. Why did everything feel right with him when she knew it wasn't? She had seen the refusal in his expression. He wouldn't come to Scotland with her.

He eased back and his dark eyes captured her. She couldn't look away. "Please…" A muscle in his jaw bulged, revealing the effort it took to force out his next words. "Please, say you will reconsider your plans. Stay with me."

An undercurrent of hurt flowed beneath those simple words. No matter what choice she made, someone would suffer. She hated bearing the weight of others' happiness on her shoulders. "If I don't take Gracie and Pearl to Scotland, what chance do they have? You know as well as I they cannot live with me in London, and leaving Gracie with Lavinia is out of the question. Lavinia and I agree it's not the best place for her. I cannot abandon my sisters again."

"You did not abandon them. Don't allow guilt to guide your decisions. I've traveled that road and it leads to no place pleasant."

She cocked her head to the side, not understanding.

"Gabrielle," he said. "I offered marriage to a woman I didn't love, because I thought it would help Eve. I knew Gabrielle didn't want to marry me, but I was driven to do right by my sister and I ignored what I knew was morally right. I should have released Gabrielle from the betrothal. Instead, I made matters worse for everyone."

"You aren't to blame for trying to make a good marriage match."

"If you know two people love each other and come between them, you are responsible for everyone's misery."

She shook her head. "No, and I don't see how this is relevant to our situation."

"Because you are coming between *us*, or rather you are letting guilt get in our way."

How could she argue? Guilt gnawed at her like a hound with a bone, but wasn't he coming between them too? "You could live at Aldmist Fell."

"I am needed here." Irritation flared in his eyes. "My land is in England, and my duties require me to be accessible. There is more involved than making an appearance when the House of Lords is in session. I am cosponsoring an act to provide housing for soldiers injured in the war and—"

She held up a hand. "I am sorry. I was not thinking properly."

His bluster died away, and he deflated on a long exhale. "No, I'm sorry, sweetheart. I didn't mean to be condescending. Fulfilling my role is important to me, and I tend to become dogmatic about it."

Dogmatic, fiery, incredibly handsome when passion lit his eyes. If he were not opposing her, she would enjoy this side of him more.

He reached for her hand. There was a twinge of sadness to his smile. "I need you to understand why it is important."

An ache throbbed in her chest. She couldn't stand the thought of him hurting. She nodded to show she was listening.

"I wasn't born with noble blood. My grandfather was only a doctor, but he was a successful one."

Helena tried to hide her surprise, but her eyes widened. His origins were not so different from hers.

"Grandfather purchased a captain's commission for my father in the cavalry when he was seventeen and charged him with distinguishing himself. Father always did as he was told and became quite the soldier, by all accounts. I was a young boy when he was deployed to Ireland to suppress the rebellions. When he returned, the King created the barony for Father as reward for his service." Sebastian's lips set in a grim line. "Mother said he was never the same after he returned from war. He had nightmares and sometimes thought he was back in New Ross. He couldn't predict the spells, and after he had one in the House of Lords, he couldn't make himself return. My father never finished the work most important to him, so I have taken up his cause."

Suddenly, she felt foolish for asking him to come to Scotland. His place was here, but where did that leave them?

He shifted toward her, a sense of urgency in his tone. "My father sacrificed his sanity for us—Eve, Mother, me. I cannot let it be for naught. I have a duty to him that I cannot ignore."

They sat in silence. She didn't know what to say. Understanding didn't make their situation easier. She squeezed his hand. "In the dining room, you said there might be a way for everyone to be happy. Is there really a chance?"

"There is always a chance, Helena."

She took a moment to roll the word around in her head. A chance implied risk. Possibly failure. And consequences if they failed. Chance had been her enemy all her life. It had taken her home, her freedom. And yet, no matter how small the chance of success, it became a sliver of hope embedded in her heart.

"How?" Her voice was almost a whisper.

His easy smile appeared. "You're the daughter of a wealthy Irish gentleman, my dear."

"You know that is a lie. My mother was Irish, but we were far from wealthy and we had no land in Ireland."

"I know," he said. "Well, I didn't know about your mother, but I know Prestwick created a different past for you. Tell me the story and don't leave out any details."

This was an odd conversation to have now, but Helena complied. "When we married, my husband told everyone I was the daughter of a gentleman, a reclusive landowner in Northern Ireland. Only the servants knew I wasn't, but they valued their positions and told no one the truth."

"Prestwick was quite the gambler, it seems."

Helena had never thought of her husband as a gambler, but it rang with truth when Sebastian said it. Was Wickie the same as her weak-minded father? She swallowed against a bitter taste rising in the back of her throat. "He said no one would question the story, and he was correct. None of the wedding guests seemed interested in my Irish roots."

Sebastian's hand rested on her leg, possessive and yet comfortable. "How did your husband explain the fact you don't sound Irish? Not even a little."

"I had an English governess, of course. Wickie told everyone I was educated at my father's estate." She rolled her eyes. "While I can guarantee my education while living with my father was *educational*, it didn't teach me to be a lady. Wickie saw to that once we reached Aldmist Fell. He hired a young woman to turn me into a lady and kept me hidden until we married."

"Why take a girl from near poverty and groom

her to become a wife? It doesn't make sense when a man in his position would have no trouble finding a suitable mate."

"Goodwill?"

Sebastian frowned, apparently not convinced of Wickie's altruistic nature. "How old were you?"

"Nineteen. For three and a half years, I was his ward, although I rarely saw him. He was active on his land and traveled often. Then one day he summoned me to his study and said it was time for me to take his name."

"Did you *want* to marry him?"

She shrugged one shoulder. "He offered security and respectability. I would have been foolish to decline his offer. It was very generous, considering he could have turned me out. I would have been grateful for a position with his staff."

And relieved he hadn't made her his mistress instead.

"Was there any mention of siblings in Ireland?" Sebastian asked.

"I don't think Wickie ever thought about creating a family history for me beyond my father. I would have told anyone who asked that I have four sisters, but no one ever did."

"Prestwick's inattention to detail could work to our advantage then."

Tightness formed between her brows, and he gently smoothed it away with his knuckle. His eyes twinkled. "How does this sound? Before you left Scotland, you received a letter from your Great-Aunt Mae in Ireland. She has been caring for Gracie and Pearl ever since your parents passed away, may they rest in peace. And soon she will be saying a tearful good-bye as your sisters depart for Dublin to catch a ship bound for England."

It sounded rather nice, honestly. And promising. "I have an Aunt Mae now?"

"Yes, and an Uncle Patrick. You and your siblings spent every Christmas at your uncle's estate. Cook made the most delicious plum puddings, and you used to sneak into the kitchen to watch her prepare them. She allowed you to lick the spoon afterwards. Don't you remember?"

She laughed and sank against the seatback. "Perhaps not as well as you, but please, refresh my memory. What else did we do at Uncle Patrick's?"

"You went riding—"

Horses? Her eyes almost popped out of her head.

"You don't ride?"

She shook her head.

Sebastian's lips turned down. "That will never do. I'll teach you to ride." He slanted his head. "I suppose Gracie and Pearl will require lessons too."

"I suppose they will. Our father—the *gentleman*— was dreadfully afraid of horses. He didn't keep a stable."

"A gentleman who doesn't keep a stable? I've never heard of such a thing. How did he get from place to place?"

"He never left home. You must remember he was a recluse." She wiggled on the seat to face him, warming to the idea of storytelling. "His fear of horses stemmed from his childhood, from the time a runaway team nearly ran him over on a bridge and he tumbled into the creek. He never taught us to swim either."

Sebastian chuckled. "What a colorful make-believe family you have, my dear."

"And those are just the stories fit to tell," she said, batting her lashes playfully. "So Aunt Mae has been caring for Gracie and Pearl and now…"

"And now her gout is acting up. She can barely walk, much less keep pace with a ten-year-old girl. In her letter, she asked if your sisters could come live with you. You enthusiastically agreed and instructed her to book passage to London. It will break her heart to see Gracie and Pearl go, but she knows they will be in good hands with her trusted maid, Edith."

Lavinia's companion. Her merriment faded as she laced her fingers with his. "For the past nine years, I've had no family history I could share with anyone. I know it's silly to feel sentimental over events that never happened, but it means a lot to me that you gave me a Great-Aunt Mae, Christmas, and plum puddings."

Sebastian lifted her hand and kissed each fingertip. "Someday we will have real memories to cherish, my love."

That sliver of hope in her heart began to work its way deeper, expanding until she began to believe perhaps it *was* possible for her to have it all. All because of this man. A rogue by reputation, but the most kindhearted soul she had ever known. And he loved her, sincerely. It showed in his tender gaze. His soft touch. The endless patience he seemed to have for her.

Her eyes misted. "Sebastian?"

He glanced down at her and sat up straighter, worry lines forming on his forehead. "Helena?"

"I love you, too."

Twenty-four

HELENA SHIELDED HER EYES AGAINST THE SEVERE afternoon sun as the carriage stood idle, waiting for a boy to urge a herd of sheep across the country lane. The carriage's sudden appearance around the bend had caused somewhat of a panic among the four-legged pedestrians, resulting in the flock darting down the lane and bleating for their lives.

"Are you certain we shouldn't offer assistance?" she asked Sebastian.

"The boy almost has them in hand. We might spook them if we try to help."

She watched the scene beyond Sebastian's shoulder, doubting his assertion as the flock appeared to be camped out on the lane. "Do you know much about sheep?"

"Not particularly," he said with a grin tossed over his shoulder, "but I've fair experience with corralling stubborn creatures."

She flopped back against the seat, pretending insult, but she couldn't hold back a silly smile. "You, sir, are treading on dangerous ground." Picking up her copy of *Belinda*, she opened the cover intending to read until the boy could convince the sheep to let them pass.

Black script jumped out from the stark page. *To a beautiful partnership. Fondly, S.* She glanced up to find Sebastian watching her with a tiny grimace.

"It's not very eloquent, I am afraid. I have been told my actions represent me better than my words." He waggled his eyebrows in jest.

"Yes, I suppose they do." Although his manner was playful, she became more thoughtful. "Every promise you have made, you have fulfilled. You have kept my confidence. You found my sisters."

He held his hand out and she placed hers in his. "You kept your word too, Helena. I only accused you of not keeping your side of our agreement because I wanted to purchase time. I wanted to figure out how to keep you with me."

"Perhaps you will be looking for a way to toss me aside soon," she said with a teasing smile, although deep inside there was a niggling fear he would do just that at some point.

"No, what I wrote is true. We have a beautiful partnership, and I would like to make it lasting."

"What do you mean by lasting?"

He held on to her hand, not allowing her to withdraw. "Marry me."

Suddenly, Helena could relate to the sheep. His proposal was like a six-in-hand coach barreling toward her. Her gaze locked on the door as she fought the temptation to run.

Marriage equaled confinement and loss of control.

It meant failing to please, consequences, and isolation. Her heart shuddered, then slammed against her breastbone as if trying to escape her body.

"Shh, it's all right." Sebastian gently stroked her hair. "Don't be afraid, love. It's all right. I withdraw my request."

The sound of her rapid breathing filled the carriage. This was ridiculous, behaving like a frightened child. Clamping her lips together, she took a shaky breath as a drop of perspiration trickled down her back.

Sebastian wasn't Prestwick. He didn't want to squire her away to a remote castle. Instead, he wanted to keep her among Society where she had formed friendships, and he wanted to make a home for her sisters. Sebastian was everything her husband hadn't been—loving, thoughtful, engaging, accepting—but marriage was a big leap.

She reached for his hand still stroking her hair and held it tightly. His strong and steady touch quieted the maelstrom inside. "M-may I have time to consider before you withdraw your request?"

His smile lit the carriage, rivaling the sun. "Take as much time as you need. I am not going anyplace."

And neither was she. She had to trust in Sebastian's plan to reunite her with her sisters.

With the sheep finally cleared from the lane, the carriage jerked forward and continued toward Springvale Manor, the home of Pearl's employer. When they had stopped in the village, Sebastian asked for directions to Mr. Mason's farm. The innkeeper, a rather chatty fellow, described a much larger estate than Helena had been anticipating.

Apparently, Mr. Mason's farm had been prosperous before his accident, but when it appeared he wouldn't survive, his hired men found other employment. With no brothers or sons to help, the farm had begun to fall into disrepair. She was uncertain what living conditions she would find Pearl living in, but her sister would have no more worries once she came to stay with Helena.

As the carriage turned onto the drive, three chimney caps peeped over the tree line. Helena scooted to the edge of the bench, anxious for her first glimpse of the house. Several steep-pitched roofs came into view, and as they approached, Helena spotted at least two outbuildings.

"It is larger than I thought," she said.

"And it's in better condition than the innkeeper led us to believe."

The grass around the house was clipped short, and window boxes dripped with flowers. A rounded door swung open and a young woman hurried to stand in the drive. She looked toward the house, dashed back inside, and a moment later returned with a gentleman at her side. His arm was draped around the woman's shoulders while a crutch supported his other side. Helena's stomach dove when she noted the bottom half of his leg was missing.

The woman smiled broadly and waved as the carriage rolled up to the house.

"That must be Pearl. She has changed so much." Pearl's hair had darkened to a chestnut brown and her manner was more carefree.

"It seems they are expecting us," Sebastian said.

"I didn't want to arrive unannounced as I did at Cora's. I think I shocked the poor girl. I sent a message yesterday."

Sebastian descended the carriage steps first, then held Helena's hand to assist her.

"Helena!"

Mr. Mason's smile was as wide as Pearl's as he nudged her. "Go on. I will be all right without you."

Pearl hesitated but a heartbeat before rushing to gather Helena in a hug. "Thank God you are alive. I never believed you were gone. I sensed you were still out there."

Cora had spoken similar words. Helena returned her sister's vigorous hug. "Oh, Pearl. How I have missed you."

Her sister's blue eyes sparkled as she took Helena's arm and urged her to follow. "I want to introduce you to someone."

Sebastian trailed behind, allowing her to have this moment with Pearl. Her sister resumed her place at Mr. Mason's side. He was a handsome man with longer-than-fashionable blond hair that fell on his forehead. And he was young. Perhaps not much older than Sebastian.

The same set of dimples Helena had inherited from their mother flashed when Pearl smiled at her employer. "May I present my sister, Lady Prestwick?"

"It is a pleasure to meet you, Mr. Mason."

He shifted his weight to his crutch and reached for Helena's hand to bring it to his lips. "The pleasure is mine, my lady. Pearl's family is always welcome at Springvale." A manservant slipped outside and Mr.

Mason nodded at him. "Show Lady Prestwick's men where to take the trunks."

"Oh! Lord Thorne and I don't wish to impose, sir. We plan to take rooms at the inn."

Pearl laughed. "Don't be silly, Helena. We have plenty of room for you and Lord Thorne."

We? Helena exchanged a look with Sebastian as Mr. Mason's men helped carry their trunks inside.

"Elliott is my betrothed," Pearl said. "Cora's husband granted permission for us to marry last week. The banns were cried on Sunday. Please, come inside."

Without waiting for a reply, she assisted Mr. Mason, her husband-to-be apparently, to swing around and maneuver back inside the sprawling home.

Sebastian offered Helena his arm to escort her. "Are you all right? You've grown pale," he whispered.

She nodded, her throat too tight to speak.

As they entered, Helena viewed the dwelling with a different set of expectations. This was Pearl's home, the place where she would raise her children and grow old with her husband. Helena noted the loose hinge when the manservant closed the door behind them, the worn carpet, and the sparse furniture in the drawing room, but the home was immaculate.

Sebastian and Mr. Mason exchanged handshakes once their host was seated. "Congratulations on your betrothal, sir."

Pearl made certain everyone was seated comfortably then excused herself to see about tea. While the gentlemen engaged in talk about Mr. Mason's land, Helena reconciled herself to the idea Pearl wouldn't be leaving with her as she had expected. She wanted her sister's happiness above all else, and she would have to be blind not to notice Pearl bubbled over with glee.

When her sister returned, Mr. Mason offered to show Sebastian his stables, which he accepted. Pearl grimaced as her betrothed struggled to stand and hopped until he gained his balance.

He winked at Helena's sister. "I can manage without your assistance. Enjoy your sister's company. I'm sure Lord Thorne will lend a hand if I need it."

Sebastian reassured her that he would be pleased to assist Mr. Mason, and then the two men left Pearl and Helena alone.

Helena accepted a cup of tea from her sister. "I am surprised Cora did not mention your engagement when I saw her yesterday."

"I am not," Pearl said as she poured a second cup. "She isn't pleased by the match."

"Why not? Mr. Mason seems like a lovely man." Although appearances could be deceiving. What did Cora know that made her oppose the marriage?

Pearl laughed and rolled her eyes. "Oh, you know Cora."

Only Helena didn't. Not really. She didn't know any of her sisters any longer, and the chance to get to know them was slipping through her fingers. Lavinia had experienced more in her life than Helena could in three lifetimes, not that she would want her sister's experiences. Cora was already married with three children. And now Pearl was to be a wife. Helena's desire to stay in England grew stronger.

Pearl set her cup aside. "Our sister wants the best

match. She has always thought of herself as prettier. Even though she hasn't met Elliott, she is convinced he is a wealthy man, wealthier than Mr. White. And more handsome." Pearl's eyes sparkled happily. "She is correct about the latter."

Helena chuckled. "Having seen them both, I agree."

"I bet she turned green with envy when she met Lord Thorne."

"I didn't introduce them. We aren't—"

"You aren't...?" Pearl's delicate brows slowly inched up her forehead.

Her heart sped up as she recalled Sebastian's proposal in the carriage. "We are not attached. At least not yet."

Pearl squealed and launched from her chair to throw her arms around Helena. Helena juggled her cup and managed to set it on the side table with minimal spilling. "I knew you were coming with good news. As soon as I read the gentleman was escorting you."

Helena wrapped her arms around her sister and laughed. "You always were a romantic, sweet pea. There is nothing to announce now, but you will be the first to know."

When Pearl returned to her seat, Helena asked about her wedding plans and the farm. "Elliott and I have managed to keep the farm afloat, but it will be easier once he gets a new leg."

"Wasn't his accident months ago? Why hasn't he been fitted already?"

"Well, he had to heal first." She lifted the tea and stared into the cup as she took a sip. She continued her examination of the contents as she said, "Once the bred-heifer has her calf, we can start selling the milk. I calculate by Christmas we will have over half of what we need for a prosthetic limb."

Helena smiled sadly at her sister. The poor dear hadn't even thought to ask Helena for the money. She didn't know if Mr. Mason would accept charity anyway, but surely he wouldn't deny Pearl a dowry. Perhaps Sebastian could approach him on her behalf later this evening. Helena would see her sister settled, and settled well as long as she had the means to provide for Pearl.

"I have a feeling there is a very romantic tale behind your betrothal. I would love to hear about it."

The happy twinkle in Pearl's eyes had returned when she looked up. "Heavens, yes. Elliott is the most romantic gentleman I ever met."

Helena smiled indulgently. Pearl hadn't known any other gentlemen in her life, and Helena was grateful the only one her sister had ever encountered was a good man. She sat back as Pearl began the story of their courtship.

Twenty-five

SEBASTIAN RETIRED TO HIS ALLOTTED CHAMBER WHEN Helena, her sister, and Mr. Mason went up to bed, but even after he stripped down to just his shirt and trousers and kicked off his boots, he wasn't ready to sleep. Instead, he began pacing the small space, his mind refusing to rest.

When he and Helena returned to Town, his first task would involve a trip to the shipping docks. Gracie's name must be on a ship's manifest—a ship arriving from Ireland—to make their story believable. There was only one man of Sebastian's acquaintance who could accomplish such a feat. Unfortunately, that man was related to Benjamin Hillary. And Sebastian hadn't ingratiated himself to the Hillary family by challenging the second eldest son to a slapping duel.

Blasted humiliating little sisters. He stopped at the window and rubbed away the tightness accumulating at his temples.

Captain Daniel Hillary was more likely to toss him from Hillary Shipping than listen to a word Sebastian had to say. How was he going to convince the man to falsify one of his ship's manifests? He didn't need money. Daniel Hillary was one of the wealthiest men in England. And he cared nothing for his social standing, although his marriage to a lovely American girl had improved his manners a great deal.

Sebastian resumed pacing, the floorboards creaking with every footfall. If he kept this up, he would wake everyone. Perhaps Mr. Mason wouldn't mind Sebastian walking the floor in his drawing room. He was always able to think better when he was moving. Grabbing the candle still burning in the holder, he slipped into the hallway and noticed a light beneath Helena's door across the hallway. It seemed someone else was not accustomed to country hours either.

He listened at her door briefly to ensure her sister hadn't snuck into her chamber for a late-night chat, and when he heard nothing beyond the settling of the house, he slowly entered the room. Helena was propped on pillows, prim and proper in a high-neck night rail, with her book open on her lap.

And she was sound asleep.

The foolish woman deserved a good scolding for falling asleep with the candle burning, but he couldn't bring himself to wake her. The past few days must have taken a toll. She'd found her sisters, but nothing was working out as she had planned. Lavinia, Cora, and Pearl had lives in England and wouldn't be returning to Aldmist Fell with her. And now he was pressuring her to stay with him.

He sidled up to the bed, set his candle on the side table, and eased the book from her hands. A soft shuddering sigh passed her lips and a bittersweet twang vibrated through him. There wasn't anything he wouldn't do for her, except let her go.

Selfish jackass.

He lowered to the side of the bed, marveling at how uniquely exquisite she was, from her sweet round face to the slight unevenness of her curved brows to the lushness of her bottom lip. Her hair cascaded over her shoulders, the candlelight giving it a subtle glow, like amber.

He had never watched a woman in slumber, never desired it, but he couldn't tear himself away. Unable to resist, he brushed a lock of hair behind her ear as she always did.

Her lashes flickered and two blue-green eyes still hazy with sleep landed on him. "Sebastian?"

"Uh…" He rubbed the back of his neck as heat scorched his face. He'd been caught gazing at her like a lovesick whelp. "You fell asleep reading. I was just leaving."

Her fingers circled his wrist as he shifted away. "Don't. Stay with me."

When a lady asked a gentleman to stay, one did as the lady wanted. He allowed a sensual smile to spread across his lips. Her eyes flared and she dropped his hand as if it were a snake.

He patted the bed, his grin teasing. "It's not a table, love."

"You said a table was acceptable." Her hand went for the lock of hair again, and his heart melted. Somewhere along the way her nervous habit had become endearing.

"Hmm…" He made a show of looking around the

room. "It seems we are short one table, so what do you recommend?"

She closed the book and rested her hands on the cover. Her swallow was audible. "I—I didn't have a chance to ask about your conversation with Mr. Mason," she said in a thready voice. She cleared her throat. "How did he take the news about Pearl's dowry?"

He sighed. "You want to talk about your sister's dowry? Now? Helena, please don't shy away from this again." He wagged his finger back and forth between them to indicate the two of them as a couple. "Let me enjoy you and you me. That is how it should be between lovers. Enjoyable. Pleasurable."

"Playful," she murmured, perhaps speaking to herself more than him.

He smiled. "Yes, playful." His hand slid to her waist and grabbed a fistful of her night rail.

She set the book aside with an almost imperceptible nod and covered his hand to still it. Taking a deep breath, she wiggled to an upright position in bed, the sway of her unbound breasts causing his cock to jerk.

She matched his smile. "So what did Mr. Mason say about the dowry?"

Sebastian grimaced and released her night rail. "He accepted." There was an unintended growl to his voice.

She wet her lips and a tightness spread from his lower belly. He couldn't force his eyes away from her mouth. He wanted to taste her again.

"Is that all?" she asked. "Didn't he say anything else?"

He blinked, trying to concentrate on what she'd asked, but thoughts tumbled in his head, and none of them pertained to this particular conversation.

He released a long exhale. "I cannot recall every-thing. There was a little of this and that, and a few other words."

She pursed her lips in displeasure. "Really, Sebastian. I hope you are never called into service as a spy. I'm afraid a report like that would be consid-ered woefully lacking."

He surged to his feet, frustrated and impatient with her.

She raised an eyebrow. A coy smile turned up the corners of her mouth. "And your ability to hide things is a bit of a problem." She nodded toward his trousers where his cock strained against the thin fabric as a furious blush invaded her ivory skin. "A-are you smuggling the crown jewels in there?"

Why, the vixen was toying with him. Playing, just as he'd asked. She was nervous and inexperienced in many ways, but she was trying. For him. His affection for her increased tenfold.

"Wouldn't *you* like to know?" he said and winked.

She smiled sweetly, her dimples showing. "Yes, please." Moving to the side of the bed, she hooked her fingers in his waistband and unfastened the front fall of his trousers. She glanced up, practically gloating. "If you had seen your expression…"

He twined his hands in her silky hair and leaned forward to kiss her. Hard. When he pulled back, he flashed a wicked grin. "You like playing, do you?" He ripped the shirt over his head. "I know a game or two you might enjoy."

Her round eyes doubled in size. "What kind of games?"

"This one is called 'Don't wake your neighbors.'"

He pounced. With a soft squeal, she scooted back on the bed, trying to evade his tickling fingers. She flopped on her belly, laughing, and tried to scramble across the bed. He caught her by the waist and dragged her back to the edge of the bed. As she halfheartedly struggled, his trousers slid low on his hips.

"Release me," she said between laughter.

"Now, why would I release you, love?" He raised her night rail over her hips to bare her lush bottom. "I think I prefer you this way."

She had a great arse, firm and full. He lightly smacked one cheek with his palm. She gasped and swung her head to peer over her shoulder. "Sebastian!"

"Shh." He held his finger to his lips. "You're going to lose the game."

She narrowed her eyes at him but couldn't maintain the pretense of scolding him. Her mouth twitched at the corners before a smug smile spread across her face. "We shall see."

He bent over and placed his lips against the small dimples on either side of her spine. She sighed and sank into the bedding. Inching her night rail higher, he licked and nibbled his way up the gentle curve of her back. Her buttocks cradled his erection by the time he reached her nape, and he held still to appreciate the softness of her skin. His eyes closed and he groaned low in his throat.

"Quiet, my lord." The imp wiggled her arse and elicited a much louder growl from him. "I'm winning," she teased.

"We just started playing, sweetheart. Come here."

He urged her to stand, her back still to him, and eased the night rail over her head. He explored the slope of her shoulder, nibbling his way to her earlobe and catching it between his teeth as his hands covered her breasts. He tested their weight, pleased with how they fit his hands. Small like apples and soft. His fingers closed around her nipples and gently tugged. Her head rolled back on his chest with an erotic little sigh.

"Isn't losing more fun?" he whispered against her ear.

She shivered. "Yes." Her voice was airy, and she raised her arms in a languid stretch before draping them around his neck. The tips of her breasts were firm buds beneath his fingers, and her hips swayed slightly, seductively, as she abandoned herself to the moment.

"You're as alluring as sin," he murmured.

She dropped her arms and slowly turned within the circle of his embrace. All traces of playfulness faded. She gazed at him with large, soulful eyes. "I don't want to lose you, Sebastian."

Her voice trembled. The mix of fear and wistfulness caused his throat to ache. He cradled her cheek and touched his lips to hers, lingering, savoring her warmth. When their kiss ended, he pressed his forehead to hers. His eyes drifted closed as a consuming tenderness coursed through him. He *couldn't* lose her.

"I want you for my bride. I want forever."

She drew back, licked her lips. He steeled himself for rejection. "So do I," she whispered.

Sebastian's heart missed a beat. "Are you agreeing to marry me?"

She hesitated a moment then nodded. "Yes. It's very sudden and others are likely to think—"

He swept her off her feet.

⁓

Helena gasped, losing her train of thought.

"Others can go hang," Sebastian said. "I don't care what they think." He laid her on the bed and made fast work of removing his trousers. His chest flexed as he crawled atop her and braced his weight on his elbows. She trailed her fingers over his lean muscles, his olive skin hot and smooth beneath her palms. He was marvelously male and splendidly made, but his intense dark gaze was the cause of her stomach flutters.

He arched a brow. "What are we about to do?"

"Make love?" She smiled, rather daftly she suspected.

His returning grin warmed her to her toes. "Does that not sound better for two people who love one another?"

He didn't allow her to answer before his mouth covered hers. She breathed deeply, the faint scent of pine soap now familiar and comforting. His mouth nipped at hers, the tip of his tongue grazing her bottom lip. She melted with him, their bodies touching heart to heart, hips to hips, his hardness to her softness.

Her tongue tentatively sought his, her exploration becoming bolder when his chest rumbled with a low moan.

When he inched down her body and circled the peak of her breast with his tongue, she arched her back, loving the incredible sensations. The heat of his mouth. The thrilling tumble in her belly. The pull between her legs. When she began to shift restlessly, his hand slid over her stomach and caressed her curls. Her hips lifted. The hunger was too much.

"Touch me," she pleaded.

He held her gaze as his fingers skated along her feverish skin. He glided over the place that brought her so much pleasure, circling and caressing until her moans grew husky and more intense. When he withdrew his fingers, she almost whimpered.

He raised himself above her, then kissed her slowly. "Not yet, angel. I want to be inside you when you come."

Her heart jolted and beat faster. When he slid into her, she arched her back and cried out with pleasure. His lips found her neck and returned to her earlobe. With each thrust, his warm breath created pleasant ripples along her skin. He filled her and she gripped his hips when he withdrew, urging him to come back deeper. After several more deep thrusts, he withdrew, ignoring her protest.

"Your turn on top." He rolled onto his back and flashed his handsome grin. Helena just stared, at a loss for words. It wasn't out of ignorance, but...

"I—do *ladies* do such things?"

"You will like it. I promise." Sebastian reached for her hand, urged her to her knees, and half lifted her atop him. She closed her eyes and sighed when he entered her.

As he guided her hips, she murmured, "So blasted good." The sensations were more intense and cloaked her in delightfully warm waves.

"Blasted *heaven*," he said with a strained chuckle. His hands traveled over her stomach and covered her breasts. A light pinch on her nipples sent a strong current to her core. She startled, pausing for a moment. He rolled the peaks between his thumbs and fingers. She moaned and rocked her hips.

"Find your pleasure, sweetheart." His lustful gaze roamed her body as his touch drove her. Her inhibitions fell away and shattered, just as she was certain she too would shatter in the end.

As her release was almost within reach, her fingers circled his wrists, holding tight. Sebastian plucked her nipples once more, and she climaxed, quietly crying out. Before her breathing evened out, he held her face between his hands and pulled her toward him for a kiss.

"Beautiful," he whispered against her lips then rolled her beneath him. He swept the hair from her face and smiled softly. "I will withdraw."

She caressed his rough cheek, certainty driving her heart. This man was to be her husband. She loved him desperately. "Please don't."

"Helena." Her name sounded like a prayer from his lips. His kiss was hard as he thrust into her. With her hands free, she smoothed them up and down his back, his muscles bunched and so powerful under her fingers. And when he reached his own release, he buried his face in her hair and softly groaned. She smiled and wrapped her arms around him, more than pleased with herself for bringing him pleasure.

"I love you," she whispered.

"I love you, too."

Settling beside her, he pulled the covers over them, blew out both candles, and tucked her against his chest. He lazily stroked her hair until her eyelids grew heavy, and the last thing she recalled before blessed sleep was counting the beats of his heart.

When she next emerged from unconsciousness, gray light was peeking around the curtains, and Sebastian was nuzzling her breast.

He lifted his head and aimed a sleepy smile at her. "Good morning, love."

Warmth radiated throughout her body. "Good morning." She threaded her fingers in his hair. "What were you doing?"

"Trying to wake you, so we can make love once more before I leave."

"Leave?"

He kissed the tip of her nose, then her chin before settling at her breast again. "I'll be returning to London today, but you should stay with your sister. You enjoyed each other's company last night. I think Pearl would like to keep you a bit longer."

Her stomach plunged. Had his proposal been true? Surely he wouldn't stoop to lies to bed her. "You could stay, too."

He aimed a smile at her. "Believe me, I am tempted, sweetheart." He nuzzled her breast again then circled the peak with his tongue.

She sighed, dissolving into the bedding when she should be on guard. But it was too difficult when he touched her like this.

He released her nipple and winked. His tousled hair lent him roguish appeal. "I could stay, but you promised to marry me. Delaying our nuptials any longer than necessary is disagreeable to me, so I plan to see to Gracie's passage from Ireland and purchase a special license. Then when you return, we will marry."

She giggled, sounding more like a girl than a woman, but it seemed fitting since the last time she recalled being this happy was when her mother was alive. Her fears slipped away. "Sebastian, you are marvelous."

"And I don't want you to forget it while we are apart." He returned his attention to her breast and caressed between her legs.

"I cannot forget," she murmured. "Ever."

"Good girl."

Twenty-six

To say the London docks were chaotic was an understatement. At least to an outsider like Sebastian upon first glance. Wagons with creaky wheels and weighed down with barrels and crates arrived simultaneously. They passed within inches of each other as they clattered over the wooden walkways. Shouts echoed on the air, some orders, others curses. Men hustled to and fro, parting to allow the wagons to pass. Miraculously, no one was run down in the process.

The ships were oddly still, like slumbering giants, while seamen swarmed the decks outfitting them for the next adventure. A group of rough-looking men had formed a queue outside the shipping office, a sprawling wooden structure that was neither fancy nor impressive. Sebastian would call it solid, serviceable. And it reinforced how he should approach the man inside.

Captain Daniel Hillary was honest. Some said appallingly so. He didn't put on airs and had embraced his grandfather's bourgeois origins with no care for what Society thought. This made him the only man Sebastian would trust with the truth about Helena.

When he had left Helena yesterday morning, she informed him that she would remain behind only one more day without him. Secretly he had been pleased by her assertion. He never wanted to come between her and her sisters, but it meant a lot that she was eager to reunite with him.

Sebastian shouldered through the group gathered outside the shipping office door and entered a large room that spanned the entire width of the building. A prim little man sitting at a table in the corner looked up from a pile of papers on the surface. "How may I be of assistance, sir?"

The seaman standing at the table swung around to gawk. Apparently, Sebastian was out of place.

"I am seeking an audience with Captain Hillary. His manservant on Curzon Street said I could find him here. I am Lord Thorne."

Placing the quill aside, the man stood and came forward. "I will see if the captain has time to speak with you." He disappeared behind a door, his voice muffled as he announced Sebastian's unexpected arrival.

A hearty laugh carried from the other room. "By all means, show in Lord Thorne."

The door swung open and Sebastian was gestured to come inside. When he entered the sparse office, Captain Hillary was on his feet. "If it isn't the man who humiliated Ben. Well done, Thorne."

Sebastian's brows shot up. He hadn't expected such an enthusiastic welcome. "Humiliation wasn't my original intention, but sisters have a way of interfering at times."

The captain's crooked grin grew wider. "I have

a sister. I well know the trouble they can cause. Fortunately, Lana is her husband's problem now." Despite his words, his eyes lit with merriment when he spoke of his sister. Perhaps Sebastian and Captain Hillary weren't so different from one another. "What can I do for you, Thorne?"

Sebastian took the seat offered to him and spotted a boy for the first time. He was sitting at a smaller desk in the corner, quiet as a ghost and engrossed in a drawing. He looked no older than Gracie.

Hillary's gaze followed Sebastian's. "This is Rafe, my wife's brother. He is learning to become a seaman. I expect he'll have his own ship by next summer."

The boy glanced up with a coy smile. "I will only be twelve. I must be a man first."

The captain went to him and ruffled his dark hair. "That's correct. Your sister would demand my head if I sent you off too early on your own."

Hillary's fondness for the boy increased Sebastian's hope that he would hear out Sebastian. "I am to marry soon, which is what brings me here. I have a favor to ask, although I realize you owe me no debts."

"But my brother does." The captain sat and leaned back in his chair, regarding Sebastian with a gaze that likely made others cower. Not Sebastian.

"Your brother has made things right for my sister, but he can never atone for the hurt he caused."

Hillary nodded. "I hope you don't expect Hillary Shipping to make amends. Ben may be part owner, but this business is my pride. I wouldn't allow my pride to be trampled."

"I have no ill will against you or your business.

The favor I ask is significant, but I will pay you for your trouble."

The captain's eyes narrowed. "I have a family to protect and anything untoward threatens their well-being."

Perhaps Sebastian's plan wouldn't work after all. He supposed he and Helena could try to hide Gracie at Mr. Mason's home for the appropriate length of time for her to have traveled from Scotland, but it seemed riskier. There would be ship records in Scotland too, and Gracie's name wouldn't be on any of them. He didn't know how to explain her sudden appearance.

He met the captain's fierce scowl. "I am protecting mine too. My betrothed has a sister, and I need to book passage from Dublin for her and a maid."

"Why didn't you say so?" Hillary's good humor returned and he leaned his elbows on the desk. "You didn't need to come to me to book passage. My man could have helped you."

"I am afraid that is where you are mistaken. My affianced bride's sister won't actually be on ship."

If Sebastian didn't require the man's assistance, he might jest about the captain needing to close his mouth before he accidentally swallowed a fly. Instead, he explained the situation, leaving out no detail. Hillary probably would sense if Sebastian withheld information. He struck Sebastian as that type of man.

When he concluded his tale, the captain made a steeple with his fingers. "If anyone finds out about your betrothed's past, it would cause quite the scandal."

"I expect it would, but my family and I have withstood scandal in the past. We would survive it again."

A corner of Hillary's mouth tipped up. "Yes, I do

recall something about a scandal at my brother's hands. Of course, I pay little notice to gossipmongers or care about providing entertainment for them."

Sebastian suppressed a frustrated sigh. It appeared he would get no help from the captain. Helena would return this afternoon, and Sebastian hated to disappoint her, but he wouldn't give up until she had everything she wanted.

"I will need the girl's name," Hillary said as he grabbed a sheet of foolscap and dipped his quill in ink. "And that of her maid."

Sebastian gave a start. "Gracie Kendrick and Edith…um…" Damn, he should have thought to ask Edith's surname.

Hillary smirked. "Perhaps something Irish would be best."

"Gallagher?"

"Gallagher it is." He scrawled their names on the paper then returned the quill to the holder. "I have a ship returning from Dublin at the end of the week or early next week. I will send word as soon as it makes an appearance."

"Can your men be trusted?"

"I don't surround myself with men I cannot trust. You have no cause for concern. The gossipmongers must look elsewhere for their entertainment. The Hillarys and Thornes have provided enough."

Sebastian couldn't agree more. He rose and shook hands with the captain to seal the agreement.

◦◦◦

Helena hadn't been back in London more than half an hour before Fergus announced Olive's arrival at the door. Wickie's cousin burst into the drawing room where Helena was enjoying a cup of tea after the long day of travel.

"Helena, where have you been? I stopped by yesterday when you didn't attend the Mayfair Ladies' meeting, and the town house appeared deserted."

Helena winced. "I forgot about the meeting. Forgive me, Olive."

She hadn't had time to concoct an excuse to explain her absence, although she hadn't realized she would need one. Foolish woman that she was. Of course Olive would notice she was missing.

Helena stood and made her way to the bellpull. "I will have another cup delivered and perhaps the cook has more of those ratafia cakes you love."

Olive pursed her lips as she tugged off her gloves and removed her bonnet. "If you think you can distract me with sweets, you are mistaken."

Fergus popped into the drawing room.

"Another cup for Olive. And a ratafia cake."

"Or two," Olive said, holding up two slim fingers.

"Yes, madam."

As soon as they were alone, Olive persisted. "Where were you? Did you leave Town?"

Helena sighed. It was clear her husband's cousin wouldn't leave without some story, so she would tell her one that was true and would surely distract her. "Please, have a seat. I have exciting news to share."

Olive sat primly on the edge of the settee and folded her hands in her lap. Helena took her seat and smiled.

"Lord Thorne and I are to be married soon. He proposed and I have gladly consented to become his wife."

Olive's jaw had grown slack the moment Helena mentioned marriage, and she still wasn't speaking.

"I realize this may be a bit of a shock, but I am *happy*, Olive." Helena's face flushed and a ridiculous smile spread across her face. "Overjoyed, in fact. I hope you will wish us well."

Fergus reentered the room with a cup and saucer in one hand and a plate of sweets in the other. Helena accepted both with her thanks and poured a cup of tea for Olive. Her hand shook as she held it out to the older woman. Helena's mother had been gone for ten years, and although she and Olive hadn't known each other overly long, there was a paternal-like bond between them. Olive had taken Helena under her care at once, for which she was thankful beyond measure.

The other woman sipped her tea and regarded Helena over the gilded rim. With care, she placed the cup and saucer on the low table in front of the settee, her expression giving nothing away. "Are you certain about the baron, my dear?"

"Yes, I have never been so sure of anything. I know your opinion of him has been low, but I love him." She hugged herself, reveling in the sound of those words. "And he loves me."

The lines around Olive's mouth softened. "I have nothing against Lord Thorne, aside from the fact he and scandal are far too familiar. I wouldn't want you to suffer because of him."

Helena's gaze dropped to her lap. If anyone was likely to suffer from scandal, it was Sebastian. Olive had no notion of how scandalous Helena was. Or how scandalous her marriage to Wickie would seem if anyone learned the truth about her.

"But," Olive said in a suddenly cheerful voice, "if the duchess and her family can survive a scandalous elopement, surely we can rise above whatever trouble the handsome scoundrel brings our way."

Helena's head lifted, her eyes misting. "Oh, Olive! Thank you for understanding."

Olive reached for a cake with a smile. "We have much planning to do. There hasn't been a wedding breakfast at Eldridge House since the former Lady Eldridge hosted one after Lord Eldridge and I married. When our sons married, the ladies' mothers insisted on hosting."

"A wedding breakfast isn't necessary. Besides, we will be marrying by special license in a few days. Lord Thorne was to purchase one at the Doctor's Commons yesterday."

Olive's eyes flew open wide. "A special license? What will people think when they hear?"

Likely that Helena was increasing, but Sebastian had lost his fiancée once before while waiting to marry. She wouldn't put him through the anxiety again. She smiled sweetly at Olive. "I suppose we will have our chance to rise above scandal from the start, no?"

"Impudent girl," Olive grumbled, but broke into a smile all the same. "A few days doesn't give me much time, but you and Lord Thorne will have an exquisite celebration. The best this town has seen all Season." Setting her cup aside, she rose and snatched her bonnet and gloves. "I really have much to do. Will you forgive me for dashing off?"

"Of course. Thank you for calling. It was a lovely surprise to see you."

They exchanged a hug and Olive bustled from the house without remembering to badger Helena about where she had been for two days.

She had just settled with her cup of tea when Fergus came in again. "The watchmaker had the baron's watch delivered. It's as good as new."

He held it aloft by the fob. It spun around glittering in the light. She had forgotten about the broken watch, but she suddenly had an idea. "I realize the jeweler just returned it today, but would you mind too much taking it back to request an engraving? As a wedding gift for Lord Thorne."

Fergus crossed his arms and frowned. "Take it back? Do you mistake me for an errand boy?"

Her heart dropped to her stomach. "No, I swear I've never thought of you as an errand boy."

He flashed a grin. "I'm teasing, lass. But I willna do it for you. I will do it for Laird Thorne. He's a decent sort, for a Sassenach."

Her hand covered her heart; her throat ached with unshed tears. He was giving his blessing and it was a most precious gift. "Thank you, Fergus."

Twenty-seven

HELENA RETIRED TO HER CHAMBERS WITH A STACK OF post with the best intentions, but no sooner had she dropped the pile on her desk than Luna dashed from under the bed to attack her petticoat ruffle.

She laughingly scooped the naughty cat into her arms and cooed to her as she scratched under Luna's chin. Luna's eyes closed and she began purring at once. "Is this what you wanted? A little attention for the poor neglected baby."

A light knock sounded at her door before Ismay entered. "Laird Thorne has arrived. Fergus showed him to the drawing room."

Helena's heart gave an excited little flip. She deposited Luna on the desk chair and swept from the room to welcome her betrothed.

"Good afternoon," she called in a cheerful voice.

Sebastian looked up from the glass of brandy he was pouring at the sideboard. "Lady Prestwick, how lovely and fresh you look after your journey." He abandoned the tumbler and met her in the middle of the room.

She tipped up her face, knowing it probably glowed

pink with pleasure at his compliment, and kissed him soundly. "Welcome, Lord Thorne."

He grinned, making her feel light and tingly inside. "Did you miss me, love?"

"Not a bit," she lied. Then to prove she didn't mean it, she twined her arms around his neck and pulled him to her for a more leisurely kiss. His hands brushed slowly to her nape then down to her buttocks where he cupped her bottom as his tongue teased her lips. She opened to him and sank against his unyielding chest on a sigh. Carriages rattled beyond the drawing room window, everyone going about their day as if life weren't suddenly extraordinary.

Olive was correct about Sebastian, of course. He flirted with scandal every chance granted him, but she wouldn't have him any other way. And she suspected he wouldn't have her either if she weren't a gentleman who embraced risk.

When she eased back, he pressed a kiss to her forehead. "If you are any more welcoming, I will carry you to your bedchamber without sharing the good news."

Helena balked. "But the sun is still up." He lifted a brow and she chuckled, heat flooding through her. "I know, there are no rules governing such things. Forgive my surprise. I am not yet accustomed to your roguish ways."

His grin widened. Holding her hand, he guided her to the crushed velvet settee then sat beside her.

She angled toward him. "What is your good news?"

"I have several items. I'm not sure where to start. Perhaps with Gracie?"

"Yes, were you able to make progress on anything?"

"Arrangements have been made for Gracie and Edith to be on a ship bound from Dublin, at least in theory. They needn't leave the comfort of Lavinia's now. The owner will send word as soon as the ship arrives."

She tossed her arms around his neck and planted a big kiss on his lips. "That is spectacular news. Thank you."

"I thought that might make you happy."

"*You* make me happy." She kissed him once more before returning her hands to her lap and silently admonishing herself to behave. "What about the special license? Were you able to obtain one?"

"It took a little doing, but the Earl of Ellis had connections he was willing to speak to on our behalf. We could marry today if we wished it, assuming I could convince a clergyman to do the deed."

She screwed her mouth to the side, uncertain how he would take *her* news. "There is a slight problem with marrying too soon. Olive came to visit a while ago, and she is insisting on hosting a wedding breakfast for us. I can't imagine she would be able to arrange anything before the end of the week. Do you mind terribly delaying the ceremony?"

"Lady Eldridge wants to host a celebration? Does she know whom you are marrying?"

"Of course she does, and she is thrilled for us."

Sebastian's eyes narrowed, as if he didn't quite believe her. "As long as it makes you happy, I can withstand a couple hours of the countess fussing over you while glaring daggers in my direction."

"She will not. She is going to adore you once she knows you better."

"I think adore is stretching it, my dear." He smirked, took a swig of his drink, and placed the tumbler on the side table. "There is one other happy piece of news to share. Eve received an offer of marriage from Sir Jonathan Hackberry. He requested an audience this morning."

"How splendid. Is she over the moon?"

He shrugged. "She seems content. I told her she mustn't feel pressured to accept his suit, but she assures me that she is fond of him."

Helena's high spirits fell a little. She wished for something more for Eve. She wanted her new friend to feel as overjoyed and in love with her bridegroom as Helena was with hers. Yet, people married for different reasons, and a sound friendship was a good basis for a loving relationship. Perhaps someday there would be more than fondness between them. "I suppose if this is what she wants, I am pleased for her. Have you told her about our betrothal?"

"Of course. Whether I want to confide in her or not, she has a way of wheedling information from me, but I was eager to tell her and Mother. I am under strict instructions to convey how thrilled Eve is you will be her sister. Mother is happy as well."

Sebastian could come home with a beaver as a bride and his mother and sister would think it a marvelous development. He could do no wrong in their eyes, and she was beginning to feel very much the same about her future husband. Granted he didn't in fact replace her with a beaver.

She chuckled at the image.

"What's so funny?"

"Oh, I don't know. You and a bucktoothed animal."

He looked at her as if she'd gone mad. "I'm sure I have no desire to know what thoughts are swirling in your head at the moment."

And because he looked so perplexed, she laughed again.

He grudgingly smiled and tugged a lock of her hair. "Someone is in a playful mood."

Memories of their recent night of play drove all silliness from her mind. She held out her hand. "Come with me, sir."

He placed his hand in hers and allowed her to lead him from the drawing room, up the curved staircase, and to her bedchamber where she turned the lock. Pivoting, she leaned back against the door. She crooked a finger and he went to her without hesitation.

Even though they had only been apart two days, it felt like an eternity. They tore at each other's clothing—day gown, coat, cravat, petticoats—until Helena was only in shift and stockings and Sebastian was down to shirt and buckskins. He lifted her to the side of the high canopied bed and unfastened his trousers. Shoving her shift high on her hips, he grasped her bottom to pull her to the edge and filled her. She wrapped her legs around his waist and held tightly as their lovemaking became a frenzied need. He urged her to lie back then found her sweet spot, circling it with his finger as he thrust.

Helena climaxed moments before Sebastian. Their cries of pleasure overlapped and melded. Both of them spent, he helped her sit and cradled her against his chest. His lips touched her hair, gently, reverently. "I missed you too, sweetheart. No more separations."

An uneasy turn of her stomach made her ease from his embrace. She forced herself to take a cleansing breath to quiet her nerves. "I need to visit Aldmist Fell at least once more. There are people I must thank, and I will want to say my good-byes."

His smile was soft, his eyes radiant. "We will visit as often as you like, assuming you will allow me to accompany you. I imagine Fergus and Ismay will be eager to return. I thought once Parliament was no longer in session we could take Gracie for a visit."

"You want to travel to Scotland?"

He swept the hair from her forehead. "I want to see where you lived. And Fergus promised to take me fishing. Perhaps you and Gracie would like to come along too. Fergus said you are quite the angler. And he said his mother, the best cook in Aberdeenshire, will bake a pie in my honor. I am not one to turn down a sweet."

She rolled her eyes, laughing, knowing sweets were not his weakness. "When did you and Fergus become confidants?"

"I'll have you know Fergus and I are the best of friends now." Sebastian tugged his trousers over his hips. "He invited me fishing when he offered his congratulations belowstairs earlier." His eyes flew open and he jumped away from the bed. "Damnation!"

Helena gasped in surprise. Luna was clawing her way up his leg, clinging to his trousers as he hopped and tried to shake her loose. When she sank her teeth into his thigh, a string of curses poured from him.

"Luna, no!" Helena scrambled off the bed to intervene, but Sebastian pried her from his leg before she reached them.

The cat hit the floor at a run, sprang onto the desk chair and desk, then slipped on the pile of post before she gained traction and dashed into Helena's dressing room. Letters plopped to the floor.

Sebastian turned incredulous eyes on Helena. "Did you see that hellcat? He tried to unman me."

A laugh burst from her. "He is a she, and Luna didn't mean to hurt you. She was playing."

His dark scowl brought about another peal of laughter.

"I'm sorry," she said, her voice muffled by her hand over her mouth. "Are you hurt?"

He lifted a brow. When his lips twitched, she knew he saw the humor too. "You could have warned me you had a guard under the bed."

"I forgot she was in here." She went to him to pull his buckskins down his thigh to inspect. "No broken skin, thank goodness. I hope you don't hold this against her. She is a very sweet cat. The poor thing was a bedraggled mess when I rescued her from the rookery."

He shook his head, smiling, as he fastened his trousers. "I suppose I didn't look much better when you rescued me."

"Even in your pathetic state, you were breathtaking." She glanced at the letters strewn everywhere. "What a mess."

Sebastian joined her on her knees to help gather the post from the floor then offered her a hand up. As she placed the mail atop the desk, an odd envelope jumped out at her. She set the letters aside and snatched it. It was addressed to her, but no sender was indicated. She turned it over and located no insignia in the wax seal either to identify who sent the letter.

Grabbing the letter opener, she broke the seal and unfolded the paper. Heavy black script was scrawled across the page.

    Dear Lady Prestwick,

    Unless you want everyone to know your sister is a whore and your husband won you gambling, come to the pleasure garden at midnight tomorrow with 130 pounds. Leave the money in a bag at the foot of the Handel statue. If you do not meet my demands, your story will be sold to the gossip rags.

The floor seemed to be rushing up at her, and she collapsed on the chair. She felt as if she was floating outside her body.

"Helena, what is it?" Sebastian's voice sounded far away. "Helena?"

Dear God, this was exactly the type of thing she worried might happen. Everyone she loved would be hurt if her secrets made it into the gossip sheets.

"Helena?" His hand on her shoulder brought her back.

She blinked and held the letter up to him. "Check the date. That is tonight."

Sebastian scanned the paper then tossed it on the desk with a glower. "You cannot go. It is dangerous and I won't have you—"

"I won't." He closed his mouth and his lips thinned. She didn't know how to interpret his response, but he seemed to be spoiling for a fight. "I won't go, Sebastian. I am aware of the risks."

His eyes narrowed. "You will not go to Vauxhall? You will not meet the blackmailer?"

"No, I swear it. I have no idea who is behind this, but I am not stupid. I only take necessary risks."

Suspicion slowly faded from his expression. "I expected more of a fight."

"Well, I hate to disappoint you then." This brought a smile to his face. "Even though I have no intention of meeting the blackmailer, I don't think it is wise to ignore his demands."

"Oh, we will not be ignoring the demands, but neither will we be paying."

It was *we* again. Not *you* or *I*, but *we*. Tears burned the back of her eyes, but she blinked them away.

Sebastian made his way to his discarded cravat and grabbed it from the floor. "I will place a bag with no money and wait for the person to collect. Then I will deal with the demands." Draping the cravat around his neck, he collected his waistcoat and jacket. "You do realize there are very few people who know the truth, which means the blackmailer is likely someone you know."

"There is only Pearl, Lavinia, and Cora. And my sisters wouldn't betray me." The answer came to her. "It was Lord St. Ambrose. He knows the truth. He was there at Lavinia's that night. She must have told him everything."

Sebastian shook his head. "St. Ambrose has nothing

to gain by drawing attention to his mistress. Besides, he has little need for money, and I feel certain he loves your sister."

She scoffed. "If he loved her, he wouldn't make her his whore."

Sebastian returned to her side and smoothed a hand over her hair. "We cannot know what has passed between them, my love. Perhaps we should both withhold judgment until we discover who the culprit is."

She nodded. Those blasted tears were clogging her throat, and she really didn't want to cry at a time like this. "We can rule out Pearl, though. I left her this morning, and she would have no place to stay."

He lifted her chin, his eyes compassionate. "Pearl is too pure of heart, of that, I am certain."

His concession lifted her spirits somewhat, but she would rest better once he realized none of her sisters were capable of such a despicable act.

"I should go, sweetheart. I will need to recall the layout of the gardens in case a chase ensues. Are you going to be all right?"

She nodded. "Please be careful. I won't be there to rescue you if footpads waylay you this time."

That smile she loved with all her heart flashed. "I promise to keep up my guard this time."

"I would feel better if you took Fergus with you tonight."

He fell silent, perhaps considering her suggestion. "That is sound advice. I will come by for him before midnight."

Once Sebastian had gone, Helena donned a wrapper and tried to sort through the pile of correspondence awaiting her, but she couldn't concentrate. How could St. Ambrose be ruled out so handily? Desperate men did desperate things. They gambled and lost. And they did things that were perhaps not part of their nature. Helena would seem like an easy mark with no husband to protect her.

Why should Sebastian risk bodily harm trying to apprehend the man when Helena felt certain St. Ambrose was responsible? She had readily agreed not to go to Vauxhall at midnight, and she wouldn't break her promise. But there was nothing stopping her from paying a call to St. Ambrose. Perhaps catching him unaware in his own territory would even the odds. She could either beg for his mercy or threaten him in return, assuming Fergus would agree to stand behind her.

Either way, she had to do something to protect Sebastian, her sisters, Eve, and Olive. None of them deserved what the gossips rags would do once they sank their teeth into this juicy bone. And neither did she. The ones who deserved to suffer were already gone, and she would be damned if she allowed her father and Prestwick's actions to hurt anyone again.

Twenty-eight

THIS IS A MISTAKE. AS THE MARQUESS OF ST. AMBROSE'S butler permitted Helena and Fergus into the marquess's Park Street town house, she knew she had misjudged the man. No one who resided in such luxury would be in the business of blackmail, unless blackmail supported his love of beautiful things.

She was actually breathless for a moment, gawking like a country lass on her first trip to Town.

The butler placed her card in a shallow Limoges bowl to carry to his employer. "Would you like to wait in the receiving room, my lady, while I inquire into whether Lord St. Ambrose is in?"

"Yes, please." Her voice was barely above a whisper as her gaze locked on the enormous colored glass chandelier dangling from the center of an ivory dome set in the ceiling. Plush crimson carpet cushioned their footfalls so they moved silently past ivory columns, two on each side of the entry, and passed through a polished oak paneled door and into another richly appointed room.

Fergus's thick eyebrows shot up when they were

left alone. He had opposed her coming to see the marquess, but forever loyal, he had done as she wished. She nodded, acknowledging her folly, and swallowed against the sickness rising at the back of her throat. For an instant, she considered dashing for the door, but the butler had her card. Lord St. Ambrose would know she had been here.

She couldn't bear to sit on either of the masculine leather chairs flanking the massive marble fireplace. That would require her to be still, and she couldn't when she felt like she might crawl out of her skin.

When the marquess entered the room several minutes later, he was smiling. "Lady Prestwick, what a delightful surprise." But one look at her cringing, and his expression changed to alarm. "Has something happened to Lavinia?" The slight break in his voice tugged at her heart.

"Oh, no, my lord. Lavinia is well." She came forward to offer comfort then thought better of it. One did not act familiar with a marquess, even if he did love one's sister. And she could see Sebastian had been correct. That momentary glimmer of fear in St. Ambrose's eyes said it all. He wouldn't hurt Lavinia or the family she loved.

Helena sensed the blood rising in her cheeks. "I apologize for coming, sir. I should not have thought to bother you. Good day."

Before she could whisk past, he put out an arm to stop her. Fergus took a step forward, giving the marquess pause. He dropped his arm so he was no longer blocking her path. "You could never be a bother, madam. Please stay. There must be a reason you sought me out." He sketched a bow. "I am at your service."

Helena bit her lip, running through plausible tales in her mind to account for her barging in on him. There were none. She cleared her throat. "I received a letter today. A threatening letter from an anonymous source."

Lord St. Ambrose stared at her in stony silence. His blank expression made her stomach quiver. "You've been threatened with bodily harm?"

"N-no." She fidgeted with the lace on her sleeve. There was something intimidating about him, a hardness she hadn't noticed in their previous encounter. "The sender is demanding money, or he will sell my secrets to the gossip rags."

His jaw twitched, but his hazel eyes remained shuttered. "And what leads you to believe I could be of assistance?"

Her mouth was too dry all of a sudden. His guardedness stirred her unease, and she inched toward Fergus for security. Perhaps she hadn't been wrong after all. "The threat was toward Lavinia, too. I—I thought you should know."

His nostrils flared, and his glare skewered her. Even Fergus sensed the animosity. His chest puffed out as he squared his shoulders.

St. Ambrose's dispassionate gaze flicked toward him then just as quickly returned to her. "You came to me for the money. How much do you want?"

"No!" It had never occurred to her that he might think any such thing. "I have money. More than I can spend in my lifetime, but Lord Thorne insists I will not give in to the demands of a blackmailer. I just thought…"

"You just thought what, Lady Prestwick?"

Her body felt engulfed in flames. She couldn't admit she thought he was the culprit without grievously insulting him or angering him to the point of endangering Fergus and herself.

Fergus closed the distance between her and him. "Her ladyship thought you might know if Miss Kendrick has enemies who would want to do her harm. Her sisters' welfare has always been first in milady's thoughts."

Lord St. Ambrose's glower was replaced with a look of confusion. "Enemies?" He scratched his head. "I can't imagine anyone wanting to hurt her, and if she did have enemies, they would not know about your family connection."

That was most likely true. Lavinia would understand the need for discretion.

The marquess gestured toward her. "The threat seems directed at you, Lady Prestwick. Have you made enemies since you've been in Town?"

Had she? She couldn't think of anyone, aside from possibly Lady Lovelace, but the widow wouldn't know about her sister. She shook her head.

"Then it seems the aim is to make money rather than cause any real harm." He sauntered toward a high round table that held a crystal decanter. He lifted it in a salute. "Do you mind?"

When she indicated he should indulge if he wished, he poured a glass.

"Would you like to sit down?" he asked. "I will ring for tea."

"That isn't necessary, sir."

He tugged the bellpull anyway. "But it is, madam. I owe you an apology, and I would be remiss if I didn't try to mend fences. Lavinia would be ashamed if she knew how I have treated you." His eyebrows lifted as if questioning if she would tell Lavinia.

"She will not hear of our exchange, my lord. I would prefer not to worry her unnecessarily."

His welcoming smile returned. "Thank you. I only hope you can understand my churlish behavior once I explain. Please, have a seat."

Helena considered declining. She didn't want to stay much longer, but she followed his suggestion and chose one of the chocolate leather chairs. He took the other. Fergus remained standing behind her chair.

"Your younger sister, Cora, has requested money from Lavinia on several occasions," St. Ambrose said. "The first time Lavinia sold a diamond broach I had given her for the money. I made her promise to never sell her belongings again. What I give to Lavinia is meant for *her* to enjoy, and she deserves it."

Helena's heart softened toward him.

"The second, Lavinia asked me for the money. I gave it to her, of course. She wanted to help her sister, and I had the means. Recently, Cora came to her again requesting money. She won't say what it is for, other than her children need it. She is always quick to remind Lavinia that her husband provided for Pearl and Gracie many years." He sneered. "Cora conveniently forgets Lavinia's sacrifice, and that Mr. White was paid to become Pearl and Gracie's guardian."

Tightness traveled Helena's jaw. She remembered

Cora as a headstrong, emotional child, but she didn't recall her being manipulative or cruel. Helena was incensed and more than a little disappointed in Cora's treatment of Lavinia.

"Did Lavinia give her the money she requested?"

St. Ambrose shook his head. "I refused. It is high time the girl learns to live within her husband's means. It wouldn't hurt for her husband to refuse her either. From everything Lavinia has said, Cora is pampered and spoiled."

Helena didn't care for the marquess's criticism of her sister, but she held her tongue. A footman responded to St. Ambrose's summons.

"Have the cook prepare refreshments for my guest."

She stood. "Please, do not trouble your cook. I really must go."

St. Ambrose rose from his chair and dismissed the footman. "Perhaps another time."

As she reached the door, the marquess said, "Lady Prestwick, I hope you will forgive me for assuming the worst about your visit. I only meant to protect Lavinia."

She turned, her hand still on the ornate handle. "There is nothing to forgive. Misunderstandings happen."

"How much did the letter demand? One hundred and thirty pounds?"

Her heart missed a beat.

"Such an odd amount, isn't it? Why ask for one hundred and thirty pounds to keep one's secrets when a much higher amount could be demanded?"

Her mouth was hanging open and she snapped it closed.

"It might interest you to know Cora requested that amount from Lavinia two weeks ago."

Helena wilted against the door. Could Cora truly be responsible for the letter? She rubbed her chest to ease the sharp pang there. If Cora needed money, she could have come to Helena. She wouldn't deny her sisters anything. And yet, it seemed Cora might not hold the same devotion to her kin. The threat to Helena wouldn't hurt only her. Gracie's future would be ruined. The burden of suspecting her sister of wrongdoing proved a heavy load on her shoulders. She needed to speak with Cora, but first she must tell Sebastian what she had learned.

With a weary sigh, St. Ambrose set his drink on the table. "If it is any comfort, I hope I am wrong about your sister."

"Me too, my lord."

❧

Sebastian arrived at Helena's town house at half past ten. He balked when she met him at the door dressed for an evening out.

"Where do you think you are going?"

"Well, nowhere until we talk. Are you coming inside?" She opened the door wide and motioned him in. Fergus stood on the edge of the foyer, his dark frown mirroring Sebastian's.

He strolled inside as if he hadn't a care when really his blood was rising. "If you think you are accompanying us to Vauxhall, you are mistaken, madam."

"Perhaps you will change your mind once you hear what I have to say."

He crossed his arms. He wouldn't change his mind.

"I think you may have been right about—" Her voice trembled and she pressed her lips together, inhaling deeply as if drawing strength from her breath. "I believe you may have been correct in suspecting my sister. I think my blackmailer is Cora."

His arms dropped to his sides. He hadn't been expecting her to come to that conclusion. She had been adamant earlier that afternoon none of her sisters could be involved.

She reached for his hand, her posture pleading. "I really must speak with her, Sebastian. Cora poses no danger. Please let me come with you."

"You cannot know that, Helena."

"I told her the same thing," Fergus piped up from his corner.

She released Sebastian's hand and threw a scowl over her shoulder. "I *can* know that. She is little more than half my height, and I have successfully fought off a man. My sister is no threat to me. Besides, it is the pleasure gardens. How dangerous can it be?"

Sebastian couldn't believe they were having this conversation. His teeth ground together. "We have no way of knowing how the meeting will play out. I won't place you at risk. And you were fortunate that night in the rookery."

"And what if she isna alone, lass?"

The fight drained from her, defeat showing in her slumped shoulders. She turned misty eyes toward Sebastian. "What if she is alone? She will be frightened out of her wits when two men accost her."

If Helena's sister was the culprit, a good scare was the

least she deserved. But Helena obviously didn't see it the same way. Perhaps he would feel the same if he were in her position and Eve was the guilty party, although he couldn't imagine his sister doing anything so despicable.

Helena took his hand. "Please, Sebastian. At least allow me to wait in the carriage, so I can talk some sense into her when you capture her."

The word "no" was on the tip of his tongue, but Fergus came forward to place his hands on her shoulders. "It canna hurt for her to wait in the carriage with your coachman."

A relieved smile spread across her pretty lips. "No, it wouldn't hurt a thing. In fact, it may help the situation in the end."

Without waiting to see if Sebastian agreed, she grabbed her bonnet from the entry table and rushed outside.

Sebastian nailed the bigger man with a glower. "You are hopelessly wrapped around her finger."

Fergus shrugged. "You canna win every battle, milaird. It's better to allow the lass some freedom so she does no' rebel."

In Sebastian's estimation, she won every battle she fought with the Scot. He was waving the white flag almost before the conflict began. "Are you married, Fergus?"

He snorted. "I canna say I am."

"Then kindly keep your advice about women to yourself," Sebastian grumbled, not nearly as disgruntled as he pretended. He liked the thought of Helena having a champion all those years at Aldmist Fell, but now it was Sebastian's turn, and he intended to keep her safe.

"I may no' be married," Fergus said as they walked outside, "but I have fair experience with the lasses. Sisters and cousins enough to drive any man insane if he does no' know how to handle them."

Helena leaned to peek out the carriage door. "I heard that."

"And the fairer sex is a nosy lot," Fergus said with a wink. "Never forget it, milaird."

Sebastian chuckled as he climbed into the carriage and sat beside Helena. "He's a good man. Very wise."

She plopped back against the seat with an exaggerated huff. "Wise enough not to make that claim in front of his kinswomen."

Fergus's laughter was muffled as he closed the door and climbed on the box to ride with the coachman.

"Are we taking the bridge or ferry?" She swiveled toward him. "Because if we take the bridge, Cora's ordeal will be cut shorter. We can wait outside the gates."

"*Cora's* ordeal," he muttered.

She sighed. "I am sorry, Sebastian. I know her threats are worrisome with Eve not yet settled in marriage, but Cora would never carry through on them."

He wished he held the same confidence in her sister's goodness. So far Cora had done nothing to prove herself worthy of Helena's loyalty. Of course there was a remote chance her sister wasn't responsible, but that begged the question of who was.

He turned to look out the window. As the carriage flew past streetlamps, the interior lit for brief moments before plunging in darkness again. The gossips would be giddy if Helena's past was revealed. A debauched gentleman stealing a young girl from a poor family. Elevating her to the status of viscountess and lying about her heritage. Any number of assumptions could, and would, be made about the years Prestwick held her at his castle, none of them complimentary.

Sebastian hadn't considered how his sister might fare if this story made it into the gossip sheets. Helena was Eve's sponsor. Certainly her fall from grace could tarnish his sister's reputation too.

He pinched the bridge of his nose, a dull pounding beginning behind his eyes. Putting his mother and sister through more turmoil was unacceptable, but even more gut-wrenching was the prospect of Helena going through the same humiliation he had suffered. The person threatening the woman he loved would be caught and dealt with tonight.

They were silent as the carriage weaved through the maze of city streets, and when they reached the bridge, Helena grabbed his hand and squeezed. He smiled to reassure her.

Colorful lanterns flickered through the trees as the carriage approached the gates to the gardens. A barouche and hired hack were the only other vehicles outside the gate. Most revelers took the ferry across the river.

"We have arrived," he said and gently tipped up her chin. "Remember, you are to stay in the carriage until I return, no matter how long it takes."

"I promise."

He kissed her quickly then the carriage door swung open. Fergus set the stairs in place and Sebastian exited. As he neared the entrance, Helena called to him. "Lord Thorne." She was braced in the doorway.

"Yes, my lady?"

"Perhaps if you mention my name, she will not give you trouble when you apprehend her."

"It is worth the effort. Thank you." He shooed her back inside, pleased when she ducked into the carriage and closed the door.

Spinning around, he collided with a woman hidden in the shadows. "Pardon me, madam."

She pulled the hood of her cloak higher to cover her graying hair. "It was my fault, sir. Forgive me." She slipped past him with her head lowered and hurried in the direction of the dock, stumbling over something on the path.

"The ferry doesn't stop running for several hours," he called. "Don't worry. You will not be stranded here."

She kept her current pace and disappeared into the dark.

Sebastian dug a few shillings from his pocket to pay for his and Fergus's admission, then they started down the dimly lit path toward the statue of Handel, the gravel crunching under their boots. The orchestra was playing in the distance and had drawn the crowd away from the Grand South Walk. Reaching their destination, Sebastian dropped the purse he'd filled with pebbles earlier at the base of the statue, and they took up positions among the trees and waited.

"Here comes someone," Fergus hissed.

Sebastian stole a peek. "It is a couple." The pair made their way down the walk at an agonizingly slow saunter. The woman's happy chatter carried on the air and eventually faded as they continued deeper into the gardens.

There were several similar incidents of people passing the statue without a glance, but no sign of anyone behaving suspiciously. After what seemed like an eternity, Sebastian leaned against the rough tree trunk. His legs were tired and his stomach had begun rumbling with hunger. "What time is it?" he asked Fergus. "I misplaced my watch."

The Scot pulled a watch from his pocket and stepped onto the path to check the time in the glow of a lantern. "Ten till one."

"The damned extortionist is late."

Fergus shrugged and returned the watch to his pocket. "I think it is fair to say the lass isna coming."

Sebastian blew out a breath, stirring the hair on his forehead. "Then we will go to her. I want this settled tonight."

Twenty-nine

HELENA STAYED CLOSE TO SEBASTIAN'S SIDE AS THEY searched the alley behind White's Butcher Shoppe for a door leading directly to the living quarters abovestairs. Fergus was ahead of them by several steps with a lantern.

Waiting close to an hour for Cora to arrive at the gardens had left Sebastian in a bit of a temper. She wasn't any happier about the wasted evening, but...

"Perhaps she had a change of heart."

His gaze cut to her. "Or became spooked and fled. Either way, we will know in a moment."

Fergus stopped in front of a battered door with peeling green paint and tried the handle. The door swung inward with a loud creak. "I found a staircase."

He held the door while Sebastian took the lantern and led the way. Helena's heart pounded as Sebastian knocked on Cora's door. It was an ungodly hour to disturb anyone, and she didn't know if Mr. White would be the type to answer with a rifle in his hand.

There was no response. Sebastian knocked again, this time louder.

"You are going to wake the children," she admonished.

A bump sounded inside then footsteps padded across the wood floors. Locks tumbled and the door flew open. "Thomas, where is your—"

Cora squeaked and slammed the door. The lock tumbled again.

With a sigh, Sebastian drummed his fingers against the door. "Mrs. White, we are not leaving until you speak with us."

"I—I am not decent, sir." Her voice was muffled as if she spoke through the crack.

"Cora, let us in so we may put this business behind us," Helena said.

"But it's the middle of the night."

"Cora," Sebastian said on a growl.

"Very well. Wait a moment."

Footsteps receded followed by a rattle before Cora returned to the door.

Sebastian urged Helena to stand back and handed Fergus the lantern as the metal clicks of the lock echoed in the small space. Cora ripped the door open and flung a cast-iron skillet above her head. Sebastian's hand shot out and grabbed the skillet. She flailed as he wrestled it from her hands. Her bare foot shot out and connected with his thigh, almost hitting his groin.

"Take this," Sebastian barked and thrust the skillet at Fergus.

Cora kicked again. Sebastian twisted to the side, and her foot slammed into his leg.

She released a painful cry and began hopping on her other foot. "Ow! Ow! Ouch! Oh, blast it all!"

Sebastian reached a hand toward her sister.

Cora slapped it away. "Don't touch me."

"Enough." Sebastian scooped Cora in his arms and stalked into the apartment. He deposited her none too gently on a kitchen chair and held her in place. "Stay."

Her chin hitched. Icy daggers shot from her eyes. "Who are you to order me about in my own home?"

"I am Sebastian Thorne. Your sister's betrothed. And most people get to know me first before wanting to bash my head with a skillet."

Helena came into the kitchen with Fergus trailing close behind. "We didn't mean to frighten you. Didn't you recognize me?"

Cora shook her head. Her face was pale and glistened in the lantern light. "I thought *he* sent you."

"Who?" Sebastian asked.

Cora reared up. "How *dare* you try to manhandle me? Lord or no, you've no leave to—"

Helena shushed her. "Let's not wake the children."

"They could sleep through the Battle of Waterloo," Cora said with a flip of her wrist.

Sebastian turned one of his charming smiles on Cora, although it didn't reach his eyes like his true smiles did, and pulled the blackmail letter from his pocket. "Explain the meaning of this."

When she didn't take the letter, Helena did. "I will read it." Their mother had taught them to read as young children, but Cora had always struggled with words.

Fergus held the lantern high to shine light on the page.

"Dear Lady Prestwick, unless you want everyone to know your sister is a whore and your husband won you gambling, come to the pleasure gardens at midnight tomorrow. Leave 130 pounds in a bag—"

Cora gasped. The hand covering her mouth trembled.

Helena continued. "Leave 130 pounds at the foot of the Handel statue. If you do not meet my demands, your story will be sold to the gossip rags." Helena's arm dropped to her side, the letter dangling from her fingers. "Cora, what do you know about this?"

She shook her head, her hand still over her mouth. "I swear, I know nothing. Where did you get it?"

"Someone delivered it to the town house while I was visiting Pearl." Helena came closer to her sister. "You must know something. Lord St. Ambrose said you had asked Lavinia for this same amount."

Her chest rose and fell rapidly. "This is the first time I have seen that letter. You must believe me, Helena."

"I believe you didn't do it," Helena said, ignoring Sebastian's soaring eyebrows. "But the amount is bizarre, and it happens to be the amount you need. Why 130 pounds?"

Cora's gaze darted toward the door and landed on Fergus. He could be an intimidating presence. "I owe someone that amount." She shifted to the edge of her chair. "Please, Helena, my husband cannot know. I made a mistake."

"How could you possibly owe that much? Cora, are you in trouble?"

She shrugged, tears filling her eyes. She swiped at them angrily. "Mr. Zachary says he will start dragging our belongings from the apartment—the furniture, our clothes, the dishes, everything—unless I pay my debts."

"Who is Mr. Zachary?"

Cora sniffled. "H-he runs a dice game in the alley.

I'd been watching for days, figuring out the patterns. I know the dice are loaded, but I thought I could beat him."

"Gambling?" Helena's stomach turned and she slumped into the chair closest to her sister. "After you saw what gambling did to our family, you still bet on a game of dice?"

Cora reached for Helena, her eyes earnest. "I thought I could win. I was going to use the money to pay my bill at the dressmaker. Thomas never would have known I had charged more than I should have. Now I don't know what I will do. My husband doesn't have the money to pay my gambling debts. If we lose our belongings, he will be humiliated."

Sebastian scowled. "What type of man tricks a woman into gambling and takes her money?"

"The kind that smells like fish." Cora sniffled again and wiped her eyes with the back of her wrist. "He is a fishmonger, and I don't think my gender matters one bit to him. He takes everyone's money."

The lantern flickered, casting long shadows on the walls. Helena couldn't believe her sister would be so foolish as to follow their father's example. Had she learned nothing from their ordeals?

Helena suppressed a sigh. She was very put out with Cora, and she would like to leave her sister to correct her own mess, but she couldn't. "I will pay your debt, but then you must promise never to do anything like this again."

Cora's eyes widened. "Do you have that sort of money? I saw you leave in a hack the other day. I thought widows' pensions barely amounted to anything."

Sebastian cleared his throat. "Helena, do you recall your conversation with St. Ambrose? You are not likely to help your sister by making this problem disappear. Another will rear its head soon enough."

Helena refused to meet his gaze, instead focusing on her sister's somber expression. She saw a flash of the troubled young girl who had lost a mother, and then slowly watched her family deteriorate, beginning with Helena leaving home. It wasn't right that her sister should lose her belongings and have her marriage ruined over a foolish choice.

"I have the means to cover your debt. I will help you."

A smile lit Cora's face as she sprang from her seat to toss her arms around Helena's neck. "Thank you! Thank you! I will repay you. I promise."

Helena eased from her sister's tight grip. "You don't owe me anything. You are my sister. I only ask that you never gamble again."

"Pfft!" She flicked her wrist. "I don't gamble that often. I'm not like Papa. I told you I only wanted to pay my dressmaker, and I could have won if I hadn't been distracted and lost count." She offered a smile to Sebastian and Fergus. "Goodness, I should make some tea. Where are my manners?"

Helena grabbed Cora's hand before she flitted away, her fingers encircling her sister's dainty wrist. "I must have your word. If I cannot trust you to pay your debt and not get into a similar situation, I cannot give you the money."

Cora's eyes hardened like a frozen lake and she jerked free of Helena's hold. "Are you accusing me of being a liar?"

"She did no such thing," Sebastian said, moving to stand at Helena's side.

Cora ignored him. "How dare you pretend you are better than me? How dare you believe you suffered more?"

"I never said—"

Cora slammed her palm against the table. "Do you truly think you are so honorable because you went off and married some bleeding toff with a castle and wealth, and now ye're a *lady*?" Her sister sneered the last word.

"That is enough," Sebastian said.

"I'll damn well decide when I have said enough." She punched her fists down to her sides and held them there, trembling. "You think you saved our family by leaving with Prestwick. And Lavinia? Good Lord, she reeks of martyrdom, giving up her virtue like she did. Well, what about me? What about *my* sacrifice?"

"We all suffered, Cora. I cannot deny the truth of that."

"Well, your suffering is over now, isn't it?"

The door swung open, and Mr. White froze in the threshold when he spotted them in the kitchen. Cora didn't see him, however. Her face was bright red, and Helena knew she could be as difficult to stop as a runaway team of horses when she lost her temper.

"Cora." She tried to alert her sister to Mr. White's presence.

"Do not 'Cora' me." She stomped her foot, reminding Helena of the young girl she had known long ago. The girl who had beat her fists against Wickie and demanded he leave her sister alone. "No one ever thanks me for my sacrifice! Have you seen the man I was forced to marry? He's *old*. And I had to throw my life away just so our sisters could have a roof over their heads and food in their bellies. It isn't fair! I gave up everything for them."

Mr. White's complexion drained of color, and his mouth hung slack. His mother stood behind him and elbowed her way into the room. Her face was a molten mask. She marched to Cora and slapped her. The crack rent the air. Helena bolted from her seat with a sharp cry of surprise.

Mrs. White snarled in Cora's face. "After everything Thomas has done for you, and you repay him by squandering his money and disparaging him? He should toss you on the streets where you belong. You ungrateful little cow."

She drew her hand back to strike Cora again, but Mr. White lunged and caught her arm. His shock had given way to outrage, and he spoke through gritted teeth. "Mother, if you ever raise a hand to my wife again, *you* will be tossed on the streets."

Mrs. White gawked. Her lips moved, but no sound came. She struggled free of his hold. "How can you take her side? Didn't you hear what she said about you?"

He smiled apologetically at Cora and rubbed the back of his neck. "I *am* old, at least in comparison to my wife. And it is true I chose her and not the other way around. I cannot fault her for speaking the truth."

"Oh, Thomas." Tears filled Cora's eyes, and she flung herself into his arms, burying her face against his chest. "I didn't mean it. I'm so sorry. You aren't too

old. You are decent and kind. And the best husband.
I do not deserve you."

She burst into sobs. Helena didn't know what to
make of her sister's display. As Mr. White stroked her
hair and whispered soothing words, Helena began to
fidget. She felt like a voyeur and retreated to a respectful distance at the edge of the room with Sebastian and
Fergus. Fergus shifted his weight from foot to foot,
appearing as uncomfortable as she did, but Sebastian
watched the exchange with his keen gaze.

"Ask her what she has done," Mrs. White said.
"Ask her how much money she owes that blackguard, Zachary."

Mr. White drew Cora under his arm and fished a
handkerchief from his pocket. "Whatever Cora has
done, it is none of your concern. We will sort it out
between us."

"You stupid man. It *is* my concern. If she loses
the roof over our heads, where will I go? And the
embarrassment she will bring on this family... You
are as hopeless as your father." Mrs. White yanked
the tie holding her cloak together and slipped it off
her shoulders.

Sebastian stiffened, his eyes darkening. "I know
you. You were the woman at Vauxhall."

Cora's mother-in-law balked. "Y-you are mistaken.
I have been here all night."

Fergus held the lantern aloft, squinting in her direction. "You were there, all right. And in a mighty rush
to make the ferry once you bumped into us."

Mr. White's forehead wrinkled. "Do you know
what they are talking about?" he asked Cora. She

lifted the letter from the table and passed it to him. He scanned the page, then lowered it, his lips thinning. "You weren't coming to retrieve me from the tavern just now, Mother. You were arriving home after extorting money from Lady Prestwick. What has gotten into you?"

His mother looked down her nose at him. "I never took a shilling from the lady. She wasn't going to meet my demands, so I did the next best thing for this family." She shoved her hand into a pocket sewn into her cloak, pulled out a stack of pound notes, and shook them at Cora. "*I* am saving my son and grandchildren from ruin. *The Informer* pays well for wicked little secrets. Enough to hold Zachary at bay for now."

The Informer? The floor tilted beneath Helena and her legs wobbled. Sebastian wrapped his arm around her to bear her weight and helped her to a chair.

"Helena!" Cora's eyes were wide as she hurried to her side. Her sister's voice sounded far away.

"I am all right." Except she wasn't. All her dreams were crumbling around her. Her wish to give their youngest sister a respectable life vanished. Her own reputation would be shattered the moment *The Informer* went to print. The room blurred as tears welled in her eyes. And Sebastian couldn't marry her now, not without ruining his family and himself.

Cora spun on her mother-in-law. "You bitch," she hissed. "No one disrespects my sister. Get out of my house."

"I am not leaving. I live here, too."

With a low growl deep in her throat, Cora pounced, but her husband caught her around the waist and lifted her feet from the floor. She shook her fist at the older woman. "I said get out."

"Quiet," Mr. White snapped. "Both of you. Cora, sit and don't say another word."

He set her down and Helena's sister did as he commanded, hatred blazing in her eyes as she glared at Mrs. White.

The woman lifted a haughty brow.

"And you, Mother." He jabbed a finger in her direction. "I have never been ashamed to call myself your son until now."

"This isn't my fault. It's all hers. She—"

"Stop! Tomorrow you will pack your belongings, say good-bye to the children, and leave for Agatha's home in the country."

She gasped. "I can't stay with your sister. She treats me worse than an animal."

"You cannot stay here either. What you have done is deplorable. I cannot imagine a poorer example to set for the children."

Reality must have hit the older woman, because her face fell and her shoulders slumped. "Who will help Cora with the children?"

"I expect she will be busy, which should keep her out of trouble."

Cora lowered her head.

Mr. White took the money from his mother and brought it to Helena. "I deeply regret what has happened tonight, my lady. This money is ill-gotten gains, and I will not allow it in my home. It cannot erase what my mother has done, but please, accept it as reparation."

Helena pushed his hand away. She couldn't stomach the sight of the small stack of bills. Was this all her reputation was worth?

"There must be something we can do," Helena said. Even as the words left her lips, she knew it was hopeless. Showing up at the editor's door demanding the story not be printed wouldn't solve anything. The truth about her past was no longer a secret, and word would spread one way or another.

Sebastian helped her from the chair. "We should go."

Cora stood too and threw her arms around Helena. "Please forgive me, Helena. Please do not disown me. I'm sorry."

Helena halfheartedly hugged her back. "You are my sister. Nothing will ever change that fact, but you need to straighten up and stop behaving like a child. You have a good man who loves you, and a family that needs you."

Her sister nodded and swiped at her tears. "I know."

Mr. White walked Helena, Sebastian, and Fergus to the door, insisting they come through the shop. He withdrew a key to unlock the metal gate across the glass-front door and apologized again.

She smiled sadly. "I do not hold you responsible, Mr. White."

Sebastian placed his arm around her shoulders and ushered her to the carriage. His warmth filled her with sadness. She didn't know how she would survive losing him.

"What time is it?" he asked Fergus.

Fergus extracted his watch with a sigh and checked the time. "It is three o'clock."

Sebastian mumbled directions, then climbed into the carriage and sat beside her. As the carriage started with a small jerk, he gathered her in his arms. "Mother and Eve will be asleep, but I am sure they will understand."

Her despair interfered with her ability to comprehend. "Pardon?"

"They should hear the news from us."

Her face flamed. "I don't know what to say. I'm so very sorry."

"Almost three weeks with no scandal. We had a nice stretch." He twirled a strand of hair that had fallen at her cheek. "Scandal is our family legacy, I'm afraid. You will grow accustomed to it in time, my beloved wife-to-be."

Her breath caught.

He smiled and kissed the end of her nose. "You didn't think this changed anything between us, did you? I have never been happier than I have been with you these last few weeks, Helena. You are my life, my meaning. I cannot turn my back on us."

Fresh tears spilled onto her cheeks. "But what about your mother and Eve?"

He swept his thumb across the wetness and sighed. "I wish I could spare them, but what is done is done. There is no going back. Mother and Eve are resilient enough to weather the storm, and so are we."

Nothing would be the way she had imagined, but he was correct. She would persevere, just as she had endured the last nine years. Only this time she wasn't alone.

Her throat felt thick with emotion. This time she had this loving, kind man by her side. Her sisters were back in her life. And she would be part of a family again.

She trailed her finger along the curve of his dark brow, the gentle slope of his nose, his lovely mouth, and his strong chin. Her hand rested on his chest. No, nothing was exactly as she'd imagined, but she had everything she wanted, and the only thing she had ever needed.

Sebastian.

"I love you so much," she whispered.

His lips brushed against hers, moist and hot like the summer evening. He enveloped her: his scent, his taste, the feel of his taut muscles beneath her palm. His hands made slow passes over her back, spreading fire through her veins. She strained into his kiss, and he lifted her onto his lap with ease; his fingers nestled into her hair. When he pulled back slightly, his mouth hovered over hers. They shared one breath, one heartbeat. His eyes glittered in the dim interior of the carriage.

"I love you too, sweetheart."

Thirty

SEBASTIAN WOKE BEFORE HELENA. SUNLIGHT STREAMED through her bedchamber windows, brightening the already cheerful yellow walls. She was half sprawled atop him in the bed, her soft hair covering his shoulder and arm like a luxurious blanket. Her bare breast was flattened against his chest. He hugged her and placed a featherlight kiss on her forehead, being careful not to wake her. He hoped she would remain in blissful unconsciousness a while longer.

The knot that had formed in his throat last night when they learned Helena's past would be exposed had doubled in size. He had feigned bravado with her in the carriage. Not that he doubted their ability to persevere. They would. But the weeks ahead would be difficult.

The ladies who had befriended her would give her the cut direct in the streets. There would be no invitations. Lady Eldridge would be forced to disown Helena if she hoped to save face herself. And they were likely looking at months of hurtful lies being printed about Helena. About him. Possibly Eve.

His sister and mother had been amazing in their acceptance of Helena last night when he woke them. His mother had sat with Helena on the sofa, holding her hand and lending quiet strength.

And Eve... She had been classic Eve.

You love her, Sebastian James Edmund Thorne, and if you do not marry her, I will crown you with this—she grabbed a three-pronged candelabrum from the sideboard and shook it. *This! You are happy. Do not muck it up.*

He had laughed and ruffled her hair to hide his swell of emotion. *I have no plans to break our betrothal, poppet, but your approval warms my heart.*

He wouldn't leave Eve's future to chance, however. Her happiness was important too. Today he would seek out Sir Jonathan and double his sister's dowry. The gentleman could take her far away, on one of his expeditions. If there were someplace safe enough Sebastian could agree to let her go.

He tried to swallow past the knot in his throat. He didn't want to send away his sister. It would break Mother's heart. And his.

They could all retreat to Aldmist Fell until the scandal died away. Sebastian would have to give up his work for the King's former soldiers, but surely his father would have wanted him to take care of family first. Perhaps Ellis would agree to cosponsor the act in Sebastian's stead.

Helena began to wake. She exhaled, her breath dancing across his skin and stirring the hair on his chest.

He stroked her soft cheek. "Good morning, love."

"Morning," she mumbled and stretched long like that worthless cat she had rescued.

Now that he wasn't smarting from the feline's vicious claws, the surprise attack was a bit humorous. He chuckled, jostling Helena.

She rose to her elbow. "Why are you laughing?"

"I was just wondering if that hellcat is going to pounce again while I am putting on my trousers."

She rolled to her back, her sweet dimples winking up at him. "I put her out of the chamber last night. You are safe."

"Thank you." He gave her a sound kiss then crawled from bed. "I should go."

"Where are you going? I thought you would stay long enough to break your fast."

He grabbed the trousers he had discarded on a chair early that morning. She sat up in bed and the covers fell to her waist. Her pale pink nipples puckered in the cooler air. His morning cockstand returned. With a soft groan, he turned his back to her and shoved his leg into the trousers. "I need to call on Sir Jonathan. He should know what has happened."

"Do you think he will break the betrothal?"

Sebastian shrugged and fastened the front fall of his trousers. "I intend to offer him more incentive to go through with the marriage."

"I'm so sorry for everything," she said with a weary sigh.

He turned toward her. "You are not to blame. Remember, we will get through this together."

"I know." She rubbed her nose as if fighting back tears. "Your mother and sister were wonderfully kind and understanding last night."

"They love you, just as I do." He pulled his shirt

over his head, moved to the bed, and kissed her. "Get dressed, love. I can stay long enough for us to enjoy breakfast together. Be quick about it."

Her dimples reappeared, and she scrambled from bed to yank the bellpull.

Belowstairs, Sebastian sent Fergus to purchase a copy of *The Informer*. He wanted to know what damage they were facing. Less than half an hour later, Helena joined him in the breakfast room. She wore a simple apron-front frock in a light green shade that complemented her eyes, and her hair had been simply arranged.

"I should call on Olive this morning," she said. "She should hear the truth from me. I hate to think of her reading the paper before I see her."

It was still early enough for the countess to remain abed if she had attended a party last night.

The front door opened and closed, and Fergus appeared in the doorway in moments. The paper was tucked under his arm, but he also held a calling card. "Milady, you have a caller this morning. Laird St. Ambrose has requested an audience."

Helena's eyes rounded. "Oh! I suppose you should show him to the drawing room."

Fergus nodded and stalked from the breakfast room.

Sebastian lifted his eyebrows. "St. Ambrose?"

Helena shrugged one shoulder, wiped her mouth with the napkin, and set it beside her plate. "I should see what he wants."

Sebastian's eyes narrowed when a dark red blush spread to her forehead. He pushed back from the table. "*We* will see what he wants."

He offered his escort and she linked arms with him.

St. Ambrose was sprawled on the settee, his arm propped along the back and his foot casually crossed over his knee. He rose in deference to Helena and acknowledged Sebastian with a slight nod.

"My apologies for interrupting when you already have a caller, Lady Prestwick."

"You aren't interrupting, my lord."

Sebastian arched a brow. "Indeed not, sir. My betrothed and I were just discussing the details of our wedding." It was rather possessive of him, he knew.

"Congratulations, Thorne." The marquess smirked. "And my sympathies, Lady Prestwick."

Helena cleared her throat and lowered to one of the chairs. "Well, I suppose we should get to the reason you are here. Or should I order tea first?"

Sebastian took up position behind her seat.

"No, please." St. Ambrose waved away her offer. "I won't take up much of your time, but I have news. It's fortuitous the baron is here, since it relates to his interests as well."

"You saw *The Informer*," Helena said. "It wasn't Cora, not that the culprit matters at this point."

St. Ambrose offered an enigmatic smile. "I know Cora is not responsible. It was her mother-in-law."

Sebastian blinked. "I'm surprised *The Informer* would divulge its source."

"It is not standard practice, no. Neither does *The London Observer*, *A Lady's Companion*, or *The Talebearer*. But as the primary investor of every gossip rag in Town, I am privy to the sources. No story is printed without my knowledge and approval."

Sebastian's body tensed, his fingers curling into a fist. "What the hell are you saying? That you approved the story about Lady Prestwick?"

"I am saying that story will *never* be printed." His eyes burned with a fierceness Sebastian hadn't known the marquess possessed. "It would ruin Lavinia's family, and I will protect her and the ones she loves with my last breath. And I will destroy anyone I must if necessary."

"You truly love her," Helena said softly.

"Yes, I love your sister." The marquess shoved his fingers through his hair, his expression miserable. "Cupid is a vindictive little creature, is he not? I love Lavinia and she loves me, but it seems our differences are an obstacle to our happiness."

Sebastian experienced a jolt of pity for the man. Even under the direst circumstances, Sebastian and Helena could be together. They might have to endure stares and whispers behind their backs, but St. Ambrose was in love with a courtesan. Miss Kendrick would never be accepted in their world.

St. Ambrose addressed Helena. "I have offered marriage to your sister. She has denied me repeatedly, but I will not tether myself to anyone else."

Helena's mouth dropped open. Sebastian didn't know what to say, but the marquess didn't seem to require a response.

"I have spoken with my brother about my wishes, and he is aware he will one day inherit the marquessate. The title will pass to my oldest nephew after him. I will never marry unless Lavinia agrees to become my wife."

What manner of insanity was this? A gentleman would shirk his duty for—for...

True love.

Sebastian had no call to pass judgment. Love made a man do any number of mad things. Even he had been willing to walk away when it came to a choice between his duties and Helena.

Helena shifted on the chair. "You own every gossip sheet in Town? How could that be?"

"I was willing to pay whatever price was presented. He who controls the gossip controls everything. Now Lavinia has no reason to worry about anything unsavory being printed in the papers when we marry."

Helena's hand covered her heart. "Has she agreed to marry you?"

"Not yet," St. Ambrose said with a smug smile, "but I am told I can be very persuasive."

Sebastian snorted softly. He had said something similar to Helena not long ago. Obviously, there was something about the Kendrick sisters that brought out a gentleman's competitive instincts.

Suddenly, it dawned on him that St. Ambrose was not only responsible for saving Helena's reputation, he had been shredding Sebastian's the last few weeks. He scowled. "What was that nonsense about dragging up my past and questioning my sanity after Lady Gabrielle's elopement?"

St. Ambrose's grin spread. "They are *gossip* sheets, Thorne. I have to allow the papers to print something to keep everyone happy."

"And I would feel happier drawing your cork," he said as he rounded the chair and advanced on the marquess.

"Wait." St. Ambrose held up a hand, laughing. "No more. I promise. We are as good as family now. You will never see your name in any of my papers again, nor anyone related to you."

Sebastian halted in front of him and dropped his fist. He wasn't likely to get a better offer. "I will hold you to that promise."

He stuck out his hand and St. Ambrose shook it. "You have no cause for worry."

After the marquess left, Sebastian had to see for himself that St. Ambrose was telling the truth. He retrieved the paper from Fergus and sat on the settee with Helena, flipping through the pages slowly. When they reached the last page without any mention of Helena or Prestwick, she closed it with a breathy laugh.

"That is it. We remain untouched by scandal."

Sebastian's lips curved up. "Is that so, Lady Prestwick? Untouched, you say. That will never do." He tugged her on his lap and grabbed her bottom with both hands. She squealed and wiggled, making the task of touching her more enjoyable.

"Sebastian, the door is open. What if someone sees us?"

"You heard St. Ambrose. We can behave as scandalously as we wish without rumors of it ever finding its way into the papers."

She stopped trying to crawl from his lap and wrapped her arms around his neck. "I look forward to many scandalous moments with you, sir. I have heard you are worth the risk to one's reputation."

"Then I shall endeavor not to disappoint you."

Her lovely eyes glowed and the dimples he had fallen in love with winked at him. "You could never disappoint me, Sebastian. In any way."

And then he kissed her like a man who loves a woman should, with passion, tenderness, and a drive to always meet her expectations.

Epilogue

OLIVE HAD WANTED TO MAKE A FUSS OVER HELENA'S wedding, but Helena took a stand and insisted the ceremony at St. George's be kept small. There would be opportunity aplenty for Society to scrutinize her and Sebastian at the extravagant wedding breakfast being held at Eldridge House afterward. Now she just wanted to be around the people she loved most.

Ismay shook out Helena's champagne-colored skirts in the church foyer before handing her a bouquet of pale pink hothouse lilies. "You look lovely, milady."

Gracie took up position beside Helena's maid and tipped her head to the side. She ran a critical eye from Helena's head to her toes and back again. A wide smile broke across her face and she nodded, bouncing the tiny curls Ismay had made with the iron before they left the town house.

Helena's youngest sister had come to live with her three days earlier. She hadn't seemed disturbed in the least by the move, but Helena was still a bit wary about taking her to live at Thorne Place after the wedding.

Her little sister had undergone many changes in her young life already.

Olive poked her head through the double doors leading to the sanctuary. "It is time. Are you ready, my dear?"

"Fergus is retrieving something from the carriage, then we will be ready."

Her loyal Scot and his sister were staying in London until the end of the Season. Then they all would travel to Aldmist Fell in the autumn.

Opening the door wider, Olive held out her hand. "Come along, Miss Gracie. I need someone to keep me company while your sister and Lord Thorne exchange vows."

Gracie went to her readily and took her hand. "Shall I help you back to your seat?"

"Oh yes, dearest. I've quite forgotten my way." Olive winked at Helena before allowing Gracie to pull her down the aisle. The door swung shut.

Tears threatened to make an appearance, but Helena blinked them back. Olive had become a most precious friend, accepting not only Gracie, but the truth about Helena's past. Helena and Sebastian had agreed it was only right to be honest with Wickie's cousin, so she could decide if she wanted to continue an association with Helena.

Olive had pursed her lips. *I always knew Wickie was hiding something. I hate to admit the truth is less damning than my imagination.*

Of course Olive refused to comment further on what sins she had imagined her cousin had been guilty of committing. But it must have been wicked indeed, for Helena had never seen the countess blush before.

Your past is neither here nor there, Helena. I shall think on it no more and neither should you.

Helena couldn't afford to be as nonchalant as the countess. In fact, she thought Olive was being too naive about the entire affair. *There is always a chance everyone will learn the truth. Perhaps it would be in your best interest to keep your distance.*

Pish-posh. Everyone has skeletons in their closets, my dear. Now eat your biscuits. All this worry has made you too thin in the face.

Ismay pulled the door open a crack and peeked inside the sanctuary. "Ooh, Laird Thorne looks more bonny than usual."

Helena hurried to peek through the crack too and melted on a sigh. Impeccable as always, Sebastian stood toward the front of the church engaged in conversation with Lord Ellis. Sebastian's black breeches and coat fit to perfection, and his gold waistcoat—which might appear gaudy on anyone else—was a spectacular choice. He was the bridegroom every bride dreamed of marrying. "He cleans up rather well."

"He isna a stray, lass."

Helena and Ismay jumped. The door swung shut and she turned to face Fergus. He held up a small box tied with a green bow. "Now, I am ready to walk you down the aisle."

Ismay gave her a quick hug and hurried inside the sanctuary to witness Helena's wedding. "Do no' let me forget to give this to you after the ceremony," Fergus said and slipped the box into his coat pocket before offering Helena his arm. "I am mighty proud of you. I know it wasna easy to let yourself fall in love. You're a brave lass."

She squeezed his arm. "Thank you, but it wasna hard to love Laird Thorne."

He chuckled. "That was better, but you still do no' sound like me."

The double doors swung open and they began the long walk down the aisle. The arched stained glass window glowed softly, creating a sense of intimacy and protection from the world outside. Helena smiled at the familiar faces as she passed. Ismay. Lady Thorne, Eve, and Sir Jonathan. Olive and Gracie. The Dowager Duchess of Foxhaven. Lord and Lady Ellis. Even Lady Norwick and her husband had come.

And waiting at the altar was her life and her meaning. Sebastian's dark eyes glimmered in the light. He took her hand and a thrill passed through her. As they spoke their vows, a golden warmth enveloped her and stayed with her while she signed her name in the parish record, all the way down the aisle, and onto the front steps of the church.

Their guests followed them outside and offered congratulations with hearty slaps on Sebastian's back and hugs for Helena. Fergus passed her the small box while Sebastian was shaking hands with Sir Jonathan. She used her bouquet to shield it from view as Sebastian assisted her into the carriage.

Helena settled on the bench; a movement across the street caught her eye. She set the box on the bench and scooted closer to peer through the window. Lavinia stepped out of the shadow of a building, lifting her hand in greeting. Her sister's smile warmed her heart. Helena pressed her hand against the glass, thankful for the small moments they could share. Even if it was from afar. Helena blew her a kiss.

Lavinia's smile widened before she turned and walked to a waiting carriage. She disappeared from sight as Sebastian joined Helena on the bench.

"My sister was there across the way just a moment ago."

He leaned to see out the window. "Lavinia?"

"She came to wish us well."

Sebastian caressed her back, creating lovely tingles that filtered through her body. "I hope she knows we missed her today," he said.

The carriage pulled onto St. George Street and headed for Eldridge House.

They both knew Lavinia couldn't have attended the ceremony or the wedding breakfast. But Sebastian's concern for her sister strengthened Helena's love for him. She reached for his hand and bumped the box sitting between them.

"Oh! I almost forgot." She lifted the small present and held it out to him.

"What is this?"

She lowered her gaze, doubting her choice a little. Perhaps she should have gotten him something more extravagant. "It's a wedding gift."

"I love it," he declared and stole a peck from her lips.

She laughed. "You don't even know what it is."

"I know it is from you," he said as he slowly untied the ribbon, "and I'm certain I love you."

His unhurried movements built her anticipation. "Open it."

"I am. I am." He tossed the ribbon aside and opened the box. His eyebrows shot up as he lifted the gold piece from its bed of blue velvet. His initials glittered in the sunlight. "It's my watch. I thought I had lost it."

"My coachman found it in the carriage after we carried you home. The glass was cracked and the hinge was broken, so it has been at the jeweler's."

Sebastian popped the clasp and opened the watch. "As good as new." He found the inscription and read it aloud. "To a beautiful partnership. Love always, HT."

Closing the watch, he slipped it into his pocket and smiled. "I was wrong. It is better than new. It comes with the loveliest wife."

She draped her arms around his neck, her smile rivaling that of any lovesick chit. "You may kiss your bride, my lord. And do not stop until we reach our destination."

Acknowledgments

I would like to thank Heather Boyd, fellow Regency author and good friend, for sticking with me from beginning to end with this book. In fact, she has been with me from the start of my writing career. Heather was my first writing partner, and it was such a treat to work with her again. It is rare and wonderful to find a friend who will be honest and uplifting at the same time.

I'm very happy to have worked with my new editor, Cat Clyne, on this book. Her guidance was appreciated, and her cheerfulness and enthusiasm made the process a lot of fun.

And lastly, I would like to thank Nephele, my wonderful agent. She is a great sounding board for story ideas and generous with her time and feedback. I feel fortunate to have worked with her on developing the Rival Rogues books.

Read on for a sneak peek of the next book in Samantha Grace's Rival Rogues series

A Good Rogue Is Hard to Find

Coming Summer 2015

July 1819

BENJAMIN HILLARY—BEN TO HIS FAMILY AND FRIENDS; "that damned heartless rogue" to most of Society—tried the back gate leading to the Eldridge's garden.

"Locked," he muttered. Of course it was. He'd had nothing but bad luck since his return from Delhi almost a month earlier.

"Balderdash." Crispin Locke, Viscount Margrave, shouldered him aside and grabbed the weathered iron handle. Gas lamps flanking the gate bathed the stone wall in a golden glow. "You have to put some brawn into it. These old gates stick." Ben's friend shot him a superior look before yanking with a loud grunt.

The eight-foot-high gate didn't budge.

"Peculiar." Margrave's brow furrowed as he smacked his hands together to clear the orange residue from his riding glove and proceeded to soil both gloves. "Why do you suppose Lord Eldridge had the gate secured?"

Ben cocked an eyebrow. "To keep out unwanted guests?"

Perhaps the Earl of Wellham had warned Lord Eldridge that Ben might show up tonight. That would explain the small army of footmen at the front door. If Wellham would stop dashing off every time Ben called on him at home or the club, Ben wouldn't be reduced to sneaking into the assemblies.

An invitation might be nice too, but he understood the reason his name was omitted from most guest lists. He had unintentionally destroyed the reputation of an innocent young lady—a lady he still pined for two years after walking away from her. Fortunately, he'd been able to set things back to rights for Miss Eve Thorne upon his return to Town. She was back in Society now, and Ben was determined to win her back into his arms.

Eventually.

She claimed she wanted nothing to do with him now, but Ben possessed the letter her confidant Mr. Cooper had sent to India stating otherwise. The clergyman had become very concerned for Eve's welfare and thought all could be set to rights if Ben would only return to England and marry her.

Ben wanted nothing more than to spend his life with Eve, but neither of them could withstand a repeat of their wedding day. He needed to find a way to make peace with the memories of his childhood sweetheart's death. For years, he'd kept the mental images sealed in a tomb he had never intended to open. Nonetheless, some tragedies refused to stay buried. Ben had never known memories could slam one to the ground or drop him in a pit of insanity, but they could. And they had chosen a hell of a time to make an appearance: while Ben stood in the vestibule with his brother, waiting to exchange vows with the woman he loved.

Ben just wanted to be free from it all, to begin anew with Eve, and he believed Wellham could help him put his past behind him.

"You won't be getting in through the gate." Margrave swiped a lock of hair from his forehead and left a smudge. Ben really should tell his friend, but the idea of Margrave bowing over Lady Eldridge's hand all pristine and proper, except for an orange smear on his face, made Ben grin.

"Why do you look so pleased?" Margrave grumbled. "I thought you wanted to get inside."

"I do, and I *will*."

Ben's sister had warned him away from the Eldridge Ball, because Eve would be here. And even though Ben had come for Wellham, she was the reason he wouldn't allow a locked gate to defeat him. He walked alongside the wall, searching for a way over.

A tree branch hung over the stone wall just low enough that he could reach it with Margrave's help.

"Give me a leg up?" Ben said.

His friend made a stirrup with his hands for Ben's foot and hoisted him into the air. Ben grabbed the branch, and when Margrave stepped out of harm's way, he swung his legs to build momentum, hooked one over the branch, and hauled himself up to straddle it.

"Well done. Wellham is in for a surprise, I think." Margrave saluted him, as if assisting a friend to scale a wall was nothing out of the ordinary.

"This seems like old hat to you, Margrave. What were you up to while I was away?"

He flashed a jaunty smile up at Ben. "Oh, you know. Things and such."

That barely qualified as an answer, but Margrave had never been the chatty type. It was probably just as well he said nothing. Then Ben might feel obligated to share his own goings-on, and some of his nights in India were better forgotten.

As his friend moved on silent feet and faded into the darkness, Ben worked his way toward the tree trunk. Once he'd cleared the wall, he dropped to the ground with a teeth-rattling thump. He rolled his neck and shoulders, then brushed off his breeches and coat.

"I am too old for this nonsense."

At three-and-thirty, he was hardly in his dotage, but he wasn't a young buck to be kicking up a lark anymore, either. He located and followed a path that wound through the garden and ended at the terrace stairs.

Several guests had retreated outdoors, taking advantage of the light breeze off the Thames. A lively melody floated through the opened French doors and flashes of color appeared through the bank of windows. Ladies dressed in crimson, plum, and emerald skipped around the ballroom floor on the arms of their gentlemen partners. Ben hadn't danced a quadrille since he'd left London, but the steps came back to him in an instant.

A footman stood just inside the doors and, noting Ben's approach, held out a silver tray. "Champagne, sir?"

Ben grabbed a glass and adopted a swagger as he entered the Eldridge ballroom. If he behaved as if he belonged there, no one would question him. They never did.

❧

"You mustn't fret," Eve Thorne's sister-in-law murmured in her ear. "He will be here."

"I'm not fretting."

Helena's blue-green gaze dropped to the handkerchief Eve hadn't realized she'd been twisting into a tight coil. It was an accurate reflection of what Sir Jonathan Hackberry's tardiness was doing to her insides. Her fiancé had promised to arrive early to Lord and Lady Eldridge's ball where their betrothal would be announced within the hour, and he had yet to make an appearance.

A thread of apprehension wound its way around Eve's heart and held it captive. What if Jonathan didn't come?

Giving up on following the conversation between Lady Eldridge and two ladies from the Mayfair Ladies Charitable Society, Eve stole another glance over her shoulder.

"Sir Jonathan will be here," Helena repeated.

Eve repaid Helena's kindness with a halfhearted smile. Her brother's new bride was more than a sister-in-law to Eve; she was a dear friend. Eve didn't want Helena to know her reassurance did nothing to calm the tempest brewing inside her.

Everything will be well. There is no cause for worry. Eve had learned long ago these were empty platitudes people tossed around when they didn't know what else to say. But Helena meant well, and Eve loved her for trying to ease her worries.

Sebastian wore a scowl as he reentered the ball-room. He pulled Eve and Helena aside when he reached them. "Sir Jonathan wasn't playing cards."

Eve knew it would be a pointless trip. Jonathan was not a gambling man. He was an intellectual, more interested in archeology and anthropology than loo. But Sebastian seemed to need something to do, so she had suggested he check the card room.

Helena looked back and forth between Eve and Sebastian, then forced a bright smile, her dimples showing. "We haven't searched the refreshment room yet."

"An excellent idea. Shall we?" Sebastian held his arm out to his wife, but Eve shook her head.

"I will wait with Lady Eldridge in case Sir Jonathan arrives and cannot find me."

"Are you certain?" Her brother drew Helena closer as if their short separation while he visited the card room had been days instead of a half hour. Helena tipped her head and gazed at him from beneath her lashes.

Eve couldn't help smiling at the newlyweds. She appreciated their attempts to include her, but it was obvious they would rather be alone. "I am certain." She shooed them away. "Go. Sir Jonathan will be here any moment."

She said a silent prayer that he wouldn't make her out to be a liar. Being abandoned by a second husband-to-be would be too mortifying to bear.

This time when she scanned the crowd, her heart-beat skipped when she thought she saw Ben. She almost wilted on the floor when she realized it wasn't him. Lady Eldridge swore Eve's former betrothed wouldn't step one foot into Eldridge Place, even though he had been turning up like a bad penny at the assemblies ever since his return to London. The earl had taken extra precautions tonight and hired extra men to guard the doors at his wife's request. Nonetheless, Eve had learned never to underestimate Ben's ability to get in wherever he wasn't wanted.

And she didn't want him here tonight.

She had waited far too long for Ben to come back to her. In two years, he hadn't sent a single word of explanation, and now that he had returned, she no longer cared what he had to say.

Liar. Eve huffed in response to the whisper at the back of her mind. Well, she didn't *want* to care. That must count for something.

Lady Eldridge and her guests moved on from a discussion of their latest charity efforts and began gossiping together. Having been the topic of wagging tongues too often, Eve had no desire to join them. She wandered a few steps away before checking to see if the countess had noticed. She hadn't.

The sea of familiar faces around her began to blur as she resumed the lookout for Jonathan. Perhaps he was lost again. He may be perfectly capable of traveling to Egypt without incident, but he couldn't navigate a town house to save his life. He often took wrong turns on his way to the men's retiring room and wound up in the host's library. Sebastian had even retrieved him from the corridor outside Lord and Lady Sethwick's family rooms once.

Eve couldn't search their hosts' town house for him,

but a quick circle of the ballroom might be wise. With Lady Eldridge occupied, Eve slipped into the crowd. She wouldn't go far, and she would be back before Sebastian and Helena returned, hopefully with Jonathan at her side. She weaved her way toward the perimeter of the room where there was no traffic and stopped to get her bearings. If she headed toward the bank of French doors at the back of the ballroom and looped around, she could make quick work of her search.

She squinted at the guests crowded onto the ballroom dancing a quadrille even though she knew Jonathan wouldn't be on the dance floor either. He preferred to observe from the sidelines. Oh, how she missed dancing with a skilled partner. A sigh slipped past her lips, and she covered her mouth with her hand.

Heavens. She hadn't meant to sound so wistful. Jonathan was a good man, a fine gentleman who accepted her just as she was, scandalous past and all. And she cared a great deal for him. A life without dancing was a small price to pay for his amiable company.

With a decisive nod, she swung in the direction of the French doors and squeaked in surprise. Benjamin Hillary, the blasted rat, was headed her way. She froze, not knowing which way to go but certain she didn't want to talk to him. He hadn't tried to speak with her since that night at Lady Chattington's ball, and she liked it that way.

Or she *should*. She hated that she was a tad bit disappointed he'd been keeping his distance.

Ben hadn't spotted her yet, since his gaze was fixed on the dance floor. Whipping her head around, she searched for a place to go.

The alcove. No, the plant!

She didn't have time for debate. Without another thought, she dashed for a deserted corner of the ballroom and squeezed behind the potted palms and ferns.

Saints above, what if she missed her betrothal announcement because she was hiding in a corner? Or worse, what if the evening ended with her brother challenging Ben to another duel? She couldn't hope to intervene a second time to save Ben's life.

Damn, the rogue. He was going to ruin her wedding again.

❧

Ben made a slow circle of the brightly lit ballroom, stopping occasionally to study the couples as they sashayed past, their cheeks pink from exertion. After several moments, he was satisfied Lord Wellham wasn't among the dancers, not that Ben was surprised. If his memory served, the earl favored gambling over gamboling.

Reaching a secluded corner near a dark alcove, he paused to check once more for his quarry before he sought out the card room.

"What are you doing here?" a voice hissed. "You are not on the guest list."

"Pardon?" Ben spun toward the speaker and came up short. His eyebrows veered toward each other. "How do you know?" he whispered back to the mass of green palm fronds.

"Because I helped make the list." The plant's fronds parted, and Eve Thorne's stern glare greeted him. What the devil was she doing?

SAMANTHA GRACE

Her frown deepened when he simply stared, at a loss for words. "Do you have a death wish, Mr. Hillary?"

The corners of his mouth twitched. "Let me guess, you've been attacked by a man-eating plant. Are you in need of rescue, kitten?"

She growled softly and the fronds snapped back into place.

One Rogue Too Many

by Samantha Grace

From the betting book at Brooks's gentlemen's club: £2,000 that Lord Ellis will throw the first punch when he discovers Lord Thorne is wooing a certain duke's sister.

All bets are off when the game is love

Lady Gabrielle is thrilled when Anthony Keaton, Earl of Ellis, asks for her hand in marriage. She's not so pleased when he then leaves the country without a word. Clearly, the scoundrel has changed his mind and is too cowardly to tell her. There's nothing to do but go back on the marriage mart…

When Anthony returns to town and finds his ultimate rival has set sights on Gabby, he is determined to win back the woman who holds his heart. But he's not expecting Gabby herself to up the stakes…

"Filled with humor and witty repartee… Grace woos readers in true Regency style as two suitors vie for one woman's commitment." —*Publishers Weekly*

For more Samantha Grace, visit:

www.sourcebooks.com

Lady Vivian Defies a Duke

by Samantha Grace

❧

The Naked Truth

Lady Vivian Worth knows perfectly well how to behave like a lady. But observing proper manners when there's no one around to impress is just silly. Why shouldn't she strip down to her chemise for a swim? When her betrothed arrives to finally meet her, Vivi will act every inch the lady—demure, polite, compliant. Everything her brother has promised the man. But until then, she's going to enjoy her freedom…

A Revealing Discovery

Luke Forest, the newly named Duke of Foxhaven, wants nothing to do with his inheritance—or the bride who comes with it. He wants adventure and excitement, like the enchanting water nymph he's just stumbled across. When he discovers the skinny-dipping minx is his intended, he reconsiders his plan to find Lady Vivian another husband. Because the idea of this vivacious woman in the arms of another man might be enough to drive him insane—or to the altar.

❧

"An ideal choice for readers who relish smartly written, splendidly sensual Regency historicals." —*Booklist*

For more Samantha Grace, visit:

www.sourcebooks.com

Miss Lavigne's Little White Lie

by Samantha Grace

—— ✧ ——

Spirited and determined to protect her young brother at any cost, Lisette Lavigne is desperate to flee New Orleans. There's only one ship sailing to England, though, and the rakish Captain Daniel Hillary will only allow Lisette's family aboard for a very steep price…

Daniel prides himself on running a tight ship, and he knows a lady will be nothing but trouble on a long voyage. Yet he can't help but break his own ironclad rules when Lisette persuades him that being gentlemanly just this once is his wisest course of action…

—— ✧ ——

"Evocative… There is a charm in Grace's prose that will delight readers." —*RT Book Reviews*

"Grace's fabulously fun debut will dazzle readers with its endearingly outspoken heroine and devilishly rakish hero." —*Booklist*

For more Samantha Grace, visit:

www.sourcebooks.com

Lady Amelia's Mess and a Half

by Samantha Grace

❧

Jake broke her heart by leaving for the country after sharing a passionate kiss.

Lady Amelia broke his by marrying his best friend.

When she returns to town a widow—pursued by an infamous rake, Jake's debauched brother, and just maybe by Jake himself—Lady Amelia will have a mess and a half on her hands.

A sparkling romp through the ton, Lady Amelia's Mess and a Half *delivers a witty Regency romance in which misunderstandings abound, reputations are put on the line, and the only thing more exciting than a scandal is true love.*

❧

"Clever, spicy, and fresh from beginning to end." —Amelia Grey, award-winning author of *A Gentleman Never Tells*

"A delightfully witty romp seasoned with an irresistible dash of intrigue and passion. Samantha Grace is an author to watch!" —Shana Galen, award-winning author of *Lord and Lady Spy*

For more Samantha Grace, visit:

www.sourcebooks.com

Miss Hillary Schools a Scoundrel

by Samantha Grace

— ❧ —

He'll never settle for one woman…

Debonair bachelor Lord Andrew Forest lives for pleasure and offers no apologies. But he receives a dose of his own medicine when his family's entrancing houseguest beds him, then disappears without so much as a by-your-leave. He'd like to teach the little vixen a thing or two about how to love a man… if he can find her…

And she won't settle for heartbreak…

After the dashing man of her dreams is revealed as a lying scoundrel, heiress Lana Hillary is ready to seek a match with a respectable gentleman—if only they weren't so dreadfully boring. Unable to rein in her bold nature for long, Lana flirts with trouble and finds herself entangled with exactly the type of man she's vowed to avoid.

— ❧ —

"With heart and humor, Grace delivers a rich and winning Regency debut. Clever and charming, this tale brings in everything Regency fans love…" —*Publishers Weekly* Starred Review

For more Samantha Grace, visit:

www.sourcebooks.com

The Captive

The first installment in the Captive Hearts series

by Grace Burrowes

New York Times and USA Today bestseller

He'll never be free...

Captured and tortured by the French, Christian Severn, Duke of Mercia, survives by vowing to take revenge. Before the duke can pursue his version of justice, Gillian, Countess of Greendale, reminds him that his small daughter has suffered much in his absence, and needs her papa desperately.

Until he surrenders his heart...

Christian's devotion to his daughter and his kindness toward Gilly give her hope that she could enjoy a future with him, for surely he of all men shares her loathing for violence in any form. Little does Gilly know, the battle for Christian's heart is only beginning.

"Burrowes deftly builds the romantic tension amid lovely layers of domestic tranquillity and honest conversations." —*Publishers Weekly*

"This is a beautiful story of redemption and love's power over evil that wrenches readers' emotions, yet leaves them utterly satisfied." —*RT Books Reviews*

For more Grace Burrowes, visit:

www.sourcebooks.com

Once Upon a Kiss

The Book Club Belles Society

by Jayne Fresina

The Perfect Hero

When handsome, mysterious Darius Wainwright strolls into town, the Book Club Belles are instantly smitten with his brooding good looks and prideful demeanor. It's as if he walked out of the pages of their favorite new novel, a scandalous romance called Pride and Prejudice. But Justina Penny can't understand why her fellow Belles are starry-eyed in the newcomer's arrogant presence—surely a wicked Wickham would be infinitely more fun…

An Unlikely Leading Lady

Justina is the opposite of Darius's ideal woman—not that he's looking for romance. But when he discovers her stealing apples from his uncle's orchard, he can't resist his own thieving impulse. A stolen kiss from the mischievous Miss Penny leaves Darius wanting much, much more. If it's a dashing villain she desires, Darius is more than willing to play the part…

Love and Let Spy

Lord and Lady Spy Series
by Shana Galen

———————— ❧ ————————

She cannot afford to fail...

Jane Bonde was raised to be a spy, but the *ton* knows her only as an elusive beauty. But if she can't find and destroy the diabolical Foncé and his French spy ring, England's defenses may fall.

However, something even more dangerous than a madman stands in her way—her fiancé.

When love conflicts with duty...

The demons of Dominic Griffyn's past make it difficult for him to get close to anyone. When his stepfather demands he settle down and marry, Dominic hopes the mysterious Miss Bonde will help him forget his troubles. He may be right— her next mission is about to plunge them both into danger.

———————— ❧ ————————

"Galen provides plenty of explosiveness, both literal and erotic, in a Regency-era romantic thriller packed with intrigue and lust." —*Publishers Weekly*

"A lively, fast-paced and wonderfully creative sensual romance." —*RT Book Reviews*

For more Shana Galen, visit:
www.sourcebooks.com

The Truth about Leo

by Katie MacAlister

New York Times Bestselling Author

— ❦ —

Can Dagmar flee Denmark

Dagmar Marie Sophie is a poverty-stricken Danish princess whose annoying royal cousin is about to have her stuffed away in a convent. When she finds a wounded man unconscious in her garden, she sees a way out of her desperate situation.

By lying to Leo?

Leopold Ernst George Mortimer, seventh earl of March, and spy in the service of the king, finds himself on the wrong end of a saber and left for dead. He wakes up not remembering what happened…in the care of a beautiful woman who says she is his wife.

Back in London, Leo—with the help of his old friends, the eccentric Britton family—sets out to unravel what he's forgotten… Is Dagmar truly the wonderful, irrepressible woman who makes his heart sing, or is she a dangerous enigma bent on his destruction?

— ❦ —

Praise for Katie MacAlister:

"Delightful… MacAlister's comic genius really shines!" —*RT Book Reviews*

For more Katie MacAlister, visit:

www.sourcebooks.com

About the Author

Historical romance author Samantha Grace discovered the appeal of a great love story when she was just a young girl, thanks to Disney's *Robin Hood*. She didn't care that Robin Hood and Maid Marian were cartoon animals. It was her first happily-ever-after experience, and she didn't want the warm fuzzies to end. Now that Samantha is grown, she enjoys creating her own happy endings for characters that spring from her imagination. *Publishers Weekly* describes her stories as "fresh and romantic" with subtle humor and charm. Samantha describes romance writing as the best job ever.

Part-time hospice social worker, moonlighting author, and Pilates nut, she enjoys a happy and hectic life with her real-life hero and two kids in the Midwest. To learn more about Samantha's books, visit her at www.samanthagraceauthor.com.